The Pulse

The Pulse

A Novel of Surviving the Collapse of the Grid

Scott B. Williams

Ulysses Press

Published in the United States by
ULYSSES PRESS
P.O. Box 3440
Berkeley, CA 94703
www.ulyssespress.com

ISBN 978-1-61243-054-6
Library of Congress Control Number 2012937119

Printed in the United States by Bang Printing

10 9 8 7 6 5 4 3 2 1

Acquisitions Editor: Keith Riegert
Managing Editor: Claire Chun
Editor: Sunah Cherwin
Proofreader: Elyce Berrigan-Dunlop
Production: Judith Metzener
Cover design: what!design @ whatweb.com
Cover photograph: © Scott B. Williams

Distributed by Publishers Group West

For Jasmine,
for being the daughter I always wanted.

ONE

ARTIE DRAGER WAS MISERABLE. He was wet, cold, and seasick, and he could not remember ever wanting anything in life as much as he wanted to be back on dry land. He huddled in the open cockpit against the back of the main cabin bulkhead to get some shelter from the wind and spray and stared at the glow of the GPS chartplotter that showed course and distance to landfall. There would be no getting off this boat ride for at least 30 to 36 hours, if the ETA displayed in a corner of the screen was to be believed.

Artie could not escape the constant sound of the crashing waves that lifted and tossed the small schooner as she shouldered her way through them in the darkness, driven onward by 20 knots of steady trade winds filling her sails. The noise and motion assaulted every part of his being, making rest impossible. He marveled that his brother could be sleeping soundly in his bunk down below, oblivious to the roaring water and horrid pitching and rolling. But Larry was a sailor, while Artie knew now, if he had not known it before this passage, that he most definitely was *not*. Though he was cold and tired of getting drenched with salt spray whenever the bow crashed into a larger-than-average wave,

Artie knew he couldn't go below even when it was Larry's turn to come on deck for his watch. Being down there in the confines of the dark teak cabin just made his seasickness worse, and each time he had tried it he had rushed back up the companionway to spew over the rail. By now there was little left in his stomach and he didn't want to think about eating more.

The queasiness had begun just hours after they'd sailed out of the anchorage near Fort-de-France and dropped Martinique astern for an offshore passage to St. Thomas. Artie had had high expectations at the start; it seemed like a fantastic idea for a much-needed vacation—a quick trip to the Caribbean to help his adventurous younger brother on an exciting yacht delivery job, sailing a gorgeous wooden schooner to her new owner. Larry did this for a living, and he had assured Artie that this would be a short, easy run. But Artie had never sailed offshore, and he hadn't counted on the seasickness. If not for that, it would have been great. *Ibis* was a beautiful little ship, and well set up for ocean voyaging.

The electronic autopilot connected to the wheel and controlled by the computer in the GPS did an excellent job of keeping the 45-footer on course. While taking his turn on watch, Artie really didn't have much to do other than scan the horizon every fifteen or twenty minutes to look for the lights of ships or other vessels that might be dangerously close. So far there had been none. Artie stood again and checked through a full 360 degrees for any flicker of light over the crests of the dark waves. There was nothing he could discern, especially through the light rain that was falling, further obscuring the night sea and adding to the discomfort he already felt from the spray. Artie would not have believed it possible to feel cold in these tropical latitudes, but being out in the wet and windy night for hours had him shivering. He looked forward to the return of daylight when the sea would seem warmer and much less menacing.

He sat back down on the cockpit seat and pushed buttons on the GPS, zooming the electronic chart out to where he could see the big picture, showing the boat-shaped blip that indicated the schooner's position in relation to all the other islands of the eastern Caribbean from Trinidad to Puerto Rico. Their destination was a waypoint Larry had selected at a channel marker outside the anchorage at Charlotte Amalie, in St. Thomas. An average speed of around eight knots made their progress to the waypoint seem excruciatingly slow to Artie, who had never traveled any distance at such painstaking speeds, but he took comfort in the fact that at least they were well over halfway through the passage. Staring at the seemingly stationary blip on the chart was somewhat depressing, though, so he huddled back against the bulkhead and pulled the hood of his foul-weather jacket back over his head, unzipping the front so he could get to his Blackberry phone, sealed in a Ziploc bag in one of the inside pockets. Through the plastic, he pushed the buttons to power it up and scroll through the text messages to the last one he had composed to Casey.

He had written dozens of such messages, each time pressing the SEND button when he was done, though he knew there was no point as long as they were this far off-shore, well beyond the reach of any cell phone towers. But it gave him something to do when he wasn't hanging his head over the rail and puking, and it made him feel closer to her even though he knew she wouldn't get any of his texts until they made landfall and the phone could reconnect to the network.

Text messaging was his lifeline to Casey. Artie had just learned how to do it five years ago when he was 42 and Casey, at 14, began using her first cell phone. He had quickly learned that phone calls were passé these days, at least among teenage girls. Even now, when she was in her second year of college, Artie found it much easier to reach Casey by text than any other means, so he'd grown used to it and did a passable job of typing with two thumbs on the tiny keyboard. He wrote to tell her what it was like out on the ocean at night, how sick he felt most of the time, and how glad he would be when they finally disembarked at St. Thomas. Writing made him feel closer to her. He wondered what she might be doing at that particular moment, hoping that at this hour she was sleeping safely in her shared apartment near campus. He ended his latest message by reminding her how much he loved her and telling her he couldn't wait to spend a weekend with her after he got back home.

After he put the phone away he was drawn again to the irresistible glow of the chartplotter screen, even though he really didn't want to know that they had only covered about three miles in the last twenty minutes. Artie checked the time on the screen and saw that his watch would be over in just one more hour. The GPS had a built-in XM satellite radio receiver, so to kill time, Artie turned it on and tuned back to a blues station he'd been listening to earlier. He turned the volume up just enough to hear the wail of bending guitar strings over the endless crash of water, but not so loud that Larry would hear it down below. Artie thought it was great that they could pick up any kind of music or news they wanted out here beyond the sight of land, and he wished his Blackberry were likewise satellite-enabled. *Maybe someday soon, all cell phones will be,* he mused.

He stood to scan the horizon again, bracing himself with one hand on the steering pedestal to keep his balance as the long, narrow hull plunged into the troughs and cut through the crests of the endless waves that marched across their course at nearly a 90-degree angle. The rhythmic motion seemed to be in sync with the Memphis blues emanating from the waterproof speakers that filled the cockpit with sound. The music reminded Artie of his home near New Orleans as he hung on and looked out into the darkness, still searching for ships that were not there. At least the rain had quit again, and the sky was starting to clear up. He could once again see the North Star hanging low on the horizon almost directly ahead on the course they were sailing. He was staring at it and thinking about Larry telling him that if you measured the angle of this star (Larry called it Polaris) above the horizon, that number of degrees would correspond to your exact latitude north of the Equator. Down here in these "little latitudes," as Larry's favorite singer, Jimmy Buffett, described them, those numbers were in the teens. Right now, according the GPS, *Ibis* was located about halfway between 16 and 17 degrees north. Artie looked back at the pole star and stretched his arm out in front of him, "measuring" with his thumb and forefinger. It was indeed a low angle, and that looked about right.

As he contemplated the challenges early navigators must have faced in the old pre-GPS days, suddenly the entire horizon in the direction of the star erupted in a blinding flash of light—first yellow and white, and then an eerie green that backlit distant clouds and reflected off the waves around him, washing the decks and cockpit in a flickering glow. Artie's jaw dropped as he watched the spectacle before him. Another brilliant flash of reddish-orange followed the green, and then there was a glow of white that lit the sky almost like daylight. The flash was over almost as soon as it began, but the light was imprinted on Artie's retinas and he couldn't see anything for a few seconds after the flash. He stood there transfixed as his vision came back, expecting to see more lights, but everything seemed to be normal again. After a few seconds he realized that part of the background noise he heard in addition to the wind and waves was static from the XM radio.

Artie glanced at the GPS unit and turned down the volume. The green display of the chartplotter no longer showed the position of *Ibis,* but instead was flashing with a message, SEARCHING FOR SATELLITES, just as it had when Larry had first powered it up. Artie pushed the menu button to scroll through the main navigation screens. Speed, distance to destination, ETA, course, heading, and all other parameters were blinking zeros, confirming that there was no satellite fix. He tried changing channels on the XM receiver but all he got was more of the same static. He was so absorbed with trying to make the unit work that he didn't notice that the yacht was changing course and heading up into the wind until he felt the pitching increase as the bow took the waves head on, and he heard the flogging of the sails as they lost the wind and luffed. In the next instant everything on deck became chaos as the mainsail and foresail booms swung wildly back and forth and the boat wallowed in the breaking swells. Artie yelled for Larry, and was about to open the companionway hatch, but didn't have to. The change in motion had awakened the seasoned skipper and he was on deck in a flash.

"What happened? Larry asked as he leapt to the helm and disconnected the autopilot linkage so he could steer by hand.

"The GPS went nuts!" Artie said. "You wouldn't believe the lights that went off to the north; red, yellow, white, orange, green.... It was so bright for a minute that it blinded me."

Larry was listening as he brought the bow of the schooner back through the wind, allowing it to fall off until the sails filled and the boat gradually eased back up to cruising speed.

"Was it heat lightning off in the distance?"

"Oh no! Nothing like lighting at all. Besides, the sky was already clearing, like it is now. There was no thunder, and this was brighter than any lightning I've ever seen. It was like daylight out here for a few seconds."

Larry was deep in thought as he listened and kept the yacht on course. "Here, take it a minute while I check the chartplotter. Just steer by the compass and keep it on about 350 degrees."

"I was listening to the XM too. It went to static about the same time the sky lit up," Artie said as he switched places with his brother.

"This is pretty weird," Larry said. "The GPS says it's still searching for satellites. It usually locks on in less than thirty seconds even when it's first powered up. Still nothing on the XM either." Larry opened the companionway hatch and turned up the volume on the VHF marine communications radio. It had been on all along, but they had kept the volume down once they were far from land and away from most boat traffic. When he turned it back up, nothing could be heard but static on Channel 16. Larry hit the scan button and found only static throughout the band.

"Nothing on the VHF either, huh?" Artie asked.

"No, *nada*. All the electronics are still working, just not picking up a signal. If it *had* been lightning, it would have fried everything. Of course, lightning striking the boat would mean we were in a big storm and that would have been obvious. Heat lightning couldn't do this."

"I'm telling you, it wasn't heat lighting that I saw. I've seen heat lighting before; not at sea, but I've seen it. This was like the Northern Lights or something. It was really kind of spectacular. Really beautiful, if I hadn't been so shocked when it happened. I wish you could have seen it."

"Maybe it *was* something like the Northern Lights. Maybe some kind of atmospheric disturbance that's temporarily interrupted radio signals. Strange that it would affect satellite signals too. It must have been really strong," Larry said.

"It was strong, all right, and it *was* in the north. I can't imagine that you'd see the real Northern Lights way down here though. You can't even see them from most parts of the United States except in unusual conditions."

"Maybe you could if it was some kind of unusual phenomenon," Larry said. "I've read somewhere that solar storms can sometimes send a disruptive pulse through our atmosphere. I hope it's just temporary, like the interruption of radio and TV signals you sometimes get during a strong electrical storm."

"How are we going to navigate without the GPS if it doesn't come back on?"

Larry laughed. "We'll just have to do it the old-fashioned way—with the compass," he said as he pointed to the big Danforth steering compass mounted on top of the wheel pedestal. "Or the stars." He nodded to Polaris, still hanging low over the horizon in the general direction they were sailing. "At least we can get the coordinates of the last position the GPS fixed on before the signal went out. Keep her on course; I'll go down and get the paper chart and my logbook. We'd better plot a DR course and start keeping track of things right away."

"DR course?"

"Dead reckoning. It's another big part of the old way of navigation. Basically involves knowing your approximate 'speed made good'—that is, the actual speed over ground, taking into account adverse or favorable currents—and the distance to your destination, then calculating how long it will take to get there assuming the same speed is maintained. Of course there are other factors, like sideways set from currents and such, but on a short passage like this it's relatively easy to get accurate enough."

"You call this a short passage?" Artie asked, at the same time noticing that for the first time on the trip he didn't feel seasick anymore. Maybe it was the excitement of all that had happened that had taken his mind off it. "What do you call a long passage?"

"Sure it's short: 350 miles? Three days and three nights, tops. Like I told you before, a long passage is a whole ocean. Like the run I did from Cape Town to Barbados last fall."

"You can have that! This is long enough for me. Seeing those lights almost made it worth it, though. I wish you could have seen them yourself. Dammit, come to think of it, I wish I had thought to get a photo! I had my phone in my pocket. Casey would have loved to see that. I just didn't think about it, it happened so fast."

"Maybe she saw it from there," Larry said.

That thought had not occurred to Artie, but of course, if it were some big event like a solar flare, it probably would have been visible all over North America as well. After all, it was in that direction. "Well, I wish she could have seen it, because it was so unusual, but the dad part of me hopes she didn't, because it happened at about two a.m., her time, and I hope she was in her room sound asleep."

"But you know she was just as likely to be out partying," Larry said.

"Nah, I know she does a little, but not on a weeknight. You know she's pretty serious about school."

"Not like I was, huh, Doc?"

"I guess you went to a different kind of school. I still don't see how you learned so much about boats, considering we grew up in Oklahoma. It's like you were born with it or something."

"I feel like I should've been. Guess I'm a lot like Buffett, just a pirate lookin' at forty; born about two hundred years too late. But seriously, you know I've been out here sailing all these years while you've been doin' the doctor thing. You learn a little out here, bit by bit. If you don't, you won't last long, because Mother Ocean doesn't care who you are."

Artie envied his carefree younger brother in a way, but he couldn't imagine living Larry's life. Initially, he had thought Larry would tire of it too and settle down into a regular job, but now, after spending just a few days with him in his element, Artie doubted it. Larry had a knack for always landing on his feet no matter how bad things got, and now, in his late thirties, he was apparently doing fine, with his skills as a delivery skipper keeping him in demand and taking him to some of the most exotic places in the world.

Artie preferred the security of a regular routine and a steady paycheck, and besides, he had Casey to think about, not just himself. In the beginning, a lot of it was about the money. After graduating from medical school and completing his specialty in ophthalmology, he was on the fast track to making the big bucks in private practice during the early years of his marriage to Dianne. But when Casey was just twelve, their family was torn asunder in one evening by someone else's impatience on a rainy interstate highway. Artie lost his wife and Casey lost her mother, and suddenly making a lot of money didn't matter near as much. He traded the long days of one surgery after another for a low-stress staff position at a V.A. hospital, where he could keep reasonable hours, have the weekends off, and spend as much time as possible filling the roles of both father and mother to his only daughter. Despite the challenges, he thought he had done pretty well as a single parent, and now that Casey was away at college, he felt the time had passed much too quickly and he often wished for the days when she was still living at home.

He kept checking the GPS and trying the XM receiver as Larry steered the boat by hand. "Still nothing," he said. "How long do you think this interference could last?"

"I've never seen anything like it, Doc. I hope not much longer, but who knows? I've been on boats that were hit by lightning. Sometimes it takes out everything electrical on board, and other times it might just be the radio or nothing at all. Seems like every strike is different. People try all kinds of tricks for preventing strikes—dissipaters on the masthead, grounding everything on board to the keel—but I have my doubts about how effective any of it is, since lighting behaves in such strange ways and is so unpredictable."

"But this *wasn't* lightning," Artie reminded him again, as if he suspected his brother doubted what he saw.

"I know that, Artie. Definitely not lightning. I would have heard the strike if it had been that close. I'm just talking about how power surges affect electronics or do not affect them, depending on unknown variables. And this was obviously a power surge. And if it took out our satellite radio and GPS signals, it had to be powerful. I'll bet they have no signal on the islands, probably not even on the mainland."

"Well, if that's the case, at least it doesn't matter to most of those people. Most people ashore aren't listening to the radio anyway, at this hour, and GPS isn't necessary on land."

"You'd think it was, from what I saw last time I was in Florida," Larry said. "It looked as if every car on the Interstate had one glowing on the dash just to find the next exit—pretty pathetic if you ask me. Do they not even teach kids to read maps anymore these days?"

"Maybe not, but Casey can find her way around. She didn't want the confusion of something else to distract her when she was learning to drive, and she still doesn't want one. I just hope this weird interference didn't interrupt her cell phone service, or her Internet access. Now *that* would be a disaster of epic proportions in her world!"

Larry laughed. "Yeah, you should have seen their faces that first night she and Jessica were anchored with me at one of the out islands last summer and they found out they couldn't text their friends back home! It was like I had just told them the boat was sinking or something. I think it was the worst thing either of them could have imagined happening!"

"Yeah, but Casey talked about that trip for weeks, Larry. Man, you just don't know how much good it did her."

Casey's raving about what a great time she and her roommate had had spending a week of summer vacation sailing with Larry was in fact the main reason Artie was here now. She had gone on and on about the clear water of the Virgin Islands and how much fun sailing was, but Artie now knew that Casey and Jessica's trip had been much different than this delivery passage he was on now. Larry had taken them on leisurely day sails among closely spaced islands where they had stopped to eat seafood and sip tropical drinks at beachfront cafés, anchoring every night in protected waters where the boat hardly rocked. It was a universe away from the hellish two days and nights Artie had already spent at sea, when the boat was like a mad carnival ride that never stopped moving, and there was nothing to look at but endless waves as far as he could see. He didn't think Casey or Jessica would have liked such a voyage either, but then again, you never knew. Larry seemed more content out here than anywhere Artie had ever been with him. When they had started the passage, his brother was nervous and stressed as he went through checklists and inspected the boat one last time. The stress stayed with him as they motored out of the anchorage and finally got the sails hoisted and set, but with each mile they put out to sea, Larry's smile got bigger until he seemed as if he didn't have a care in the world and the land astern slipped beneath the horizon. This was his world out here, and the place he felt at home. For Artie, the passage was just an ordeal he had no choice but to endure once he was committed to it.

But now he was free of the awful seasickness for the first time since they'd left the anchorage. He didn't know why it had suddenly gone away, but Larry had said he'd seen people instantly cured of seasickness before when there was some sudden crisis such as a storm that demanded action and somehow snapped the body out of the throes of nausea. Artie figured it was the shock of seeing the incredible lights as well as the "boat crisis" that had occurred when the autopilot went haywire. Now that he didn't feel like he had to throw up all the time, he was hungry, and he reached inside the companionway for a bag of pretzels and pulled a soda out of the built-in ice box under one of the seats.

Larry stayed at the helm as the sky gradually lightened in the east, and soon a new day was breaking, the early light casting a slate-gray sheen on the rolling waves the schooner slashed through on her course to the north. When the sun climbed above the horizon and began to burn away the chill and dampness of the night, Artie felt better than he had on the entire voyage, and offered to spell his brother at the helm so Larry could go below and brew a pot of coffee in the galley.

When Larry returned with two cups in hand, the sun was already hot, the start of another tropical day that would soon have them both crowded into the scant shade of the small Bimini top that covered the cockpit.

"Still nothing," Larry said as he pushed buttons on the GPS unit that was still displaying a flashing SEARCHING FOR SATELLITES message. Larry sat back in the cockpit and made another entry in his logbook, checking the compass as he did so.

"Do you know where we are?"

"Close enough. We'll reach St. Thomas in time to enter the anchorage about this time tomorrow morning. We should get a visual by the glow from all the lights there early tonight. At night you can see the more populated islands from a long way out at sea."

"What if this power surge, or whatever it was, caused their electricity to go out?" Artie asked.

Larry chuckled at the thought. "Not likely. That would take one hell of a powerful event—though it doesn't take much for the lights to go out anyway on those islands. But this wouldn't have anything to do with that, I wouldn't think. My best guess is that it was just some kind of space interference or solar flare-up or something that messed up the satellites. Although I'm surprised it would affect local VHF radio reception, unless it somehow disrupted the big transmitter stations on the islands. We don't know if we can talk to other vessels or not, since we haven't seen any. But there's usually some boat-to-boat chatter going on even this far out, and I should be able to get the NOAA weather radio channel in St. Thomas, so that's kinda weird."

"I just wish I could call Casey and ask her what's going on up there in the Big Easy. I guess she's getting dressed for class by now," Artie said as he looked at his watch.

Despite all the caffeine, Artie was exhausted from being awake and sick for so long, so when Larry told him he didn't need any help steering, he stretched out on the cockpit seat and slept through the morning. When he woke shortly after noon he felt even better, and the nausea still had not returned. As he stretched his arms and stood against the cabin bulkhead, he asked Larry if they were still making good progress and glanced at the GPS to see if it had started working again.

"I guess not, huh? You decided to just turn it off?"

"No," Larry said. "It looks like we've got an even bigger problem than the lack of satellite reception. The whole chartplotter unit just went off as if it had been powered down about two hours ago. I can't get it to do anything when I push the power button. The VHF radio did the same thing. Without the autopilot to hold course, I didn't want to go below and check the 12-volt circuit panel, but if you'll take it a minute, I'll go do that now."

Artie got another cold Coke out of the ice box and moved into position behind the helm. Larry disappeared down the companionway steps and reappeared five minutes later.

"This is the strangest thing I've ever seen, Doc. The VHF is dead as a doornail. The stereo is dead. The single-sideband radio receiver is dead. Even my personal handheld GPS receiver that was turned off and stuck in the locker under my bunk is dead. Not only is the autopilot disabled because it can't communicate with the chartplotter, but the unit itself won't even power on. I tried to power up my laptop and it won't come on either; ditto for my cell phone. But we still have ship's power. The batteries are apparently still working, and the LED cabin lights still come on, but there's nothing to that but a simple 12-volt circuit and a single switch from the breaker panel. It's apparently everything with sensitive electronic circuitry that's shut down."

"What could have caused that to happen? That stuff didn't shut down right after I saw the lights last night. It was just the signals that were lost. Did you see anything else this morning?"

"No," Larry said. "But that doesn't necessarily mean anything. It was daylight and you can see how bright the sun is. If whatever caused those lights to appear last night had happened in the daylight, I'll bet you wouldn't have seen them at all. For all we know, this could have been an even stronger second surge."

Artie's Blackberry was still in the pocket of his foul-weather jacket that was now bunched in a corner of the cockpit. He was reaching for it as Larry pondered the cause of the strange shutdowns. He took it out of the Ziploc and pressed the power button. It normally took a couple of seconds before it would light up when it had been turned off, but press as he might, nothing happened this time. The expensive smartphone was an inert object in his palm. He removed the back cover and took out the battery, waiting a few seconds before replacing it and trying again. Nothing—the phone was dead.

"What in the world?" Artie asked as he stared at his dumbfounded brother.

"I can't imagine what could cause this," Larry said. "Like I told you before, I've been in electrical storms on boats and seen everything on board fried. A good lightning strike could do this—and even take out stuff like the hand-held GPS and computer that were not connected to the vessel's electrical system. But I'll be damned if I know what could do it on a clear sunny day like today."

"I don't see how even lightning could affect a device that's not plugged into something. Isn't that why they tell you not to leave the TV and stuff like that plugged in during a thunderstorm at home? Remember how Dad used to run around unplugging stuff every time a summer rain came up back when we were growing up?"

"In a lot of cases, unplugging stuff does save it. But sometimes if a sailboat like this takes a direct hit to the mast, it can send enough of a power surge through the whole boat to fry everything. I've heard of strikes melting all the 12-volt wires in the vessel. Hell, there have even been cases of lightning running down the mast and blowing a chunk out of the bottom of the hull—sinking the boat!"

"I guess I can see how that could happen with a really powerful bolt of lightning. But as you said, the sky is blue and clear. What could cause a power surge like that on a day like this? It has to be something to do with those lights I saw, but how?"

"It had to be some kind of electromagnetic pulse thing," Larry said. "I don't know enough about the science of it to know what's possible. But I have read something about how solar flares could disrupt radio signals and such on Earth.

I couldn't imagine one powerful enough to short out electronic circuits though—but that could be what happened."

"What if it was something intentional? Some kind of terrorist attack or something?"

"I suppose that's possible too, but I don't know how. Unless maybe if it was a nuclear attack, but the way you described those lights, it seems more like some freak of nature event to me."

"Whatever it was, I just wonder how far-reaching the effects were? I sure hope it hasn't done the same thing back home where Casey is."

"Well, South Louisiana is a long way from the eastern Caribbean. I guess we'll find out more when we get to St. Thomas in the morning. Surely it will be in the news."

"I'll just be glad to get to a working phone so I can call Casey and make sure she's all right."

Artie took another turn at the helm as Larry worked out their approximate position on the paper charts and made detailed entries in his logbook. The steady trades continued to bear *Ibis* to the north-northwest along the rhumb line that Larry plotted on the chart. He said they were making good progress and should arrive as predicted shortly after daylight the next morning. The afternoon wore slowly on under the tropical sun as the two brothers separately pondered reaching land again and finding out the source of the strange electrical pulse.

They passed one ship sometime around mid-afternoon but it was so far away on the horizon they could not distinguish any details other than that it was a freighter of some type and that it was moving slowly, if at all. The sea was otherwise devoid of traffic and they saw nothing but the occasional breaching dolphin until nearly sunset, when Artie noticed several objects floating in the waves several hundred yards ahead, and just slightly east of their course. He assumed it was floating garbage or debris of some sort until they sailed closer and saw how much of it there was. Many of the floating objects were shiny, reflecting the light of the late afternoon sun. Pointing it out to Larry, Artie asked what he thought it could be.

Larry stepped up to the cabin roof and leaned against the mast to get a better view through his binoculars. After a few seconds he told Artie to steer for the debris.

"What is it?" Artie asked, "Can you tell?"

"Some kind of wreckage. I can't be sure, but maybe parts of a boat—or an airplane. We'd better check it out. There could be someone in the water. Head up a bit so I can ease the sheets. I want to slow down and be ready to heave to if we see anyone."

As they closed the gap, it became obvious what the floating objects were. "Oh my God, it *was* a plane," Artie said, astonished, looking at a clearly recognizable wing tip floating, half awash, dead ahead of the schooner. He steered past it as Larry scanned the water for any sign of survivors.

"Looks like it was a small private jet, maybe a corporate aircraft of some type.... Definitely not a commercial airliner," Larry said as they passed more recognizable pieces of fuselage and a tail section.

"You think it broke up like this when it hit the water, or could it have exploded first in the air?"

"Hard to say, but since there's more than one piece here in the same place, it probably hit the water first. A lot of the parts may have sunk."

"Maybe whoever was on it was already rescued," Artie said hopefully, as they both scanned every wave for any sign of life, half-expecting to see the bobbing heads and waving hands of life-jacket-wearing survivors any minute now. "How long ago do you think this happened?"

"My guess is not all that long, considering that these pieces are still floating together. It wouldn't take but a few hours with this much wind to scatter them miles apart. I'll bet it happened when all the electronics shut down this morning."

"You mean that you think that power surge or pulse or whatever it was that shut down our electronics could have also caused the plane to crash?"

"Absolutely. It might not have affected an older prop plane with manual controls, but this was obviously a late-model, high-tech jet. Aircraft like this have so many computer-operated controls and instruments that a total loss of on-board systems would have doomed it, no matter how good the pilot was."

Larry grabbed the helm as he was talking and brought the bow of the small schooner through the wind to change tacks. "We had better crisscross through the area a few times and look carefully. If this plane crashed because of the pulse, no one has been here to look for survivors, and no one likely will, at least any time soon. They would not have been able to make a radio call before they went down, and anyway, air traffic control on the islands may be down too."

Artie was stunned at the implications of what his brother had just said. "What about commercial airliners? Would they crash too if they were close enough to the source of the pulse to be affected?"

"Yes," Larry said. "Let's hope this thing was just local, but if not, I'd hate to think of how many jets would have been flying just in and out of the island airports in the area. St. Thomas is especially busy, with all the tourists connecting to the cruise ships there. You know, come to think of it, I haven't heard any jets overhead at all today, or seen any vapor trails. There are usually so many you don't give 'em any thought, but I *know* I haven't seen any."

Artie climbed to the cabin top and began desperately scanning the waves for any sign of life among the floating wreckage. "You'd think we would see them if they were still here, even if they were dead. Wouldn't the bodies float for a while?"

"Maybe, maybe not. The waves could have carried the wreckage at a faster speed than floating bodies. But from the looks of these pieces and parts, I honestly don't see how anyone could have survived the impact. Then there are plenty of sharks in these waters too. You know that from the ones we've already seen."

Artie shuddered at the thought of being in the water for a long time without a boat. He knew Larry was right. He thought that if he had been in that situation, he would have preferred to have died in the crash rather than be eaten alive later.

"I know in some of the big airliner crashes over water they've picked up survivors who had been more than a day in the water," Larry said, "but this jet might have gone straight down with an impact no one could have survived. That, and the fact that there was probably only a pilot and perhaps a copilot and two or three passengers on board makes it even less likely we would find them even if they were still afloat."

Larry tacked the schooner twice more and made a couple of passes upwind of the debris, just in case any swimmers or floating bodies were drifting at a slower pace than the remains of the aircraft. They both scanned the rolling seas on both sides of the boat continuously as they sailed, but saw nothing else, and soon the sun was rapidly sinking to the horizon, taking with it the last chance of seeing anything they hadn't already spotted.

"We may as well get back on course to St. Thomas," Larry said. "Maybe we can find the answers there."

"It worries me what we *will* find out," Artie said. "This is the most bizarre thing I've ever heard of. And I certainly never expected to sail through a plane crash site when I came down here for a tropical vacation. This delivery trip is turning out to be more of an adventure than I had bargained for."

"You and me both, Doc. All we can do at this point is carry on and get to the anchorage. I don't think the radio, the GPS, or anything else is going to suddenly start work-

ing again, so we won't get our answers until we get there."
Larry went below and grabbed his logbook and paper
charts to work out the approximate position of the crash
site, and entered it in the log so they could report it to the
authorities when they reached the island. He then hauled
in the sheets as Artie steered back on course, and soon the
schooner was back up to hull speed, carrying them northeast into the growing darkness as the short tropical twilight
faded to night.

Without the formerly familiar glow of the GPS in the
cockpit, Artie's gaze was fixed on the big steering compass.
At least its backlight still worked, as it was a simple 12-volt
bulb wired through a switch to the vessel's storage batteries. Larry had said the batteries would continue to provide
ample power for a few lights, including the running lights
and interior cabin lights, until they reached the anchorage.
They couldn't recharge them because the engineless schooner had no alternator, and the charge controllers and volt-
age regulators that connected the batteries to the large solar
panels mounted on the stern rail had been taken out by the
pulse. Larry wished that the owner had allowed the builder
to install a small auxiliary diesel engine, but he had stub-
bornly insisted on keeping *Ibis* a true sailing ship.

Artie reflected on what his brother had said earlier that
day about how men had been crossing oceans in small
boats without the benefit of electronics for centuries, and
how they were lucky they were on a seaworthy sailing vessel
instead of some posh motor-yacht with intricate systems
dependent upon technology. The schooner worked now

just as her predecessors had, and as long as the trade winds blew, they could depend on her to carry them to their destination. The sight of the plane crash had really unsettled Artie, though, and he longed to be able to contact Casey to make sure she was okay, and to tell her that he was. He knew he had to somehow maintain his patience, but as his four-hour watch dragged by, he had no doubt it was going to be a long night.

When Larry came back on deck at 2200 hours to relieve him, he said that the glow of St. Thomas should be visible by now, but it wasn't. The skies were clear and stars arced over the masthead in such density they looked like clouds of light, but at the level of the horizon the darkness was the same through a full 360 degrees.

"I was afraid of this," Larry said.

"So, the power is out on the islands?"

"At least in this part of the Virgins. Who knows where else?"

"Can we find it in the dark?"

"Oh yeah, no problem there. We won't be close enough to it to hit it before well after daylight even if we couldn't see it. But with this much starlight tonight, we should see the outline of the mountains from several miles out."

Artie went below and stretched out in his bunk, trying to get some sleep during his time off watch, but instead he spent most of the four hours tossing and turning, his mind racing with thoughts of the horrors of the plane crash and what it implied about what could have happened since he saw the lights. He thought about Larry saying that all jet airliners would be affected if their electronic controls went out, and he began to wonder how he would get back home. He had a ticket for a flight from St. Thomas to New Orleans by way of a connection in Atlanta, and he had been planning to leave the afternoon after their arrival at the anchorage. What if the power were still out then? What if the strange pulse had damaged the instruments of all the planes sitting at the airport? What if some of them had been in flight when it happened and had crashed? There was no way Artie could get any sleep with all this on his mind. He gave up and went back up on deck. It was two hours after midnight.

"There it is," Larry said.

Artie looked over the bow and saw the dark silhouette of distant ridges and peaks rising out of the sea. "That's St. Thomas?" he asked.

"Yes, and a couple of smaller islands that lie just outside of the harbor. Normally, the whole mountainside above Charlotte Amalie Harbor would be lit up like a Christmas tree. The lights were out on St. Croix, too. We passed within about 12 miles of it a couple of hours back while you were below, and there was nothing—no glow or anything. That tells me the power is definitely out in the whole island group. I still haven't seen any air traffic either, and only a couple of vessel lights. I've never seen anything like this as long as I've been down here. Even after a hurricane hits, there are helicopters and all kinds of planes flying around."

"That's why I couldn't sleep," Artie said. "I've been wondering just how I'm supposed to get back to New Orleans if my flight got canceled."

"No use worrying about that right now. We'll find out more later this morning. I've reefed the main and staysail to slow us down some. We'll take it nice and easy on the approach and should be just outside the harbor entrance when the sun comes up. No use taking a risk running too fast in these blackout conditions. I'm glad you came back on deck, because we both need to keep a good lookout until dawn. You never know, there may be big ships out here steaming with no lights—if they're able to run at all."

"I can't believe this is happening," Artie said. "Especially the one week-and-a-half period of my entire life that I decided to take a Caribbean vacation."

"Hey, you're on island time now. Not to worry, mon. Everyt'ing gonna be all right."

"Yeah, I hope you're right. But you live your whole life on island time. Some of us have to *work* for a living. I've got to be back at the V.A. Monday morning. I have patients to see."

"I wish you could meet my friend Scully. You think *I* live on island time? Scully could teach us all something about not worrying."

"Yeah, I heard all about Scully from the girls after their trip last summer. Casey got on a reggae kick I didn't think would ever end. At least she and Jessica didn't start smoking marijuana—as far as I know anyway—but she talked about Scully for weeks."

"I suppose he was the first real Rasta that either of them had ever met. Scully's a good guy, definitely one of my best friends in the islands. The Rastas smoke their ganja, all right, but it's different with them. It's not about getting high and partying. It's more of a spiritual experience—part of their religion—a path to enlightenment or something like that."

"Enlightenment? They seem like just another version of dope-smoking hippies to me. You don't mess with that stuff, do you, Larry?"

"I'm more into good island rum, especially when I'm anchored in a nice spot for the evening. I'm not saying I wouldn't take a hit off the pipe now and then, but Scully knows better than to bring it on board a boat when we're doing a delivery, and certainly not to bring it on *my* boat. It's not worth the risk of getting a boat confiscated, and I won't tolerate it at sea."

Artie figured drinking rum and taking a toke now and then sort of went with the territory for a yacht delivery skipper. Looking at his lean and tanned younger brother standing at the helm, his full beard and wavy hair bleached blond from the sun, Artie thought maybe Larry *had been* born two hundred years too late. He was an adventurer at heart, and this sailing life he'd chosen seemed to suit him well, and apparently agreed with him, as he looked much younger than his 38 years. Artie couldn't imagine Larry in any other setting, as these islands had been his home since he had caught a ride on a boat out of Fort Lauderdale during his first Spring Break, and he never went back to college to finish out the semester.

"It's too bad Scully won't be in St. Thomas while you're here," Larry went on. "But then again, who knows how long you'll be here? Maybe you shouldn't have come to the islands in 2013, Doc. Didn't you know the world was supposed to end sometime around the end of 2012 or, at the latest, by 2013?"

"Hah, hah; very funny, Larry. So the lights went out, and now it's the end of the world?"

"It would be for most people up there," Larry said, referring to mainland America, a place he rarely even visited. "What would they do without their DSL connections? What would they do without TV? Yeah, it would be the end of the world for sure."

"I know it would be for Casey," Artie laughed. "But seriously, if this were some kind of weird power surge or electromagnetic pulse from a solar flare, or whatever, and it really did knock out the power grid, it might take awhile to fix it, huh?"

"Your guess is as good as mine. I know it takes a while after a hurricane comes through. Happens down here all the time, but they bring in crews from other places with all the stuff to repair the damage. Let's just hope this is local to this part of the islands. Otherwise, it could be a real problem."

"I just hope there's a landline or something working when we get to St. Thomas, so I can call Casey. If it was something local to the islands, she may have heard about it today and may be more worried about me than I am about her—if that's possible."

Larry stayed at the helm for the rest of the approach to St. Thomas in the pre-dawn darkness. Under reefed sails, *Ibis* reached to the north at barely five knots, the fastest speed Larry dared to sail under these eerie blackout conditions where there could be more wreckage like the crashed plane anywhere along their course. They saw the 12-volt running lights of three other small sailing vessels as they neared the island, and as dawn broke with *Ibis* some seven miles south of the steep coast, they could see the silhouettes of an anchored U.S. Navy ship and half a dozen cruise ships lying outside the harbor. Larry said there were always navy vessels in the vicinity, as well as plenty of cruise ships waiting to dock to load and unload passengers, but he said he had never before seen an unlit cruise ship. He said that by sunrise there would also be a lot of fishing and dive boat traffic heading out of the harbor on a normal day, but today nothing was moving.

"It's sort of like coming in here after a hurricane, but with the harbor full of boats and without all the buzz of activity that would already be going on from the cleanup," Larry said as they sailed into the anchorage. Artie could see hundreds of moored yachts filling the natural harbor. There were sailing vessels of all descriptions and sizes, from traditional-looking schooners like *Ibis* to weird, spaceship-like catamarans and trimarans, as well as motor-yachts that looked like floating palaces. Larry expertly piloted the schooner through the maze of boats until he spotted the numbered float that marked the mooring that *Ibis*'s owner had rented in advance. Artie took the boat hook forward to the bow, and following Larry's instructions, snagged the mooring line and slipped it over one of the bow cleats just as Larry eased all the sheets and then quickly sprang into action to release the halyards and drop the sails to the deck. The passage was over. *Ibis* was secured solidly to the heavy mooring at the bottom of the harbor, and Artie breathed a sigh of relief as she swung downwind and settled down for the first time since they'd sailed out of the harbor at Martinique. He looked at the surrounding green hills dotted with houses, hotels, restaurants, and shops that reflected the morning sun from their shiny windows and created an illusion that everything was normal and as it should be. He looked forward to stepping onto the solidity of that dry land and its promise of shelter, momentarily forgetting the incomprehensible events that had completely altered his reality during his first ocean voyage.

TWO

CASEY DRAGER PULLED the covers over her face and rolled over, annoyed that her dream was interrupted by bright sunlight filtering through the thin curtains hanging in her window. She couldn't return to that place though, as much as she wanted to, and slowly she became conscious that it was only a dream. She threw the covers off and sat up with a start. The sun wasn't supposed to be up! Jessica was supposed to call her at 6:00 a.m. so she would have time to study for an hour before she showered, ate breakfast, and headed for her eight o'clock class. The way the light was filling her bedroom, it had to be eight already. She grabbed her iPhone off the table by her bed to make sure she hadn't silenced the ringer volume by mistake. She couldn't believe Jessica would let her down, because she had to get up early today too. She was mad at herself more than she was at her roommate, though. She knew Jessica wasn't coming in last night and she should have set the alarm on the phone as a backup.

The phone lit up, and the digital clock on the screen read 8:07 a.m. Oddly, there was a blinking message at the top corner of the screen that indicated the phone was not connected to the network. This had never happened since she got the new iPhone a year ago, and it certainly shouldn't happen in a city the size of New Orleans. It brought back bad memories of the lousy service she had had with her first cell phone back in junior high. So that was the reason Jessica hadn't reached her. She had probably tried but couldn't get through.

Casey didn't have time to beat herself up for not setting her own alarm, though. She rushed into the bathroom to hurriedly work on her hair and makeup. There would be no time to shower or eat today. She stepped out for a second to turn on the TV so she could hear it while she got ready. The screen lit, but all that it showed was a blue background and an error message. The sound coming from the speakers was white noise. She grabbed the remote and flipped through several channels. They were all the same. *Weird*, she thought to herself. *No cell service, no TV. WTF?* There was no more time to give it much thought now, though. It would be working again any time, of that she was certain. Right now, all that mattered was getting to class.

Casey supposed Jessica's phone could be off the air too. She had an Android phone on a different network, so it seemed unlikely, but it was also unlikely that the cable TV would be out at the same time too. Jessica had spent the night with her boyfriend, and Casey wondered if they could have overslept too. She would find out when they met at lunch. She slipped the closed MacBook that was lying on her table into her small backpack that doubled as a book bag and purse, slung it over one shoulder, grabbed her key ring, and rushed out the door. Her bike was cable-locked to the wrought-iron balcony rail of the second-floor apartment that made up half of the small wood-frame house fronting Webster Street. She opened the combination lock, quickly carried the bike down to the sidewalk, and pedaled off. It was just a short three-quarter-mile ride to the Tulane University campus, and the bicycle was the only sane way to go with the parking situation being what it was.

As she turned onto St. Charles Avenue, Casey was surprised to see large numbers of cars stopped everywhere in both lanes of the broad, live-oak-shaded boulevard. There was no moving traffic besides other students on bicycles, and some drivers were opening their doors and getting out. She narrowly missed wiping out when a man in a large SUV opened his door right in front of her. Why all these vehicles had stopped in the street was beyond her, but it was not her concern either, late as she was. It was already vexing enough that her phone service was out. She steered onto the broad sidewalk away from the cars, weaving among pedestrians as fast as she dared until she reached the main campus entrance from St. Charles and hung a quick right into the breezeway to the bike racks in front of Dinwiddie Hall.

She locked the bike in an empty slot and made for the front doors, pushing her way through a cluster of students on the steps. Once inside, she was surprised at how dark it was, and she realized that all the overhead lights in the hallway were off. More people were milling about outside several open classroom doors.

"What's going on? Why are the lights out?" Casey asked the first student whose eyes met hers.

"We were wondering that too," the girl said. "They just went out all at once, like they were switched off."

"When?" Casey asked. "I had power at my apartment over on Webster Street when I left just fifteen minutes ago."

"It was, like, less than five minutes ago. That's why everyone left class. The windows in this building suck. It's too dark to do anything without the lights. I think most of the classes in here were dismissed."

"I wonder if this has anything to do with my phone not working? When I got up this morning my phone had no signal, and it still doesn't. My TV was just static too."

"Tell me about it! Everyone I've talked to this morning said the same thing about their phone. *Everybody's* phone quit working right after that freaky light show last night."

"Light show?"

"I didn't see it, but everybody who did is talking about it. The whole sky lit up like daylight at about two o'clock in the morning. They said it was awesome, like all kinds of colors and flashes—lasted nearly a minute. After that, all the phones went out."

"That's freaky! What was it?"

"People are sayin' it was something like the Aurora Borealis, you know, the Northern Lights. They say it messed up electronic signals somehow."

"I didn't think it was possible to see that from New Orleans," Casey said.

"I don't know. All the geeks and Star Wars nerds are talking about it. I heard some of them this morning. They're all excited about it, saying it was caused by the sun or something from outer space."

"Great. So when exactly can we expect AT&T and all the rest of the cell companies to get their signals fixed? There's no telling how many texts I've missed this morning. And now the power is out in Dinwiddie Hall. Or do you think it's all over campus?"

"I don't know. I was just heading over to the library to find out if the lights are still on there when you asked. I sure hope so. I've got a ton of research to do."

"Well, thanks," Casey said. "I guess I freaked out for no reason over being late for Anthro."

Casey walked back out to the sidewalk and glanced back at St. Charles Avenue out front. The entire street was still like one big parking lot. No vehicles were moving, not even the streetcar that was still stopped on the tracks right where it had been when she had entered the campus. Most of the cars in the street had their hoods raised now, their owners standing around looking helpless. Casey wondered if the strange power outage had anything to do with all these apparently stalled cars, but she couldn't think of any reason why it would.

She turned and walked down the shaded sidewalks of Gibson Quad. Its park-like expanse was crowded with groups of students talking about the power outage and the strange lights during the night. Looking at the other surrounding buildings, she realized that the power probably *was* out all over campus. No one was in class, it seemed.

She decided to keep walking to the breezeway at the other end of the complex and see if PJ's Coffee was open. She knew Jessica had a nine o'clock class and would normally be stopping by there about this time to get her morning caffeine fix first. Casey thought Jessica might have seen the lights if she and Joey had been out that late, but when she got there, despite her hopes that it would somehow not have been affected, PJ's was closed. She sat on a park bench across the breezeway and opened her backpack to get out her MacBook. Usually, on the rare days she had time to stop for a vanilla latte, she would sit in the café and check her e-mail or post something to her Facebook wall. She didn't really expect the campus WiFi to be working with everything else shut down the way it was, but the laptop was fully charged and she could think of no reason why it shouldn't come out of hibernation when she opened it up. She pushed the power button repeatedly with no effect, and then noticed that the little green light that indicated that the battery was charged was not lit. It was just one more WTF moment in a morning that seemed to hold no end of new surprises.

"Hey, Casey!"

She looked up to see Grant Dyer walking her way at a brisk pace. His wavy blond hair was even more disheveled than usual this morning, and he looked as if he hadn't slept all night. But like every other time he was near, she felt something come over her that was hard to describe, something between nervousness and excitement. She had met him only last semester, when she went on a field trip for extra credit in a freshman cultural anthropology class. A graduate student, he had been assisting her professor on a visit to an ancient Native American village site near the mouth of the Mississippi River. From the first day she met him she had experienced the same reaction when he spoke to her. Today was no different, and as she turned to greet him she felt herself blush a little.

"Hi, Grant! I didn't see you in Dinwiddie Hall, but I was late getting there. I guess you left when the lights went out, huh?"

"Yeah, I wondered where you were this morning, Casey. I figured there was no use hanging around when I saw the whole building was shut down."

"I overslept. My roommate was supposed to give me a wake-up call, but of course I didn't know the cell phones were going to go out. Did you see those lights last night that everyone is talking about?"

"Oh, yeah, I saw them, Casey. You mean you missed them? It was the most incredible thing I've ever seen. It was amazing. I had just walked out of the House of Blues with my friend Jeff and was about to go home. We just stood there in the parking lot tripping out. The whole sky lit up; then it just glowed, and waves of colored light ripped across the city like some kind of explosion, but there was no sound. It was just an eerie, silent, flashing light show. I've never seen anything like it."

"What was it? Do you know?"

"No one knows for sure. But I'm hearing a lot of talk that it could have been some kind of mega solar flare. It disrupted every kind of radio communication, and no one seems to know how extensive the disruption was, because there's no way to get any news."

"My TV was out too. I didn't check the radio, though. But now my MacBook won't even power up. What's up with that? I know the battery was charged because it was plugged in all night before the power went off."

"Weird! I don't have mine with me, but it should come on, even it you can't get online." Grant took his cell phone out of his pocket as he looked at Casey's laptop to verify that there was no way to turn it on. "Hey, my phone's completely dead now. Not only does it not have a signal, it won't even come on."

Casey reached for her iPhone and discovered that it was likewise shut down and would not come back on.

"This must have just happened at the same time as the electrical shutdown a little while ago. Wow! What kind of force would it take to do that?"

"Did you see all the stalled cars out on St. Charles?" Casey asked. "It looked like they had stopped just about the time I turned onto the street this morning on my way here. That would have been about the same time the lights went out, according to what everyone in Dinwiddie Hall said."

"No, I haven't been back off campus. If cars have gone dead because of this, then it was definitely worse than I thought. And the fact that our phones and your computer are stone dead confirms it."

"How can the power going out affect things that were not plugged in?" Casey asked. "And what does any of that have to do with causing cars to stop?"

"Because it's much more than just a power outage, Casey. First it was radio and satellite signals right when those lights flashed. Then the electricity went out this morning. That must have been a separate event. If it shut down cars, then it was one hell of a strong electromagnetic pulse that must have fried the computers in them."

"I still don't see what that has to do with cars. Surely most of them don't have computers in them?"

"I don't mean regular computers like your laptop…just the little 'black boxes' that control the ignition and other things that keep the engine running. Without those devices, most cars won't even start."

"Oh. I'm really stupid when it comes to cars, I guess."

"You're not stupid, Casey. I don't know that much about them either. I don't even *own* a car. I just read about that somewhere. Oh, and there was some documentary I saw about how the police were experimenting with some kind of pulse device on their cruisers that could be used to shut down the engine of a vehicle they're chasing. It worked on the same principle."

"I guess my car probably won't start, then."

"I don't know. What is it? What year is it?"

"It's an '03 Camry. Why?"

"If it were an older car—no fancy electronics—it might still run. At least that's what I read. But yours is much too new."

"I tried to get Dad to buy me an old Volkswagen Beetle, but he insisted I needed something newer and 'more reliable.' So much for that, huh?"

"Who could have known this would happen? We still don't know the full extent of it. This could be a lot bigger than we think. It could have affected the whole country, or even the entire planet."

"I didn't know the sun could do all this. Has it happened before?"

"Maybe it has, just not since people have had electricity. It wouldn't have mattered before that."

"Is this dangerous?" Casey asked. "I mean, can't the sun, like, burn up the planet or something?

"No, I don't think so," Grant laughed. "I should say, not right now anyway. Of course it will eventually, when it expands and burns up every planet in our solar system, as scientists say all stars do, but that's a few million years down the road, I believe."

"That's comforting. So, what are we supposed to do now? No electricity, no cell phones, no WiFi…how do we find out how bad this is?"

"All we can do is go have a look around. Hey, since we can't go to class, do you want to go see what we can find out?"

"Sure, I guess so," Casey tried to sound nonchalant, hoping Grant couldn't tell there was nothing she would rather do than hang out with him for a while. "Where will we go?"

"I don't know, maybe off campus a bit, see if the power is out in other parts of the city. You've got a bike, right?"

"Yeah, it's locked up over in front of Dinwiddie Hall." Casey knew Grant had one. She had passed him in her car a couple of times far from campus, flying down city streets, weaving in and out of traffic like a New York bike messenger. Looking at him, anyone could immediately see that he was in great shape. "I won't be able to keep up with you, though, on my heavy mountain bike."

"We don't have to go fast," Grant said. "I won't run off and leave you, I promise."

"Hey, can we just go by my apartment first and at least check my car? We won't know for sure that it won't start unless we try it."

"Sure thing; it won't hurt to try. Where do you live?

"It's not far. Over on Webster Street just a couple of blocks this side of Magazine."

Grant walked with her back to where she'd left her bike, and then she pushed it along as they walked to get his where he'd left it near the library. When they rode off the campus together and turned onto St. Charles, there were so many people standing and walking in the road and on the sidewalks that they had to slow to a near-walking pace to avoid hitting them. Stalled vehicles were still blocking the lanes everywhere, most with their hoods up and their frustrated owners talking with each other and wondering what to do next.

"These cars haven't moved since I came by on the way to class," Casey told Grant.

"This is unbelievable," he said, as he scanned both ways at the first cross street they came to. There's not a moving car in sight. Good thing we have bicycles."

"Yeah, I never drive my car to campus anyway. It would be too crazy trying to park. But when I have to get around town, it's nice to have it—especially since I can't ride insane miles on a bike like you do."

"I just like riding, especially since the weather's so good here most of the time. And when I'm here during the semesters, I rarely leave the city anyway, there's just no time. Grad school's like that."

"I can imagine," Casey said.

They turned onto Calhoun Street, dropped a couple of blocks down from St. Charles to avoid the snarl of cars and people, and soon reached Webster Street, where Casey lived. Six blocks farther on, Casey pointed out her car parked on the street near the stairs that led up to her apartment. They pulled the bikes up beside it and Casey dismounted and rummaged through her backpack for her keys. When she found them she looked at Grant with a shrug.

"You might as well try it, at least," he said.

Casey first tried the electronic door opener on her key, but nothing happened when she pushed the button. She had to use the key itself and manually unlock the door. When she slid behind the wheel and turned the ignition switch, it had no effect whatsoever; there was not even the click of the starter relay.

"I guess we won't be cruising around town in this," she said, almost apologetically.

"Yeah, too bad you didn't get that VW Bug you wanted. I'll bet it would still run."

Just as he said it, as if to prove his point, they heard the sound of an engine winding out and saw a dilapidated diesel work truck weaving its way up the street around the stalled cars and their stranded drivers. It looked to be a relic from the '60s, if not older.

"Nothing electronic under the hood," Grant answered when Casey gave him a questioning look. "People with old vehicles like that are in luck, but the problem is, the roads are so clogged up with all the new ones that they likely won't be able to go anywhere. We're better off with our bikes."

"I suppose, as long as we don't need to go far. Hey, I need to see if my roommate Jessica came home. Do you want to come up to my apartment with me to check? Then we can go ride around some if you want."

"Sure. There's certainly no hurry. Not much else I can do anyway."

Casey was grateful for this unexpected turn of events that gave her an opportunity to hang out with Grant. She hoped it didn't show in her body language because she was embarrassed for him to know that it mattered to her. She led the way up the stairs and unlocked the door. "It's going to be hot in here without the AC, but at least it's not summer yet."

"Yeah, it's actually pretty pleasant today. Usually when the power goes out down here, it's because of a hurricane, and in hurricane season, it's always hot."

"I want to hear more about what it was like here after Katrina, if you ever have time to tell me about it."

"Sure, I'll be glad to, but we got out ahead of the worst of it and didn't come back for a long time."

"I can't imagine what it must have been like to lose your home and everything in it."

Grant just shrugged and said that wasn't the worst part of it. He said that growing up the way he did he was used to being uprooted and moved to new places. As a result of that lifestyle, he said, he didn't have a lot of possessions that he was attached to, like most people did. The worst part was that all his close friends had moved out of New Orleans and even out of the state after they were displaced and none had come back. He was essentially alone on campus, and though he had new acquaintances in his graduate classes, none of them were people he spent time outside of class with. He promised to tell her more about Katrina soon, and said that what he learned in the aftermath of that storm might come in handy considering what had apparently happened now.

It was obvious that Jessica was not in the apartment, and Casey could see no sign that she'd been back. She told Grant that she must still be at her boyfriend's place or else had gone straight to campus from there without coming by the apartment.

"What about yours?" Grant asked.

"My what?"

"Boyfriend, significant other, or whatever."

"No, I'm afraid not. I haven't really dated since I started classes here. I just didn't need the drama with all the work I have to do. I thought I would end up with my high school sweetheart, but he dumped me when he went to LSU."

"That was a dumb move on his part, I'd say."

Casey blushed. "Thanks, but it happens to everyone, I think. That's why I haven't bothered again for now."

"I know what you mean. I keep myself free too these days. If not, I couldn't do all the traveling I do between semesters."

Casey started to say something but reconsidered. She was lost in thought for a moment but suddenly changed the subject. "If we can't get the news on TV or the radio, and cell phones are not working either, how are we supposed to find out more about what happened to cause this? How will we know if other places outside the city are affected?"

"We won't know anything by staying here…unless someone makes it here from areas that were not damaged. I don't know, but if it *was* what I think it was, and it *was* caused by whatever caused that light display last night, I can't imagine that it only affected our region. And if it was more widespread, how would anyone send a message here or get here? This could be a very serious situation, worse than any hurricane."

"Well, I don't see how it could be worse than a hurricane. I mean, no one is getting hurt because the power's off and the phones don't work. It's not like there's wind blowing houses apart or flood waters filling the streets. How can it be that bad?"

"Think about it for a minute, Casey. Think about all the people in the hospital, for instance, depending on machines that run on electricity to keep them alive. Think about people that need to *get* to the hospital, but now can't. Think about all the stores that will have to stay closed and can't sell food or anything else. What will everyone do when they can't get anything?" Grant paused for a minute. "You can be sure people are getting hurt or dying because of this." He suddenly got quiet. "You don't even want to think about all the people who must have been flying in jets and other airplanes when this pulse or whatever it was suddenly hit."

"What would it do to an airplane? If they stopped like all these cars did, couldn't the pilots still glide them down or something? I've seen them do that in movies."

"Maybe some types of small planes; not big jumbo jets, from what I understand. They don't glide well at all, and there are not many places they could safely land. Besides, big airliners are even more dependent on computer controls than cars are. They can't navigate without all that stuff to tell them where they are, how high they are flying, and how fast they are going. I think they would all crash if all that went out. At least that's what I read somewhere."

"Oh my God, if this had happened just a couple of days later, my dad could have been in a crash!"

"Is he flying somewhere then?"

"He's supposed to be coming back here from St. Thomas on Thursday. But he couldn't have been on a plane today, because he's out in the ocean with my Uncle Larry on a sailboat. What would this do to a sailboat?" Casey suddenly looked frightened. "What if their GPS went out? How will they find their way back to land?"

"Where were they going?" Grant asked.

Casey told him all about the delivery trip, about how she and Jessica had sailed with Larry in the islands the previous summer, and how Larry had been sailing all over for years and years, but it was her dad's first offshore voyage.

"I wouldn't worry right now, Casey. It sounds like your dad is in good hands with his brother, and a real sailor like that can navigate without fancy electronics. They're probably in about the safest place anyone can be right now, out on the open sea."

"But how will I *know*?" Casey was distraught. Grant put his arm around her and she turned to him and hugged him with both of hers. "He won't be able to call me when they get to land. I won't even know if they made it or not."

"I hope I'm wrong about the extent of this, Casey. I really do," Grant said as he returned her hug with a reassuring squeeze. "I hope this was somehow local and just affected the city. That way, they can get outside help in here fast and get things running again."

Casey had never given much thought to how much everything in modern life was dependent upon electronic devices and the power that made them work. Like everyone else, she imagined, she just took it for granted that all these things would keep on working just as they always had. Most people had never considered the possibility of a situation like what was going on today. She was grateful that Grant was with her and that he seemed so knowledgeable. She wanted to just stay in his arms where she could momentarily forget her worries, but she felt his embrace relax, signaling an end to the hug, and she reluctantly pulled away.

"So what do we do now?" she asked, hoping that whatever it was, they could do it together.

"Do you still want to ride around some on the bikes? Maybe we can look for your roommate, and listen to the talk on the streets."

"Of course. We could try going by Joey's place to see if she's there. He lives in a little cottage on the grounds of an old mansion on Philip Street. It's about three miles west of here, over in the Garden District."

"I know the area. It's where the rich people live."

"It's just a rental, but yeah, his parents are loaded, I think."

"Let's go, but I'm getting kind of hungry. We'd better find something to eat first."

"I've got pizza in the freezer," Casey said, "but no way to cook it."

"Let's see what we can find somewhere on the way. We're going to have to start thinking about more than lunch too; if the power stays off, food will run out fast."

"I didn't think about that," Casey said.

"You haven't been through a hurricane. It's okay. Leave that to me. I know all about this stuff."

Casey was becoming more impressed with Grant all the time, and in a twisted kind of way, she was almost glad the lights had gone out. When she thought about it, she knew he lived alone, and with everything shut down, he probably didn't have too much else to do right now. This would give them a reason they otherwise would not have to spend time together—time that she hoped would help them get to know each other even better. It seemed that Grant liked her company and wanted to help her. If not, he would just do his own thing, as he was used to being on his own.

They made their way to the busy maze of Magazine Street, which was much narrower and seemed even more crowded than St. Charles Avenue, with stalled cars, pedestrians, and throngs of other people riding bikes. They found a line outside a pita sandwich shop that was serving what food they had left and the rest of the semi-cold sodas from their coolers to customers who could pay in cash. Casey never carried bills on her, always relying on her debit card to make even the smallest of purchases. Once again she felt stupid and embarrassed and had to admit to Grant that she didn't have any money. Grant told her not to worry, he had money on him, so they were in luck and got in line standing beside their bikes, where they could overhear all sorts of wild speculation from those around them about what could have happened. Theories ranged from terrorist attacks to government conspiracies and even an alien invasion. Many people in this city that never sleeps had been outside and had seen the bizarre lights that flashed across the sky in the wee hours of the morning. It was obvious that there was a growing sense of frustration at all the unknown aspects of the situation, and even though it was only March, by late morning it was getting hot and humid. Gathering clouds threatened the afternoon rain that was typical in the Big

Easy. When the rain started falling it would only add to the annoyance of all the suddenly stranded drivers who found themselves unable to get to wherever they had been trying to go that morning.

Grant bought all the bottled water and Gatorade they could stuff in their book bags, along with some one-serving bags of baked potato chips, the only extra snacks the shop still had a supply of. Then they pedaled off to make their way to Joey's house, where they hoped to find Jessica. Along the way, Casey told Grant that the relationship between Jessica and Joey probably wasn't going anywhere. It was more of a physical attraction than anything else. Joey was arrogant and impatient and didn't seem to care much about listening to what anyone else had to say. He didn't have much time for her roommate anyway, Casey said, adding that he was a pre-med student barely keeping his GPA above the minimum, thanks to all the time he spent partying with his friends.

"Sounds like she should have dumped him already, if you ask me," Grant said.

"Yeah, I keep hoping she'll move on. She deserves better."

Casey set the pace as she led the way down Magazine until they came to Philip, where she turned right, heading towards the river. "Here's the house, just ahead on the right." She pointed.

They pulled into a narrow drive that led into a beautifully landscaped semi-tropical garden of date palms, philodendrons, and oleander, and followed it past the white two-story mansion to a separate guest house in the back of the grounds. Joey's black Audi was parked in front, but Jessica came to the door alone when Casey knocked.

Casey reintroduced Jessica and Grant, though they remembered meeting briefly one morning when she and Casey were walking through campus together.

"I was just getting ready to start walking home, since Joey's car wouldn't start this morning," Jessica said. "He flipped out about it pretty bad. I tell you, I've had about enough of his temper. We both had nine o'clock classes, and by that time, whatever caused the electricity to go out and all the cars to mess up had already happened. Joey just went nuts. I don't know if you noticed it in the driveway or not, but he kicked a big dent right in the driver's door of his car, blaming it on his dad for buying him a *used* Audi. Then he took off running towards campus. I decided not to bother. I didn't have anything I couldn't skip today and besides, I knew they wouldn't have class with no electricity. I went back to bed, because I sure didn't get any sleep last night, and I was a bit hung over."

Grant glanced back in the direction of the car and rolled his eyes. Jessica was a beautiful girl by any standard, and he was surprised she put up with such an asshole. "Did you guys see the lights last night?" he asked.

"Yeah, through the windows. We had just gone to bed and it was so bright it flashed through the whole house. I had no idea what it was. Joey didn't either. But we were both pretty bombed from the party we went to."

"I slept right through it. Grant was outside though, and saw everything," Casey said.

"What in the hell was it?" Jessica asked. "What's going on? I can't believe everything just quit working like that. I can't make a call, listen to the radio…nothing."

"We don't know for sure," Casey said. "But the rumor is that it was some kind of disturbance from the sun. It could have affected a lot more than just New Orleans. Grant said that it could be a serious thing. A lot of people might have already died, and if the power doesn't come back on soon, things will get bad, like after a big hurricane."

"What are we supposed to do now, then?" Jessica asked.

"We need to start thinking about that," Grant said. "Hey, if you're ready, why don't we head back over to your apartment? Mine's close by campus too. I've got some stuff there we're gonna need. Do you have a bike, Jessica?"

"Yeah, but it's locked up by McWilliams Hall on campus. I left it there after play rehearsal and rode here with Joey in his car yesterday."

"No problem. We'll walk back with you. Casey and I can push our bikes so you can keep up."

"Geeze, Casey," Jessica whispered as they went inside to grab her bag out of the bedroom. "How come I can't find a nice guy like that instead of a jerk like Joey?"

During the three-mile walk back in the direction of the Tulane campus and their apartments, Grant related some of what he had experienced in the aftermath of Hurricane Katrina to Casey and Jessica and began speculating about what could happen next in a city the size of New Orleans with no power, no communications, and few working automobiles. He said it would likely become dangerous to stay in the city if these conditions continued for more than a couple of days. He mentioned the post-Katrina violence that took place throughout New Orleans after the levee broke and the city was flooded and cut off.

"But those people didn't have a choice," Jessica said. "They were stuck in the Superdome and everywhere else in the city and our own government screwed up and didn't get them out in time."

"It was a combination of things," Grant said. "Yeah, the local, state, and federal governments could have done better, but it was really an overwhelming event no one could have prepared for. It's also a fact that some of those people stayed behind on purpose to take advantage of the situation. Even members of the police department were looting stores and stealing new cars from the dealerships. The people who truly got stuck here against their will were mainly just waiting in the Superdome—in bad conditions to be sure, but most didn't have bad intentions. People who had their own transportation and wanted to leave generally got out before the hurricane even hit, and well before the city flooded."

"But don't you think a lot of the looting and stuff happened because people lost their homes?" Casey asked. "This is different. Yeah, the lights are out and the phones don't work, but I don't see why it would get bad like it did after a hurricane."

"When you think about it, Casey, what are people going to do for food in a city this size? You saw how long we had to stand in line just to get a sandwich and something to drink at lunch. And this is just the first day. I wonder how long shops like that will have anything left. I'll bet that one we went to is already completely sold out. Think about the grocery stores. If the power is out everywhere and most vehicles are not running, the shelves will be stripped bare in no time, and with the delivery trucks not running, they won't be restocking. There are a *lot* of people in New Orleans, Casey."

"So what are we supposed to do?" Jessica asked.

"The only sensible thing to do is get out of the city," Grant said. "There are simply too many people here. There's no way order can be maintained. It's just a short time before most people start panicking."

"I don't know where else I would go," Jessica said. "I don't know how I could get home if cars aren't working and the airlines are shut down."

"She's from Los Angeles," Casey explained to Grant. "And I don't know where I'd go either…. It's not as far to my dad's house in Mobile—well, at least not in a car, where it would be like two and a half hours, but that might as well be L.A., if you had to walk."

"What day was he supposed to be back?" Jessica asked. "Did you hear from him last night before the phones went out?"

"No. They left Martinique on Sunday afternoon. I think they were supposed to get to St. Thomas like tomorrow, so his flight back here was on Thursday. I knew I wouldn't hear from him last night because they were still at sea, but now he has no way of reaching me to let me know when they get to St. Thomas. I'm worried about him, but like

Grant said, a good sailor like Larry doesn't need electronics to navigate. I'm sure they'll be fine, but how will he get back to the States when they do get to land? I know he's going to be worried sick about me too."

"We can still hope the effects are not that far-reaching," Grant said, as he started walking again to encourage them to keep moving in the direction of their apartment. "But they're probably better off there than most anywhere else they could be, if this thing *is* that widespread. We're the ones in a situation we have to worry about. I think we need to start getting ready to go and make a plan now. But regardless of when we leave, we had better get what food we can carry now."

The only store along the way that was open was a small corner grocery on Magazine Street that was already packed with people buying everything they could snatch off the shelves. Like the sandwich shop Casey and Grant had stopped at earlier, the grocery could only accept cash purchases because there was no way to verify credit or debit cards. Grant had a little over forty dollars left in his wallet and Jessica had a single twenty-dollar bill.

"Jessica's a vegetarian," Casey said as Grant reached for the last two packages of beef jerky remaining on an end display.

"It's okay," Jessica said. "Go ahead and get what you want, it doesn't bother me as long as I don't have to eat it."

"The thing is, we've got to get things that are lightweight, will keep without refrigeration, and, ideally, don't require extra water to cook."

"Hey, how about these?" Casey asked, holding up a two-pound bag of almonds.

"Those are great," Grant said, "And vegetarian-safe," he added with an amused smile.

They were out of cash before they had purchased more than they could carry. Grant said they had done well, though, scoring a supply of several kinds of nuts, raisins and other assorted dried fruits, some bulk-packaged granola, a couple of large boxes of oatmeal that he said could be eaten uncooked if necessary, the jerky, several packages of tuna in foil, some boxes of whole-wheat crackers, two jars of peanut butter, and a couple of large blocks of Swiss cheese that he said would hold up well without refrigeration. Most of the other customers were loading up on bulky canned goods and other items that would be impossible to carry far on foot or on a bicycle. Despite their small haul, it took nearly two hours to get in and out of the grocery store. While they were in there the dark clouds that had been threatening rain since late morning finally broke open and drenched the streets, but the downpour had let up to a light drizzle by the time they were out in it.

They tied the plastic bags on Grant's rear rack and around the handlebars of both bikes and, pushing the bikes, made it back to Casey and Jessica's apartment by late afternoon. Casey opened all the blinds to let in as much light as possible, and at Grant's urging the two roommates began sorting through their clothes and shoes to find a few items that would be suitable to travel in. Casey was overwhelmed at what Grant was suggesting—that they might actually have to leave the city on *bicycles*. She knew Grant could do it, but she couldn't imagine how she or Jessica could pedal for miles and miles on the open road to anywhere. But Grant wasn't talking about just anywhere. His parents, who were currently working on an archaeology project in Bolivia, owned a small cabin on a river not too far from New Orleans. They'd used it as a weekend getaway when they were living in New Orleans for a couple of years while Grant was still in high school and his father was teaching at Tulane. That was before the hurricane destroyed their home in the city and his parents left for good.

"It's only about 90 miles from here," Grant said. "It's to the north, not far across the Mississippi state line, on a beautiful stream called the Bogue Chitto River. It would be a safe place in a situation like this. My dad thought of everything. There's a well and generator and lots of food and other supplies stored there all the time. I was up there over the holidays to get away and work on a research paper."

"Ninety miles! I could *never* ride a bicycle 90 miles!" Jessica blurted.

"Sure you could, Jessica. If you can ride a bike at all, you can ride it as far as you need to. You just have to take it one mile at a time," Grant explained.

"That's easy for you to say," Casey said. "You could probably ride that far in a day. But we aren't in shape for it like you are and our bikes suck compared to yours."

"I'm not talking about a race, Casey. We'll take our time, and go at the pace of whoever is the slowest. If it takes two or three days, that's okay. The main thing is that we'll be getting out of here. We can ride out of the city and get across the Causeway the first day for sure."

"The Causeway is 25 miles long by itself!" Jessica said.

"Yeah, you're right. But it's also the shortest route north to where the cabin is. When you think about it, if you can ride a mile, then you can ride two miles, three miles, and on and on. You just keep pedaling and the miles will slide on by. We'll stop and rest whenever we need to. One good thing, with few vehicles running, there won't be any traffic. I'll bet there'll be other bicyclists though—at least those who are smart enough to think of it and start moving now."

"I just hope it's not a mistake to leave," Casey said. "Can't we just go back now and buy all the groceries we can carry and bring them back here? I've probably got at least thirty or forty dollars in change if I dig through all my drawers and boxes in my closet. We can come back here and stay inside and lock the doors. The lights *have* to come on soon, don't they? Maybe it won't be too long before everything is back to normal."

"I think it would be a mistake to stay here," Grant said. "I mean, we don't have to leave immediately, but we'd better get ready. I don't think we can count on this being resolved or back to normal any time soon. If we didn't have the option of going to a well-stocked cabin within a reasonable distance, it would be one thing. But I know we would be safe there, and we would at least have a supply of food and water. We wouldn't have to worry about the angry mobs of looters that are bound to start roaming the streets here when they figure out no one's gonna bring them what they need and the police are powerless to stop them from taking it wherever they can find it. If I'm wrong and it turns out to be no big deal, then there will really have been no harm done, and we will have had some good exercise riding up there."

"But this isn't the Ninth Ward, Grant," Jessica said. "This is *Uptown*. It's *nice* here. People here don't loot and rob. I think you're being a bit paranoid."

"I know it's nice here now. And yes, it's relatively safe. But this kind of stuff would happen anywhere after a disaster like this. When people get desperate, they'll do anything. And besides, the people in the truly bad areas like you're talking about know that with everything shut down, nothing is going to stop them from coming here. And they know there's money and other goods here."

"He may be right, Jessica," Casey said. "He's been through hurricanes and lived all over."

"But why us, Grant? You hardly know us—well, me anyway.... Don't you have other friends or family that will need to go there?"

"Not now, I don't. My parents are much too far away to get any good out of it. And as I already told Casey, after Katrina all my close friends left New Orleans and never came back. I suppose I would go alone to the cabin if I didn't know anyone who wanted to go with me, and I still will if you two aren't interested. I'm certainly not staying here in the city, regardless. Casey and I just kind of ran into each other today; it's been a really weird day, and, well, here we all are at your apartment. I don't really have anyone else to spend the first day of the total shutdown of the grid with."

"We don't know that it's a *total* shutdown," Casey reminded him.

"No, but we should assume that it is in the immediate region, anyway. Look, I don't want to try to talk either of you into anything. But I've got a few of the things we need over at my apartment, and whether you leave the city with me or not, it would be safer to stick together for now. I'd like for you to both come over after you get your things together. I've got battery-powered lights and candles in my camping gear. At least we'll be able to see after dark at my place, and we can talk it over tonight and see how things are looking in the morning. What do you say?"

"That's fine with me," Casey said. "I hate blackouts even when they're just for a few hours. It'd be scary over here with no flashlights or anything."

"I'm okay with that too, I just don't know about going to some cabin in Mississippi," Jessica said. "And what about Joey? If I go, can he come too?"

"Of course," Grant said.

"If he would even want to," Jessica added.

"He may stop by here looking for you before he goes home tonight," Casey told her. "Why don't you leave him a note telling him we'll be at Grant's place and that he can find us there?"

They locked the door to the apartment at dusk, slipping a small piece of paper with Grant's address in the crack just above the deadbolt, where Joey couldn't miss it. Jessica and Casey had both emptied their backpack/book bags and stuffed them with as many items of clothing as they could possibly jam inside without breaking the zippers. The groceries were still tied on the bikes in the plastic bags. They walked them on campus, to the bike rack near the theater where Jessica had left her bike the day before. Grant's place was an efficiency apartment in back of a house on Freret Street, so after a short ride of a few blocks they were there.

"Wow, you've got some cool stuff in here," Casey said after Grant let them into his apartment and lit up the living room with a battery-powered Coleman lantern he dug out of a closet.

"Thanks. It's mostly stuff I traded for during summer field study in Guyana. These things are all that made it home. A lot of the artifacts I shipped got lost, or more likely stolen, somewhere along the way."

"What were you studying?" Jessica asked as she looked around the room at the collection of carved wooden drums, masks, blowguns, and bows and arrows hanging from every wall.

"Grant is an anthropology grad student," Casey explained. "I forgot that I hadn't told you. He spent three months last summer in the Amazon jungle."

"Actually it was in the highlands of Guyana, not in the Amazon Basin," Grant said. "I was working on a project our department is conducting among an indigenous tribe called the Wapishana on the upper reaches of the Kamoa River."

"That's crazy," Jessica said. "Do those people still use this stuff? Are they cannibals or something?"

Grant laughed. "No, they're not cannibals, but they're still mostly naked. And yes, they do use primitive tools and maintain most of their ancestral ceremonies. They are true hunter-gatherers, and really don't need anything but what the rainforest provides."

"Hunters? That's just wrong!" Jessica said. "Why do they still do that? I thought the jungle was full of tropical fruit and stuff."

"It is, but not enough to live on and get a balanced diet. They eat everything the forest provides, from the smallest insects and fish, to monkeys, snakes, wild pigs...you name it."

"It must have been an awesome experience staying in their villages and seeing how they live," Casey said, before Jessica and Grant could get into an argument about the ethics of eating animals.

"It was quite the experience, but this particular subgroup of the tribe has such a nomadic way of life they don't even live in villages. That's one reason we know so little about them. Our department is the first group of anthropologists to study them. Their first contact with the outside world was just in 1995. Anyway, there'll be time to tell you more about it later, if it doesn't bore you to death. I need to sort out some stuff and we need to talk about a plan, that is, if you two are still in with me after seeing all my jungle headhunter gear."

Casey and Jessica waited while Grant pulled a large duffel bag out of the same closet where he had gotten the lantern. He said it was the gear that he took on the jungle expedition and also occasionally used for weekend canoe camping on the river near his parent's cabin.

"The problem is, we can't carry all this stuff on the bikes, plus the food and water we're going to need for the trip. I can carry much more on mine, since I've got a rack on it and it's a lightweight bike anyway, but you two are going to have a hard enough time just pedaling those heavy clunkers you have even without any weight."

"Can't we just wear our backpacks?" Casey asked.

"Yeah, but it's not ideal. If you keep them light with just your clothes and things like that, I suppose it will have to do. But too much weight that high up will wear you out and keep you off balance. It's better to let the bike carry the weight. I think if you both carry your clothes in your packs and we strap some of the lighter, bulkier stuff like sleeping bags on the handlebars and under the seats, I can manage everything else we need."

"Didn't you say the cabin would have everything we need?" Jessica asked.

"Yes, but we can't head out on a trip that far and count on getting there in a certain length of time. A lot of factors could delay us, considering what has happened, so we need to be prepared to be as self-sufficient on the road as possible."

"I would have never thought like that," Casey said. "I guess that comes from what you learned in the jungle, huh?"

"Just travel in general. I learned more from my parents than from anywhere else. We were always on the move, it seems. I learned that real travel, not the tourist stuff, requires flexibility in your thinking and the ability to adapt to changing circumstances. We're not going to be tourists. If we go anywhere while the grid is down, we'll be *travelers,* and we had better be ready for anything."

THREE

THE ARRIVAL OF *IBIS* in the harbor at Charlotte Amalie brought most of the occupants of the other vessels near her mooring to their decks to wave and shout questions to the newcomers. Most simply wanted to know from where the two men in the schooner had sailed, and what they had seen or heard of the bizarre flash in the northern sky that was the first sign of the series of events that took out communications, the power grid, and most forms of transportation. Artie was still reeling from days and nights of constant motion, and felt his body still compensating despite the calm of the harbor in which *Ibis* floated peacefully, tethered to her mooring without rolling, pitching, or bobbing. He fought to steady himself while Larry was busy securing the sails and sorting out lines. When asked how far to the southeast of St. Thomas they'd been when they saw the flash, Artie replied with the numbers of the last coordinates the GPS had displayed before it lost satellite reception. These were numbers he would never forget, as they marked the point where Larry began navigating by dead reckoning.

"We have no way of knowing how Martinique might have been affected," Larry added after saying that those coordinates from when the event occurred put them over a hundred nautical miles from their departure point.

They were directing most of their answers to an older couple aboard a sleek, 50-odd-foot sailing yacht of modern design, with immaculate white topsides and polished metal fittings that indicated it was nearly new and well maintained. This boat, with the name *Celebration* displayed on her stern above the hailing port of Norfolk, VA, was the nearest vessel to *Ibis*, and the owners lost no time introducing themselves as Pete and Maryanne Buckley, inviting them to come aboard for a cup of coffee and more conversation.

"Our dinghy's already in the water," Pete said. "I'll come pick you up."

Pete rowed the rigid-bottomed inflatable alongside *Ibis*, explaining that the EFI-equipped 25-horsepower Honda outboard on the stern hadn't started since the power surge.

"It's not just the dinghy motor either," Pete said. "We're pretty much dead in the water. *Celebration* is just too dependent on high-tech equipment. But oh, wow! What a beauty you guys are on! She looks like you just sailed her in from an era before all this stuff was needed."

"Yeah, *Ibis* is pretty sweet," Larry said. "I wish she were mine, but as usual, I'm just doing a delivery."

"We thought we were doing the right thing," Pete said, "setting the boat up for our retirement with all those gadgets to do the work for us. You know, when you're an old fart like me, cranking a sheet winch by hand ain't the fun it looks to be. Now all this technology has come back to bite us on the ass, now that it won't work anymore. Maryanne's not taking it too well, but I told her, at least we're safe out here on the boat, even if we just stay here in the harbor."

"So nothing is working on the island?" Larry asked.

"As far as we can tell, no. We went to town several times yesterday, talked to a lot of people, tried to find out what we could. There's no contact with the outside world at all. And no way to get off the island, unless you're among the lucky few like us out here who have our own boats."

"What about the airport?" Artie was almost afraid to ask.

"Burned all day and into the night yesterday. People on that end of the island say that right after the power went out, a Delta flight coming in from Fort Lauderdale crashed right into the terminal. Nothing has flown over here since."

Artie's hopeful expression upon asking the question faded to a blank look of solemn acceptance. "I was afraid of that," he said.

Larry told Pete about the wreckage they had discovered late yesterday.

"This isn't gonna fix itself," Pete said. "Hell, even most cars are shut down because of their electronic ignitions, just like my Honda outboard. People around here are saying that if that surge was strong enough to knock out practically *everything* with any kind of electrical or electronic circuit, then there won't be any way to fix the damage for a long time."

"I guess it depends on how far-reaching the damage actually was," Larry said, as he and Artie climbed into the dinghy for the short row back over to *Celebration*.

"That's the real question, isn't it?" Pete agreed.

Pete secured the dinghy to the stern platform of the gleaming yacht and they all climbed into the cockpit, greeted by Maryanne, who had brought out a tray with four cups of coffee and a loaf of fresh-baked local bread along with a knife and butter dish.

"We bought as much bread and fresh fruits and vegetables as we could find in the market yesterday," she said. "The lines were already getting long and they were selling out fast."

"This is wonderful!" Artie said as he took a seat in the plush cockpit and reached for his coffee. I've barely eaten for the past three days."

"Offshore sailing didn't agree too well with my brother," Larry said. "But the light show he saw the other night cured him."

"So you saw it yourself?" Pete asked Artie.

"Oh yeah. I was on watch when it happened. Couldn't have missed it if I tried. The whole sky just lit up like daylight, except that there were all these different colors."

"We slept right through it, regrettably," Maryanne said.

"Yeah, that's another thing about a boat like *Celebration*," Pete said. "Our stateroom is so well insulated down there that half the time you couldn't tell if there was a hurricane blowing topsides."

"So this is a Tayana 54?" Larry asked. "First one I've been aboard, but I delivered a Tayana 42 Cutter from Annapolis to Antigua once. Solid boat."

"She's comfortable, for sure," Pete said. "Probably more boat than two people need for a retirement home, but you know, everybody is cruising bigger boats these days. You don't see many people out cruising the world on anything under 45 feet anymore."

"I do," Larry said, "but not in the popular anchorages. You probably can't get into many of the out-of-the-way places. What does she draw, anyway?"

"Seven feet, two inches," Pete said.

Larry whistled. Artie was just listening, not knowing enough about boats to really have an opinion. "I guess you didn't see much of the Bahamas then. Not many anchorages there that carry seven feet of water."

"No, but our goal was to get down here to the Virgins first," Pete said. "Then we were talking about trying to do a passage over to the Med if everything worked out. Out there in the Atlantic, draft doesn't matter, does it?"

"That sure is a pretty little schooner you guys are sailing," Maryanne said, "It's amazing how well-maintained it is. How old is it?"

"Less than a year," Larry said. "She looks like an old-time classic, but she's really a new custom build, a Reuel Parker design. She only draws four feet. It's all cold-molded wood-epoxy construction. The owner was supposed to meet me here tomorrow, but I guess that isn't going to happen. He lives in Tampa, so unless he changed his plans and flew in early, it's doubtful he'll be picking up his boat."

"Tampa? Was he planning to sail her all the way home from here?" Pete asked.

"No, he's apparently got another boat he keeps there. He had this one built to keep here for cruising around the islands. She was built in Trinidad. I picked her up there and did a shakedown cruise through the Grenadines before my landlubber big brother here came down to meet me in Martinique."

"It wasn't so bad, after I got my sea legs," Artie said, the memory of the awful seasickness already fading to the back of his mind.

Larry changed the subject back to the power outage as he stared across the harbor to the island. "I wonder how long it will be before people start to panic. If what we typically see after a big hurricane is any indication, it won't be much longer."

"We haven't been here for one of those yet," Pete said. "This is our first year of cruising since we both retired and bought the boat. We just got here right after Christmas. We spent the fall in Key West."

"I've been down in these islands long enough to see it all. You're right to say all of us out here on boats are better off. It's probably going to get ugly ashore pretty quick. Especially here in Charlotte Amalie and the other crowded places. Even this harbor probably won't be safe, so you ought to think about moving somewhere more remote. Only thing is, you don't have many choices with that seven-foot draft."

"I don't see how we could be in any danger out here," Maryanne said. "There are so many other boats around. Who's going to bother us?"

"Well," said Larry, "to people ashore, especially the gangs that don't need an excuse like this anyway, a boat like *Celebration* is a gold mine. They know it's full of expensive hardware, not to mention the food and water everyone is soon going to be desperate for. Cruisers have been targeted here before, and especially in St. Croix after Hurricane Hugo and some of the other really bad ones. I'm talking robbery, murder, gang rape, you name it."

Maryanne shuddered and looked at her husband. "Sounds like a realistic scenario to me," Pete said. "The question is, where *do* we go? I thought we might be better off here than back home, depending on how big this thing really is. I mean, if the same pulse took out everything in the States, it might be even worse there. Look how dependent everything up there is on the power grid, not to mention transportation."

"It's hard to believe this has shut down automobiles," Artie said. "I never would have thought about that. Of course, I never would have thought about it causing airplanes to crash either. I can't believe I'm stuck here now with no way to get back to New Orleans or even to call Casey and check on her."

"His daughter," Larry explained. "Artie was just with me for a few days of vacation."

"If you're going to get back to the mainland, you'll probably have to sail," Pete told Artie.

"*Sail?* All the way back to America? How long would *that* take?"

"Not as long as it took us to get down here, that's for sure," Pete said, adding that going back to the mainland was a downwind run with the help of the trade winds, while getting *to* the islands from Florida was a difficult, upwind bash.

"He's right about that," Larry said. "I've done it both ways many times. It's an easy run from here to Fort Lauderdale. If you don't stop along the way, you can get there in a week or so, depending on the boat."

"And your daughter is in New Orleans," Pete said. "At least that's a port city and you *can* sail there. You're lucky she's not at Kansas State or something. It might take another week or two to get around the Keys and across the Gulf, depending on the weather, but it could be a lot worse if she were inland. My guess is that a lot of people will be walking if they got the same effects up there that we got here."

Artie was overwhelmed. He had never considered the possibility of having to sail all the way to New Orleans in order to get back to Casey. Despite what Larry and Pete said, a *lot* could happen in a matter of two weeks or longer. How could he live that long not knowing if she was okay? What would she do in the meantime? If her car wouldn't start, she probably couldn't leave, but what dangers would she face in a blacked-out New Orleans? Artie couldn't believe the circumstances that could put him so out of touch with the person he loved most on this Earth. He knew Larry couldn't fully understand, even if he thought he did, because he had never had children. Casey was the light of Artie's life. He had to do whatever it took to get to her and protect her, even if it meant another voyage much longer than the one he'd just endured in miserable seasickness.

"If it's going to take that long, then we need to leave immediately," Artie said to Larry, his entire attitude about ocean voyaging completely changed now that he accepted the reality that it was the only way home and the only way back to his daughter.

"It's not quite that simple, Doc. For one thing, we can't take off on *Ibis* and leave the owner hanging, even if he is still in Tampa and has no way to get here. First, I have to make sure he's not already here."

"If he's not here, then it won't do him any good. Couldn't you drop the boat off in Tampa later, after we go to New Orleans?"

"It's a few hundred miles back to Tampa from New Orleans. I've done that crossing before. But no, I don't want to risk his boat like that considering the conditions, and my contract was to deliver her here. I've met my obligation as far as that goes, but if he is here, I need to find out. Besides, my boat is better suited to the voyage."

"But it's not even finished, you said. Aren't you still building it?"

"She's built and could be launched as she is. The main thing I have left to do is step the mast and set up all the running rigging. She's not painted yet, but that doesn't matter, I've got a solid coat of gray primer on everything and we can slap a coat of bottom paint on right before we splash her."

"You've built your own boat?" Maryanne asked. "What kind of boat is it?"

"A catamaran—a Wharram Tiki 36, to be exact."

"I've heard of Wharrams," Pete said. "We saw an old di-lapidated one in Key Largo. They sure are funky-looking boats. Aren't they homemade out of plywood?"

"A lot of them are homebuilt, and yeah, its plywood, but it's a composite construction with everything laminat-ed with epoxy resin and fiberglassed over. Some of them are built rough by people who don't know what they're doing, but I've taken my time with mine. All the materials are to Lloyd's specs and I've cut no corners. She'll look like a million-dollar yacht when she's all painted up and fitted out."

"Can a boat like that make it all the way to New Orleans?" Artie asked.

"Of course she can! You well know how long I've been sailing, Doc. I've sailed just about every kind of boat you can think of in my deliveries. Would I spend my hard-earned cash and most of my spare time building something that wasn't seaworthy? *Alegria* will be at least as capable as *Ibis* there. These cats have crossed every ocean in the world. There's no boat I would trust more when it gets re-ally nasty out there. The big difference, though, is that she can go where almost no other sailboat can. She only draws two feet."

"Two feet! Wow!" Pete said. "That's like a dinghy."

"Yep, I'll be able to put her right on the beach if I need to. That's the other thing—she's light. No lead keel, and construction from the finest okoume marine plywood brought her in at less than four thousand pounds, ready to cruise." Larry turned to Artie: "You see, *Ibis* is relatively shallow too, and she would get us there in a fine style, but we don't know what we might encounter in all this mess with everything shut down. My boat will have a lot of advantages if we need to go up a river or get to other places regular boats can't reach. And—she's much faster than a monohull. And—you're gonna love this, Doc—the motion of a catamaran is a lot different and a lot easier. None of that deep rolling that had you puking your guts out on the way here. You're gonna like multihull sailing a *lot* better."

"Where is your boat?" Pete asked. "I'd like to take a look; she sure sounds interesting. Is she close to the harbor?"

"Unfortunately no," Larry said. "I did the building under a tarp shed on the beach at Culebra. I'm sure you're familiar with it; it's one of the islands between here and Puerto Rico."

"Oh yes, there's a lovely anchorage there," Maryanne said. "We stayed there a couple of nights on the way here."

"I like it," Larry said. "It's much more laid-back than St. Thomas. I can actually leave tools lying around without having to worry about them walking off when I turn my back."

"How far is it from here?" Artie wanted to know.

"Not far at all, really," Pete said, "about 20 nautical miles west. You can see the island once you get out of this harbor and past Water Island."

"Still, if Culebra's an island, even 20 miles is a long way. If we have to leave *Ibis* here, how are we supposed to get there so we can even get started?" Artie asked, unable to conceal his anxiety about each new obstacle that seemed to come between him and Casey.

"I'm thinking," Larry said. "But first, I need to go ashore and ask around to make sure my client is not here."

After inviting them to come back that afternoon for drinks, Pete took Artie and Larry back over to *Ibis* so Larry could offload the schooner's dinghy for the trip to shore. Pete promised to keep an eye on *Ibis* while they were gone, so Larry could relax a bit about leaving her. Artie had question after question for his brother about their proposed voyage to New Orleans, and Larry did his best to answer each one as they lowered the sleek wooden dinghy into the water and Larry got the ship's paperwork and their passports in order. Normally, clearing back into St. Thomas as American citizens meant a brief visit to the U.S. Customs and Immigration offices at the western end of the harbor, but considering the circumstances, Larry wasn't sure anyone would be there. Still, they had to try, and they had to go ashore anyway.

Larry did the rowing as Artie sat in the bow of the dinghy. Each time they passed another occupied vessel in the anchorage they were hit with the same barrage of questions about where they had come from, what they had seen, and what they might know of what was happening in the world beyond the harbor. When they reached the ferry dock near the government offices, Artie lost no time clambering up the ladder as Larry tied them off.

"Land!" Artie said. "At one point a couple of days ago, I swore I'd kiss it if I ever set foot on it again."

"So go for it!" Larry said. "I've been waiting to see this."

"What's the point? At that time I thought I'd never have to get on a boat again if I ever got here. Now, this is just a temporary stop. I guess I shouldn't get too excited about it or get too used to it."

"Probably not, I don't want to waste any time here; this place is gonna turn to shit in another day or two. It's bad enough in normal times with all the cruise ship tourons and gangs of punk-assed dreads."

As Larry suspected, they found the customs and immigration offices closed. Artie followed as Larry led the way back east along the waterfront to the Yacht Haven Marina and Hotel complex to see if the owner of *Ibis* had arrived before the pulse hit. If he had, he would be stranded among the thousands of other tourists stuck there in miserable conditions in hotels without lights or air conditioning. If not, it was certain that he wouldn't be coming to the island until after power and communications were restored, and who knew how long that would be?

They found the hotel lobby full of frustrated guests unsure of what to do next, many of them killing time while they waited by drinking warm beer or the local Cruzan rum. The clerk behind the desk could not look for the name Larry gave him because all guest information from before the power outage was in their computer registry system. They went to the marina office and no one there remembered anyone asking about a yacht named *Ibis*. Larry said that most likely the owner was not on the island. There was nothing else to do but leave the yacht on the mooring as he had contracted to do, and hope that eventually her owner would be able to get to St. Thomas to claim her—if someone didn't steal her first. But they had to get to Culebra, as there was a lot of work to do to get Larry's boat and make it ready for the passage to New Orleans.

"I guess we'll have to sail over there on *Ibis* and then sail both boats back here so we can leave her once we get *Alegria* shipshape," Larry said, when Artie asked how they were going to get to Culebra.

"That's going to take a lot of extra time, isn't it—coming all the way back over here?"

"We'll lose most of a day doing it, but it won't make much difference in the end. What else can we do? Besides, my cat is a lot faster than *Ibis*. We'll have the trade winds in our favor once we leave here for good, and we'll make a fast passage to Florida. You'll see."

They left the exclusive Yacht Haven complex and Artie followed his brother to a seedier part of the waterfront, where they found his favorite bar still open for business, despite the lack of power. Larry was well acquainted with the owner from his many stops in the harbor taking yachts up and down the island chain.

"We're open until we run out," the man said. "At the rate people have been drinking since yesterday, that won't be much longer. What are you two having?"

"Nothing," Larry said. "It's way too early for me. We're getting out of here real soon, I hope. I just had to make a quick check and be sure my client wasn't here."

"Brought another boat in, huh?"

"Yeah, a pretty sweet little wooden schooner—new custom build and all that. Too bad the owner probably won't get to see her any time soon."

"If he wasn't on the island before five minutes after ten yesterday, he won't. Man, this is one bizarre scene. *Nobody* knows the extent of it. There's just no way to get any news. We don't know if anybody's coming to help us get things back up and running or not."

"We intend to find out, one way or the other," Larry said. "We're gonna sail to the mainland and try to get some answers. I hope you're not staying around here yourself."

"Liz and I have already talked about it. Our boat is pretty well stocked up all the time. We won't stay in Charlotte Amalie more than another day or two. There's already been some looting and a couple of house fires. It won't be long before the gangs are running the streets with machetes, taking whatever they want. We've seen it before. We're thinking of sailing over to the BVI and maybe hanging out at one of the out islands, maybe Peter Island."

"Probably a good idea," Larry said. "Good luck to you, man. We've gotta scoot. We've got a lot of work to do on my boat before we can leave."

Outside the yacht club, Artie and Larry stood for a minute taking in the scene on the city streets leading up the slopes from the harbor. Throngs of pedestrians, locals and stranded tourists alike, were moving among the stalled cars that filled the roadways. Everything was in a state of chaos as people walked around looking for friends and family they couldn't call on the phone, or for water or food they could no longer drive to get. The enormity of the disruption over-whelmed Artie as the reality before his eyes sunk in. It still didn't seem possible that all the advanced communications and much of the machinery of modern civilization could just be turned off like flipping a switch. He watched for a few moments, and felt truly sorry for the thousands of vacationers who were caught on the island in this mess and had no idea how they would get home. At that moment, he began to realize that despite the fact that he too was a stranded tourist, he was lucky to have a brother like Larry and the prospect of a sure, even if somewhat slow, ride home.

It was shortly after noon when they left the ferry dock at St. Thomas and rowed back out to *Ibis*. Pete was in the cockpit of *Celebration* and saw them coming. He waved them over to talk for a few minutes. They sat bobbing in the din-ghy while he held the bow painter to keep them from drift-ing away. Pete had the best news that Artie had heard since they made their decision to sail Larry's boat back to the States. He said that while they were ashore, he and Mary-anne had talked it over and decided that they didn't really feel good about staying in Charlotte Amalie. They decided that Culebra would be a better place to hunker down for the time being, as the population was much smaller there, and they had liked it when they stopped there before. Since they were going back anyway, Pete wanted to offer Artie and Larry a ride with them on *Celebration*. That way, Larry could leave *Ibis* on her mooring as he was obliged to, and they could get going on Larry's boat as soon as possible. Besides, Pete said he and Maryanne would have a hard time moving the big Tayana alone without the aid of her electric windlass, depth sounder, GPS, and all the other amenities they were so dependent upon to handle her.

Artie was delighted with this, as it meant they wouldn't have to backtrack to St. Thomas later. Larry agreed that Pete and Maryanne would be safer in Culebra, and said he would introduce them to some of his friends there. It was already too late in the day to get underway, get there, and settle into the anchorage before dark, though, so Larry said they would have to wait until morning to sail. It wouldn't be safe to enter Culebra's reef-guarded harbor at night with all aids to navigation unlit—especially with *Celebration*'s seven-foot draft. But they could get their personal belongings and the remaining supplies off *Ibis* and move aboard the bigger yacht that afternoon.

"We'll have dinner around five thirty," Maryanne said. "It will be steaks on the grill tonight, if that's all right with you guys. We've got to use up what's in the freezer. It won't stay cold much longer in this heat."

Artie helped Larry finish the job of sorting out *Ibis* and stowing all her gear in preparation for leaving her. They carefully furled the mainsail and foresail, secured them to their booms with sail ties made of nylon webbing, and then buttoned on the canvas covers to shield the sails from the sun's damaging UV light. They removed the big genoa from the forestay and bagged it to be stored below, and furled the smaller staysail, secured it in its fitted cover, and hoisted it just clear of the deck by its halyard. They folded up the cockpit Bimini and lashed it to the grab rails on the coach roof. They put all loose gear away in the cockpit lockers, and then Artie scooped up seawater in a canvas bucket attached to a line to rinse the decks as Larry scrubbed them with a long-handled brush. When they were done, *Ibis* was as neat and clean as any yacht Larry had ever left with her owner, even though he knew that she would likely remain unattended and unused for a long time to come.

They packed their clothes in their bags down below, and Larry cleaned out the ice boxes and lockers, bagging up all of the remaining food on board. He figured it was more than enough for the two of them to make the passage to the mainland if they took it all.

"There should be enough stuff for a couple of weeks already on board *Alegria*; I hope Scully thought to pick up what he could when the lights went out."

"So he'll be there when we get to your boat?"

"Oh yeah. He's living aboard while he's working for me, at least some of the time. Scully doesn't hurt himself working *too* hard. He wouldn't do it at all if he didn't like me and want to see that boat completed."

"So what will he do when we launch it and leave for New Orleans?" Artie asked.

"Go with us, of course," Larry said as if that should have been obvious to Artie.

"Is there enough room for all three of us?"

"Of course, and we need Scully. He's a good sailor and navigator, and even better, a great fisherman. Everything about the trip will be easier with him along."

"How do you know he'll want to go?"

"Because he doesn't have anything else to do. You already know he's a Rastafarian. His favorite thing in the world is simply observing what's going on, watching other people, and prophesying doom to the modern world and our way of life. He's been expecting something like this very event for years. There's probably nothing he'd rather do about now than sail to Babylon itself and see what has happened."

"You mean he'll be happy about all this? I don't know if I'm going to get along with this guy or not."

"Not happy—just indifferent. It's like what I told you about living on 'island time.' Scully doesn't *need* any of our modern technology. His life would be about the same with or without it. But you'll like him okay, and we do need him and his skills at a time like this."

When they were done packing, Artie handed down the bags of food and gear to Larry in the dinghy, and Larry made a couple of trips to shuttle it all over to *Celebration*. Once everything was transferred, Artie helped him haul the dinghy aboard the schooner and lash it upside down in its fitted chocks between the masts; then Pete came to pick them up in his inflatable.

They had dinner and rum drinks in the cockpit. Inevitably, the conversation centered around the profound changes that had taken place within not much longer than the past day. But Artie and Larry were both tired from their inconsistent sleep on the passage from Martinique, and asked to be excused early so they could catch up before the short sail to Culebra the coming morning.

Celebration was only the second sailboat Artie had ever been aboard, and he soon found out why Larry preferred smaller vessels for his own use when they prepared to leave the harbor the next morning. With the complex electrical control systems throughout the vessel rendered useless by the pulse, there was no way to start the inboard diesel engine. It was not set up for manual cranking the way some smaller marine engines are. They would have to sail out of the crowded anchorage, maneuvering among dozens of other vessels while taking care not to run across their anchor rodes with the seven-foot-deep keel. Just getting underway was a task Artie was unprepared for. With Pete taking the helm and Larry having to manually hoist and trim the huge sails that would normally be controlled by electric winches, he had the grunt job of hauling in the heavy, all-chain anchor rode. That, too, would have normally been done with a push of a button to start an electric windlass, but today Artie had to manually crank the windlass with the emergency backup handle, hoisting over a hundred feet of three-eighths-inch chain inch by inch, heavy labor that had him soaked with sweat in the tropical humidity.

Larry expertly trimmed the main with a manual winch as Pete steered off the wind just at the moment the anchor broke free. Artie continued to crank at the windlass as he pulled in the remaining few feet of chain and then struggled to control the big plow-shaped anchor as it spun in the air and swung back and forth, threatening to slam against *Celebration's* pristine bow. He somehow wrestled it aboard without smashing his fingers and pinned it in its chocks as

Larry had instructed him before they started. He felt the boat suddenly heel to starboard as the mainsail filled, and then Pete brought her about on another tack to pick a clear line between all the boats in their path. Most everyone in the anchorage was awake and on deck to wave and call out to them as they sailed past. Word of their plans had spread fast, and the other boat owners wished them luck and offered last-minute tidbits of advice. Artie stood on the pulpit watching the bow cut through the clear aquamarine water, wondering if he would soon be in the miserable throes of seasickness once they reached the open water. But at least today's trip was a short passage and would be over in a few hours. He hoped what Larry had said about the motion of catamarans was true. He had been so sick on the previous voyage, and he tried not to imagine being that sick for two weeks on their way to New Orleans. But above all, as he watched the buildings and green hills of St. Thomas slide by, he was grateful to at last be in motion and going in the right direction—the only direction that mattered to him—west to Culebra and one step closer to New Orleans and Casey.

Larry joined Artie at the bow, where he could see better into the shades of green and blue water to pick out the deepest channel and give hand signals to Pete at the helm to tell him which way to steer. He had been in and out of this harbor countless times, but was taking no chances, considering the circumstances and the vessel's deep draft. He relaxed a bit once they passed Water Island, a smaller outlying cay that guarded the main entrance. Once it was abeam to port, Culebra was visible on the horizon ahead, hazy blue with distance, and obviously hilly, though not as large or steep as St. Thomas. Larry said it was made up of mainly brush and rock, more desert than anything else, but it was renowned for its pink sand beaches and clear waters. It was also much less accessible than St. Thomas, lacking an airport for commercial jets and reachable only by ferry or small plane in normal times. But there was a good harbor, safe from all but the strongest hurricanes, and big enough to accommodate many cruising boats.

"So it's technically part of Puerto Rico?" Artie asked his brother.

"Yes, and so is Vieques," he said, pointing to another outlying island farther south. "See that big mountain way past them in the distance? That's El Yunque, the highest peak on the main island of Puerto Rico. There's a rain forest preserve up there that's pretty awesome. I *like* Puerto Rico. It's about my favorite place in the Caribbean. The people are great—especially the women," he grinned. "There's more happening on the main island, but Culebra's quieter and better suited for building a boat."

"You've been at this project for a while, haven't you?"

"A little over three years now; I keep getting pulled away on these delivery jobs, so working on my own boat is kind of hit or miss. I put in a month here, two weeks there, that sort of thing. But hey, it's all good—I'm on island time the whole time—and the best thing about it is I pay for the boat as I build it. I'll own her free and clear, unlike our friends here on this monstrosity."

"What does a boat like this cost?" Artie asked.

"This one? I don't know, roughly around six, seven hundred grand, I reckon. Maybe more, the way they've got her set up. Way outta my league, I'll tell you that, but chump change for a doctor like you."

"Yeah, right. She *does* seem to sail well, though."

"Oh yeah, and I'm sure she's fast too, in the right conditions, with her long waterline. Out in the blue water she would be quite comfortable compared to *Ibis*."

The route to open water took them right past the airport, where they could see smoke still rising from the rubble of the terminal, and a few undamaged jetliners that had been far enough away on the runway to avoid the explosions and fires. There was no sign of activity there, as the airport now had little to offer to anyone on the island. A few miles beyond the waterfront runway, the westernmost point of St. Thomas slipped by to starboard and soon they were off soundings with nothing in the way and 20 knots of favorable trade winds to bear them swiftly to Culebra. With no need to keep a lookout off the bow for now, Artie and Larry made their way back to the cockpit to join Pete and Maryanne for snacks and conversation as they all took turns steering the yacht by hand. Artie was glad to be moving, but he also couldn't help thinking that in the few hours that would elapse from they time they left the mooring until they were anchored at this first waypoint on their voyage, he could have flown all the way to New Orleans and driven his car to Casey's apartment—if only there were an airplane that could fly, or a car that would start....

But despite his impatience, the crossing to the other island went surprisingly quickly, and Artie soon found himself back at the bow with Larry to help spot the channel as they rounded a barren rocky point and entered a narrow opening on the south side of the island that led into a large and well-protected harbor. Boats were anchored on both sides of the channel and off the beach that fronted the small town surrounding the basin. Artie guessed there were at least fifty large cruisers and some smaller day boats, most of them sailing vessels. As soon as they were safely inside the anchorage and past the reefs, Larry took over the helm and guided *Celebration* to a spot deep enough to accommodate her draft and give enough swinging room at anchor, whatever the wind direction. He said he was anxious to check on Scully and his boat and Pete said they could borrow the inflatable dinghy, as he and Maryanne were in no hurry to go to shore and could wait until the next day.

Larry rowed, pointing the blunt bow of the clumsy inflatable at an opening in the mangroves on a stretch of the shore away from the main cluster of houses and stores. As they neared a narrow beach, Artie could see a large white tarp stretched over a framework of two-by-fours and posts. Protruding from under the makeshift workshop roof were the upswept bows of two slender hulls that brought to mind giant canoes, more than any other kind of boat. They pulled the dinghy up on the sand and Larry secured it with an anchor.

"There she is," he said. "*Alegria*: our ticket to New Orleans."

Artie walked across the sand to get a closer look before saying anything. The two V-shaped catamaran hulls were supported by heavy wooden cradles blocked up over the sand by various bits and blocks of timber. Workbenches and sawhorses surrounding the hulls were cluttered with other miscellaneous assemblies and fabrications that were obviously part of the boat, and tools, assorted hardware, jugs of epoxy, and cans of paint were scattered in haphazard piles on every available work surface. A stepladder stood next to one of the hulls, giving access to the deck, which was at least eight feet from the ground. Artie's anticipation of getting underway to New Orleans turned to dismay, which was written all over his face when he looked back at Larry.

"This isn't a boat, it's a construction project! It'll take forever to put all this together and get it in the water."

"It's closer than you think, Doc. Look, I know you can't visualize how it's going to be—most people can't when they see it this way. But when these 36-foot hulls are spread apart to assembly width, the overall beam will be 20 feet—that's a big platform with an easy motion at sea. All the beam and deck components are built. We just have to install some hardware here and there, step the mast, do some bits of rigging, and we'll be ready to launch. Cosmetics be damned, I'll paint her later after all this shit is over with. She's one hell of a boat. You're gonna see once she's in the water."

"It all just looks so overwhelming to me. I mean, how are we supposed to even move these huge hulls apart to put them together? How do we get it in the water without a crane or something?"

"It's all downhill to the water, Doc," Larry said, pointing out the barely perceptible slope from the boat shed to the high-tide line. "Trust me, I know how to get it done."

"So where's this friend of yours, Scully, who's supposed to be working on it?"

"Right there," Larry said, pointing to the harbor.

Artie saw a lone figure paddling a long sea kayak with bright yellow decks and two separate cockpits, the front one empty. The paddler was coming from the direction of the main town, across the harbor. As he ran the bow of the kayak up on the beach and stepped out, Artie could see that he looked just the way his daughter had described him. He was shirtless and barefoot, clad in nothing but a pair of ragged cutoffs that had once been camouflage military fatigues. There couldn't have been a spare ounce of fat on him. As he pulled the boat up above the tide line, wiry muscles rippled under his skin like knotted cords. That skin was a shade of ebony rarely seen today with so many generations of mixed blood lending lighter tones to the color of most people of his race. Scully looked like he could be purely African from some untouched equatorial tribal lineage, but what stood out even more than his striking dark color and outstanding physique was his wild hair. As he walked up to them, dreadlocks that hung nearly to his waist swung like tangled lengths of rope across his shoulders and behind his back.

"Scully! What the hell have you been doing, mon? Why don't you have my boat in the water yet?" Larry grinned as he stepped forward to greet his best friend.

"A mon got to have a break sometime. I an' I goin' to de town to find out de news and den I look bok dis way an' see dis rubber dinghy on de beach. T'ink some pirate be comin' to steal de boat, so I comin' bok fast to put a stop!"

"I *am* a pirate, don't you know, Scully. Hey, this is my brother, Artie. He's Casey's father. You remember Casey, don't you?"

"How can a mon forget de most beautiful girl ever comin' down de island? Pleased to meet you, mon. An' your daughter, she wid you?"

"No, I wish she were."

"Casey's in New Orleans at the college," Larry said. "Artie's not supposed to be here in Culebra with me. He came down to help me deliver a boat to St. Thomas. You remember that new little schooner I was telling you about when I left here to take that Beneteau to Trinidad? Well, we were halfway through the passage when the lights went out. What about you, did you see anything when it happened?"

"You know a mon not supposed to be up all de night 'cept when he navigating on de boat. No, I an' I sleepin' when dem seh dey seen de flashin' lights. Only in de mornin' when I put on de radio an' de music don't play, I t'ink somet'ing hoppen. But I got work to do on de boat an' not to worry, until later in de mornin' when I try de drill press...an' she don't turn. Den I check de cable...and den try de saw. No juice to de shop an' no light shinin', so den I paddle to de town an' find same t'ing everywhere in de island. No mon he can seh what is de reason, but some of dem talkin' of de lights in de night sky. An' some of dem say dat mehbe it's de sun gonna burn up, or mehbe it's some nuclear missiles fired up by de evil dictators in Bobbylon. But I seh Jah, he strike de Earth wid his mighty hand, 'cause he is displeased wid all dis desecration of his creation."

Artie could barely understand what Scully was saying. He was obviously speaking English, but in some strange West Indian dialect that was so foreign it almost sounded like another language. Larry obviously understood him perfectly, though, despite how fast he was talking.

"You've been saying that for years, Scully," Larry said. "But whatever it was, as far as we know it's widespread. In St. Thomas, everything's out. Have you heard any news from anywhere else beyond here?"

"Some mon comin' on de sailboat from Fajardo yesterday. He seh all de lights dem dark on Puerto Rico. Lights dem don't work. Cars dem won't go. Bus too, an' de planes dem can't fly. He seh he comin' to Culebra because he afraid to stay on Puerto Rico. T'ree million people an' dem got not'ing to eat on dat island."

"Yeah, Puerto Rico would not be the place to be about now, just like I told Artie about St. Thomas. I guess a lot of people from over on the main island will be coming here and to Vieques too when it gets bad, but only those who have sailboats or some kind of old, really basic engines will have a way to get here."

"So wot you gonna do, Copt'n? You t'inkin' to put dis boat in de watah?"

"We've got to, Scully. Sailing is the only way to go. Artie has no way to get home, and he can't stay here, because Casey is in New Orleans. We've got to sail there and try to find her. We need your help, Scully. We're sailing to the States."

"New Orlean? Dat's in *Bobbylon*, mon! America de very place dat displease Jah so much he shut off de lights all over de world. A mon not supposed to be sailin' to dat place in de end time like dis."

"Maybe not, but we can't leave Casey there. What else have you got to do, Scully? You always said Jah was going to destroy Babylon anyway. Maybe now you can see it for yourself. We don't plan on hanging around after we find Casey. I figure things are going to get real bad up there if the power stays off long enough, too many people who won't know what in the hell to do. It's bound to get ugly. But if we get going fast, we hope we can find Casey quickly and get the hell back south to St. Somewhere, where there's not so damned many people."

Scully looked out over the harbor and then back to the disassembled catamaran in the shed. He pushed his long dreads back over his shoulder and reached out to shake both Artie and Larry's hands. "Okay. I t'ink it's crazy but if you goin', I goin' too. Can't leave a girl like Casey in dat evil place. We need get her on de boat and wid she friend too. Nice girls dem, and need to bring dem bok to de island. But dis boat she can't sail like dis."

"Absolutely, Scully. So let's get to work so we can go!"

FOUR

WHEN THE TWILIGHT FADED away in New Orleans, the blacked-out city was darker than Casey could have ever imagined. Standing on the balcony outside Grant's apartment, the three of them watched as night enveloped the neighborhood, cutting them off from the world beyond the streets out front. Stars they had never noticed before in the perpetual light pollution of the city now filled the sky in the gaps between surrounding trees and houses, providing the only illumination to be seen other than a few candles and battery-powered flashlights visible through some of the nearby windows. Casey wasn't afraid of the dark, but this complete absence of electric-powered lights was just creepy in such a dense urban environment. Adding to the closed-in feeling of near complete darkness was the unsettling quiet caused by the lack of automobile traffic and other mechanized sounds. She had not been aware until now of how pervasive the constant hum of machinery in the city had been until it was silenced, and now she heard human voices from the streets and nearby buildings that would have been drowned in the background noise before. They each stood looking and listening, lost in their private thoughts for a few moments, saying nothing until Grant suggested they go in and eat something.

Inside the apartment, Grant's battery-powered lantern illuminated the small living room where he had begun sorting through his camping gear and organizing it into several piles according to each item's priority. Casey was surprised at how much stuff he had, and wondered how they were supposed to carry all this on bicycles if they really had to leave the city that way. Once the compact sleeping bags and other items were unpacked from the duffel bags he kept them in, Grant's equipment practically filled the room. Casey had only been camping a couple of times with her dad, and that had been years ago in a state park campground where they were able to set up the tent just a few feet from the car. There had been hot showers and vending machines, as well as lots of other friendly people around. She couldn't imagine what it would be like to camp along the road while riding bicycles, as Grant suggested, since 90 miles would be too far for them to travel in a day. Unlike Jessica, she could see that it was *possible* to ride that far, but she sure hoped they wouldn't have to. Casey still held out hope that they would wake up in the morning and the lights would be back on—just as they had been after a tornado had ripped through the neighborhood and taken down the power lines when she was a little girl. Grant was convinced this couldn't happen.

"This is different than any kind of conventional wind storm or lightning damage," he said. He went on to explain that though wind can blow down power poles or trees and take out big areas of service by disrupting the transmission lines, and lightning can short out transformers and destroy other components along the lines or at the power sub-stations, the areas of damage in both cases are usually pretty limited. Katrina was an exception, to be sure, he said, because the power grid throughout most of Louisiana, Mississippi, and Alabama was taken out in a single day by that storm. It took a staggering amount of work to get all those power lines that were pulled down by falling trees rebuilt and back online, even with utility companies from all over America pouring into the region and crews working around the clock for weeks. In some of the hardest-hit areas, it took nearly two months to get all the power restored—and that was with the resources to do it. Plenty of replacement parts were available everywhere outside the hurricane damage zone, as well as running vehicles and manpower to operate them and do the work. Grant asked them both, if this solar storm or whatever it was took out a bigger area than Katrina had, maybe even most of the United States, where were the crews and parts going to come from? "I don't think we need to entertain false hope that this is going to be fixed any time soon," he said.

"So you think it could be a few weeks before they can get it fixed?" Casey asked.

"No, I don't even see that happening, more like a few *months* if I had to guess. But we really just don't know the extent of it, so who knows?"

"I can't just sit in some cabin in the woods for months," Jessica said. "How am I supposed to let my parents know

I'm okay? How am I supposed to know if they're okay? And how is Casey's dad going to get home? And if he does get back here, how will he find us?"

Grant was about to answer when he was interrupted by a loud banging on the door that startled all three of them. He picked up the long machete that he had shown them earlier—another souvenir from his trips to the South American jungles—and walked over to the door.

"Who is it?" he asked, before reaching for the knob.

"Is Jessica in there? She's supposed to be at this address," an impatient voice on the other side demanded.

"Joey!" Jessica jumped up.

After glancing in her direction and seeing it was obvious she knew his voice, Grant opened the door and introduced himself to the visitor standing on the porch. Joey looked as if he had been drinking all day, which he had. He was holding a beer in one hand and half a six-pack of cans dangling in their plastic rings in the other. He was wearing a New Orleans Saints T-shirt, flip-flops, and shorts, and looked as if he were coming to yet another in a long series of parties.

"I've been looking for you all afternoon!" he said to Jessica as he pushed past Grant, barely acknowledging him. "I thought you would stay home until I got back, or at least stay at Casey's."

"Well, I guess you can see that the lights are out, Joey. What was I supposed to do, sit there in the dark?"

"We came over here because my friend Grant has all this stuff," Casey said, pointing out the lantern, the piles of gear, and the bags of groceries they had bought earlier that day.

Joey glanced around the room at all the gear and the three bicycles leaned against walls where they had brought them inside to keep them from getting stolen. "You must be a freakin' Boy Scout, huh?" he said to Grant. "What the fuck are you gonna do with all this shit?"

"We were just making plans to evacuate the city," Grant said calmly. "Things are not going to get better here before they get a lot worse."

"That's bullshit! I don't know why everybody's tripping out about a little blackout. They'll have the lights back on tomorrow or the next day. Besides, how the fuck are you going to evacuate when nobody's car will run? Mine sure won't. They say we're all gonna to have to get new computers in them because they're fried. All we can do is wait 'til the lights come on and the parts stores open."

"I don't think they're going to get this fixed any time soon, Joey." Casey said. "Stop and think about it for a minute. What could we do if we stay here? What are we going to eat? The stores are already running out of everything."

"Well, they still had beer back at the Circle K a while ago, even if it was just Coors Lite piss. But I've got a half a case of Abita back at my house, and plenty of sandwich stuff and chips. Come on, Jessica. Let's go home. I can think of things we can do without lights."

"I'm not walking all the way back to your house tonight, Joey. It's too far in this dark. I'm staying here, and you should too. I don't want anything to drink. I'm scared and I just want to be with friends until it's daylight again. You need to just stay here with me; I'm not leaving tonight."

Joey put up an argument but seeing that Jessica was not going to change her mind, he acquiesced, and opened another beer for himself when no one took him up on his offer to share the three that remained. Casey could tell that Grant would have been happy to see him go and she would have too, but since Jessica wanted him there Grant offered the two of them his room, where the only bed in the apartment was located. Then he stretched out his sleeping bag on the living room floor, giving Casey the couch, which was a bit narrow, but comfortable enough. Casey spent at least another hour awake that first night, lying in the darkness listening to Grant's steady breathing from the floor and thinking of her dad, wondering if he and Larry had made it to land yet, and if so, if they had found the electricity still on in the islands. She also thought about how strange it was that here she was sleeping on the couch in Grant's apartment, just a few feet away from him—a guy she barely knew but had thought about often since first meeting him. It was so strange how circumstances had brought them together in a situation where almost anything could happen. So much had happened already since she woke up this morning, she could barely comprehend it, and if this much could change in one day, she wondered what might be in store the next morning. Sleep did come at last despite her worries. When she woke and sat up on the couch it was daylight, and Grant was standing in the apartment's tiny kitchen, pouring hot water he had boiled on his propane camp stove into a French press sitting next to it on the counter.

"Coffee will be ready in about five minutes," he said when he looked her way and saw that she was stirring.

"That sounds great! Good thing you had that stove."

"Yeah, I would imagine quite a few folks here in the city are going to be doing without their morning brew today."

"Are they still asleep?" Casey asked, nodding towards the closed bedroom door.

"I guess. I haven't heard anything from them."

"I'm sure they were both exhausted since they didn't get any sleep the night before."

"I can see why you don't like that guy," Grant whispered as Casey stepped into the kitchen where they waited on the coffee to steep another minute or two.

"Like I told you, he's a real jerk. I can't believe Jessica hasn't already dumped him."

"There must be something about him she likes."

"His looks, I suppose. I'm afraid he's going try and talk her into going back home with him today."

"That would be a dumb idea," Grant said. "I think we need to be getting ready to leave, and maybe even head out later today."

"Do you really think we have to leave this soon? Isn't there some possibility help will be coming, and maybe we ought to wait just a little longer and make sure we really have to evacuate?"

"Based on how things were after Katrina, I have to say no, that's not a good idea. Even with outside help coming in and a large portion of the population already gone, things got really bad early on and stayed bad for a long time. We simply *have* to go where there are not so many people crammed into one area. These people are going to get desperate, and it's not just because they'll be missing their morning coffee, either."

"I just hope we can get to your cabin and it will be as safe as you say it is."

"We'll get there all right, assuming we get moving soon enough. I can't guarantee it'll be safe, but I think it's a way better choice than staying here."

"I've got to somehow let my dad know where I'm going. I know he may not be able to get here, but if he does, he's going to be looking for me. I need to leave a note with detailed directions to the cabin. I need to leave one in my apartment and one in his car at the airport. Can we go by the airport on the way out? It's not that far out of the way, is it?"

"It's several miles out of the way, but doable. I don't want to make this trip any harder on you two than it has to be. I'm actually more concerned about Jessica than you. I don't think she realizes the danger, and I wonder if she has the stamina to make it."

"She'll be okay," Casey said. "I don't know what either one of us would do without your help, though. I guess we would just be stuck here like everyone else."

"I'd hate to leave you two here in this mess if I can do something about it. And as I said before, if I didn't bring you along, I'd just be making the trip alone. Speaking of which, why don't you write that note for your dad's car now—I'll draw a map of the route to the cabin to go with it—and I'll ride over to the airport alone this morning. That way I can scope out what's going on today and see if I can hear any news of things beyond the city. Do you have a key to his car?

Casey said she did and went to get her key ring out of her backpack. She told Grant about her mom's accident and how after they lost her she and her dad had been nearly inseparable throughout her teen years. Though it hadn't been easy, Casey thought her dad had done a great job as a single parent. Hardly a day went by that they didn't talk for at least a few minutes, and she knew her dad would be frantic with worry about her after being completely cut off from all communication. He had not liked the idea of being out of touch even for the three days he would be sailing offshore with her Uncle Larry. Though it might be impossible for him to get to New Orleans any time soon, she had to leave him as much information as she could about her plans on the off-chance he would somehow find the notes before she could return to the city.

"Just let them sleep for now," Grant said when Casey mentioned Jessica and Joey as he was readying his bicycle for the 24-mile round-trip ride to the airport. Maybe by the time I get back they will work out what they're going to do and he can decide if he is going with us or not. Please stay here where it's safe, Casey, and try to keep her here as well, even if Joey tries to get her to leave. Today will be a lot worse than yesterday, and it could get dangerous out in the street. There won't be any traffic holding me up, so I should be back in two hours or so if I don't run into any problems. We can leave the other note at your place when we head out for good, since it's right on our way.

With no one to worry about or hold him back, Grant Dyer zipped through the stalled cars choking every street and headed west from the university area, easily keeping his lightweight Cannondale hybrid at a cruising speed of 18 miles per hour. He could maintain this pace for hours on an unloaded bike, but as he pedaled he wondered how long it was going to take to get to the cabin on the Bogue Chitto River with two or three riders in tow who had probably never pedaled a bike more than five miles at a time? Aside from their lack of conditioning, Casey had an entry-level Trek mountain bike that was hardly suited to long-distance riding on pavement, with its fat, knobby tires, and Jessica's bike was basically department store junk. He didn't know if Joey had a bike at all. Grant knew that he was taking on an enormous burden, trying to get these two girls and a guy he barely knew to safety on loaded bicycles, but doing anything less was simply not an option. And what would be the point of going alone anyway? He knew if he were traveling solo, he could leave now and probably be at the cabin before night fell again, but then what? He had already spent too much time alone, of that he was certain, even in normal times when he lived surrounded by the city and spent most of his days in classrooms or the library around other students.

There was something about Casey Drager that intrigued him and made him want to get to know her better. She was attractive, for sure, and he could tell she thought he was too, but there was more to her than her looks that made him want to know more. Grant figured most guys would think that Jessica was even better looking, if appearance alone was the kind of sex appeal that could turn heads on any campus or street. She had the body, the face, the smile, and the eyes—everything—but though it was going to be nice to look at her every day, it was already obvious that she was a lot higher maintenance than Casey. She didn't seem as grounded in reality and certainly had not accepted the seriousness of the situation they were in. Grant wondered how she would cope when the going got really tough. It was also a major hassle that she was a vegetarian. Food was going to be hard enough to obtain even for those who did not have restrictions on what they could or would eat. On top of that, there was the issue of Joey. Grant went out of his way to avoid guys like him. There was no question that Joey was only into Jessica for one thing, and other than that, his main interest was partying and having a good time. He was going to be one unhappy camper when it finally sunk in that the party was over and the cold beer was gone. Grant wished he would just go away, but that was mostly up to Jessica. If she wanted him to tag along too, Grant wouldn't tell her he couldn't—because if he did, she might refuse to go, and if she stayed behind, Casey might too.

No matter how many problems and obstacles the trip would entail, Grant was convinced that they would all be better off in his parent's rural cabin than just about anyone would who chose to stay behind in New Orleans. He knew that taking these two girls anywhere in the unrest that was sure to follow the shutdown would expose them to danger, but he felt the risks of travel were preferable to the risks of staying in the midst of so many people, especially if they left soon, before everyone else got the same idea. Grant was under no delusion that he was any kind of expert who could guarantee their safety and survival, but he did feel better knowing that he had *some* experience living and traveling in extremely remote areas with few of the conveniences of civilization. The field work in Guyana was fresh in his memory and something he thought about almost every day. He had been surprised at how easily he'd adapted to life in the jungle, and how little of modern technology he'd actually needed. He had learned from observing the Wapishana, and those lessons might be the most valuable knowledge he possessed in the new reality they had all awoken to the day before. Leaving the narrow, live-oak-shaded streets of the Garden District and Audubon Park area behind him, Grant made his way towards Metairie and Kenner along the old road paralleling the Mississippi River. Normally, this would be a dangerous place to be on a bike, with a high likelihood of getting taken out by a speeding car. But today, cars were not a threat, and the road was faster than the bike path that ran along the top of the levee. He saw other people riding bikes, just as he had expected. Some were just moving about around the city, while others were carrying stuff in handlebar baskets, on racks or in backpacks or bags slung over their shoulders. A lot more people were in motion today than had been the first day after the event. Most were scrambling to get stuff they needed and move it back to wherever they lived or planned to stay. Many more were on foot than on bicycles, and a few were still using motorized vehicles if they were fortunate enough to have older models that would still run. Grant was passed by several still-functioning motorcycles, most of them older-model Harley Davidsons with loud exhaust pipes and simple engines of decades-old design.

On the larger thoroughfares, people had pushed most of the cars and trucks blocking the streets out of the roadway to the curb. Many of these had been broken into already, as evidenced by smashed windows and pried-open fuel doors. Grant assumed that those who did have motorized transport that was still working would soon or already had run out of options for buying fuel and would find a ready supply in the tanks of all these abandoned vehicles. He was glad he didn't have to worry about such things. Though a working vehicle would make it easier for him to get his friends out of the city and to the safety of the cabin, he knew such a vehicle would be a target. Those without options would soon become desperate enough to try to take what they needed by force. Even the possession of bicycles put them at risk, and Grant knew they would have to remain vigilant against potential attackers. As he made his way to the airport, he scanned the roadway ahead, looking for groups of people congregated in one place and detouring around them, even if it required going several blocks out of his way. He knew he could outrun any pedestrian attackers with his bike, but only if he had a clear escape route and they could not cut him off or surround him.

He felt he was in less danger when he reached the wide four-lane roadway of Veterans Memorial Boulevard. From there it was a straight shot west to Kenner and the New Orleans International Airport. Grant rolled into the long-term parking area when he got there and scanned the rows of vehicles until he found a silver Chevy Tahoe with Alabama plates and a "Life is Good" sticker on the rear bumper. Like Casey's late-model Camry, the Tahoe had an electronic door opener that no longer worked, but he was able to unlock it with the key. Grant left Casey's note in the center console where she said he would certainly find it if he made it back to his vehicle, as that was where he kept his driving sunglasses. Sitting behind the wheel of Casey's father's car, Grant wondered what it must be like for him to be stuck somewhere among islands so far away with no likely prospect of getting back home or even getting in touch with his daughter. Grant hoped he was up to the task of protecting her until she and her dad could be reunited. While thinking these thoughts, it occurred to him to look around the vehicle a bit for anything of her father's that Casey might want. Opening the locked glove box with the key, he found several photos of Casey, including some obviously taken at a recent birthday celebration. There was another pair of sunglasses in a case, and the vehicle owner's manual packet was resting atop something else.

Grant reached under the booklets and was surprised to see that the something else was a gun. Casey had not mentioned anything about her father having a gun in the vehicle. Grant took it out and examined it. It was a stainless-steel automatic pistol with dark brown, checkered wooden grips, the barrel and most of the receiver protected inside a soft nylon holster. He unsnapped the strap that secured the pistol in the holster and pulled it out. The stamp on the receiver said "RUGER 22 CAL. LONG RIFLE AUTOMATIC PISTOL." The pistol had a solid heft to it and a long barrel fitted with adjustable sights. Grant hadn't owned another gun since he'd lost everything in Katrina, but he was familiar with the .22 caliber because it was the same cartridge used by the well-worn Colt Woodsman pistol his father had taught him to shoot shortly after they bought the land on the Bogue Chitto. He depressed the magazine release catch at the bottom of the grip and removed the slim magazine. It was fully loaded with hollow-point ammunition. He pulled back the slide and checked the chamber to make sure it was empty. Grant knew enough about guns to know a .22 pistol was not really intended for defensive purposes, but he figured Casey's father kept it handy, just in case, and he knew it could do the job in a pinch, at least in some circumstances. Looking deeper into the glove box, Grant found a hundred-round box of hollow-point ammunition, labeled "CCI Stinger," the container full except for the ten rounds already loaded into the magazine.

Grant wondered again why Casey had not mentioned that her father kept a gun in his vehicle. Maybe she simply didn't know about it, or perhaps it didn't occur to her that a gun was something they might need. Grant knew that while Jessica seemed clueless about what they were facing, even Casey had not come to the full realization of the hardships that could lie ahead. She probably couldn't fathom that they might actually have to defend themselves with deadly force, or kill animals for food. Though he didn't believe in taking things that did not belong to him, there was no way Grant was going to leave something as potentially useful as the pistol in the vehicle. He knew that Casey's father would understand, and would probably be glad that someone with her had it to protect her. Grant found a pen and quickly scribbled his explanation on the bottom of Casey's note, adding that he would do his best to take care of the pistol until it could be returned when this was all over. Then he locked the Tahoe and remounted his bike, the Ruger and its ammunition zipped inside his handlebar bag.

When Grant returned to his apartment, he found Casey there alone. In the short time he'd been gone, she said, Jessica and Joey had gotten out of bed and immediately started arguing about what they should do next. Joey had insisted on going back to his house and Jessica had left with him. She told Casey she would be back in a little while, but Casey was not convinced, especially since Joey was adamant about not leaving the city.

"We can't wait around to find out, Casey. Do you think she really wants to go with us or not?"

"I think she does, but she doesn't know what to do about Joey. He's not going anywhere. He said it again this morning. He thinks you're full of it and he's blaming you for putting stupid ideas in Jessica's head."

"From what I saw out there, we need to hurry, Casey. On the way back I passed a group of looters coming out of the broken windows of a CVS pharmacy with armloads of stuff. I also saw a fight with at least five people involved, and someone on the street threw a bottle at me that just barely missed my head."

"Where are the police? Aren't they trying to do something about all this?"

"Sure, they're trying, but most of them are on foot too. I saw some officers on mountain bikes, and even a few on horseback down near the riverfront, but the mobs are getting bigger and getting out of control. There aren't enough cops, Casey. After Katrina, it took the National Guard and even members of the regular army to restore order here. And they were sent in from areas that were not affected. They may not be coming this time, as far as we know, anyway."

"So what do we do, go to Joey's and try to talk to Jessica?"

"I'll go. You stay here and keep the door locked. I've got to go tell her how it is, and she's either going to have to come back with me or stay with him. When we get back, assuming she comes with me, we need to all get on the bikes and head for the Causeway. I want to be out of the city before dark."

Grant left without telling Casey about the gun and rode as fast as he could to Joey's house. Jessica had taken her bike with her, but Casey said she was pushing it, since Joey didn't have one. Walking, they would barely have time to get to the house before Grant could catch up.

As he turned into the upscale neighborhood where Joey lived, Grant smelled smoke and heard several loud bangs that could only be gunshots. Before he reached the driveway to Joey's house, he saw two New Orleans police officers in tactical gear running across a side street with rifles at the ready. One or more houses were burning somewhere in the direction they were headed, and from the sound of it, a gun battle had broken out between the police and whoever was responsible. He hopped off his bike and leaned it against Jessica's, which was propped unlocked against the rail on Joey's back porch. Grant knocked on the door. When no one answered, he began banging on it louder and calling their names.

"It's Grant!" he heard Jessica yell from inside. "Open the door, Joey!"

"Son of a bitch! What the hell is he doing here?"

Jessica unlocked the door herself when Joey wouldn't do it. "Grant! Am I glad to see you! I've been scared to death ever since we got here. Did you see what was going on in the neighborhood? We got in here and locked the door as fast as we could when the shooting started."

"I did, Jessica. It's starting even sooner than I thought. This area is a target for looters because it's so upscale. I came to tell you we've got to go, and now."

"Screw you, man!" Joey came to the doorway, pushing Jessica aside. "Who are you to say what she needs to do, or Casey either for that matter? You think we all wanna go ride bicycles freakin' 90 miles to stay in some cabin in the middle of nowhere? I'm not leaving my house and letting a bunch of thugs come in here and clean it out—maybe burn it down too."

"How are you going to stop them, Joey?" Jessica yelled. "You saw the same thing I saw. They're shooting at the *police,* and you don't even have a gun."

"You can't stop them," Grant said. "No one can. There will be far too many of them. It would be crazy to stay here just to protect your property."

"I *am* staying!" he yelled back at Grant, and turning to Jessica: "If you want to be with me, you'll stay here too, where you belong. Let Casey go with this asshole if she wants to. No girl of mine is going to run off on a camping trip with some dude I don't even know."

"I'm not staying here, Joey. People are *shooting* at each other! If you loved me you wouldn't want me to stay where I am in danger...."

"If you loved *me,* you wouldn't leave me to go run off to the woods with some prick who doesn't know what the fuck he's talking about."

Grant stood in the open doorway, disgusted, but not wanting to step into the middle of the argument any more than he had to. He glanced around to make sure no one else was coming up the secluded, tree-lined driveway. The gunshots had stopped and he thought maybe the looters who had engaged the police in a firefight had made a run for it and were looking for places to hide anywhere they could find them.

"We need to get out of here before more of this starts, Jessica."

At this, Joey turned away from Jessica and charged through the doorway, pushing Grant so hard that he fell over the porch railing into the hedges planted on the other side. "No, *you* need to get out of here, asshole, and stay the fuck out of our business!"

Grant was caught by surprise, but unhurt by the fall, and quickly scrambled to his feet, expecting to have to defend himself as Joey came outside to follow up. But before Joey could come down the steps to the lawn where he waited, Jessica slapped him in the center of the back, causing him to turn around to face her, which opened him up perfectly to catch her other open hand right across the side of his face. "I'm done with you, you bastard!" Jessica yelled. "You're the asshole, and I'm not going to be with anyone who treats my friends like this and cares more about their stupid stuff than my safety. You can sit here with it from now on. I'm *leaving!*"

Jessica grabbed her bike and pulled it away from the railing to get on it. "Let's go, Grant."

Grant half expected Joey to try to grab her or attack him again, but as they rode out of the driveway, all he did was vent his anger at her by yelling and kicking the wooden porch rail so hard that it broke: "Fuck you, you fuckin' little bitch! You'll wish you hadn't left when all this shit is over and the lights come back on and you try to come running back to me. I'll find someone who deserves me!"

As she pedaled away with Grant, "I hope not—for her sake!" was the last thing Jessica ever said to Joey.

Grant was nervous as they made their way out of Joey's neighborhood at a much slower pace than he would have if he had been traveling alone. It was all Jessica could do to manage 10 miles per hour on her heavy Wal-Mart bike. Grant felt vulnerable on the mostly deserted avenue they were following. His worst fear became reality when two young men in their late teens stepped into the street from the sidewalk to intercept them before they could think about turning around or making a detour.

"Give us those bikes, man!" the first one demanded. He was lean and athletic, dressed in baggy shorts and a tank top that revealed sleeves of unintelligible gang tattoos that left little of his white skin showing. His black partner wore a Nike sweatshirt with the hood pulled over his head, despite the heat. They clearly were outsiders to the neighborhood on the prowl for targets of opportunity. Grant knew that, with Jessica holding him back, any escape would be impossible. They would catch her even if he could elude them, and there was no question that they were serious about taking the bikes. Grant knew that if they gave up their only means of transportation, getting replacement bikes would be impossible, and walking out of the city to his parent's place would take days, if not an entire week.

But fighting back was out of the question too. Grant was no fighter, even though he was aerobically fit from constant bike riding. The idea of tangling with even one of these guys, much less both of them, was not something he relished. Though they were younger, they had the look of experienced street fighters, and probably wouldn't hesitate to pound him into the pavement or even kill him, leaving Jessica at their mercy. He had to buy a few seconds to get the gun out—it was his only chance. He locked up both brakes before he rode into the leader's reach and quickly dismounted, pulling his bike to the side of the road. Jessica didn't know what to do and couldn't react quickly enough. She was still on her bike when the guy in the sweatshirt reached her handlebars and pulled her to a stop. Jessica screamed and struggled but the tattooed guy came to his buddy's assistance and grabbed her from behind in a bear hug, pinning her arms and pulling her away from the bike. This distraction gave Grant just enough time to unholster the Ruger pistol inside his handlebar bag and draw the slide back to chamber a round. He wished now he had test-fired the gun at least once to make sure it would function properly, but he had no choice but to trust it now. The attackers had made the mistake of discounting him as a threat and probably assumed he would either run and leave his bike behind, or make a hopeless attempt to help his female companion empty-handed, giving them the opportunity to work him over. They thought they were looking at clueless college students whose bikes were easy pickings. What they didn't expect was to face a gun. The last thing Grant wanted to do was kill someone over a couple of bikes, but he was determined not lose them.

"LET HER GO AND BACK OFF!" he yelled as he leveled the long target barrel of the .22 at the head of the one holding Jessica's bike.

Both of them turned to look in his direction, the leader quickly pushing Jessica aside and turning to face him, with no intention of backing down. Grant raised his point of aim ever so slightly and pulled the trigger, sending a bullet whizzing right over the hooded guy's head to strike the side of a brick-walled house across the street, where it ricocheted skyward with a high-pitched whine.

"I won't miss next time; that was your warning! NOW BACK OFF!

The attackers didn't argue. Grant figured that if they had been carrying weapons, it must have been only knives rather than handguns, as neither made a move to reach for anything. Seeing that Grant was willing to use his weapon gave them reason enough to move on to easier prey. They both backed away with their hands up while still facing him, and Jessica picked up her fallen bike and rolled it behind Grant to where he'd dropped his on the curb. He covered the two retreating assailants with the pistol until they reached the other side of the street and turned to walk quickly out of sight.

"Are you all right?" he asked Jessica.

She was shaking and had started to cry. "I wasn't expecting anything like this," she said as Grant put his free arm around her, still holding the pistol in his right hand. "Why are some people so mean?"

"It's just human nature, I'm afraid. Something like this often brings out the worst in some people. That's why I've been saying it's better to get away from the majority of people as much as possible. No crowded city anywhere will be safe as long as the power remains off."

"I can see that now," Jessica said. "I can't believe you have a gun, though. Why didn't you say something about it? Where did you learn how to shoot guns?"

"I *didn't* have it until this morning. It belongs to Casey's dad. I got it out of his car when I rode my bike to the airport to leave her note in it."

"I didn't know he had guns either. Casey never said anything about her dad owning guns."

"Maybe she didn't even know herself. Anyway, it's just a target pistol, and only a .22 at that, but still, it may save our lives—and maybe it already has. I don't think he'll mind that I borrowed it. I'm going to tell Casey about it when we get back to my place."

"But won't it get us in trouble with the police if they find out we have it?"

"It could, but I'd rather take my chances than not have a weapon. Where were the police just now? They obviously have their hands full, and they can't be everywhere all the time. After Katrina, they confiscated all the guns they could find in New Orleans from citizens who had them, but this is so much bigger than a hurricane, I think they have a lot more to worry about than going around door to door collecting guns. And when we get north of the city, there will be even fewer police. I'll keep it hidden unless we need it." Grant put the pistol back in his handlebar bag before they remounted the bikes, but this time he kept the zipper partly open for quick access and left the weapon ready to fire, with a round still chambered in the barrel and the safety on.

The ride back to Grant's apartment seemed to him to take forever, nervous as he was about the possibility of another attack at any point along the way. They passed through areas where lots of pedestrians were crowding the streets, but no one else threatened them, and when they reached the apartment, they found Casey locked inside and waiting.

"I'm glad you're back," she said, hugging each of them in turn. "It's been scary being here alone. I heard something that sounded like gunshots a couple of times, and lots of cursing and screaming. I couldn't tell what was going on out there and didn't want to go find out."

"Some people are starting to go nuts already," Grant said. Then Jessica filled her roommate in on what had happened at Joey's and on the street on the way back.

"I don't know why I didn't think about it," Casey said when Grant showed her the pistol. "Of course I remember it. It's probably older than I am. He took me to a shooting range a couple of times when I was probably 10 or 11. I forgot that he kept it in his car."

"I just thought we might need it more than he will, especially since he's unlikely be able to get back to the airport until all this mess is straightened out anyway."

"It's okay. You're right; he would want us to take it. I'm glad you had it today."

"We would still be walking on the way back here if I didn't," Grant said, "if they had left us in any shape to walk at all. I'm going to feel a lot better armed on our trip to the Bogue Chitto. Besides that, this kind of pistol is accurate enough that we may be able to use it to supplement our food supply if this goes on long enough that we need to."

Jessica look puzzled. "How can we get food with a gun? You're not thinking about robbing a grocery store or something, are you?"

Casey laughed. "I think he's talking about hunting with it, Jessica."

A look of disgust crossed Jessica's face. The idea of having to hunt and kill for food had not even crossed her mind. "I'm not eating any animals, no matter what happens!" she said.

Grant said nothing. He knew that both of the girls were overwhelmed by the events unfolding around them and he figured that both, even Jessica, would adapt to the changing circumstances as necessary. All they could handle right now was one challenge at a time, and for now, they had enough food to travel on if there were no unexpected delays in the journey to the cabin.

He set to work immediately, completing their preparations to leave. As his bike was the only one set up to carry luggage, there was no way to carry all the gear and equipment he owned, so he had to leave behind many items that would have been nice to have but were not essential. This included the French press, his expensive North Face tent (which was too small to accommodate all three of them), and the battery-powered lanterns. He did pack the propane stove and one extra bottle of fuel, along with a single cook pot that would serve for everything from making coffee, to cooking rice, to purifying questionable water. In place of the tent, he packed a lightweight nylon tarp that could be rigged as a lean-to or an A-frame shelter, and he carried his two sleeping bags for the girls and a lightweight wool blanket for himself. Other essentials included his machete, a couple of flashlights, matches and butane lighters for starting the stove and making fires, a pocketknife and multi-tool, his bike pump and tool kit for roadside repairs, and their clothing. With the food and water bottles they would also have to carry, there was no room for anything else. The cabin contained most of what they needed anyway, and they would be roughing it only during the journey there. By keeping their loads as light as possible, that journey could be shortened and, he hoped, not be too unpleasant.

Even with their luggage pared down to the minimum, their loads were awkward. Grant lashed the heaviest items on the rear rack of his bike. All three of them wore the backpacks that had been used as book bags in their previous lives as college students. In addition, Grant had lashed the stuffed sleeping bags and rolled-up items of clothing to the handlebars and seat posts of Casey's and Jessica's bikes. In the end he was carrying at least twice as much as either of them, but that was only fair, he thought, as he was in better shape for riding, and his bike had a stronger frame and wheelset that could stand up to the load. A brief stop by Casey's apartment gave her a minute to leave her second note for her father in her bedroom nightstand, where he would find it on the slim chance he made it back to the city and happened to come there first instead of to his car.

"I sure hope it won't be too long before we can come back home," Casey said as she locked the deadbolt on the door and walked back down the steps to the street. Grant led the way as the three of them pedaled north, making their way past the university campus and towards the elevated expressway of Interstate 10. He wanted to avoid the narrow streets and crowded residential areas along the river, and figured there would be little foot traffic on the expressway. This route would take them directly west to Causeway Boulevard. From there, it was just a couple of miles of wide four-lane to the start of the 24-mile-long bridge spanning Lake Pontchartrain. Before nightfall Grant hoped to get well onto the bridge, where he felt the three would be far removed from the gangs of looters in the city and would likely be sharing the route only with others who were wise enough to try to get out while they could.

He set an easy pace, spinning in one of his lowest gears to stay beside Casey and Jessica, who were having a hard time controlling their bikes with the unaccustomed weight of gear tied on the handlebars as well as in their back-packs. Jessica's bike, with its cheap components, wouldn't stay in the gear she selected and made grinding noises as she pedaled, adding to the work she had to do to keep the pedals spinning. Grant knew her rear derailleur wouldn't last long, but could only hope the bike would hold together long enough to get them to their destination. It was just something else to worry about along with the vulnerability he felt at such a slow pace and the fear that they wouldn't be able to travel far enough before dark. These thoughts fed his urge to occasionally reach inside his handlebar bag as he pedaled, simply to feel the cold polished steel of the Ruger for reassurance that it was still there. It had proved its worth already, but he still felt suspicious of just about every pedestrian they passed, especially any groups of more than two males, and he imagined them sizing him up and feasting their eyes on his pretty companions and the three laden bicycles that, although slow, would be enticing prizes to many who had no better option than to walk.

When they reached I-10, Jessica and Casey had to get off their bikes and push them up the steep entrance ramp to reach the elevated freeway. At the top of the ramp they remounted and wound their way among the cars, SUVs, pickups, and tractor-trailer rigs frozen in place in the lanes or parked against the retaining walls, where their drivers had coasted them to a stop when the pulse hit and killed all the engines. All of them were abandoned now, with no one in sight on this shadeless concrete bridge two stories above the offices and stores where people had worked until the power went off. It was obvious that everyone stranded on the expressway the morning before had long since given up on getting their vehicles started and had walked to the nearest exit to get relief from the heat and find food and water. Depending on where they were along the way when their vehicles stopped, getting off the elevated sections could involve a bit of a hike.

As Grant and his companions pedaled along one of these long stretches between exits, several large black birds hopped to the top of the retaining wall while others took flight at their approach. There was no mistaking what they were—vultures—and they had been crowded around something lying along the shoulder of the right lane, which took shape as they drew nearer.

"Oh my God!" Jessica said, turning her eyes away as soon as she saw the figure clearly. It was the body of a very obese man, with graying hair, sprawled belly down on the hot pavement. He was dressed in business clothes, a tie around his neck, but his jacket was missing, probably discarded somewhere along the way as he walked in the sweltering heat. His sweat-stained Oxford shirt was untucked at the waist; one leather shoe was lying a few feet behind him, the other still on his right foot. His head was turned so that his missing eyes were unavoidable as they passed, as were the flies that swarmed around his open mouth. Grant felt a wave of nausea and dizziness sweep over him, and he got off the bike to push it to the far side of the left-hand lane and past the horrid sight. Casey and Jessica did the same; then Jessica turned pale, bent over, and puked. Seeing this, Casey couldn't hold it back either. Three of the vultures still sat on the low concrete wall just a few feet from the body, watching them with beady black eyes, reluctant to fly away from their newfound meal unless seriously threatened.

"What do you think happened to him?" Casey asked Grant as she spit and coughed, trying to get the awful taste of vomit out of her mouth.

"Probably a heart attack or stroke," Grant said. "It looks like he was trying to get to the exit like everyone else, but he was in no shape for that kind of exertion in this heat."

"His eyes...did the...?"

"Yes, the vultures," Grant finished for her. "They fight over them, from what I've seen of dead cows and such."

Casey pushed her bike faster. She just wanted to get away from the scene as quickly as possible.

"Why did they just leave him to lie here like that?" Jessica asked.

"Who would have moved him? It's not like anyone could call for an ambulance. The other people stuck here on this bridge would have been concerned with their own safety. He might have died before he even hit the ground. He's too heavy for anyone to carry or drag very far, so where he fell is where he stayed."

"That poor man," Casey said, trying to visualize him as a living, breathing human being rather than the gruesome thing that she knew would be an image forever burned in her memory. "He probably has a family somewhere in the city, wondering when he's coming home."

"I'm afraid we're going to see more of this," Grant said. "The Causeway will probably be worse. There'll likely be a lot of live people still stranded there too. Some of them will be too old, too young, too out of shape, or too disabled in some way to walk the long distance back to either end, especially if they were unlucky enough to be caught in the middle when the pulse hit. Others will probably already be dead. I wish we didn't have to see that, but be ready for it. Just try to remember, we have to focus on our own survival. We probably can't help them, and there's probably not anyone who can really help us either."

FIVE

"WHO CAME UP WITH the stupid idea that these islands are some kind of paradise?" Artie yelled as he shook the water from his hair after another frantic plunge into the harbor. Incessant attacks from the tiny biting sand fleas that plagued their beach worksite in the otherwise calm early morning were driving him insane. They swarmed around his eyes, ears, scalp, and every exposed part of his body, biting with infuriating persistence that could only be relieved by diving underwater to wash them away, which was essentially futile, as it seemed a million more were ready to take their place as soon as he resurfaced.

Larry laughed at his brother's antics. "You get used to them after awhile. Just learn to ignore them."

"How am I supposed to ignore them when they are all over me? Damn! This is worse than being out there on the boat, throwing up day and night." The passing of several days had pushed the memory of his miserable *mal de mer* far enough back in his mind that it now seemed like a minor inconvenience.

"Not'ing to be done 'bout de no-see-um," Scully said. "Dem always on de beach when de air be still. Dat's why a mon needs dreadlocks. Shake de dreads 'round an' de sand flea, he got nowhere to stop. Keep de herb pipe handy too. Dem can't fly in de smoke, mon."

"And if they did, you wouldn't feel the bite, right, Scully?" Larry grinned.

"Dats for true. A mon *need* de ganja smoke here in de island."

Despite all the talk about Scully's ganja smoking, Artie had only seen him light his pipe in the evening around the campfire they built on the beach near the boat shed. During the day, he was a tireless worker, which came as a surprise after all Larry had said about the Rastafarian philosophy, religion, or whatever it was. He was still confused about the unlikely friendship between his brother and this islander, but they certainly both knew boats, and their progress on putting Larry's big catamaran together was astounding.

Most of the work consisted of installing hardware and fittings that Larry had previously purchased and had been planning to install after all the final painting and other cosmetic work was completed. With no time to worry about aesthetics or even the proper drilling and marine bedding techniques for long-term protection against rot in the wooden structures, these installations went fast. Scully drilled the holes with a manual brace and bit Larry had bought at a flea market years ago, and assorted hand chisels were used where mortises were needed to install flush fittings. Larry said the hardest part of building a boat from scratch was all the detail work that went into the final sanding, fairing, and painting to get a perfect finish, and since they were skipping all that, it only took a day to finish these installations. Then they were ready to assemble the major components—two hulls, bridge decks, crossbeams, and the mast—that as a whole made up the catamaran.

The second morning of work was consumed by this assembly. They used jacks and timber skids to move the hulls inch by inch out of their supporting cradles and slide the keels apart, and then aligned them fore and aft at the correct spacing so that the four massive connecting beams could be fitted. With the beams in place, Artie could see that *Alegria* was a much bigger vessel than at first it had seemed. The deck space was enormous. The central cockpit area between the two hull cabins was fitted with seats with storage lockers under them, while other deck areas fore and aft were made up of slatted wood planking or fabric trampoline material to allow breaking waves to quickly drain off. The cockpit area where the helm station was located was shaded by a curved, rigid Bimini cover, which Larry said he had molded from foam-cored fiberglass. The cabins inside the hulls were narrow and tunnel-like, but deep enough to allow standing inside without the need to duck. The forward area of each cabin featured a four-foot-wide, wall-to-wall double berth, with lots of locker space under for storing provisions. An additional single berth was fitted into a separate section of the port hull, forward of the main cabin area. The port hull also contained the galley, with a countertop, sink, and alcohol stove making up the area aft of the bunk. This same space in the starboard hull was taken up by the navigation station, which included a chart table, electrical circuit panels, and now-useless electronics such as the VHF and SSB radios, XM radio and MP3 player, and laptop with navigation software.

The bulk of the internal wiring was left undone, as they couldn't use most of the electrical equipment anyway. Larry said it was just as well, as he had expected to take at least a week to do a proper job of the wiring. Like most sailors, he had amassed quite a collection of flashlights, LED lanterns, and other gear such as portable navigation lights that could run off of disposable batteries. He made it a point to always keep a fairly large stock of these batteries stored for his voyages. This way, he said, at least they would have lights when they really needed them.

The main propulsion system for the Tiki 36 was an aerodynamic mainsail that fit over the round aluminum mast by means of a sewn-in sleeve. Larry said the sleeve was like that of a windsurfer sail, providing a clean air flow and functioning like the much more expensive rotating wingmasts found on million-dollar racing catamarans. Headsails of various sizes could be fitted on the forestay, which, like all the standing rigging, was made of a high-tech synthetic rope, rather than heavier stainless-steel wire, which Larry said was now passé in the performance sailing world. Auxiliary propulsion for maneuvering in harbors and through calms was supposed to be provided by two Yamaha 20-horsepower four-stroke outboards, fitted in motor wells under the cockpit decks port and starboard. Larry said that since the Yamahas were brand new and over-reliant on technology, with electric starters and alternators, and electronic fuel injection, they would be leaving them behind. In their place, he mounted in the starboard motor well a single Evinrude 25-horsepower two-stroke that dated back to the late 1970s. "It'll be enough to get us out of a tight spot if we need it," he said, "and it'll usually crank after a few pulls. But you'll see, this boat will sail so well I doubt we'll ever bother. Losing the weight of those two Yamahas will help too."

When the time came to launch, on the third day after they'd arrived in Culebra's harbor aboard *Celebration*, they dismantled the temporary tarp shed on the beach and cleared away the workbenches and ladders from the hulls. They stepped the mast by hoisting it up with a temporary gin pole lashed to its base and hooked to a block and tackle system. Then Larry rowed out into the harbor with the main anchor and set it at the limit of his longest rode, which was three hundred feet. It was Artie's job to climb up into the cockpit and man the big manual winch that doubled as an anchor windlass "...since you did such a great job hoisting *Celebration*'s anchor," Larry said, while Larry and Scully worked at each keel, maneuvering the jacks and shifting skids from the sterns to the bows as the big cat slowly inched down the beach to the water. When they were within a foot of the wet sand above the tide line, Larry said they needed to stop to officially christen the boat before she went in. He disappeared into the starboard hull and came back down to the beach a minute later with a bottle of golden 10 Cane rum. "Trinidad's best! I've been saving it for this moment. Here's to the *Casey Nicole*," he said, as he splashed most of the bottle on the dull gray primer coating the twin bows and then offered the bottle to his brother. "Drink up, for a safe and successful voyage!"

Artie was surprised at what he heard. "I thought you were naming her *Alegria.*"

"That was then, this is now. My niece is the reason I'm launching today. Otherwise, I probably would have dragged on another year, piddling with this and that, trying to get everything perfect. Now I'm going to sail her today, and when we get Casey on board, everything *will* be perfect. Until then, I don't think there's going to be much *alegria* aboard anyway, especially not for you, Doc, and I totally understand."

They took turns sipping from the bottle, Artie offering it to Scully only to learn that he wouldn't touch alcohol. "A Rastaman don't to drink, mon. Dat's not I-tal. Only smoke de herb of wisdom. De rum is poison to de brain an' not put on de Earth by Jah like he put de the ganja plant for a mon to use."

"You're full of shit, Scully, you know that?" Larry said as he took another pull from the bottle.

Once again, Artie was baffled by the strange ways of this character, Scully, and his confusing version of the English language. What kind of religion advocated smoking dope while prohibiting alcohol? He was learning something new about his brother's friend every day. Despite that, he knew Casey would be thrilled to learn that her uncle had named his pride and joy after her. He couldn't wait to see her face when she found out, and he asked Larry if they were going to paint the name on the sides.

"Absolutely! Normally I wouldn't launch a boat without doing that first, but since we're kinda in a hurry, I'll paint it on temporarily from the dinghy tonight when we're anchored. This gray primer will get covered up later with topside paint, and then I'll do it right."

"So, we're not going far today, you said?"

"No, I want to shake her down, make sure everything's sorted out enough for the voyage. There will still be work to do all along the way, but as long as we have good weather, I can do most of that at sea. Today we're going to get the rig tuned and work the stretch out of the stays and halyards, then tighten up the beam lashings and everything else before we head offshore tomorrow. There's a pretty little island you're gonna love just a few miles off the east coast of Puerto Rico. We can be there by late afternoon, drop the hook and make our adjustments, and still get a good night's sleep before we head out."

Back on deck, Artie cranked on the windlass handle while Larry and Scully maneuvered the jacks and skids. The newly christened *Casey Nicole* slid across the wet sand, sliced into the gentle chop of the harbor, and floated free, sitting nicely on her lines, with just a couple of inches of bottom paint showing all around. Larry and Scully high-fived it and jumped up and down cheering. Artie couldn't contain his grin as the big platform beneath him glided away from shore, hovering like a giant magic carpet over the sandy bottom that seemed close enough to touch through the crystalline water. He had to admit he was pretty impressed with his younger brother's handiwork. It was simply amazing to him that anyone could build such a vessel from scratch under a makeshift tent on the beach.

They spent the remainder of the morning loading the rest of Larry's tools and spare parts on board. This included just about everything needed to maintain and repair any component of the boat, and even to fabricate broken parts. Larry said that all Wharram catamarans were designed to be built and kept shipshape with simple tools and easy-to-find materials, and that even in normal times many had been built without the benefit of power tools.

"It's really the perfect design for sailing in the post-apocalyptic world," he joked.

But seeing all the stuff he was putting on board, Artie wasn't so sure he was joking after all. It was amazing to him what a relatively small cruising boat could carry, as he had first noticed during the trip on *Ibis*. A seaworthy offshore sailing vessel really was a self-contained world of its own, capable of traveling great distances for extended periods of time without the need to visit land or take on any of the goods to be found there. His brother was obviously well versed in the art of provisioning and equipping such boats, having made a career of passage making. Artie saw that his checklists were extensive and often doubly redundant, as well as impeccably organized so that nothing could be overlooked or forgotten. Much of the equipment on these lists was already on board in the individual hulls before they were assembled. The only thing lacking was a fresh supply of food items, but the stores aboard already contained plenty of non-perishable goods, and when they had moved all the groceries off of *Celebration* that they had taken from *Ibis* before leaving her in St. Thomas, Larry figured they had enough to last the three of them for at least a month, especially if they could supplement the stores with fish caught along the way—and much of the gear on board was dedicated to that purpose.

This included conventional tackle such as rods and reels for trolling astern and casting, as well as drop lines, collapsible bait and crab traps, and the underwater spear-fishing gear that most cruisers in tropical waters carried as standard equipment. In addition, Larry said the big tandem-cockpit sea kayak Scully had been paddling the day Artie had met him would be invaluable for fishing and other forms of seafood gathering if it came to that. The 20-foot wide overall beam of the catamaran made it a simple matter to lash it across the decks forward of the mast. Larry said he'd bought this 19-foot kayak specifically for the purpose of serving as a dinghy on the catamaran, as it was faster and easier to paddle long distances than any conventional rowing dinghy.

"It's more seaworthy, too," he said. "Heck, with two strong paddlers, this thing can go out in about any conditions the big boat can handle."

"But there's only room for two," Artie said.

"Yeah, well, considering how things are now, I doubt we'll all want to leave the boat at the same time. Someone needs to stay with it to keep an eye on things anyway. Speaking of which, I've got a special place for this." Larry unzipped a nylon carrying case that was among the last items yet to be stowed and pulled out a stainless-steel Mossberg 12-gauge pump shotgun.

"I sure hope we don't need *that!*" Artie said.

"I've always kept a shotgun on board whenever I could," Larry said. "Never had to use one, but things could be different now—a *lot* different. I just wanted to let you know where I'm keeping it. There's a hidden compartment right under the shelf that's over your bunk in the nav station. I'm sleeping in the galley hull myself—where the food and coffee is."

"What about Scully?"

"He's got the forward single bunk cabin in the port hull when we're at sea, but he prefers to sleep on deck in all but the roughest weather."

Before they left the harbor, Pete and Maryanne rowed over from *Celebration* to where the *Casey Nicole* was anchored to share a cup of coffee and wish them luck on the voyage. By the time they left, the afternoon trade winds had kicked in, and Larry said it was time to go see what the new boat could do. Getting underway was much easier than it had been on the larger *Celebration*. As soon as Artie had the anchor on deck, Larry and Scully working together had the main and jib set and Larry steered off the wind to let them fill. Artie was totally unprepared for what happened next. Instead of heeling over and slowly gathering way like the schooner *Ibis* and the big cutter-rigged Tayana had, the catamaran simply accelerated, converting wind power to forward motion with a suddenness that almost caused him to fall. The twin bows sliced through the chop of the harbor with spray flying on both sides and made for the opening to the sea. Larry and Scully whooped with delight and Artie joined in. It felt like they were practically flying over the clear water, and he thought that if they could just keep this up, he would be reunited with Casey in no time.

Once they put Culebra astern, Larry aimed the bows toward the big mountain on Puerto Rico and soon they were in the heaving swells of the open ocean, the boat pitching fore and aft but not rolling from side to side as had the only other sailboats Artie had experienced. The distant island grew more distinct by the minute as they closed on it at 17 knots, changing from a hazy blue outline to a landscape of mountains that rose sharply behind slivers of sandy beach interspersed with condos, houses, and hotels. Larry was clearly pleased with his new boat and was grinning from ear to ear as he pointed out various design elements that contributed to her seaworthiness and speed. When they were about six miles from the main island, he steered for a tiny outlying islet that rose like a mirage from the coral-studded waters not far from a larger cay to the north. The islet was the postcard-perfect image of a deserted tropical isle—a rounded, sandy hump of beach, shaded by a grove of tall coconut palms and little other vegetation. It was the kind of place a cartoonist might draw to depict a scene in which a castaway is washed ashore in paradise.

Larry and Scully doused the spinnaker and brought the cat around to sail up to within 20 feet of the shore, where the water was only waist deep. Scully leapt in and carried the bow anchor up on the beach, while Larry hauled in on the rode of a stern anchor he'd deployed as they approached. When the lines were adjusted, the *Casey Nicole* floated almost motionless over transparent waters alive with multicolored fish.

"Welcome to Isleta Palominito," Larry said. "This is one of the coolest little islands in this part of the Caribbean."

"It *is* beautiful," Artie admitted. "I didn't know there were still uninhabited islands like this, especially so close to a crowded island like Puerto Rico."

"Oh yeah, there are a lot more than you'd think. This one is one of the best, though. I've brought more than one of my *Puertorriqueña* girlfriends over here for a night or two of playing 'castaway.'"

"I'll bet you have."

"It gets crowded with weekend boaters from the main island, but even in normal times it's usually deserted during the week. And now—I wouldn't expect anyone to bother coming over here. It'll be safer than anchoring near Fajardo, and there's nothing we need from a city like that anyway. So enjoy your evening, Doc. It'll be your last chance to go ashore for a few days."

Larry and Scully worked on tightening the rigging and making other adjustments necessary after the first sail, with Artie helping as much as he could, following their instructions, but not really knowing what to do or how to tie the fancy nautical knots they both made look effortless. Then Larry was in the water with his mask, snorkel, and spear-gun, while Scully climbed two of the tall coconut palms ashore and cut down more than two dozen green drinking nuts, bringing them back aboard to store for the voyage. At sunset, Artie walked around the sandy perimeter of the tiny island, which only took a few minutes, as it was less than an acre of total land area.

That evening they cooked the grouper Larry had speared over a small fire on the beach, the smoke and the steady sea breeze keeping away the no-see-ums that had tortured Artie on the beach at Culebra. Artie realized that in other circumstances, if he had not been so desperate to find out if Casey was okay, nothing could have persuaded him to hurry away from such an idyllic setting, and he began to understand his younger brother's obsession with boats and the island lifestyle. He wished Casey could be here experiencing this with him, and that this nightmare was really just a bad dream they would wake from to find themselves all together on a vacation in paradise.

When he crawled into his bunk later that night, with the smoked acrylic hatch over his head open wide to give him a view of the uncountable stars arcing overhead in the Milky Way, he felt a sense of peace and assurance that Casey was okay and that he would soon be with her, whisked across the sea on his brother's wonderful boat. Sleep came easily, and the noise and confusion that shattered his dreams after midnight didn't seem real, until finally he was wide awake and realized they were.

Voices of strange men, yelling orders in a language he recognized as Spanish…. Scully yelling back in his West Indian accent…. A scuffling and stomping of feet on deck…. Something banging against the side of the hull…. A ringing clang of steel hitting steel…. A muffled scream of pain and then a big splash….

Artie sprang to the main hatch leading to the deck and looked out. Scully was crouched on the forward slatted deck, wielding the machete he had used earlier to open coconuts like a sword, as he parried the blows of a smaller man slashing at him with a similar weapon. When Larry yelled as he started out of the port hull where he'd been sleeping, a second stranger in the cockpit, also armed with a machete, turned in his direction and attacked him with a murderous downward blow. Artie saw his brother raise his right arm in an attempt to defend himself just as the blade came down, causing him to fall back into the companionway opening and out of sight. At that moment, he remembered the shotgun Larry had placed near his bunk and ducked back below to grab it. He hadn't handled a 12-gauge pump since the last time he and Larry had hunted pheasants with their father when he was still in high school, but neuromuscular memory took over when it was in his hands, and he racked the slide to chamber a round and pointed the muzzle toward the opening to the deck just in time to see the assailant who had stricken Larry looming over his own hatch. He'd seen enough in the brief seconds he'd looked on deck to know that he had no choice but to pull the trigger. He winced at the blast of the 12-gauge buckshot shell, so loud inside the tiny confines of the cabin that he heard nothing but ringing that felt like a vise tightening on his brain from the outside in. The muzzle flash in the dark blinded him temporarily, and when his eyes readjusted, the man trying to get at him from the deck was gone. Artie racked the slide to chamber a fresh round and climbed up the steps to help Scully. He expected to see the man he'd shot sprawled across the cockpit floor, but there was no body there. The white paint of the cockpit floor shone brightly in the moonlight, unmarred by blood or any other sign of the intruder whom he was certain he'd hit point blank.

Looking to the forward deck, he saw that the wild-haired Rastaman didn't need any help and that he was the only person still standing on the boat. The smaller man that had engaged him in a deadly machete duel was now draped lifelessly over the forward crossbeam. Scully pushed the body the rest of the way overboard with one foot before he noticed Artie had come on deck.

"Scully! Are you all right?"

"I an' I okay, but you miss dat udda mon. Quick, don't let him go. Shoot 'im in de boat, 'cause he be comin' bok wid he friends if he get away!"

Artie turned in the direction Scully was pointing. He could make out a small boat in the darkness—a rowboat manned solely by the last of the assailants, who was pulling desperately at a pair of oars to get away from the scene of the foiled attack.

"I can't just shoot him. He's running away," Artie said. He still couldn't believe that his shot from down in the hull had not blown the man's head off. Apparently he had seen the muzzle of the 12-gauge pointing at his face just in time to move out of the line of fire and had decided to abandon the attack.

"How many were there, Scully? Just those two?"

"No, t'ree, mon. I kill de first one before you an' de Copt'n wake up. Den dis last one keep tryin' to cut me up, so I killing him too. You missed dat one an' now he escapin' to come bok again."

All Artie needed to know was that the attack was over and he could focus on his brother. He passed the shotgun to Scully and rushed to the port companionway, terrified of what he might find after witnessing Larry receive such a vicious blow with such a big blade. Quickly descending the steps into the hull, he heard two more blasts from the shotgun as Scully fired at the man in the rowboat, but he couldn't be concerned with that now. He held his breath as he dropped to his knees on the cabin sole, where Larry was curled up in a fetal position, clutching his right forearm with his other hand in an attempt to stanch the flow of blood that was welling out from beneath his fingers, soaking his shirt and pooling on the floorboards around him. He reached for the battery-powered lantern Larry had mounted over the galley stove and turned it on. He saw that his brother was also bleeding profusely from a long cut across his forehead that extended from his hairline to his right eyebrow. His attempt to parry the machete blow that would have split his skull succeeded in absorbing most of the force, but at the expense of a wicked cut to the blocking arm.

"It's all right, Larry. I'm here now. You've just got a couple of little cuts."

"Scully?"

"He's fine. Not even hurt. He took out two of those guys single-handedly. The other one's gone, or maybe he got him too."

Larry grunted approval, but didn't reply. He was clearly racked with pain. The blood from his scalp wound ran over his face and eyes unchecked until Artie reached for a roll of paper towels near the sink and wadded up a bunch of them to form a temporary compress.

"Scully! I need your help down here!"

When Scully reached his side, Artie instructed him to keep pressure on Larry's head wound while he went to work on the far more serious slash to his brother's arm. Holding pressure above the cut to control the blood flow, he pulled Larry's left hand away so he could see the extent of the damage.

"It's bad, huh, Doc?"

"Yeah, but at least you still have your arm." Artie could see that the machete had cloven nearly halfway through his brother's arm. Probably the only reason it didn't sever it completely was that his arm gave with the force of the blow, like a shock absorber, allowing some of the energy to reach his forehead.

"Can you fix it?"

"I don't think you'll lose it, if that's what you mean, but we need to get you to an ER, and ASAP."

"You know we can't do that, Doc."

Artie had momentarily forgotten the larger situation in his haste to take care of this immediate crisis with his brother. His trained response was to rely on hospitals and the rest of the infrastructure supporting them, but he knew Larry was right, that was not even an option now. "Larry, I haven't dealt with trauma patients since my internship. But I do know that you can't fool around with a wound like this. You could lose your arm or even die if this gets infected."

"I've got everything you need to take care of it in the ship's first aid kit, over in the nav hull. Look under the chart table. Go! Scully and I will hold pressure on this 'til you get back."

Artie returned with a big yellow Pelican case with a plain red sticker on it in the shape of an emergency cross. His brother was shivering despite the warm tropical night, so he grabbed a blanket off the bunk to cover his bare legs and feet. There was barely room in the slender catamaran hull for him and Scully to crouch, with Larry taking up most of the narrow cabin sole. Artie didn't want to move him to the bunk until he knew the bleeding was under control.

His assessment of the damage led him to the conclusion that the ulna, the outward of the two forearm bones, which had been facing upward and outward in his blocking motion, was almost cut in two by the chopping blow of the sharp blade. It was no wonder that his brother was in severe pain and borderline shock. The damage to the bone would heal, much like a clean break, but Larry was facing a long recovery from the inevitable nerve and tissue damage. But the more immediate concern was stopping the flow of blood from the severed ulnar artery and numerous smaller vessels that had been cut.

"This is good," Artie said, as he opened the case and examined the contents in surprise.

"It's not your regular Boy Scout first aid kit," Larry agreed, grimacing in pain as he spoke. "When you're delivering boats across oceans, you've got to have what you need."

"Got some good medicine in dat box," Scully said. "De Copt'n, he know where to buy de good stuff."

"I'll say. Having the tools and supplies that I need will certainly make this easier."

Artie ripped open a QuikClot sponge compress and pressed it into the deep slice in Larry's arm.

"There's a tourniquet in there too, Doc, if you think I need it."

"No way, not if you want to keep your arm. We can keep the blood in check with pressure. The worst bleeding is from the ulnar artery, which is one of the main arteries in your arm. You're lucky it's a clean cut. The artery will seal itself off on its own if we keep up the pressure. Then we'll clean this wound out and make sure it's disinfected, and bandage it so it can't open up again."

"You gonna sew 'im up, Doctor?" Scully was still holding the makeshift compress on Larry's head gash. Artie opened another sterile compress from the kit and gave it to Scully to replace the blood-saturated wad of paper towels.

"Not his arm, Scully. This cut is so deep, and into the bone, there's too much chance of infection if we seal it completely, especially out here on a boat. I'm going to close it up with those butterfly sutures in the kit, and hold everything in place with some heavy tape over that. That way we can check it every day for signs of infection, in case it is still contaminated. We'll keep the bandages changed and keep an eye on it. Do you have any duct tape on board, Larry?"

"You bet. Enough to put the whole boat back together if need be."

"Good. Now that cut on your forehead, that's another story. I think we can stitch that up with the suture kit in here so it won't scar too badly."

"De Copt'n gonna look like de pirate fo' true now, mon. Scar on de face, big scar on de arm. De girls, dey like dat, dem." He grinned at Larry, who didn't look quite so amused at the prospect of a new, more rugged look.

"You oughta at least wait for daylight to sew it up," Larry grunted. "You might be able to do a better job if you can see what you're doing, Doc."

"It'll be less painful if we do it all in one go, little brother. We have enough of these battery-powered lanterns so I can see all I need to. Let's get this arm bandaged up and make sure the bleeding has stopped, then we'll get you up in your bunk. You can have a couple of shots of rum to ease the pain, and I'll make it as quick as possible. It's all gonna hurt right now, but if we get this over with now you can focus on healing after that."

When Artie was finished, Larry was tucked into his sleeping bag in his bunk, his arm no longer bleeding and a row of fresh stitches closing the gash across his forehead and face. Dawn was breaking and the wind was calm, making the stuffy confines of the cabin stifling with all three of them down below. Artie told Larry they were going back up on deck, and that he would be checking on him every few minutes. He had been so focused on tending to his brother's wounds that he temporarily forgot about the last of the attackers, the one fleeing in the rowboat that Scully had fired at with the shotgun. Looking around from the cockpit, Artie saw that the sea was calm and empty, with no trace of the rowboat or any other vessel. He looked at Scully and asked him what had happened after he fired.

"I t'ink I wounded 'im, mon, but he still pullin' de oars and don' fall out de boat. T'ink by de time I shot he too far away from de buckshot in dat Mossberg. Too bad I got no AK, or I kill him dead."

"I don't think he'll be back, then, whether you wounded him or not. With two of his friends dead and no weapon but a machete, he would be stupid to try something else. I just can't believe this happened though. Those guys were trying to *kill* us."

"Want de boat, mon. Dem got not'ing to eat, no way to go someplace bettah. T'ree million people livin' on dat Puerto Rico, dem got no hope wid no ship an' no plane comin'. Dat be a dangerous place to be, mon. Lot a people from dat island happy to steal a boat like de *Casey Nicole*, loaded as she is wid food an' watah an' havin' sails to go wid de wind."

"Larry thought we'd be safe anchored off this little out-lying island, but I guess he was wrong. I just wish we could get him to a doctor. He needs several days to recover from those wounds, and in a clean environment. He's gonna need physical therapy too, and still may not get full use of his arm back. That machete cut a major nerve."

"De Copt'n gonna be okay, mon. Rest on de boat while she sail. De Copt'n, he strong from livin' on de sea an' workin' de boats. Not to worry, mon. We let him sleep an' we do de work."

"So you think we can continue on without his help? You know I don't know what I'm doing. I have no idea how to navigate, or set the sails, or anything."

"Navigation no problem, Doc. I an' I sailin' dis route wid de Copt'n many times. Deliver boats to Miami, Fort Lauderdale, Palm Beach.... Lots of time we sailin' dis route. De islands, dem like steppin' stones across de sea, mon. Hop to one, den cross to de next, all de way to Bobbylon. First Puerto Rico, den Dominican Republic, den Caicos, Exumas, Bimini...dem islands reachin' all de way to Florida."

"But Larry said we wouldn't be stopping until we got to Florida. I thought we were going directly there instead of all those islands in the chain. And besides, we might get attacked again if we stop somewhere."

"Not stoppin', mon. Just pass 'em by. Dat way we be knowin' de way. Wid de GPS dead we gotta sail de old way. Larry, he can use de sextant an' get he position wid de stars, but I an' I cannot cipher dat black magic. But wid de compass, de sun in de day and de North Star in de night, and passin' close by some of de islands along de way, findin' de way to Florida, no problem."

"I guess he can help us if we *do* have a problem. He'll probably feel like coming up on deck when the initial shock wears off and we know there's no chance of the bleeding starting again. So which way do we go when we leave here? We're obviously not going to stop in Puerto Rico," Artie said, looking at the mountainous island to the west.

"No, we be sailin' past de island on de north side. Got to stay maybe 10 mile off de coast, safe from the reef and safe from any mon in small boat tryin' to cut us off an' intercept. Puerto Rico 'bout a hundred mile long. Den we hop across de Mona Passage another hundred mile, den follow de coast of Dominican Republic same way. Dem got big mountains on dat island, and can see it maybe twenty mile from de ocean. No mon there he gonna catch de *Casey Nicole,* if de wind she hold and we stayin' out dat far. An' den we turnin' north an' pass through de Caicos an' de Bahamas. Lot of little island in dem chain wid no mon livin' on dem. Find good fishin' an' good divin' for de lobstah if we stop for de break."

"I don't care about taking a break, Scully. I just want to get to New Orleans as fast as possible and make sure Casey's okay."

"Dat I understand, mon. Fo' dat, we gonna need de Copt'n. I an' I not knowin' dat city or de way 'round anywhere in Bobbylon but dat east coast of Florida."

"Well, I know enough to know that we've got to somehow sail *around* Florida to get to the Gulf of Mexico, I guess around the Florida Keys. And then we either follow the coast or cut straight across the Gulf to New Orleans. Larry will know which is best. After that, I don't know how close we can get with the boat. I know people sail in Lake Pontchartrain, and there are marinas on the lakeshore, but I've never paid much attention to the water there. I'm always either driving or flying when I visit Casey."

"De boat is de best way, mon. Jah nevah intend no mon to fly in de air like a fockin' bird, and de car, dem always crashin' on de road an' killin' de driver an' de passenger too—an' sometime killin' some child walkin' in de street. I an' I t'ink dis de will of Jah to put a stop to dis madness an' t'ink it's why he send a mighty flash from heaven to put out de lights."

"Well, I don't know about that, Scully, but I do know that this has put a lot of people in a bind, and in real danger. Look what has happened already. I never dreamed I would sail through the wreckage of a plane crash, or that we would be attacked in the night by pirates with machetes. I certainly never dreamed I would be shooting at someone in the middle of the night when I went to bed, or that you would have to kill two men right here on the deck of this boat. And look at Larry…. I sure hate to think about what could happen next, and I'm worried to death about my daughter."

"Jah he protect de righteous mon, Doc. Dem evildoers comin' to justice now or later, and dem two pirate not de first I kill," Scully said. "Lots of bad mon in de streets of Kingston when I growin' up. A young mon got to fight to survive in dat place, but I leavin' to find a bettah life in peace on de sea. Now I t'ink mehbe de peace it hard to find. I t'ink anyplace we goin', an' especially dat New Orleans, gonna be a dangerous place, mon."

"All I want to do is get Casey out of there, and as soon as possible. I don't know what we'll do after that, but this won't last forever, Scully. Whatever caused the lights to go out is probably over, and the grid will be rebuilt. Cars and planes and everything else will be fixed, but I know it might take some time—maybe even *a lot* of time—but it *will* be fixed, Jah or no Jah."

An hour after dawn the tropical sun was already beating down on the decks and Artie was anxious to get underway. The trade wind had died down significantly overnight, but there was still a five-knot breeze out of the southeast, and Scully said that was all they would need to leave Isleta Palominito and sail for the open Atlantic north of Puerto Rico. Using a bucket to dip up seawater, Scully rinsed the forward decks where the blood of one of the slain assailants had stained the teak slats. Before he began his task of hauling in the anchor, Artie went below to make sure Larry was reasonably comfortable. He was relieved that his brother's bleeding had stopped, and thankful that he was trained in what to do and that Larry's medical kit contained what he needed to do it. A wound like his was certainly life-threatening. Things could have turned out much worse. A cloud of dark thoughts swept over him as he thought of all the people who would not be getting proper medical attention for all manner of ailments and accidents in the aftermath of this shutdown. Hospitals like the one where he worked would be flooded with people trying to get help, if they could even get to one, and then most, if not all, of them would be turned away. Some hospitals might have functioning generators that could provide basics such as lighting, but with so much dependence on electronic equipment for diagnostics, treatment, and life support, their ability to respond to the situation would be overwhelmed. If only he knew Casey was okay, he knew he wouldn't hesitate to jump right in and do his part as he had sworn to do, and he was sure there would be opportunities later, but for now, sailing to New Orleans had to be the only goal.

Artie knew he had a lot to learn about sailing and navigating, and now it was no longer merely a recreational pursuit. He was determined to absorb everything he could from Scully. Seeing how quickly last night's attack had rendered his brother incapacitated and could as well have left him dead, Artie realized he had to take responsibility for finding their way and operating the boat on his own, as something could certainly happen to Scully too. From that morning on, he resolved to master the skills of seamanship, and when he came back on deck, he became an eager apprentice, giving Scully his full attention and following his directions just as he would defer to a senior physician explaining a complicated new surgical procedure.

"Dis boat she don' point so high in de wind and she don't tack like dem racin' yacht, but she gonna fly off de wind, mon. Get out on de Atlantic side away from de island few miles, an' de wind gonna pick up. I t'ink we makin' 200, mehbe 220 miles a day like dat."

Once he helped Scully get the sails trimmed to his satisfaction and all the loose ends of the sheets and halyards coiled neatly, Artie ducked into the navigation station in the starboard hull and brought out his brother's chartbooks for the Greater Antilles and Bahamas. He wanted to study the route while the winds were light, the sun was shining and the *Casey Nicole* was skimming along the surface of nearly smooth seas almost as steadily as she had rested at anchor. Feeling her sails harness the wind like a great winged bird gliding in the breeze; Artie again marveled at the tremendous amount of work and ingenuity that went into building her. He knew then, if he hadn't known before, that Larry could have done anything in life he set his mind to, and the skills he had learned in this sea vagabond's life were as complex and intricate as those required for his own career path. And one thing was certain: such skills and knowledge would be invaluable in the days ahead.

Isleta Palominito faded in their wake as they sailed past the northwestern point of Puerto Rico and the condos and hotels of Fajardo that crowded the beaches and reflected the morning sun from their glass and white stucco facades. Scully was careful to keep their course well offshore here, far enough that they could see no details on the coastline and, presumably, would only be seen as a distant white sail from eyes ashore looking seaward. Scully pointed out on the chart where the reefs and other hazards to mariners were indicated, and explained how to triangulate their approximate position from landmarks ashore by using Larry's binoculars with the built-in compass to take bearings. While it wasn't quite as easy as looking at the moving blip that had indicated *Ibis*'s position on the electronic chartplotter before the pulse, Artie found that triangulation worked well and would make it possible to measure their progress as long as they were in sight of land. For the hops between islands, they would depend on the dead reckoning method Larry had explained to him during the last leg of their trip into St. Thomas without instruments. Keeping an accurate log was the main thing—that and keeping up with the time and knowing how to judge the boat's speed through the water— something that Scully assured Artie he was very good at.

That speed increased just as Scully had said it would after ten a.m., when the trade winds freshened to the steady force five that Larry had said could be counted on in these latitudes at this time of year from late morning until well after dark. By now they had rounded the northeast corner of the island and were running before the wind to the west, staying well north of the coastline. Artie was alarmed to hear disconcerting creaks and groans from the mast foot and the connection points of the beams and the hulls as the rig was stressed and the boat surged forward, doubling her cruising speed to more than 12 knots.

"No problem, Doc! Dis boat she happy to get de wind, and not'ing gonna break in dese conditions. She can take a blow lot stronger widout to worry."

"I just wondered if maybe we should reduce sail a bit, that's all."

"You want to go to Bobbylon or sit out on de watah an' watch de fish? Not to worry 'bout de sail. She runnin' off de wind, an' de seas dem not too big. If de Copt'n be on deck right now he put up de spinnaker too!"

"He always was a daredevil. Yeah, I want to get there as fast as possible, but let's not break something trying."

"Everyt'ing on dis boat built strong, mon. I an' I see to dat myself. You brotha, he pick a good design to build, an' she goin' take us to New Orlean an' den anywhere we want to go. Not to worry 'bout de boat no more, Doc. Jus' enjoy de sailin' and de freedom to ride de wind across de sea."

Artie did feel the sense of freedom that held so much attraction for Larry and Scully, but more importantly, at the speed they were now making, he felt a sense of *progress*. That progress was easily measured without the need to take bearings, by simply watching as the city of San Juan and the rest of the rugged north coast of Puerto Rico slipped past them to the south over the course of the day as the wind bore them west. By late afternoon, the entire island was astern, and well before sunset it had dropped below the horizon in their wake. For the first time since he'd arrived in St. Thomas with Larry, Artie was once again at sea beyond the sight of land. Full darkness fell and the visible horizon closed in to the limits of what could be discerned by starlight. No lights from anything man-made could be seen, though that didn't mean there were no other vessels sailing in the vicinity. Though they had Larry's backup LED navigation lights to use if necessary, Scully said it would be best to save the batteries and instead keep a sharp watch, on rotating shifts. With any ship or other vessel they might encounter likely to be unlit as well, sounds would be as important as visual cues to alert them to dangers close enough to worry about.

Larry remained in his bunk through that entire first day and night, in a lot of pain but still wanting regular progress updates whenever Artie or Scully went below to check on him or get something out of the galley. During Scully's watch, from eight p.m. to midnight, Artie changed the bandage on Larry's forearm and sat with him, discussing routes and options for the trip.

"We still have no way of knowing how bad it is up there, or even knowing for sure if the grid is down on the mainland. If it is, we don't know how much else may have changed. I'm worried about even being able to enter U.S. waters."

"I thought it wouldn't be an issue since we're sailing directly from U.S. territorial waters in Puerto Rico to the mainland. As long as we don't clear in to the Bahamas or anywhere else, we shouldn't have a problem, right?"

"In normal times, no, but how will they know where we're coming in from? If there are Navy ships patrolling or blockading the coastlines, they may have orders to intercept any vessel sailing in from international waters."

"But why would they do that? If this surge or pulse or whatever it was came from the sun, they couldn't blame some other country for an EMP attack, like Pete was speculating about."

"No, but you know it's still going to be an urgent matter of national security up there. You've been living there since 9-11; I haven't. You know how things got right after that, and then again after every minor incident. I know this is going to cause all kinds of security issues, but I have no idea how this may or may not have affected the military's capabilities. I know that in normal times, it had gotten to where nothing could get in from the islands undetected, even from way back in the '80s when Reagan cracked down on the cocaine and grass smugglers running goods over from Bimini."

"But so much of their surveillance relies on high-tech electronics. I don't see how they can seal off the coast like they did after 9-11. And even if they do, we're both American citizens. They would have to let us in, wouldn't they?"

"One would think so, but Scully doesn't have a U.S. passport. He's from Jamaica, but now his official citizenship is in Grenada. That could be a problem, but as you can see, we need him more than ever now. I'm gonna be pretty useless for a while with this bum arm."

"All I know is that *I'm getting in*, one way or the other. I'm going to find Casey in New Orleans and get her out of there, but I don't know what we can do after that."

"I don't know either, Doc. I'm just glad we've got the boat. I think we ought to sail somewhere pretty remote and lay low for a while after we leave there. Anywhere near New Orleans is not gonna be the place to be, Florida either, or just about anywhere in the Gulf, except maybe a few stretches of the Mexican coast on the north side of the Yucatán. Wherever we go, it needs to be some place with good, protected anchorage for the boat, a fresh water supply, and good fishing and foraging. I've got a feeling we're gonna have to be self-sufficient for a while. I just can't even contemplate what a mess it's going to be up there in the bigger cities if this goes on for a few months."

"But don't you think everyone is going to have the same idea about getting out of the cities? It looks like there would be a mass exodus from just about all of them. I mean, everybody knows that food comes from the country, even city people. Won't they head out any way they can and try to get to farms hoping to find something to eat? I guess that's what I would do, if I were in that situation with no other choice."

"Nah, some will, but you gotta remember, most people are conditioned to expect a government handout when some disaster strikes, like a hurricane, for instance. I think most of them will hang around hoping help is on the way until they finally realize it ain't coming. Besides, from what I've seen my last few times in the States, most people these days aren't in shape to walk out of their neighborhoods, much less far enough to get to the rural areas. And even though some could do something like that, far fewer have access to good, seaworthy boats that could reach the kinds of places I've got in mind. No, Doc, we don't have to worry about that. As long as some other freak of nature doesn't come along and shut down the wind, the world is our oyster here aboard the *Casey Nicole.*"

"I just hope we get there before Casey decides to leave," Artie said, suddenly worried about this new possibility. "If she were to evacuate or something before we get there, I don't know how I would ever find her."

"We're *gonna* find her, Doc. Just try not to worry too much about all the what-ifs. Just help Scully sail this boat and when we get there we'll figure it out one step at a time."

SIX

CASEY GLANCED OVER her shoulder one last time at the terrible place on the Interstate where a dead man was sprawled face down on the concrete slab. She shuddered to see that at least a dozen of the big black vultures they had disturbed in their passing had returned to swarm over the body, while more circled downward, gliding in for the feast in lazy, spiraling loops. Casey looked ahead with apprehension for signs of more winged scavengers, as Grant had said it was inevitable that they would pass more dead bodies, but, at least for now, she didn't see any.

By the time they reached the exit to Causeway Boulevard, where they would get off the expressway to turn north, the mid-afternoon sun was baking the hot concrete beneath their tires. New Orleans's heat and humidity, even in March, could sap the strength of the fittest athlete. Sweat dripped on her handlebars as she rode, and her quadriceps burned from spinning the cranks. Jessica was struggling even more than she was, while Grant made it look effortless.

"I don't think I can go much farther without resting," she said, as they coasted down the ramp at their exit.

"It's only a little over two miles from here to the start of the Causeway Bridge," Grant said. "If you can just try to push on that far, we'll stop there and take a real break before we start the crossing. We need to eat something to keep our energy up, but I'll feel a lot better if we don't stop until we're on the bridge."

Causeway Boulevard, like every other road they had seen in the city, was packed with stalled cars and trucks, but in the short ride north to the start of the bridge, they had to move out of the way several times to make room for the occasional running vehicle as well. Most of these were pickup trucks, station wagons, or sedans twenty years old or more. Without exception, all were bound north, out of the city, most jam-packed with families and as many of their belongings as they could pile in the back or lash onto the roof. All of them faced a 24-mile-long obstacle course of more stalled vehicles blocking the bridge, but Grant said that by now people had probably pushed enough cars to one side or the other to open a route. Most of those few lucky enough to be riding in motor vehicles were focused on the obstructions ahead of them and hardly gave Casey, Grant, and Jessica a second glance. While a lone traveler without much stuff might have had some chance of hitching a ride, no one was going to stop for three people loaded down with gear. There were other bicyclists riding out of the city too, as well as a few people walking with large backpacks or duffel bags slung over their shoulders. The refugees moving north that first day were the vanguard of what would surely become an exodus from the city when more of the population of the greater New Orleans area figured out that help was not coming. Grant said it would probably be several days before many people accepted that reality and decided that their survival was up to them, and even those who realized the truth would likely hesitate due to indecision until it was too late.

"I've never seen anything like this in my life," Jessica said, "except in a movie or something. This is just unreal."

"It's sort of like a hurricane evacuation, but without the traffic jams. You should have seen what it was like here just before Katrina hit. Every road north was backed up bumper-to-bumper for a hundred miles. It was that way all the way across Louisiana to Mississippi and Alabama. But the big difference was that the cars were running. Everyone who had access to a vehicle and any common sense at all got out and got out early."

"But they also had someplace to go, right?" Casey asked. "I mean, all they had to do was drive far enough inland from the Gulf to get out of the danger zone. Where will all these people who are leaving go if the power is out everywhere? I don't imagine most of them have a cabin like yours to go to."

"No, but a lot of them may have relatives or friends nearby. Maybe they think everything will be normal somewhere else within reach, or at least they can hope. But they're making the right choice to get out of New Orleans while they can."

"Don't you think there will be someone willing to help all these people, like there are when hurricanes hit?" Jessica asked. "Surely there will be some somewhere."

"It's possible, but we just don't know the scale of this. If it's as bad as the worst-case scenario, I just can't imagine how anyone could do much, no matter how much they may want to. I think you'll see small groups of neighbors joining together to help each other, especially in the smaller towns and rural areas to the north of the city. But I don't see how they can do much to help a bunch of outsiders flooding in with nothing to eat. I'm just glad we have what we need with us and a place to go so we don't have to depend on anyone's generosity, because it will probably be in short supply."

At the edge of Lake Pontchartrain, the broad northbound and southbound lanes of the boulevard disappeared and the roadway transitioned into two separate, parallel bridges, with two lanes going north and two going south. Low concrete retaining walls bordered the edges of the lanes on either side, allowing a good view of the water from the height of a bicycle seat. The three of them pedaled onto the bridge, leaving land behind for an open horizon of empty water for as far ahead as they could see. Driving across the Causeway was about as close as a person could get to being out at sea without a boat, and Casey had found it interesting the few times she'd crossed it, especially in the middle sections of the span where no land other than the bridge itself could be seen in any direction. She had never dreamed of riding across such a bridge on a bicycle, and knowing how long it seemed to take in a car, she felt a good deal of apprehension about pedaling such a distance.

Grant said he thought it was okay to stop once they'd ridden about half a mile onto the bridge. He was visibly more at ease now that they had this small bit of isolation between themselves and the streets of the city. Casey and Jessica followed his lead and leaned their bikes against the rail. They all drank from their water bottles and sat in the shade of an abandoned delivery van to get some relief from the hot concrete. The three shared peanut butter and crackers, some dried fruit and almonds; Casey and Grant ate some of the beef jerky Grant had bought at the store. Grant said they would have a hot meal later that night when he felt they had gone far enough to camp safely. High-energy snacks would get them through the miles until they could rest.

As they sat there eating, an occasional car or pickup motored by headed north, and one young couple on expensive touring bicycles with a covered baby carrier hitched behind the man's bike made their way by as well. The trailer was occupied not by a child, but rather by a small dog that looked to be some sort of schnauzer.

"They'll probably be eating him before this is over," Grant said. Seeing Jessica's expression of horror, he felt bad about bringing it up. "Well, they eat dogs in a lot of other cultures," he explained. "It's weird how we have such a strange attachment to some animals while we slaughter others. What's the difference really, between a dog and a pig?"

"Dogs are cute!" Casey said. "That's what."

"I know. Man's best friend and all that. But still, they are just another variety of animal that our particular culture has chosen to live with as pets rather than raise as meat-producing livestock like pigs or cows."

"That's why I don't eat meat," Jessica said. "There's not really a difference and it's not our place to decide which species are better. All animals have a right to live, just like we do."

"Agreed!" Grant said. "Except that it's not a *right*. Humans are the only animals able to comprehend such complex concepts. In the animal kingdom it's all about survival of the fittest. We just happen to be at the top of the food chain—for now. In the overall scheme of things, we haven't always been, though, and we're still not in some places, like out there." He pointed to the empty expanse of sea over his shoulder. "In the sea, it's all about who's the biggest and who has the most teeth. Now, I'm afraid a lot of people are going to see that survival of the fittest applies to us, too, once you take away all the technology that has made our lives so easy. I'll never forget how my first undergrad anthropology professor put it. He said if you compared the entire span of human history to the span of a single twenty-four-hour day on the clock, then the advent of the Industrial Revolution would not occur until about five minutes to midnight."

"Really? I never would have thought about that," Jessica said.

"Interesting, isn't it?"

"I feel like survival of the fittest is already about to apply to us," Casey said. "I'm not looking forward to riding all the way across this bridge."

"Me either. It already hurts just to think about getting back on that bicycle seat. I don't think I can go much farther today."

"You both are doing just fine. We'll take it easy and stop as much as we need to.

If we have to keep going after dark, that's fine too, but I want to get past the main navigation channel under the bridge before we stop. There's a drawbridge there, and if for some reason the authorities decide to open it, we'll be screwed. I'll feel a lot better if we camp on the other side of it, even if we are still on the Causeway."

"How far is it to the drawbridge?" Casey asked.

"It's closer to the north shore, really, I think about two-thirds of the way across. So figure maybe 15 or 16 more miles."

"Ugh! That's a long way."

"You can do it. We'll find a place to camp after we pass it and sleep long enough to be refreshed for tomorrow. We should easily be able to push past Mandeville and Covington in the morning and get out in the country, where I'll feel a lot safer."

"I hope you're right about that," Jessica said. "Places like that scare me. When I think of rural Louisiana and rural Mississippi, all I can picture is a bunch of rednecks with guns."

"Well, there *are* some rednecks there to be sure, and most people out there have guns. But those are the kind of people who generally won't mess with anybody who is not messing with them. As long as we're not trying to steal something or trespass on somebody's land, we'll be fine. I know you're from California and all, but it's not quite like *Deliverance* down here."

Grant got them back on the bikes before they had time for their tired muscles to cool down and stiffen. They continued north on the bridge as the late afternoon sun began to sink, casting a glaring reflection on the watery horizon to their left. Casey couldn't imagine doing something like this on her own, without Jessica's company and Grant's encouragement and guidance. She wondered as she rode what she and Jessica would have done if he had not offered to help them, and she still wasn't quite sure why he wanted to be burdened by them. She guessed that without him, they would have just stayed put like almost everybody else and waited—but for what? If Grant was right about all the things he'd told them, life in New Orleans would be a lot harder than riding a bike 90 miles. She didn't want to think about the entire distance, but the least she and Jessica could do was make their best effort, considering all he was doing to help them. She gritted her teeth and focused on riding 15 miles; just 15 more miles and then they could stop for the night, eat something, and get some sleep.

Before they reached the drawbridge they crossed three smaller navigation channels where the Causeway rose to elevations ranging from 22 to 50 feet to allow the passage of smaller recreational vessels. At each of these places, the roadway rose in a steep hump that forced Jessica and Casey to get off their bikes and push, while Grant shifted to his lowest gear to spin along at a speed that matched their walking pace. They reached the crest of the second and highest of these elevated spans as the sun was beginning to set over the water in an impressive display of reds and golden yellows.

"I don't think I've ever seen a more beautiful sunset," Jessica said.

"Sunsets over the water are the best," Grant agreed.

"It sure makes me miss my dad," Casey said. "I just hope he's okay. I hope they found their way safely to land and that things in the islands are not as bad as they are here."

Grant was about to reply when they all became aware of a distant roar of engines to the south, in the direction of the city but obviously much closer, as they were now a good 12 miles from the south shore. The sound was growing louder, and it became clear that it was coming their way. From their vantage point on the elevated section of the bridge, they were soon able to see movement, and moments later that movement was distinguishable for what it was—a long line of motorcycles—winding among the stalled cars and trucks and coming their way at a rapid pace.

"Quick! We've got to find a place to hide," Grant said. "I don't like the looks of this. There must be nearly a hundred of them! I don't think they can see us yet. Let's get the bikes down there behind that pileup of cars and get out of sight before they get here."

The pileup he was pointing to was the scene of a multiple-vehicle accident that must have occurred just as the pulse hit and the drivers lost control. Some were smashed against the guardrail, and an overturned GMC Yukon was halfway on top of a crushed compact car. As they made their way around it and pulled the bicycles out of sight into the jumble of vehicles, Casey saw to her horror that there was a dead woman hanging upside down from her seatbelt in the Yukon. A pool of blood had dried beneath the crushed car under it but Casey turned her eyes away before she saw another body. It was a gruesome place to hide, but they had no other options. The lane to the far right was just clear enough to allow passage of one vehicle at a time, and they could only hope the motorcyclists would go on by.

"Is it a motorcycle gang?" Casey asked in a whisper, as the first few in a seemingly endless line of loud Harleys reached the foot of the elevated section.

"Probably," Grant said. "Or a motorcycle *club*, as they would prefer it."

"What would they do to us?" Jessica whispered.

"Maybe nothing. But I don't want to find out. Two beautiful girls out here with no law and order and no one but me to try and stop them...it's not worth taking the risk. Now keep down, and don't move!"

The first of the motorcyclists crested the rise in the bridge and streamed by the pileup in pairs and groups of threes and fours. They slowed down, gawking at the wreckage, but none of them stopped. Some of the riders had female passengers behind them. All of the bikes were loaded down with saddlebags, duffels, and other luggage strapped to sissy bars, forks, and handlebars, and without exception, all were Harley Davidsons from the 1980s or earlier, running obnoxiously loud straight pipes. Some of the riders were carrying guns in plain sight: pistols in holsters at their sides or shotguns and rifles slung over their backs or strapped to their machines. As they passed by, Casey could see from the patches on the backs of their jackets and vests that they were indeed members of an organized club. She had heard of the name *Bandidos* somewhere before, probably in a movie or something, but it didn't mean much to her. Whatever Grant called them, they looked like a gang to her, and she was really glad that they were hiding right now instead of pedaling along in plain sight of these bearded, tattooed, and greasy-looking bikers. When the last of them finally rolled past their hiding spot, she felt a flood of relief. Grant was right, there must have been more than a hundred motorcycles in the roaring procession, but all of them were focused on getting to wherever they were headed to, and soon were far enough away that it was safe to come out.

"Bandidos," Grant confirmed. "They're the dominant club in New Orleans and most of the Gulf Coast region."

"Are they like the Hells Angels or something?" Jessica asked.

"Yep. Definitely an outlaw motorcycle club. They usually don't mess with regular people unless they get in the way of one of their criminal enterprises, but in this situation, it's not worth taking a chance."

"I'll say. They sure look like they could take on anybody. Where do you think they're going?" Casey asked.

"Who knows? Probably somewhere to hook up with other chapters in their organization; there are thousands of Bandidos here in the South, and other, rival clubs as well. Riding those old Harleys with their simple engines, they've got an advantage now over most people, including law enforcement agencies. There's no telling what they're up to."

"I'm starting to think I'm going to like staying at your cabin in the woods," Jessica said.

"I'm telling you, any place away from people is the place to be in a situation like this. That river is not on the way to anywhere, and most people with criminal intentions would have no reason to go somewhere they wouldn't expect to find lots of people to take advantage of. We'll be so much better off when we get off the highway. The cabin is at the end of a dirt road that is miles from even the nearest crossroads. We'll be safe there—or I should say at least as safe as anywhere I could imagine, in this country, at least."

The sound of the motorcycles had completely faded when they remounted their bikes and started moving again. Daylight was fading fast, but Grant insisted on getting past the drawbridge, even though he admitted it was unlikely that it would be opened. They had not seen any sign of ship or barge traffic on the vast lake all afternoon, and there was little reason to think that the authorities would deliberately open the bridge and cut off one of the main evacuation routes out of the city. But still, he didn't want to take a chance.

"Once we're past that drawbridge, we're past the last potential major obstacle between us and the cabin. If I sleep at all tonight, it will be because I know that. But I probably won't sleep, because there's no way of knowing who else may come along in the night."

"I think we should keep a rotating watch, the way Uncle Larry says you have to do on a boat at night when you're out at sea."

"That's a good idea. Yes, let's do that every night until we are safe at the cabin."

The last few miles they covered in the twilight took them across the middle reaches of the Causeway, where land on either end was at its most distant. There were other people in this desolate stretch of roadway over the water—refugees from the city who had made their way this far and also stopped for the night to camp, and others who had been here since their cars stopped, still waiting for someone to come and help. Most of those in the latter category were too weak to move by now and had little chance of survival. Riding past them was heartbreaking to Casey, but she understood that she could do nothing for them. They barely had enough water between the three of them to last until the next morning, after exerting so much energy in the afternoon heat. Grant said they would cross some streams shortly after they reached the north shore the next day and that they would have the opportunity to refill their water bottles then.

When they finally pushed their bicycles across the steel grate of the drawbridge, full darkness had descended upon

Lake Pontchartrain. Though they were now only eight miles from Mandeville, where there should have been a blankct of city lights covering the shoreline, there was nothing but blackness, making it impossible to see land to the north. Likewise, there was no glow from the direction of New Orleans to the south. Instead, in the absence of man-made light pollution to obscure the heavens, the stars that filled the sky overhead were more brilliant than Casey had ever seen them. Out here in the open with no trees or buildings to block her view, she could see even more of them than she had the night before on Grant's front porch. It was simply amazing to her how much of the natural world she had missed before while living in the artificial insulation of modern technology. She couldn't help but marvel at this newfound natural beauty, but she would trade it back for her old familiar world in a heartbeat, and she knew Jessica would too. Grant, she wasn't so sure about. He seemed almost in his element in this new reality, and she was more impressed with him all the time as she saw how he seemed to have an answer for every problem that arose. She attributed it to his unusual upbringing with his adventurous parents, and of course, to his own chosen field of study that promised a continuing life out of the ordinary, mundane working world that most people had to fit into. He reminded her a lot of her Uncle Larry, who certainly had carved out a lifestyle for himself that most people wouldn't have dared to dream of. People like Larry and Grant may have been outsiders in some ways in the "normal" world, but she was beginning to see that in this new reality they might have a distinct advantage over those who had chosen more conventional lives. She knew Uncle Larry could take care of himself in just about any kind of crisis. She just hoped he could do the same for her dad as well.

The three of them huddled together behind a stranded tractor-trailer rig where they would be out of sight of anyone passing by in the night, and took turns keeping watch while trying to get some sleep during their off-watch hours. Jessica slept better than Casey or Grant did. She still had not caught up from being awake almost the entire night of the pulse event and she was exhausted from her long day that began with walking to Joey's house and later being attacked by the would-be bicycle thieves. Casey finally got a couple of hours of deep sleep before dawn, but it seemed to her she had just closed her eyes when Grant gently shook her shoulder and said it was time to get up and get ready to move out. He wanted to get in a full day of travel, and hoped they would be able to cover enough ground so that they would only have to stop one more night and then could reach the cabin the following day.

"You would probably already be there if not for us holding you back," Casey said as they each drank coffee and ate a bowl of oatmeal with chunks of almonds and dried fruit in it to give it more flavor and substance.

"I might be, but that's not even a consideration. You're not holding me back from anything. We'll get there when we get there."

"I don't think I can even sit on that bicycle seat today," Jessica said. "I can't believe how sore I am."

"The pain goes away after the first mile or so when you get warmed up. You'll be fine. We'll keep on at about the same easy pace as yesterday and before you know it, we'll be off this bridge, through all the towns on the North Shore, and out in the countryside."

Grant was right about the soreness going away. Casey couldn't believe how much it hurt to sit down on the narrow bicycle saddle when she first got back on it, and her legs felt so stiff she didn't think she could turn the cranks. But ten minutes into the ride she was starting to feel better, and the cool morning air made it a lot easier to breathe than it had been in the heat and humidity of the previous afternoon. The ride might have been pleasant if not for another gruesome reminder of the new reality they passed before they got off the bridge. This time the victim was a young man who didn't look unhealthy or out of shape at all, nor had he died in a car accident. His body was lying between an undamaged pickup truck and the concrete retaining wall. A stain of dried blood darkened the bridge deck beneath his head, and when Grant looked more closely he saw what could only have been a bullet hole. The back window of the truck was covered in a large Mossy Oak camouflage clothing logo, and the bed was empty except for some nylon ratchet straps that looked like they had been cut with a knife.

"He had something in the back of this truck somebody wanted," Grant said. "It looks like he was into hunting; it was probably some kind of four-wheeler ATV with a pull-start engine they were able to get running."

"Somebody killed him for it?" Casey asked in disbelief.

"It sure looks that way."

"Those motorcycle guys?" Jessica asked.

"No. They wouldn't have wanted or needed a four-wheeler, and this guy's been dead longer than that. It probably happened the first day, when everyone first realized they were going to have to walk if they ever wanted to get back to land. My guess is that it was someone with about the same mentality as those punks that tried to take our bikes. He probably put up a fight and lost."

It was still early in the morning when they left the Causeway for good and rolled onto the smoother pavement of the four-lane highway that began where the old bridge ended. Like Grant, Casey felt a lot better now that they were off that narrow route. It had felt like a trap, where the only avenue of escape was straight ahead or back the way they'd come. At least now that they were back on a regular road they could turn off in any direction if they had to, or even cut across a parking lot or yard to get away from any potential attackers.

Highway 190 mostly ran through an area of strip malls, gas stations, car dealerships, and fast-food restaurants, all built with automobile access in mind, unlike the older environs of New Orleans such as the Tulane campus area. Because of this, there were far fewer pedestrians and bicyclists out and about. Just as in Metairie and the other suburban areas of New Orleans, all of these businesses were closed. Some were boarded up with plywood as if in anticipation of an approaching hurricane; others were guarded by owners sitting or standing by the entrances with shot-guns and rifles. A few stores, especially the convenience stores that sold food items, had obviously been broken into and looted already, their windows shattered and merchandise and packaging strewn out in the surrounding parking lots. But as they pedaled north, they saw more of a police presence on this side of the Causeway than they had to the south, mostly in the form of small groups of well-armed officers patrolling on foot. In addition, a few older vehicles that would still run had apparently been rounded up by the Covington Police Department and the St. Tammany Parish Sherriff's Department. Some of these were nicely restored antiques that had probably once been proudly displayed at car shows by their owners but were now pressed into utilitarian service as patrol and rescue vehicles. However they were doing it, it was obvious that the authorities in this smaller city on the north shore of the lake were doing a better job of maintaining some semblance of law and order than the overwhelmed law enforcement agencies of the Big Easy to the south. As Casey remarked on this, Grant said it was a good thing they had gotten here when they did, because the citizens of this town might decide to put a stop to an influx of desperate evacuees from New Orleans if the volume started increasing. As he had suggested the evening before, one measure the authorities could take would be to simply open the Causeway drawbridge, using Lake Pontchartrain itself as a moat to protect them from invading hordes of refugees.

Their passing was not unnoticed by these watchful authorities, but since they stayed on Highway 190 and did not stop except to get off their bikes and drink some water and eat from the supplies they were carrying with them, they were not questioned or hassled. Grant said the best thing they could do was to appear focused on where they were going and ride through these patrolled areas as if they had every right to be there. Hesitation and the appearance of confusion or uncertainty might get them unwanted attention.

"The last thing we want to do is end up in some refugee camp," he said. "It could certainly happen. Right now, there's no organization or coordination among different levels of authority, but I would expect that they will eventually try to work out some system to control all the displaced people."

"How would they do it?" Casey asked. "I thought you said that without communication and with the whole country likely shut down, they wouldn't be able to send in the National Guard or any outside help like they did after Katrina?"

"No, probably not, but who knows? I would be more worried about the local police and county sheriff's departments taking things into their own hands. They're going to have to set up some kind of control systems if they expect to keep any power at all and protect their immediate concerns. I just think it could get out of hand and I wouldn't want to be among those who they might detain because they think they present a threat. That's why I kept saying we had to get out early. We're ahead of the curve so far and I want to stay that way."

"Me too," Jessica said. "Even if it kills me to keep riding this bike all day, I've seen enough now to know I've got to."

They passed the intersection where Highway 21 splits from Highway 190 and runs northeast, and crossed the bridge over the Bogue Falaya River. Two more miles took them through the north end of Covington to where Highway 190 makes an abrupt turn to the west to connect to Hammond and Baton Rouge beyond, but Grant led them north onto Louisiana State Highway 25. This arrow-straight two-lane route would take them away from the large human population centers surrounding Lake Pontchartrain, with only a few small towns and semi-rural neighborhoods separating them from the real boonies Grant assured them they would find when they crossed the Mississippi state line. Shortly after they left the city limits, they came to another bridge over a small, fast-running creek that looked much more inviting than the murky waters of the Bogue Falaya had. Though the water was far from pristine and unpolluted, Grant said it would be safe enough after chemical treatment and that it would also be nice to wash their dishes from last night's camp.

"How does that work?" Jessica asked as she watched Grant fill each of their water bottles and then add a capful of some liquid he carried in a small glass bottle that looked like a medicine bottle.

"The bottle contains iodine crystals," he said. "They are kept inside it by a particle trap, so they can be re-used over and over. I filled the bottle with water before we left my apartment, and it mixes with the iodine to form a concentrated solution. A capful in each quart bottle of water will make it safe to drink after about 20 minutes."

"Are you sure it works?" Casey asked.

"I'll bet my life on it," Grant said. "I've used this stuff everywhere. Even in the muddy Essequibo River in Guyana, where villagers dump their crap directly into the river and every kind of exotic tropical parasite known to man is likely to thrive. This stuff works for any kind of biological pathogens. And the best thing about it is that when this bottle of solution is empty, like right now after treating our bottles, you just simply refill it with more water and shake it up, and in an hour or so, you've got another bottle of solution ready to go. You can't beat it. This one bottle could last us for months, if need be. But I've got two more in my bags too."

"I'm impressed!" Casey said. She was indeed impressed and growing more so all the time—not with Grant's water treatment solution in particular, but with Grant the person. She knew it was probably obvious, and it was becoming obvious that Jessica was impressed with him too. She just wondered what he really thought of them and then it occurred to her that he might very well decide he liked Jessica more than her. After all, she turned guys' heads everywhere she went more than most any girl Casey had ever known. She wanted to think that Grant wasn't that superficial, but he was, first and foremost, a guy, and guys noticed girls like Jessica. Even though Jessica came across as mostly clueless when it came to dealing with a situation like the one they found themselves in, Casey knew that Grant might overlook that and that Jessica might come around to reality sooner than she had first assumed. The more time Jessica spent around Grant, the more time she would have to learn from him—and the more time he would have to notice how beautiful she was—despite not being able to properly do her makeup and hair or even take a bath every day.

The creek did give them an opportunity to wash their faces and freshen up a bit, though, and with full water bottles and the clean cooking pot and utensils packed away, they set out north again on Highway 25. The pedaling was easy here on a mostly flat highway with smooth pavement. Housing developments began to give way more to empty fields and wooded areas the farther they rode from the city. Interspersed here and there were larger single homes surrounded by expansive lawns, many with horse barns and ponds. They were now in the outlying areas. This was where the commuters with good jobs in the city would drive home each day, to their semi-rural retreats. And each day they would get up and do it again the next—that is, until three days ago, when that entire automobile-dependent lifestyle ceased to be viable for the indeterminate future. Along the roadway, shiny BMWs, Hummers, and other status-symbol rides were left abandoned alongside the well-used utilitarian brands of the less affluent. These now-useless relics proved that the failure of technology made no distinction between marks of manufacture when it came to anything dependent upon modern electronic circuitry. The playing field had been leveled once again as it had been briefly in the aftermath of Katrina, putting wealthy and poor alike at an equal disadvantage. Many of them probably habitually complained about spending hours in traffic to get to and from work, but were now faced with the even more discouraging prospect of walking for hours just to travel a few miles. There was no choice for anyone, no matter how wealthy, but to adapt as best they could from a life of comfort, ease, and security to one of ever-increasing hardship and danger.

For Casey, Grant, and Jessica, this discomfort was multiplied exponentially a half hour later when the clouds that had been building all morning finally opened up in a steady downpour. Grant said it didn't look like it was the kind of rain that was going to go away in a few minutes or even a few hours, like a typical summer thunderstorm in southern Louisiana. Instead, rain like this in mid-March usually indicated a large storm front moving into the area. Without any access to a weather report of any kind, they had left New Orleans not knowing such a weather system was coming their way. Grant had hoped they could make the entire trip to the cabin in the fair weather they had started out in yesterday. He didn't have enough rain gear at his apartment for all three of them, though there were ponchos stored with the canoe gear in the cabin. Stuffed in his backpack was a decent waterproof cycling jacket that he frequently wore when commuting around the city, but with the three of them caught out on the open road and the rain already falling, there was little good one jacket could do. He didn't feel right about riding in dry comfort while his companions got soaked, and there was no practical way for them to share the jacket, as everyone would get wet anyway when it wasn't their turn, so he didn't mention it or bother to get it out. Likewise, the tarp he brought for bivouacking along the way would keep them dry if they stopped, but would do little good on the road. Besides, the weather was warm enough that they were in no danger of exposure from getting wet; it was just unpleasant.

"It won't do any good to try to wait it out," he said. "This rain may last two or three days. We'd be soaked by the time we found a place to set up camp anyway, and then we'd just be stuck there with nothing to do. We might as well keep riding. I wouldn't normally want to ride far in the rain, but at least we don't have to worry about being hit by cars that can't see us."

"Oh wow, this *really* sucks!" Jessica said.

"You can say that again," Casey agreed. "Everything we have on is going to get drenched!"

"Yeah, but it'll all dry out again when this is over. The main thing is that our food and the really important stuff is packed away safely in plastic bags. It may be kind of miserable spending the night out in this tonight, but if we keep on pushing today until dark, we should easily reach the cabin by tomorrow," Grant said. "It may turn a lot cooler after this front moves through, but if we keep going, we'll be there before that happens. Just tough this out and soon, I promise, you'll be warm and dry, sitting by the heat of the woodstove and eating a good hot meal that will make you forget all about today."

He could give all the pep talks he wanted, Casey thought, but there was no way to describe riding in this heavy rain as anything short of misery. She had to squint and keep her head down just to keep from being blinded by the pelting drops that splattered on her forehead. The pavement beneath her tires was two inches deep in standing water that couldn't drain off the roadway as fast as it came down and made steering and braking treacherous. As if that weren't enough, the fenderless front wheel threw spray in her face from beneath while the rear wheel kicked up a rooster tail of more spray that soaked her back side from the bottom as thoroughly as the falling rain drenched her from above. In less than twenty minutes, everything she had on was soaked through and through.

The highway took them through the town of Folsom, but in the rain their passing was hardly noticed, a decided advantage of traveling in these conditions. "Not many people are going to be out in this unless they really have to be," Grant said. Though they continued to pass disabled vehicles on the side of the road, no one was out and about in Folsom except for a handful of people standing around here and there under the shelter of awnings in front of darkened storefronts and gas stations. Some waved as they passed, and one man yelled out to ask where they'd come from and if they had any news about the power outage, but no one harassed them or asked if they needed anything. Once they were north of the city limits, they had the road to themselves again, though in the limited visibility it was hard to be sure there were no potential threats lurking just ahead, out of sight. The terrain had changed from flat to rolling hills, and with every climb Casey and Jessica slowed to a crawl.

"It's only about nine more miles to the river," Grant said as they passed a fork where Highway 450 split off to the northwest and 25 curved away to the northeast. "Highway 25 will take us almost parallel to it for a while, and then it crosses over on the bridge at Franklinton. We'll camp for the night somewhere before we get to the bridge, though. Franklinton is a bigger town than Folsom and I don't want to be close to it tonight. We can ride through tomorrow morning and then keep going north until we get to the state line. Then it's only a few miles to the cabin."

Two more hours of slogging through the rain at a slow pace put them past the side road leading to Bogue Chitto State Park. Grant said it would normally be a good place to camp, but considering the conditions, it would be better to avoid any kind of developed campground and 'stealth camp' somewhere just off the highway where no one would see them. They found a spot on a dead-end logging road leading off the highway to the east. The muddy dirt track was too slippery to ride on in the rain, so they dismounted and pushed their bikes a hundred yards to where it ended at the edge of a dense forest of river-bottom hardwoods. Pushing on a short distance into the trees would have made them completely invisible to anyone passing by on the highway even if it had not been raining, but, much to Casey's disappointment, a steady shower continued to fall. Grant dug the nylon tarp out of his backpack and began unwrapping the cords attached to the grommets in its corners. Then he stretched another piece of rope that was wrapped up in the tarp between two trees that were spaced about 10 feet apart. This line he pulled tight and tied off so that it was parallel to the ground and about four feet high. "This is our 'ridgepole'," he said. "Help me pull the tarp over it and we'll pitch it so that it's like an A-frame tent."

Casey and Jessica did as he asked and Grant secured the two corners on one side to the bases of nearby saplings. There was nothing convenient to tie the remaining two corners to, so he took out his machete and quickly cut two stakes from another inch-thick sapling, sharpened the ends with a few deft strokes of his blade, and then pushed them into the soft ground. When he had pulled these last two corners tight, the tarp did resemble an A-frame tent, only one with no walls and no floor.

"Wow, you know what you're doing, don't you?" Casey said.

"It's just basic stuff," Grant said. "We used plastic tarps similar to this in Guyana. Our Indian guides there were the real experts in setting them up in no time flat. To them, any piece of plastic is a luxury. They can build just as dry a shelter with palm fronds or other foliage, but it takes a little longer."

"But this is hardly going to be dry," Jessica said, pointing out the wet leaves and muddy ground under the tarp as they crawled under it to get out of the rain.

"No, it's not going to be all warm and cozy, but at least it'll keep the rain off of us while we try to sleep."

"I don't know," Casey said. "It seems pretty cozy to me. Especially with all three of us crowded under here."

"Just be glad Joey didn't come too," Jessica said. "I know I am. He couldn't have handled this anyway. He would have freaked out so many times already."

"Yeah, you're right about that," Casey said. "I'm glad it worked out this way. He wasn't good for you anyway. You're better off without him—we all are."

"Well, I want you both to know I'm really proud of you," Grant said. "You two have been real troupers ever since we left the city. I knew you could do it, though."

"Not without you making us, Grant," Casey said. "I still can't believe you wanted to be burdened with us tagging along. You could be sitting by that woodstove right now, in the comfort of your cabin."

"And then what, sit there with no one to talk to for no telling how long until this gets fixed? No, thanks. I spend enough time alone in everyday life. I wouldn't have this any other way. I'm just glad you two were insane enough to come along with me, and I hope you don't go stir-crazy from being stuck there with me."

"After what we've seen since we left yesterday, we'd be crazy to do anything else but go with you, I think."

"Yesterday…" Jessica said. "I can't believe it was only yesterday that we left. It seems forever ago…so much has happened. That dead man…the motorcycle gang…crossing the Causeway…. It's hard to believe that just yesterday morning I was stupid enough to follow Joey back to his house."

"Time does seem distorted," Grant agreed. "That happens with this kind of stress."

"I just have to wonder what tomorrow will bring?" Casey asked. "Besides more rain, that is."

"The rain is a given, I think. But so is getting to the cabin if our luck holds out. Right now, I think we should try to get a little more comfortable and get some hot food inside us. That does more to make a person feel better in these kind of conditions than anything else."

Grant unpacked the sleeping bags and Casey and Jessica spread one of them out and temporarily suspended it from the overhead guy line for some semblance of privacy so she and Jessica could get out of their wet clothes on one side while Grant changed his on the other. They all still had some dry items of clothing protected by the garbage bags lining their packs that Grant had given them before they left. With dry clothes and sleeping bags, the night under the tarp would be much more tolerable. The garbage bags and their wet clothes under them provided some insulation from the ground and a relatively clean surface upon which to spread out the sleeping bags. This done, Grant assembled the stove and boiled water to cook a couple of packages of rice pre-mixed with dried cheddar and broccoli, and they ate huddled together under the tarp as night closed in and swallowed their hidden camp in inky blackness. A compact LED headlamp that ran on two AAA batteries provided enough light to eat by when Grant hung it overhead, but beyond the tiny circle of illumination it cast, the darkness in this dense stand of forest was more complete than anything Casey and Jessica had ever experienced.

"This is scary," Jessica said, her voice barely above a whisper, as if she were afraid something unseen out there in the night forest might hear her and come their way.

"It is creepy," Casey agreed. "Are there bears or anything like that in these woods?"

"There's nothing to worry about," Grant said. "The only animals we need to fear are the two-legged kind, and we're way out of sight of the road here. But to answer your question, there are a few bears around in the river-bottom swamps in Louisiana and Mississippi, but they are so rare you hardly ever see one. And they're certainly too shy around humans to be a threat. They're not like the bears in the mountains and places where they are plentiful. Snakes are the biggest wildlife danger in these woods, but unless you're walking along through here at night without watching where you're stepping, you don't have to worry about them either."

"Who would be stupid enough to walk out here at night?" Jessica asked. "You can't see *anything* out here."

"Just take the light and watch where you step if you have to go out to go to the bathroom tonight. But most likely, even the snakes won't be moving around in this weather."

"There's *no way* I'm going out there for anything tonight. I'll hold it 'til morning."

But when they had finished eating and the cooking pot was empty, Grant scraped it out and washed it in the rain running off the edge of the tarp, then boiled more water for tea. After drinking a couple of cups of hot tea Casey and Jessica did have take a short trip out from the tarp before going to bed, but they went together and stayed close, checking the ground carefully with the beam of the light after what Grant had said. When they were back in their sleeping bags, Casey found it hard to believe they could be so comfortable in such miserable conditions with so little. The night wouldn't be half as bad as she had imagined, and besides, she was so tired she felt like she could sleep anywhere.

When she awoke the darkness was replaced by the foggy gray of dawn, and the heavy downpour of the night before was now lighter, but a steady, soaking shower was still falling and showed no sign of letting up. Grant already had the coffee ready, and after they all had a cup he made a pot of oatmeal. The hardest part of the day, he said, would be leaving the shelter of the tarp and getting back out on the road. The hot breakfast would help, but after that there was nothing to do but face another day of riding in the wet. When Grant had taken down the tarp and helped repack the bicycles, they pushed them back to the highway along the muddy logging road and set out to the north again. The highway was still deserted, and riding was a bit easier in the gentler rain compared to the afternoon before.

They hadn't gone a half mile when there was a loud popping sound from Jessica's bike and then her chain came off the gears, forcing her to stop.

"What happened?" Casey asked.

"Looks like that cheap Chinese derailleur finally broke," Grant said. "I was afraid of that, as much noise as it's been making."

"What am I supposed to do now?" Jessica asked. "Does this mean I won't be able to ride it?"

"I think I can get you going again," Grant said. "You just may not be able to shift gears, at least not on the rear cassette. Hold on, let me get my tools."

Grant dug around in his pack until he found what he was looking for. It was a chain-breaker tool that allowed him to remove enough links from the chain to shorten it so that the rear derailleur could be bypassed altogether. After doing this, he then took the broken derailleur completely off and placed the chain on the middle cog of the eight-speed gear cluster.

"That should do it. I've put it in the gear you'll probably need the most on these roads. If we come to a hill you can't climb in that speed, you can still use your other shifter to drop down to the smaller chainring up front."

"Ingenious," Casey said.

"Bicycles are simple enough. No big deal really. A lot of people prefer single-speed 'fixies' anyway. It's kind of a trend, even."

Grant's repair worked fine. With the inferior rear derailleur gone, Jessica's bike ran much more quietly. The terrain became flatter again anyway, as the highway here ran in the bottomlands of the Bogue Chitto River. When the route finally took a right-angle turn to the east towards the town of Franklinton, Casey and Jessica got their first look at the river that was to play such an integral role in their lives in the near future. Riding across it on the bridge in the rain, they saw its rising waters swirling among fallen trees and stumps, coursing through a jungle-like forest of tall hardwood trees that leaned over its current from walls of greenery along the banks. Both upstream and downstream of the highway crossing, there was nothing but wild, dark woods on both sides of the river.

In the outskirts of Franklinton, the highway turned north once again. They stopped for a few minutes under a large open roof covering gas pumps at a convenience store, when two local policemen who had switched from cruisers to horses waved them over and asked where they had come from and where they were going.

"What do you mean, they won't let us in?" Grant asked, in disbelief.

"I'm just telling you what we've heard," one of the officers said. "Officials in Mississippi are turning back refugees from Louisiana. They say they can't take care of their own people, much less hundreds of thousands of people coming up from New Orleans and Baton Rouge. They're afraid it's going to be like another Katrina, where they'll have a flood of people coming in who won't leave for months—or maybe ever."

"This situation is a lot worse, and they do have a point," the other policeman said. "Nobody has power, either here or north of the state line, so what would they do with a bunch of refugees?"

"But we're not refugees," Casey said. "We have a place to go. He has his own cabin, on his parent's land."

"I understand," the first officer said. "But they *are* turning people back. We've already seen people coming back here through Franklinton. You're the first we've seen today, out in this weather, but a couple of days ago some people who had running vehicles were reporting they couldn't get in."

"The thing is," the other man said, "you all have to have proof of Mississippi residence or they'll turn you back. You have to show them your Mississippi driver's licenses or some other official I.D."

"We're screwed," Jessica said. "All I have is a California license."

"And mine's from Louisiana," Casey said.

"Mine too," Grant said. "But we *own* our own land there. It's right on the Bogue Chitto. My parents bought it more than fifteen years ago."

"I'm sorry to be the one to bring bad news, but I just felt like we ought to flag you folks down and tell you. I figured you were planning on passing on through when I saw the way y'all were loaded down. I hated to see you ride on up to the state line only to be told you can't cross it."

"I appreciate it," Grant said. "But we've got to try. I've got to see this for myself. Everything we need is in that cabin. I don't know what we would do or where we would go if we couldn't go there."

SEVEN

BY SUNRISE THE SECOND DAY after leaving Isleta Palominito, the *Casey Nicole* had sailed some 220 miles in just under 24 hours and made landfall off the Samaná Peninsula, on the rugged north coast of the Dominican Republic. Scully insisted on keeping their course several miles offshore, and from that distance it was impossible to tell in daylight whether or not the electricity was out on the first part of the island they could see. But from what Artie could glimpse of the land they were sailing past, there might be little indication even at night. Much of the coast here appeared to be a rugged wilderness of steep, jungle-cloaked mountains, with jagged cliffs of gray rock looming like the walls of a fortress over the sea. In only a few places were there breaks in those cliffs, and in some there could be seen the openings to small bays or coves, where Scully said there were a few tiny villages and farming settlements.

"Dem Dominican in some of dis place got no light even before Jah strike down de technology of Bobbylon," Scully said, as Artie scanned the wild-looking coast with Larry's binoculars. "Lot o' dem livin' de simple life. Catch de fish, grow de coconut, spend time wid dem family. Livin' de way Jah people supposed to live."

"That looks like a village we're passing now. I can barely make it out, even with the binoculars, but it looks like a bunch of small houses or huts under that grove of palm trees beyond the beach there. I can see smoke too. I wonder what that's all about?"

"Always fires in dem village like dat. Cooking fire, burning some brush, making charcoal."

"So that's not a sure sign the lights are out?"

"No, but by dark we sailin' past de big cities on de island. Puerto Plata got about 150,000 people. Lot of light in dat place. But I t'ink all de lights made by man, dem out all over de world."

"Well, I hope you're wrong, but we shall see tonight then. I guess it doesn't matter much one way or another to those villagers. I suppose you can't miss what you don't have. But tell me, Scully, do you really think people would be better off without technology? I know modern civilization is not perfect, but still, isn't life the old way a hell of a lot harder?"

"Life in de island not so hard as you t'ink, Doc. In dis place we got de sun. Nevah cold all de year. Good weather for a mon and good for crops too. In dis place we got de sea an' all de fish it provide, and wind to make de boat go. Not so hard dis life in de island, but bettah in de old days when all Jah people livin' dis way. Now dem got big city even here. Cut down de forest, catch all de fish, an' pushin' Jah people into de bush to build de big hotel and casino on de beach. De youth of de island, now dem don't want to live de simple life. Now watchin' TV an' computer too, an' want de flashy cars of Bobbylon. Too much stealin' goin' on and killin' too, because dem not content wid de ganja herb. Want de cocaine and de money dem get to sell it. I t'ink it's good now de TV, it can't play."

"Well certainly there are some ill effects brought about by technology and civilization, but still, there's a lot of good too. Look how much freedom and opportunity we have now. Never before in human history have individuals had access to as much knowledge and as many choices in how to live their personal lives. I continue to be amazed by all the changes brought about in my lifetime—but especially most recently, with the advent of the Information Age."

"But where dat information now, Doc? De radio, it don't talk. GPS, it don't track. Cell phone, dem don't call. Airplane, dem can't fly.... All dat technology...gone away wid a flash of light. But de wind, she still blow.... De sun, it still shine bright.... Fish, dem still swim.... An' dis simple boat, she still sail."

"You're right, of course, but all that will be fixed. It's just a matter of repairing or replacing the damaged parts. The knowledge and technology is still there."

"But what dem forget is de *useful* knowledge. Knowledge to live in de world of Jah creation widout all dat technology. Not many in de islands, but some of de roots Rasta dem choose to live de simple life in de bush, just like de ancestor dem in Africa. I spent time in dat life too, deep in de Blue Mountains. Growin' de food on de land, an' de ganja too, watchin' de sun come up each day an' go down too. Not to worry 'bout de money or t'ings it can buy. Jah will provide if a mon is just willing to learn."

"But isn't that just getting by, Scully? Sure you can grow enough to eat, and keep a shelter over your head. But how long can you live that way before you get bored out of your mind? You didn't stay there, did you? You've been out seeing the world with my brother. Would that have been possible without modern technology? Sure, this is a simple boat, based on a simple design that is thousands of years old, if what Larry said is true, but what about the modern epoxy used to hold it together? The fiberglass covering the plywood hulls? The synthetic Dacron sail cloth? The stainless steel hardware? All these things are better than anything you could fashion from nature, right?"

Scully just shrugged and grinned as he stood at the helm and steered. "Good stuff, dat—not to argue. But all I an' I sayin' is maybe now some people gonna have to learn to live a more simple life. Only time will tell, Doc."

"Yeah, we'll see. Let's just get to Casey while we've still got a new boat to do it. I don't plan on having to carve out a dugout on the beach just yet."

Ten hours later, as darkness fell on the coastline they were sailing past, it became apparent that the electricity was indeed out all over the island. They passed several larger towns, and finally, Puerto Plata, which should have been brightly lit by city lights, but instead they could see scattered campfires against the dark silhouette of mountains. At Larry's insistence, they adjusted their course to put more distance between themselves and the land, as insurance against the possibility of a collision with some small, unlit fishing boat or other vessel operating near shore. There wasn't much point in risking sailing in closer anyway, as there was little to see in the darkness and they had no compelling reason to stop anywhere in the Dominican Republic.

"Luperon is a great place to drop the hook," he said, pointing out a harbor entrance they passed a couple of hours west of Puerto Plata. "At least in normal times, there are always a lot of cruising boats there: American, Canadian, and European. It's well protected in all weathers there too. The rum is cheap, the food is great, and the girls are beautiful. What more could a sailor ask?"

"Sounds like your kind of place for sure, little brother."

"I've been known to stay there a few weeks at a time, between delivery jobs."

"Ah yes, the life of a delivery skipper, I know. Like I said, most of us have to *work* for a living."

While Scully steered the boat, Artie ordered Larry down into the galley cabin where he could change the bandages on his arm and inspect his wounds for signs of infection. He was pleased to see that there were none so far and that the deep cut was in the early stages of the healing process, although it would be a long time before he could leave it unwrapped. He had fashioned a sling for the arm from some canvas and webbing material Larry had on board, as it was pretty much useless at this point, and securing it in a sling would make it easier for his brother to avoid further injury while getting around on the moving boat.

"It still hurts like hell, Doc. I can't even move my fingers on that hand."

"That's normal. I told you it was going to hurt. The swelling will gradually go down in your hand and fingers. Like I said, you've got nerve damage too. You have a long road ahead of you."

"Good thing I don't play the guitar for a living, huh?"

"Yes. Good for you and for your audience!"

"Damn, that hurts worse than the cut, Doc. You know how hard I tried to learn."

"Well, at least you figured out you didn't have an ear for it before it went too far. Anyway, I don't think any lasting damage you might have from this will affect your present career too much."

"Nah, even if I lost the whole arm I could always get a hook. Sure beats a split skull any day of the week."

"I'll say. And that's what would have happened if you hadn't put that arm up."

"How do my stitches look, Doc?

"Beautiful! You'll always have a visible scar, especially considering how dark you stay working out here in the sun all the time. But I don't think it'll detract too much from your dashing good looks, and like Scully said, it might even add to your appeal as a rugged, adventurous boat captain. One of these days, in one port or another, some pretty little lady is going to set the hook and drag you aground permanently, and your sailing days will be through."

"That'll never happen to me, Doc. I've steered clear of those reefs this long; I'll be damned if I'm going to wreck my ship now."

"Well, couldn't you at least find another one who wants to sail with you? I know they're out there. Colleen hung with you for three years. Surely you've thought about finding another one?"

"Nah. What I finally figured out, Doc, is that bringing a woman on a boat is like bringing sand to the beach. Kinda redundant, if you know what I mean. Best to leave 'em on the dock and look forward to the next landfall."

"So it's true what they say about a girl in every port?"

"Absolutely," Larry grinned. "And what about you, Doc? It's been, what, seven years now? Casey's out of the house now; you've got to be lonely."

"Just dating occasionally has been enough for now. I don't want to live alone forever, I know that, but it wouldn't be fair to get married for that reason alone. I just can't stop comparing every woman I meet to Dianne, no matter how hard I try. It just doesn't seem real to me that it's been seven years. It seems more like seven months or so to me."

"I know you miss her. I can't imagine. You've done a great job with Casey, though. And I know she knows it too."

"I just can't lose her too. You know that, little brother."

"I do, and you won't. That's why I'm here. We're going to get you to her and we're going to keep her safe."

"I'm sorry it's already cost you so much," Artie said, looking at his brother's arm again. "I could never do this without you and Scully. I don't know what in the hell I would do, still stuck in St. Thomas with no way to get back to the mainland. I would go insane worrying about her.

I'm worried as hell now, but at least we're doing something about it. At least we're in motion, thanks to you, and I can feel hope that she will still be okay and will be there when we get there."

"I'm sure she's fine, Artie. The campus is probably one of the safest places to be in New Orleans. Casey's got a lot of sense. She's not going to go wandering around town getting in trouble in a situation like this. I'll bet she and Jessica are hunkered down at home with their friends, keeping a low profile and waiting to see if help is coming. They'll be okay until we get there."

"What's your best estimate at this point? How many days?"

"Given that we can count on favorable winds this time of year on this leg of the trip, I'm going to say we'll reach the Keys in three and a half more days, give or take a few hours. We're going to shoot straight up the Old Bahama Channel, just north of Cuba. That will keep us from having to thread our way around all the reefs and islands in the Bahamas, other than the Cay Sal Bank. There is a place on the bank I want to stop at though. The spear-fishing there is some of the best in the world."

Artie looked at the chart Larry showed him. The Cay Sal Bank was a huge area of shallow water far to the west of the main Bahamas archipelago, situated between Cuba and the Florida Keys. Larry said it was one of the few coral atolls in the Atlantic, and like the atolls of the South Pacific, it consisted of a lagoon of shallow water protected by an encircling fringe of reefs and low islets.

"I've never even heard of it," Artie said. It's amazing how many of these places, not all that far from Florida, I've never heard of. It sounds interesting, but do we really have time to stop and fish?"

"In this case, we can't afford not to. See that tiny string of islets and cays there?" Larry pointed to a line of specks on the edge of the shallow bank labeled *Anguilla Cays*. "That area sees so few human visitors that the grouper and yellowtail hardly know what a diver looks like. It's also so far from Nassau and Bimini that even in normal times the Bahamians rarely patrol there. We won't have to worry about clearing into the Bahamas and all that hassle. Just drop the hook and go hunting. With my arm out of commission I don't think I would do much good, but give Scully a speargun and he can load this boat with a few hundred pounds of fish in a couple of hours. And he can show you how to help. Think about it, Doc. We only have so much food on board, and the local Winn-Dixie in New Orleans ain't likely to be open when we get there. And the muddy water up there doesn't exactly offer the promise of spearing fish there if we get hungry."

"Yeah, but assuming it is that easy to spear them, how will we keep all that fish fresh? It's not like you have a deep freezer or even refrigeration on board."

"No problem, mon. You see how much wind and sun there is out here at sea, and all the open deck space we have around us, being that we're on a cat. We'll preserve the fish the old way. We'll dry it. People in the islands still do it all the time. Anyway, you'll see. A brief stop to anchor there for a few hours will hardly make any difference in the grand scheme of things and will hardly affect our arrival time in New Orleans, but it will make a huge difference in our provisions."

"Okay, fine with me if you say so, but you never did answer my question. How long do you think it'll take to get the rest of the way, from the Keys on up to New Orleans?"

"Five days, tops, assuming we have wind. Weather in the Gulf is more fickle than here. We won't have the trades, but we might get a lift from the Gulf Loop Current, and the wind should still generally be out of the southeast or east unless there's a northern blowing, and that's not likely this late in the year. We'll leave the Anguillas after we take on our fish and cut right through the middle of the Keys under the Seven Mile Bridge at Marathon. I don't plan on stopping there at all for any reason unless we run into some Coastie or Florida Marine Patrol boat and get pulled over. Once we clear that bridge and get in the Gulf, I aim to set a straight course for the Mississippi Sound, just east of the entrance to Lake Pontchartrain."

"The direct route then, that's good. How far is that?"

"About 550 nautical miles. It's wide open sailing until you get to the oil fields about a hundred miles off the north coast. Normally, that's a dangerous area, with all the crew boats and other vessels that serve the rigs running 24-7. There shouldn't be any activity at all out there now, though."

They passed the border that separates Haiti from the Dominican Republic later in the night, and by dawn were north of Tortuga, a Haitian island Larry said was made famous by the buccaneers who used it as a base of operations in the seventeenth century. After another jump of roughly 80 miles out of sight of land, they were abeam of the eastern end of Cuba. It was now late afternoon on their third day of sailing since the attack at Isleta Palominito. Larry said they would parallel Cuba for some 350 miles to the Cay Sal Bank. The trade winds were holding steady, and by staying 20 or so miles off the coast of the island, they would avoid the land effects that would interfere with the wind and be able to maintain an average speed of 10 knots as they had been doing since they left. Larry calculated this would put them near the southeast corner of the bank and the Anguilla Cays at dawn the day after tomorrow.

"If we happen to reach the banks before daylight, we'll just have to heave to until there's enough light. Even with just two feet of draft and a working GPS, that would be a risky area to enter without good light. The coral heads just about reach the surface in a lot of places, and they're everywhere."

For the most part, the waters they had traversed north of the island chain had been deserted except for a few sails spotted on the horizon off Puerto Rico and near Samaná Bay. Cuban waters were no exception. Larry said that no sailing vessels leaving the U.S. were likely to be seen this far south, as it was a dead beat to windward to go from Florida to the islands in the Old Bahama Channel. He figured a lot of people on the mainland who were lucky enough to own cruising boats would indeed leave for the islands to get away from the chaos, but most would cross the Gulf Stream to Bimini or the Abacos since they wouldn't likely have the benefit of a working engine to help them motor-sail a more direct course to windward.

Other than an occasional visit to the cockpit to get some fresh air and look around, Larry stayed below in the port cabin most of the time, reading or sleeping in his bunk. He was still in a lot of pain, and Artie insisted that he take it easy and not try to do too much. By now, Artie had adapted to a four hours on, four hours off routine of alternating watches with Scully. But there wasn't a whole lot to do while on watch. The wind vane took care of the steering, and the steady trade winds allowed them to sail a downwind run with the sails set wing on wing—the jib poled out to starboard, and the main eased out as far as possible against the port shrouds.

Cuba, by far the longest of all the islands in the West Indies, seemed to go on forever. The main island was out of sight by night at their distance, but the following day Artie caught occasional hazy glimpses of the higher mountains inland.

By carefully recording their dead-reckoning position each hour in the logbook and marking off a rhumb line on the chart, Artie and Scully were able to keep track of their progress along the island coast. They were able to check their calculations against charted landmarks, especially along the long outlying island of Cayo Lobos, which they passed much closer to than the main island. One more night at the consistent speeds they were sailing put them at the

Cay Sal Bank around dawn, just as Larry had estimated the day before. As they neared this area of reef-studded shallow water, Scully reduced sail at around 0400 hours to slow the boat down to six knots, a speed that felt to Artie like sitting still on the catamaran, but still a respectable average on many sailboats. Scully told Artie that this would ensure they would not arrive at the banks too early.

"Got to wait for de sun come up to enter dat bank, mon. Only one way to navigate de banks—dat's by de eyeball. Even when it's workin', de GPS no good in a place like dat."

"I thought it wasn't that big of a deal on a catamaran. Isn't our draft so shallow we can hardly hit anything anyway?"

"Shallow draft, but on dem bank de reef sometime all de way to de top. Even a skiff got to find de channel. Coral like dat tear out de bottom on a plywood boat. Dem banks no place to get in trouble like dat. No watah on dem cays and even before now not many people going dat place."

"So the diving is really good here, huh?"

"Bahamas best diving in de world, mon, and Cay Sal best in de Bahamas. Fish in dat place not afraid because most of dem nevah see a mon before."

When the sun did come up, Cuba was no longer in sight to the south and the only visible land was a sliver of a low-lying cay of rock and sand roughly three miles ahead. The transition from the ocean to the edge of the bank was marked by a dramatic change in water color, from deep indigo blue to transparent aquamarine green through which Artie could see every detail of the sand bottom 20 feet below. The water over the bank was impossibly clear, the underwater visibility far exceeding even that around the coral reefs of Isleta Palominito. When they passed over an isolated patch of coral formations that reached to within 10 feet of the surface, Artie could clearly see that it was teeming with a dazzling array of tropical fish. A large black-tip shark darted away at right angles to their course as the catamaran's twin bows passing overhead startled it. Larry was clearly excited to be here, and had come on deck to eagerly scan the line of cays ahead with his binoculars.

"Where are we going to anchor, near the island?" Artie asked.

"No, just past it, off the north end, on the edge of the banks. There's an extensive patch of reef there you won't believe, huge elkhorn and brain coral formations, lots of deep crevices and canyons, all in about 30 feet of water. It's thick with big grouper and yellowtails. We can clean up there in short order. Damn, I just wish I could dive!"

"Sorry, little brother, but you're going to have to sit this one out—doctor's orders. I'd like to try it myself, but I don't know after seeing the size of that shark back there."

"Plenty shark," Scully said, as he steered them closer to the cays, "but not to worry too much. Best t'ing is to spear de fish and get dem on de boat quick."

"Yeah, that's a good idea, diving in shark-infested waters and then calling the sharks to dinner by poking bloody holes in a bunch of fish!"

"They don't usually mess with you if you don't hang around too long," Larry said. "Like Scully said, as soon as you spear a fish, get it out of the water as fast as possible to minimize the blood."

Artie was still skeptical a half hour later, when, anchored over the reef, he put on a mask and snorkel and sat on the edge of the deck with a pair of fins. Scully was already in the water, and Artie could see him free-diving effortlessly into the winding and convoluted canyons between the coral, his dreadlocks streaming behind him as he cruised 20 feet below, with his speargun at ready.

By the time Artie was in the water, still swimming by the boat and looking around beneath the surface with his mask, Scully was on the way back to the boat with a two-and-a-half-foot long, heavy-bodied fish impaled on his spear. Artie found out later it was a Nassau grouper, a reef fish much sought after in the Bahamas that is much more scarce near the populated islands. The Anguilla Cays were so far from the rest of the Bahamian islands they may as well have been in another country, and from what Artie could see as he snorkeled along the surface, Larry had not been exaggerating about the possibilities for stocking the boat with fresh fish. The only problem was that, for Artie, handling the awkward Hawaiian sling spear gun underwater was difficult enough, on top of the fact that to get within range of the fish, it was necessary to hold your breath and swim down to at least 15 feet or deeper to reach the coral. Artie had little experience using the snorkeling gear, and even less free-diving to any depth. By the time he got close enough to start looking for potential prey, he invariably felt the need to return to the surface for air. When he did get a shot at a grouper, the stainless-steel spear missed by a wide margin and went into a patch of sand on the bottom, a good 25 feet deep. He tried twice to reach it, each time having to abandon the attempt and lunge for the surface for another breath before he could reach the bottom. Finally, Scully came to his rescue and got the spear. By this time, Scully already had more than a half-dozen fish on the decks of the *Casey Nicole*, and when Artie saw a 10-foot shark swimming around just on the edge of his visibility limit, he made for the boarding ladder as fast as he could.

"Sorry, little brother, but I guess we would starve to death if we were dependent upon my abilities as a hunter."

"That's all right, Doc. It takes practice. You'll get your chance again."

Artie marveled at the array of fish Scully had lain out on the teak slats of the forward deck. When he finally came aboard and took off his gear, he had one last prize—a huge spiny lobster, which he held up for Larry with a grin.

"You're the man, Scully!" Larry was ecstatic about the lobster. "Scully won't eat lobster," he explained to Artie. "But he got one for us, since I couldn't do it myself."

"Dat's not I-tal, mon," he said when Artie asked if he did not like lobster. "A Rasta don't to eat dem lobstah, crab and animal like dat—only fish. But if I an' I got not'ing to eat, not to worry 'bout dat, gonna eat dem too."

"Well, too bad for you, Scully, but the Doc and I are going to have lobster tail for breakfast, so we need to get going." He said to Artie, "I told you this place would be worth a short stop, didn't I?"

An hour and a half later, with drying fillets of fish spread out on the decks, they were underway again on a broad reach, sailing over the smooth waters of the banks just inside the reefs that break up the swell from the open ocean. This was some of the best sailing of the whole trip, the wide, stable form of the catamaran gliding over a transparent sheet of smooth crystalline water that stretched as far as they could see over the shallow, sandy bottom of Cay Sal Bank.

They were approaching the Damas Cays, the next islets north of the Anguillas on the rim of the atoll, when Scully spotted a sail out on the banks to the southwest. Closer inspection through Larry's binoculars, which they all passed around for a better look, revealed that it was not just a single sail, but rather a two-masted schooner. It didn't take long to ascertain that the distant vessel was coming their way, and Larry said it appeared to have adjusted course to intercept them if they continued on their present heading.

"Who do you think they could be?" Artie asked.

"It's still too far away to tell, but it doesn't look like your typical cruising yacht to me," Larry said. "I'd say it's over 60 feet, and probably built somewhere in the islands."

"Could be dem Cuban, mon."

"You're right, Scully. Or Haitian. Or from the west, maybe Honduras or Belize. It's been long enough now since the pulse that people who are able are probably starting to get on the move. There's just no telling, but I don't like the looks of this. Let's bear off and get all the speed we can out of these sails while I look at the charts. There are some dangerous shoals just to the south of those cays ahead."

Scully eased the genoa sheet and adjusted the mainsheet traveler to leeward. They were on a broad reach, which was generally a faster point of sail on a catamaran than a dead downwind run. The morning breeze had been light while they were anchored over the reef, but now, as it was getting toward noon, the trade winds had freshened to 15 knots again. Artie glanced at the distant schooner and then at the wake behind their twin sterns. At its fastest speeds, the Tiki 36 created quite a bit of turbulence astern, and Larry estimated they were hitting 16 or 17 knots. The schooner wouldn't be able catch them in an even race, no matter how much sail they piled on, but it had an angle advantage on them in relation to the wind, and it appeared it would intersect their course if they continued to the northwest inside the reefs of the bank. Artie could tell that Larry and Scully were both getting nervous about the situation, and he felt knots in his stomach thinking about the attack at Isleta Palominito.

"I don't like this," Larry said, as he stared at the schooner through his binoculars. "They've adjusted their course again to account for our increased speed, and it looks like they're trying to cut us off before we can reach the north end of the bank."

"What can we do?" Artie asked.

"First of all, you can get my shotgun and bring it up on deck. There's a couple of extra boxes of buckshot and slugs in the locker under the chart table."

This was the last thing Artie wanted to hear. The thought of having to use the gun again twisted the knots in his stomach even tighter. "How do we know what their intentions are?"

Larry handed him the binoculars. "Take a look. It's definitely not a family cruiser or vacation charter boat."

The schooner was now within a mile of the *Casey Nicole*, and with the binoculars, Artie could see that it was anything but a modern yacht. It looked as if it had been built back in the days when all ships harnessed the wind, and its peeling paint and stained and patched sails proved it was an island fisherman or cargo vessel, probably from Cuba. Despite its condition, it had obviously been built from plans that came from the drawing board of a skilled naval architect, evidenced by its graceful lines, raked masts, and purposeful bowsprit. It was clearly well sailed by its unknown crew, and Artie could see that if they didn't do something different, they would be cut off soon. He handed the binoculars back to Larry and went below to get the gun as his brother had asked. When he came back on deck with it, Larry was grinning as he studied the chart while Scully steered. His new excitement had nothing to do with the gun being on deck.

"You look too happy for a captain about to be run down by pirates, little brother."

"I've got a plan now, Doc. I'm about to show you why catamarans rule. Then you'll know why I spent so much time building one."

"Aren't we already going about as fast as she will go?"

"I've got more tricks than speed up my sleeve," Larry said. "Hang on. Just another quarter of a mile and we'll be home free."

"Dat boat full of Cuban, mon." Scully had the binoculars now while Artie took the helm and kept them on course. "Must be ten, maybe twelve on de rail. Probably got dem AK too. I hope you got a good plan, Copt'n."

"Just pray to Jah the wind holds, Scully. We're almost there."

Artie couldn't see what "there" was. There was nothing ahead but more of the same pale green water and white sandy bottom clearly visible beneath it, while to their starboard side there were occasional rocks and crashing breakers where the open Atlantic was separated from the bank by reefs. He looked at the schooner again and was shocked to see how close it appeared. Just as it seemed hopeless to try and outrun it, he found out what Larry had in mind as his brother took the helm with his one good hand.

"Okay, Scully, get ready. Just past those two rocks ahead I'm going to put her hard over to starboard. We'll jibe and run off to the northeast straight outside. Artie! I need you on the forward deck. Help me look for coral heads. The chart shows an area with about two feet of water over the reef at low tide, but that's still six hours away. We should be able to slide over as long as we don't hit something sticking up where it's not supposed to be."

Artie scrambled forward and crouched low on the deck as Larry brought the stern through the wind and Scully sheeted the genoa on the other tack. For a moment, the boat slowed dramatically, and seemed to be coming to a stop, but as soon as the wind filled the sails from the other side, it surged forward as only a light multihull could, and was quickly up to at least 10 knots again. Artie stood and hung onto the forestay where he could look around the luff of the sail and study the waters ahead. There were breaking waves outside the reef and dark patches of brown under the clear water all around them. He held his breath as they passed over rocks that looked like they would tear the bottoms out of the hulls, but depth was deceptive in the clear water and they never touched bottom, despite the appearance that it was only inches below the surface.

He heard a series of loud cracks that had to be rifle shots from the schooner, but didn't dare take his eyes off the course ahead to look back. Pointing with his free hand, he motioned for Larry to adjust course to dodge a rock just close enough to the surface to hit, and when they skimmed past it, he saw that he had been right to do so. It was a near miss, but now the water color had changed to sapphire blue and the reefs were astern. The bows pitched as they sliced into a four-foot swell, and Artie hung on to the forestay with both hands to keep his balance. At this point, he could relax and look back.

The schooner was dead astern and coming right at them, having altered course to follow the catamaran off the banks. Artie wondered if such a big vessel could possibly clear the reefs over the route they took, then he began to understand why his brother had been grinning. If the crew of the schooner were not familiar with the area and did not have proper charts on board, they might have assumed that if their prey was able to sail off the banks at that point, they could too. He rushed back to the cockpit where Scully and

Larry were also watching to see what would happen next. Someone on board was still shooting in their direction, but Larry said the range was still too great for ordinary rifles.

"Come on, baby!" Larry said as they sailed east. "That's right, just keep on coming and try to catch us!"

"Dat copt'n is a fool!" Scully said. "Got no chart and no common sense too!"

"He's still coming," Artie said. "How much does a boat like that draw? It's got to be more than Pete and Mary-anne's *Celebration* that we were on."

"Actually, no. These fishing schooners were designed to work the banks and are considered shallow-draft vessels at four feet. That's a lot more than us, though, and they're about to get a surprise!" And soon after he said it, when the *Casey Nicole* was nearly a half mile east of the reef, the big schooner came to a sudden stop with a sound of splintering and breaking wood. With the bow plowed up on the reef, the stern swung around until the hull was nearly at right angles to the direction it had been sailing, then heeled over until the masts were leaning at a 30-degree angle to the horizon.

"Yes!" Larry shouted, shaking his fist in the direction of the wreck. "Serves you right, you stupid son of a bitch!"

"Damn! They hit the rocks at full speed."

"Dat boat is finished, mon. Nevah gonna get dat hull off de reef again!"

"I love it, Doc! See what I told you about Wharram cata-marans? Fast under sail, seaworthy, and shallow draft too! What's not to like?"

"That was scary, though. They almost got within rifle range before we crossed that reef."

"Almost, but almost doesn't count, does it, Doc? We're home free, for now at least. Let's point this vessel to Florida and get out of here."

"Sounds good to me. I never wanted to stop, anyway, but I guess it was worth it to get all this fish."

Larry gave Artie the course to steer while Scully moved the drying fish from the forward decks to the netting stretched between the sterns behind the cockpit. There it would be safe from getting washed overboard by the occasional large wave and be out of the spray from the bows. To avoid the reefs and the possibility of running into other aggressors on the banks, Larry wanted to head nearly due north for another 20 miles before setting a northwest course directly for Marathon, in the middle of the chain of islands making up the Florida Keys.

"It's nearly noon now. That's good and bad at the same time," Larry said. "It's nearly 90 miles to Sombrero Key light, which is where I want to make landfall. The good news is that we'll get there after dark. The bad news is also that we'll get there after dark."

"I don't understand, the logic, but go ahead."

"Well, we need to cut through the Keys just west of Marathon to get to the Gulf for two reasons: one, it's a more direct route than sailing all the way around Key West, which is another 70 miles west, and two, we have to cross the Gulf Stream between here and the Keys, and its current will be setting us to the east of our rhumb line. Trying to sail directly to Key West or points west of there would be even more difficult. Anyway, going through the Keys at night might be a good thing because we won't likely be noticed and it will give us a look at how things are in U.S. waters, and whether everything is totally blacked out or not."

"And the bad?"

"It's a treacherous area to be sailing through at night—especially with no working channel markers or other aids to navigation, and no GPS. I wouldn't even attempt it in any kind of deeper-draft sailboat. And I also wouldn't attempt it if I weren't intimately familiar with that area. There are reefs, rocks, wrecks, derelict boats, and no telling what else on the Atlantic side of the chain, and about a million crab traps with their floating buoys scattered all over the Gulf side for miles and miles. But the good thing is, I've been in and out of Boot Key Harbor in Marathon in more conditions than I can count: day, night, squalls, approaching hurricanes, you name it. So considering all the pros and cons, I'm willing to risk it, especially since we'll have nearly a full moon tonight."

By mid-afternoon, Cay Sal Bank was far astern and they were once again sailing off-soundings through an inky-blue sea with empty horizons for a full 360 degrees. Larry had plotted a course that would compensate for the lateral drift they would experience crossing the Gulf Stream, and he calculated they would reach the outlying reefs of the Florida Keys by 1800 hours, considering they were still averaging 10 knots throughout the afternoon. By the time the sun was approaching the horizon to one side of their course, the almost-round moon, just two days from full, rose from the sea on the other, and with only a few scattered cumulus clouds in the sky, promised to light their way through the night.

All three of them were still wound up from the encounter with the schooner, and with another landfall approaching fast, no one wanted to leave the deck to take a turn off watch. Sleep could come later, once they were clear of the Keys in the wide-open waters of the Gulf of Mexico. As the last hint of twilight disappeared, the moon lit a silvery path across the waves and a pod of dolphins joined them, leaping and broaching ahead on both sides of the boat and between the bows, seemingly delighted to lead them home to U.S. waters. As the distance to land had to be closing, according to Larry's dead reckoning, he constantly scanned the horizon ahead and through 180 degrees to port and starboard with his binoculars.

"There it is!" he said at last. "Another half mile to the west and we'd have run right into it!" He handed the binoculars to Artie. It was incredible how much light these high-quality German-made navigation binoculars gathered even on nights lit only with starlight. Under the moon they had tonight, looking through them was almost like viewing in daylight. He saw what Larry was pointing at: it was a steel tower rising out of the sea, the 142-foot Sombrero Lighthouse. Larry said it was the tallest light in the Keys. While the flashing white light that would have enabled them to see it from much farther out had been extinguished, the tower itself was an adequate landmark on an otherwise empty sea to mark their position. More significantly to Artie, it was a major milestone in their voyage. It meant they were back in mainland U.S. waters and that he was that much closer to Casey.

"I don't know how you do it, little brother," he said, as he handed the binoculars back to Larry. "That was an incredible feat of navigation with nothing but a compass."

"Nah, no big deal. I just followed the dolphins," Larry said, but as he looked around, he saw that they had disappeared. "The good news is we made it to the U.S. It looks like the bad news is that the lights are out here too. From here you would normally be able to see a whole string of towns lit up along the Overseas Highway, dead ahead. You'd also see the glow of Key West off to port and the glow of Miami way up there to the northeast. But I don't see anything. This is truly bizarre."

"I guess every place we come to that has no lights just proves how incredibly widespread this event was, whatever it actually was. I don't guess there's any reason to hope it's not the same in New Orleans."

"Nope, I wouldn't think so. We all need to keep a sharp lookout now. There aren't any reefs to worry about if we hold this course, but there could be other obstructions. We should be able to see the Seven Mile Bridge soon. It will be to the left of the closest key we'll pass on this route, where Marathon and Boot Key Harbor are located. We want to aim for the high-rise span in the bridge that's about three miles from the eastern end. The vertical clearance there is 65 feet, so we don't have anything to worry about there."

Though they had no working depth sounder, it was obvious from the change in the wave patterns when they crossed into the shallower waters of Hawk Channel as they passed the Sombrero Key light tower. From the edge of this area of somewhat protected waters inside the scattered reefs that paralleled the Keys, it was less than five miles to the Overseas Highway, a road that consisted of numerous bridges stringing the island chain together from Key Largo to Key West.

"There's only a few places in this part of the Keys where a boat with a tall mast can get under the bridges," Larry said, "and this is one of the highest spans."

Artie could see the bridge looming ahead out of the darkness as they closed the gap. Scully eased the sheets to spill some wind and reduce speed as they approached the channel under the elevated section of the span. It was a surreal scene after being so long at sea and among less-developed islands. Here was a modern concrete and steel highway bridge that was totally silent in the absence of traffic and totally dark without the lights on its lampposts lit or the headlights of cars shining. As they drew nearer, they could see parked vehicles spread out at intervals on the roadway overhead.

"They've been there since they stalled out, I suppose," Artie said.

"Yeah, I'm sure. All the traffic to and from Key West has to come this way. It wouldn't be the best place to be right now, unless you had a boat."

"My God, can you imagine how many cars must be stuck on the Causeway? It's much longer than this. I hate to think of what it must be like for anyone to get stuck in the middle of a bridge like that and have to walk to the shore."

"It would be a nightmare for sure," Larry said. "But you don't have to worry about Casey being in a mess like that, at least. From what she and Jessica told me during their vacation last summer, most of their life in the city revolves right around the campus and the immediate area nearby."

"Yeah, unless she tried to leave. After this many days without electricity and phones, I don't know if she and Jessica could sit still that long."

"Just try not to worry; we'll be there in just a few more days now. Soon as we pass under that bridge, we're in the Gulf!"

Artie was elated to be back in U.S. waters, two-thirds of their voyage behind them. But he still couldn't help but worry about Casey, especially now as he saw the reality that even a country as modern as the United States was shut down and blacked out. Looking up at the rail just before they sailed under the bridge, he was startled to see movement. There were two people leaning over to look at them.

"Hey! Stop that boat and give us a ride!" one yelled. The other one threw something at them that they could not see, but a couple of seconds later there was a huge splash in their wake as something heavy hit the water.

"Rock! Watch your heads!" Larry said.

"Fockin' kids, mon." Scully said as he looked up.

Just then they moved out of danger as the boat slid under the overpass and was hidden from the view of anyone above. Scully hardened the sheets as soon as they were between the pilings, and the *Casey Nicole* accelerated out from under the other side, but whoever had thrown the rock didn't follow up and in a few minutes the bridge was receding astern.

Larry said there were still several scattered keys and shoal areas to the north of the bridge that they would have to be careful to avoid as they made their way to the open Gulf, but he knew the waters, and the moon was now high enough to provide good visibility, especially in the absence of lights ashore. The crab traps he had mentioned before were evident everywhere on this side of the island chain, marked by floating white buoys that were so numerous Scully had to constantly steer around them. With no inboard engine and consequently no prop in the water to hang up on the buoy lines, the markers were really no threat to the *Casey Nicole*, but since they showed up clearly in the moonlight, Scully avoided them anyway out of long habit on other boats. By midnight, they were back north off the extensive shallows and shoals on the Gulf side of the Keys and in the open sea once again. Larry went back below to retire to his bunk now that they were beyond the navigation hazards of the Keys, and Artie and Scully took turns keeping watch. Artie stayed on deck to rest even when he was off duty, the night being so nice with the light of the moon and the barely perceptible swell of the Gulf as the boat moved north at eight knots in a light breeze. He was elated that no other major obstacles stood between him and New Orleans. If all went as planned, they would be sailing into the waters of Lake Pontchartrain in four days or less.

EIGHT

"WHAT IF WHAT THEY SAID is true?" Jessica asked as the three of them pedaled north out of the town of Franklinton in the drizzling rain. "Where will we go if we can't get to the cabin?"

"I don't see any reason why policemen here would have made it up," Casey said. "They probably don't want us hanging around here either, and wouldn't do anything to encourage us to stay. But still, it's unbelievable that they would close a whole *state* to non-residents. Can they do that?"

"I don't know," Grant said. "I guess all bets are off as to what people may do and what may happen in a situation like this, mainly because it's never happened before." Grant was reeling with the impact of what the police officers had told them. If it were really true, he had made a terrible mistake to bring his two trusting companions all this way for nothing. If they couldn't reach that cabin, he had no idea where they would go or what they would do. They were already low on food and he had no alternate plan for obtaining more. Turning back to New Orleans certainly wasn't an option. Riding out of Franklinton in the continuing rain didn't do anything to improve his optimism, but until they received this news, the cabin had seemed so close it had felt as if they were already there, and he could put up with any amount of discomfort knowing they would not have to spend another night out on the road. Now, everything had changed. They had come all this way only to learn they might not even be allowed to ride the rest of the way to their safe haven.

For now, it seemed as if the only logical choice was to continue on to the state line to see for themselves whether or not they would really be turned back. Maybe they could somehow convince the officers at the roadblock to let them in. It certainly didn't seem fair that only those with Mississippi driver's licenses could enter the state. His parents were landowners there, and the land and cabin were his to use any way he wanted while they were out of the country. But he also was painfully aware he didn't have any way to prove the place even existed, other than by a verbal description and the address, which was on a remote rural lane in the middle of nowhere that few would likely be familiar with. It had never occurred to him that he would need to carry such proof. And of course, as his actual place of residence was the apartment in New Orleans, his driver's license was issued in Louisiana, just like Casey's, so neither license would do them any more good than the California license Jessica carried, if what they'd just learned was true.

At least they wouldn't have far to go to find out. He couldn't remember exactly how far it was to the state line, but a quick check of the map showed it was less than 12 miles. They could stop under a bridge or somewhere out of the rain and eat lunch, and still be there in two hours.

As they pedaled he began to ponder a new idea. There was no way he was going to give up on reaching the cabin just because of some stupid roadblock that was probably illegal and unconstitutional, despite the circumstances. Grant figured they were blocking Highway 25 at the state line because it was a logical route from most of the populated areas to the south. Although there were some alternate smaller roads that also crossed the state line in the vicinity, he knew they would likely be watching those too, as there weren't many of them and it would be easy enough to set up checkpoints at all of them if they were serious about keeping non-residents out. But what they likely would not be watching, he reasoned, was the river.

Like most rivers in the region, the Bogue Chitto flows mostly unseen through deep forests, swampy bottomlands, and other areas accessible by only a few roads. Although the river was popular with weekend canoeists and fishermen, few people in the area would think of using it as a travel route. And since recreational paddlers seldom bother trying to fight its sometimes swift current to travel upstream, the authorities would hardly suspect anyone would try slipping into the state by that route. Grant knew they could get away with it, and besides, the cabin they were trying to reach was right on the banks of the Bogue Chitto. There was a bridge crossing the river just a short distance south of the state line, and from that point he knew it was less than 10 miles upstream to the cabin. It would take a lot longer to paddle that distance than it would to ride the bikes to the cabin on the road, but it would be a sure way to get there undetected. The only problem was that they would need a canoe and paddles. He had one at the cabin, of course, as floating the stretch of river down to the next bridge was one of his favorite pastimes when he spent time there. That one wouldn't do them any good, now, but an alternative might be found, if he remembered correctly. It still wasn't his first choice by a long shot, but thinking about it gave him something to do while he pedaled.

Five miles north of Franklinton, they met a refugee family that had indeed been turned back at the state line. Seeing them riding their bikes in the rain, heading north, the driver of a southbound antique Ford pickup pulled over and rolled down the window to wave them over.

"I hope y'all ain't tryin' to go to Mississippi," the man said.

Grant brought his bike to a stop and Jessica and Casey did the same. The truck was in great condition for its age, and had probably been kept in a garage and only driven occasionally or displayed in car shows prior to the family's current need for it. The driver looked to be perhaps in his late thirties or early forties, his face weathered and tanned like that of a man who earned his living working outside every day. On the bench seat beside him was a boy of about six, and on the other side sat the boy's mother, an overweight but pretty brunette who looked quite a bit younger than her husband. The back of the truck was covered with a blue tarp secured by an assortment of old ropes and bungee cords.

"We are," Grant said. "My parents own a cabin not far across the state line. Is it true they are turning people back?"

"Yep. I got a brother lives out from Columbia, about an hour from here. Got a big place in the country and raises about everything he needs. I was taking the family up there to get away from that mess in Baton Rouge. I was raised up there myself but moved down here years ago for the work. I'm a roofer by trade. Now I wish I had never seen that place. A big city like that ain't no place to be with the lights out an' all. I never would have thought they'd turn us back at the state line though. I lived in Mississippi more than 20 years until I moved down here. Now I can't even get in. I don't know what we're going to do now. We ain't really got no place to go and no way to get anything we need. I sure don't want to take my family back around all them people. Heck, I don't even have any way to protect 'em anymore since they took all my guns away."

"Took your guns? Who took your guns?"

"Them sheriff's deputies up there at the roadblock. Said I broke the law trying to bring weapons into the state, and they didn't even let us in to begin with. Heck, all I had was an old 12-gauge pump I figured would come in handy for huntin', with all the grocery stores cleaned out, and my Smith .357 revolver that had belonged to my daddy."

"How could they just take them? Doesn't just about everybody around here in Louisiana and Mississippi have a gun in their vehicle? It's not illegal to own one or transport it."

"Naw, but everything's changed now. Some of these gung-ho law enforcement officers act like they're in a war zone or something. Do whatever they feel like doing, and there ain't nothing you can do about it. Heck, they even *look* like soldiers, standing around out there with their BDUs on and carrying those M-4s. I tell you, there ain't no arguing with 'em, and it's only gonna get worse. If I was you, I wouldn't be ridin' up there on no bicycles trying to get across that line with them two pretty girls you got with you. I'd be gettin' off the road too, unless you're packing yourself."

"I *am* armed, and I intend to stay that way," Grant said. "I'm really grateful you told me they were confiscating weapons at the roadblock, though. We won't attempt it now."

"Well, I hope y'all have good luck trying to find some place to go. I'd give you a ride somewhere, but as you can see, we're loaded down. Don't know really what we'll do, but my wife's got some friends that's got a place out in the country a bit north of Hammond. I reckon we'll go there and see if they'll let us camp out on their property. I've just barely got enough gas left to get there."

"Good luck to you too. I hope it works out that you can stay there. I've got a couple of alternate ideas, and the info you gave me helps a lot."

The man put the pickup back in gear and drove off. Grant turned to Casey and Jessica, who were expectantly looking at him, waiting to see what he had to say about all this.

"Can you believe that? Confiscating guns, closing a state line to non-residents…this is crazy. It's like I told you before about New Orleans after Katrina. The cops there were going around collecting weapons, even from innocent citizens who only had them in their homes for self-protection."

"So now we can't even try to cross the state line," Casey said.

"Why not?" Jessica asked. "We won't need a gun when we get to the cabin, will we? I mean, I know it's your dad's gun and all, but we could just buy him a new one later, after all this is over, couldn't we?"

"That's not the issue," Grant said. "Right now, in this situation, any gun is priceless and cannot be replaced for any amount of money. We can't risk losing it. And yes, we may well need it for self-defense, even at the cabin, and if not for that, then certainly for small game hunting."

Jessica was exasperated. "So a gun is the reason we can't try to cross the border. What are we going to do, then?"

"It's not just about the gun, Jessica. It's clear that they wouldn't let us in anyway. They turned that guy down and he has a wife and small boy with him, not to mention that he's *from* Mississippi, even if he doesn't live there now. Besides that, there's no telling what those lawmen will decide to do next. They're obviously on a power trip and are making up new rules on their own. Like the man said, you two attract a lot of attention, even if you do look like a couple of soaking wet rag dolls right about now."

Casey smiled. The rain was letting up so there was hope they wouldn't have to stay soaking wet much longer. "So what is the alternative, if we can't even *attempt* to cross the state line?" she asked.

"I didn't say we couldn't attempt to cross it. I just said we can't risk trying that roadblock, or any other roadblock for that matter. That means we won't be crossing into Mississippi by road."

"So how are we supposed to get there, then?" Jessica asked.

"The river. I've been thinking about it since we left Franklinton. The river goes right to the cabin, and nobody will be watching it because there's nothing but woods where it crosses the state line. In fact, it's so remote between bridges you really don't have any way of knowing that you've crossed from one state to another."

"What do we do, walk along the banks pushing the bikes or something?" Casey asked.

"No, that would be impossible. You couldn't walk the banks at all, much less with a bicycle. It's too swampy and the undergrowth is far too dense. It's almost like a jungle, in fact, and you'd need a machete to go a hundred yards. It would take days to walk it and in places you'd have to wade or swim across sloughs and side creeks. Nope, we can't walk it, we've got to go by canoe, that's the only way."

"But where are we supposed to get a canoe?"

"I'm not a hundred percent certain, but I think I have a pretty good idea. But first we have to keep going north just a few more miles. Then we'll turn back west on the last road that crosses the river on the Louisiana side of the state line."

They continued riding on Highway 25 into an increasingly rural setting, where large pine plantations and other wooded areas outnumbered pastures and clearings. The turn-off to the west that Grant wanted to take was less than a mile south of where 25 crossed the state line and became Mississippi State Highway 27. In the flat, wooded terrain, though, it was impossible to see that far, so despite their curiosity about the roadblock, Grant led them west onto Highway 438, the northernmost east-west road in Louisiana to bridge the Bogue Chitto, and the closest river access to the cabin on this side of the state line.

It was only a short ride on 438 to the river from the turnoff, and when they reached the east end of the bridge, Grant pulled over on the wide gravel shoulder and dismounted. There was a deeply rutted dirt and gravel access lane leading down the steep bank and curving out of sight under the bridge. The river was wide here, flanked by heavy woods on either side, and swollen above normal levels by the rain of the past two days, its current running strong, especially in midstream.

"Let's push our bikes down the bank and get them out of sight of the road, in case someone comes along."

"Wow, this river is bigger than I thought," Casey said. "From the way you described it, I thought it was more of a creek."

"It is, normally. The rain's got it up. It rises fast in rains like this, but goes down fast too. It looks like the rain is about over now, and if it is, the river will be back to normal in a couple of days or so. It's a lot nicer when it's lower. The sandbars in this stretch are normally a lot wider, but you can't see all of them because they are partially underwater right now."

"How could anybody paddle a canoe upstream against that?" Jessica asked. She had never been canoeing, but remembered how hard it was to paddle against the wind when she and Casey were out playing on Larry's kayak during their island vacation the summer before.

"You can't go against the main current," Grant said. "But you can play the eddies close to the bank, get out and pull it in some shallow places, and use a pole to push off the bottom in others. It's doable, you'll see."

"But I still don't see any canoes, Grant," Casey said. "Where do you plan to get one?"

"Downstream. There's a camp not too far up below the bridge on this side of the river. I remember seeing it last time I paddled this stretch from our cabin and we took out down in Franklinton. There must be a private road leading to it from somewhere off of Highway 25, I'm not sure, but it's one of those really nice weekend getaway camps, not a full-time residence. Probably owned by someone in New Orleans or Baton Rouge. I remember seeing a separate boathouse up on the high bank next to it, with a whole rack of canoes in it. I seriously doubt whoever owns that camp was able to get here after the lights went out. It's probably vacant unless someone local is using it."

"You're not thinking of stealing a canoe, are you?"

"Not stealing—buying. I wouldn't do it if they just had one, but there must have been at least six in that boathouse. I figure our three bikes are worth a lot more than one canoe, and besides, after all this is over we can bring it back and maybe even get our bikes back. But we sure don't need them as bad as we need a canoe right now."

"How will you ask them to trade if no one's home?" Jessica asked.

"I don't plan to ask, and I'm counting on the odds that no one will be home. We can't get these bikes through all the undergrowth downstream to the camp anyway. I figure we can hide them somewhere partway up there and leave a note for the owners of the canoe, telling them where to find them, and explaining what we did."

"Isn't that still stealing, in a way?" Casey asked.

"It's survival, Casey. If we don't find a way to get to my cabin soon, we're going to be out of food and in real trouble. Do you have a better idea?"

"No, I guess not. I just don't want to get in trouble, and I don't want to get shot by somebody for trespassing and stealing from them."

"We'll be extremely careful. Here's what I had in mind. I'll need one of you to go with me to help me carry the canoe down the bank and paddle it back up to here. Someone needs to stay behind with the bikes and our gear just in case we can't get a canoe and still need them. Casey, I think that should be you, since you know how to use your dad's pistol. I'll leave it with you and take Jessica with me to get the canoe."

"Shouldn't we all just go look for it?" Jessica asked. "Can't we just hide the bikes and our other stuff?"

"We'll hide everything, but I'll still feel better if one of us is with it. It shouldn't take more than an hour to get there and get back with the canoe, assuming we can find paddles, which should be stored in the boathouse too. We've got to be quiet. If we all go, it will be harder to sneak up to the cabin, just on the off chance someone *is* home."

"I'll stay," Casey said, "but in case someone is there, don't you need to take the gun with you?"

"No, I hardly want to get into a gunfight with the owner. If anyone's around, we'll forget the whole thing. But I don't want you staying here alone near the bridge unarmed. Someone could come down to the river at any time. Let's get the bikes out of sight, and all you have to do is sit tight and wait. We'll be as quick as possible."

When they had rolled the bikes into a patch of tall river cane where they could not be seen from the bridge or the dirt lane leading under it, Grant set out, picking his way through the woods downstream, with Jessica following him. He carried his machete, but didn't want to make noise by cutting vines and brush out of their path, so they had to weave their way through the worst of the undergrowth. The rain had turned all areas of the bank that were not sand into mud, making the walking difficult, but because everything was so wet, they were able to move quietly without the worry of crackling leaves or snapping twigs.

Grant was beginning to wonder if his memory was playing tricks on them by the time they had worked their way maybe a half mile down the river. Then they came to a clearing in the riverside forest, and carefully approaching the edge while staying in the cover of the trees, he saw that it was the camp he remembered. The cabin, which was as big as many regular houses, was situated on a clay bluff that overlooked the river from maybe 20 feet up. He could see the boathouse on the other side of it. It would be too risky to simply walk out across the open yard to it, as they would have to walk right past the front of the house to reach the canoes and it was impossible to tell if anyone was home or not. He whispered to Jessica and she followed him as he began to circle the property, staying out of sight within the edge of the woods as they worked their way all the way around to the other side to the boathouse.

When they crossed the gravel driveway leading into the house from the east, Grant could see no sign that anyone was there. They waited and watched for a few minutes, and when he was completely satisfied that they were alone, they walked to the boathouse and, much to his delight, found the canoes on the racks he'd remembered, overlooking the river from the bank where he'd seen them as he'd floated past over a year ago. Four of them were well-used Grumman 17-foot aluminum canoes, the kind that was popular with canoe rental outfitters for their durability and low maintenance. One was a short solo canoe made by Mad River, and the other was a 16-foot Kevlar-hulled Mohawk. The Mohawk was the best of the lot, but a little small for three adults. All of the canoes were locked to the wooden racks with light chains and padlocks. Grant selected one of the Grummans that looked to be in the best shape, and, with his machete, easily liberated it from the chains by simply hacking through the two-by-fours they were passed around. Jessica helped him set it outside, then he picked out three decent wooden paddles and a spare, as well as three life jackets, and put all these in the canoe. This done, he hastily scribbled out a note explaining his actions and describing the location of the bicycles. He didn't mention their destination in the canoe, of course, and figured anyone would assume it was downstream somewhere anyway, as no one in these parts ever paddled upstream. He wedged the note into a gash he cut in the canoe rack and looked around the shed one more time. One item that looked too tempting to pass up was one of a dozen fishing rods and reels hanging on one wall. He grabbed one and also found a small tackle box with a few artificial lures and hooks in it.

"You don't eat fish, either, do you, Jessica?"

"No. I used to, when I was growing up, but not since I became a vegetarian."

"We're getting pretty low on supplies, and I don't know how long it's going to take to buck that current up to the cabin. We may be reduced to what we can catch before long. I hope you don't get hungry."

"I'll be all right," Jessica said. "I don't eat much anyway."

Grant dropped the topic. He felt certain Jessica would be changing her diet sooner than she thought, but there was no point in pressing it now. Satisfied that he had what they needed for the trip, he was ready to get the canoe to the river and get going. There was a path winding down from the boathouse to a small deck built at the water's edge; it had turned to slippery mud after two days of rain. By the time they got the canoe to the bottom of the high bank, both of them had slipped and fallen and had gotten mud smeared all over the knees and seats of their pants. Grant pushed the bow of the canoe into the river pointing upstream, and held it steady so Jessica could step in.

"Shouldn't I be in the back, since I don't know what I'm doing?" she asked.

"No, that's exactly why you need to sit up front. The stern paddler is the one who does all the steering and keeps the boat going straight. All you have to do from the front is paddle to provide extra power. It'll take both of us to paddle against the current."

When Jessica was situated, Grant grabbed the gunwales with both hands and put one foot in the boat while he shoved them off with the other. The canoe immediately started drifting backwards until he dug in with his paddle and began stroking hard to gain momentum against the river. Jessica splashed her paddle awkwardly until Grant told her how to properly hold it and how deep to dip it on each stroke. They made progress at a crawling pace at first, slowly leaving the cabin behind them as they paddled past the woods they'd crept through on foot to get there. The river made a gradual bend to the right and it was not until they had followed that curve around to the end that they could get a glimpse of the distant bridge where Casey would be waiting with the bikes.

"There it is!" Jessica said. "We made it, but this is a lot harder than riding the bikes, even uphill. How far did we paddle, a mile?"

"Not hardly," Grant said. "More like a little over a quarter of a mile. It'll be a half by the time we get to the bridge."

"Oh wow. We'll *never* get to the cabin at this rate then. Didn't you say it was like 10 miles?"

"It is, but it's still just like riding the bikes. Remember when we left New Orleans? I said don't think about the whole distance. Just focus on riding and the miles will slip by. It's the same with paddling, it's just a lot slower—but we don't have nearly as far to travel by canoe as we did by bike. We'll get there, probably by tomorrow night, in spite of the current."

As he spoke these words of encouragement to Jessica, he knew it was going to be a hard slog upstream, but had no doubt they would make it. By the time they got to the cabin, Jessica and Casey would know how to paddle a canoe, he figured. Now that they had a canoe, he felt a whole lot better about their overall situation than he had earlier that day when faced with the prospect of being turned back at the roadblock. It had always amazed him how practically no one in this country utilized the rivers any more for anything other than occasional recreation. In Guyana, the rivers were the highways of the jungle. One seldom traveled far without passing local dugouts, going both upstream and down. He was just wondering if anyone else would be using the Bogue Chitto as a travel route when he saw the flash of a reflection off a wet paddle under the bridge ahead. Sure enough, it was a canoe coming downstream. Jessica saw it too as they continued to paddle, hugging the bank next to the woods to stay out of the strongest current. The downstream-bound canoe, however, was closer to the other side of the river, taking advantage of the main flow. As it came closer, they could see the hull was a dull aluminum color, identical to the one they were in. It was guided by a lone paddler with a mountain of gear in front of him, all of it covered by a camouflage tarp lashed over it. The other canoeist saw them too; there was no way to avoid it. Grant hoped he wasn't a local resident who knew the owners of the cabin they'd "borrowed" their boat from, but from the amount of stuff he had with him it seemed unlikely. This guy looked like he was planning to stay in the woods for a long time, and was just passing through here as quickly as possible.

The solitary paddler looked right at them as he went by going downstream, and Grant waved. The distance was a little too far for comfortable conversation, and Grant figured if he had wanted to talk, he would have steered his canoe closer to their side of the river when he first saw them. Instead, he waved back, watching them as he paddled by, but showing no intention of slowing down. Grant wondered if Casey had seen him go by or if the man had seen her when he paddled past the bridge.

"I wonder where he's going?" Jessica asked.

"I don't know, but it looks like he knows what he's doing. See how he's only paddling on one side of the canoe? He's using a guide stroke to keep it tracking straight, and he's right in the middle of the current for better speed. Not at all your typical weekend canoe renter like you usually see around here. He's probably traveling the river to avoid people, which is a smart idea. It looks like he's loaded to bug out to the woods for a long time too. He may be headed for the big swamps downstream, where the Bogue Chitto runs into the Pearl River."

★ ★ ★

When Grant and Jessica were out of sight, Casey began thinking about how nice it would be to clean up a bit while she had the privacy. The rain had stopped and the afternoon sky was starting to brighten a bit in the west, giving her hope that the cloudy overcast would soon give way to sunshine again. She felt awful after riding in the rain for two days, and knew a quick bath and changing back into dry clothes would do wonders for her attitude. The river did not look inviting at the edge of the canebrake where they had hidden the bicycles. The bank there was muddy and it looked like it dropped off into a deep hole with swirling currents where she could not see anything below the surface. But when they had pushed the bikes down the bank from the highway, she had noticed a large sandbar just upstream of the bridge. Part of it was probably visible from the roadway above, but it looked to her like it continued on, beyond where the river curved around out of sight to where it would be obscured by trees and secluded enough for a quick dip before Grant and Jessica returned. She knew Grant wouldn't want her to wander off and leave the bikes, but they had seen no one on the road in the vicinity of the bridge and she couldn't imagine anyone finding them before she got back.

Scott B. Williams

She sorted through her gear and made sure she had dry clothes and shampoo in her backpack, then she put her father's pistol in it as well and started up the bank, passing beneath the concrete pilings supporting the bridge. She had to push her way through more river cane on the other side of the bridge to reach the sandbar, but once she was there, she saw that it was ideal for her purpose. It did indeed stretch around the bend, its edge sloping off as a sandy beach into the river, where she could sit or crouch in two feet of amber-colored water that was translucent enough to allow her to see what was on the bottom.

She walked until she found a convenient log to put her backpack on to keep it out of the sand, then looked back to make sure she was completely out of sight of the bridge. She felt a little self-conscious taking her clothes off on the wide-open sandbar in broad daylight, but told herself that was silly as there was no one around and nothing in sight of the sandbar but the river itself and the surrounding dense woods. Besides, it felt great to peel off her soggy long-sleeve shirt and cargo pants, which she hung on a nearby branch. It was even better to remove her wet socks and feel the soft sand between her toes. She continued stripping down until she was completely naked, hanging her sports bra and panties next to the rest of her clothes and wading into the river with the bottle of shampoo. The water was colder than she expected, but she was determined to have a bath. She walked in until she was knee-deep and gradually eased herself down to a sitting position on the bottom. Once the water was up to her waist, it didn't feel quite as cold. She held the shampoo bottle between her knees and used her cupped hands to dip water over her head to wash her hair. Lathering up and washing away the greasy feeling and road grime of the last three days was wonderful. When she was done with her hair, she stood and used the shampoo to wash her entire body, then, after rinsing the shampoo by kneeling back in and splashing herself with her hands, she stepped back onto the sandbar to drip dry. She rinsed and squeezed out the bra and underwear and hung them back up on the branch. Even though she was sure she was alone, she still felt uncomfortable standing out in the open naked, and slipped on the sweatpants and last clean T-shirt from her backpack. Grant and Jessica would be jealous to learn she'd had a nice bath and changed into her last dry clothes. She was sure they would want to do the same when they came back, hopefully in the canoe that would take them to the cabin.

Thinking about the canoe, she looked out at the river and wondered how hard it was going to be to travel upstream against the current. Grant had said that it was less than 10 miles by river from this bridge to the cabin, but it sure looked to her like it wouldn't be easy to paddle that far going the wrong way. Grant had said the strongest current was usually in the middle and along the outside edge of bends, and that by sticking to the inside edges of the river's curves they could play the eddies and patches of slack water to make progress. Looking upriver along the sandbar on which she stood, it *did* appear that there was a reverse current flowing the other way near the bank. Curious, she left her backpack and drying clothes where they were and walked a bit further in that direction to get a closer look at the eddy and see how far it went. The river seemed to curve on around almost like a horseshoe bend, and she thought if she walked upriver another hundred feet or so she might see where it straightened out again. Then it would be time to head back to the bicycles and wait for Grant and Jessica.

The sandbar narrowed as she went upstream, and in places tall river birch and sycamore trees leaned out of the forested top bank and forced her to duck under to pass. She could see now why Grant had said they couldn't walk upstream following the river. The sandbars were not continuous, and in the places where there were none, this hardwood forest would be extremely difficult to travel through, as the understory beneath the trees was a choked tangle of vines and bushes forming a wall of greenery at the water's edge. She looked at the river as she walked, fascinated by the counter-current and marveling at how much Grant knew about rivers and so many other things relevant to their situation. It felt liberating to be walking barefoot in such a pristine place after bathing naked in the river, and she imagined that Grant would feel right at home doing exactly that. Then she thought about what it would be like if he were here now, just the two of them, without Jessica. It was a momentary pleasant daydream, but she was suddenly startled out of it when she ducked under another big tree and was stopped in her tracks by what she saw just a short distance upstream, at the upper limit of the sandbar. Pulled halfway up on the bank ahead of her was an old aluminum canoe that clearly had not just washed up there on its own. A paddle was leaning against it, and a green canvas backpack and two large duffel bags were lashed down to the thwarts inside it. Casey felt suddenly exposed and vulnerable, not believing someone could have been this close all this time without her knowing it, especially when she was bathing naked in the river just around the bend. She took a faltering step backward, suddenly wishing she had not left the backpack and the gun that was in it behind. As she did, she backed into something solid that had not been there before, and faster than she could react, she felt an impossibly strong arm encircle her waist and a steely hand close over her mouth to stifle the instinctive cry of alarm that would have come next.

Before she could even struggle, she felt herself pulled backward and off her feet by her unseen assailant. The next thing she knew she was on the ground and belly down in the sand, both arms pinned behind her by an immovable weight that she soon realized was her attacker's knee as he forced some kind of fabric in her mouth and used both hands to tie it tightly behind her head. She tried desperately to spit it out and scream, but it was no use. She couldn't even turn her head to see what he looked like before she felt yet another piece of cloth being wrapped and tied over her eyes and forehead. The weight shifted and she felt hands working at her wrists, tying something around them, securing them behind her back so that she was totally helpless, blindfolded and gagged. She tried to use her feet to flip herself over and kick at her attacker, but when he had finished securing her hands, she felt her ankles locked together in a vise-like grip and then the constricting force of something being wrapped and tied around them as well. The next thing she knew, she was lifted from the sand in strong arms, carried a short distance, and put down on the sand again. She heard movement that she realized was the sound of the canoe sliding in the water, and then felt herself lifted again. Twisting and squirming did nothing to prevent her from being picked up and set down again, this time on a hard surface, with softer objects under her feet and head. She heard a crackling sound as something was pulled over her, and then could feel it being tucked around her and pulled tight as the other objects in the canoe were shifted around and positioned so that her movements were even further restricted. She realized that she being covered by something, as it shut out what little light she had seen before through the blindfold. She felt the canoe slide some more until it was free of the bank, then she could feel it floating free and tipping sharply to one side as someone stepped into it and sat down. She heard a paddle dip into the water, then felt the canoe surge beneath her, then pick up speed to the sound of rhythmic stroking as it moved into the river current.

Casey was terrified. She could not believe how suddenly and completely she had been subdued and abducted and was now being taken away. She was alone with this wordless stranger who had her in his canoe and had her completely and totally at his mercy. Grant and Jessica would have no way of knowing what had happened or where she was. How could anyone find her? She knew a canoe was silent, and, traveling the river, it would leave no tracks or trace of its passing. She would have to somehow get out of this fix on her own, but there was absolutely nothing she could do right now. She realized that, bound and gagged as she was, there was no way she could swim if the canoe tipped over, so it was best not to struggle at this point, because the idea of drowning with her hands tied behind her back was no more appealing than the thought of what this man might do to her. All she could do was lie there and think about how unfair it was that something like this could happen now, after they'd already been through so much in just three days.

She knew Grant and Jessica wouldn't know what to do when they came back and she was gone. This would put them in more danger and keep them from getting to the cabin, because she was sure they would spend a lot of time looking for her around the bridge without success. She thought about her dad as well, knowing he must be terribly worried about her and would be going crazy by now, because he most likely would have no way to even get back to the United States mainland, much less New Orleans. But even if by some miracle he had made it there and found her note, and then set out for Grant's cabin to look for her based on the directions in the note, she would not be there. If that happened, he would be in constant danger traveling there to look for her in vain.

The thought sickened her with worry and regret. Maybe she'd done the wrong thing after all to leave New Orleans with Grant. Now she'd gotten her best friend, Jessica, out here in the middle of nowhere too. Something bad could just as easily happen to them and she would be partially to blame. These dark thoughts filled her mind as she lay helpless in the canoe, like just another piece of baggage piled in the bottom as cargo to be taken wherever the owner intended to go.

NINE

WHEN ARTIE WOKE AGAIN it was because of the heat
of the late-morning sun on his face. He had fallen asleep on
one of the cockpit seats sometime before dawn while Scully
was on watch. Sitting up, he saw that they were far out in
the Gulf, surrounded by empty horizons in all directions.
Scully was slumped against the starboard cabin side, doz-
ing off as well, while the wind vane kept the *Casey Nicole* on
course. Artie stood and looked around for any sign of ships
or other dangers, but there was nothing. He knew they had
a long way to go before they had to worry about hitting anything associated with land again, at least until they reached
the offshore oil platforms of the northern Gulf. This would
be his longest crossing yet beyond the sight of land, as the
past few days they had sailed a course that frequently was
close enough to the islands they passed to allow an occasional visual reference.

Not wanting to disturb Scully, Artie peeked though the
port companionway hatch to check on his brother. Larry
was asleep as well, undoubtedly exhausted from yesterday's
tense encounter on the Cay Sal Bank and the tricky passage through the middle of the Keys the evening before. It

had been a long day and night for all of them, but now they all could relax a bit and let the wind do the work as it bore them to the northwest for at least another three, and possibly four days.

Artie looked at the fillets of fish spread out on the rear netting to dry and saw that they were still there. The swell was gentle and there was barely a chop and certainly no danger of any seas big enough to sweep them overboard, at least for now. After sailing this many miles on the *Casey Nicole*, learning from Larry and Scully, he could now estimate their speed based on how the wake behind the hulls looked, and he guessed they were still making about eight knots. It certainly wasn't the best the catamaran could do, but considering the nice conditions and light but steady wind, it was not bad. His thoughts turned to Casey and he wondered what she might be doing at this moment. He knew she would be thinking of him too, and probably worrying about him a lot as well, but he doubted it would occur to her that he would try to reach New Orleans by sailboat. She would probably assume he would hunker down in the islands with Larry until some more conventional mode of transportation was available again. And he likewise hoped she was hunkered down as well. If she had tried to leave New Orleans, as he sometimes thought she might have, he didn't know how he would ever find her. He knew they couldn't get very close to the Tulane campus by boat unless they entered the mouth of the Mississippi River and followed it upstream to where it penetrated the heart of the city, but Larry had ruled that out because it would require lots of motoring. The outboard would work if they needed it, but they had a limited amount of fuel and Larry wanted to save that for emergency maneuvering. He said the only feasible way to approach the city was via Lake Pontchartrain, which they could enter under sail from the Mississippi Sound. From there, it would be possible to anchor off or beach somewhere on the lakeshore near Metairie and then hike to the campus on foot. Someone would have to stay with the boat, and that would be Larry, because of his injury.

During that first full day and the following night on the open Gulf, little changed with the state of wind and sea, and the three of them slipped into an easy routine of alternating watches while the steering vane did all the work of keeping them on course. Their speed made good stayed about the same, averaging eight knots or so, which put them approximately 250 miles north of the Keys by their second morning waking up at sea. In such benign sailing conditions, they had been able to relax with the easy motion of the boat and enjoy better meals than they had eaten while on the passage through the Caribbean. The thin-cut fillets of grouper dried quickly on the netting, greatly increasing their stores of protein to go with the large amounts of stored staples such as rice, pasta, and corn meal that Larry already had aboard.

Larry's comments about the unstable nature of the Gulf from their earlier discussions of the voyage proved accurate by their third evening out. Dark clouds loomed on the horizon to the west before sundown and quickly overtook them, much to Artie's consternation. They appeared as dark blue and almost gray-black walls hanging just over the horizon and ominously growing larger as they neared. Their most frightening aspect was the frequent flashes of lightning that streaked out of them in all directions, appearing to continuously strike the water directly below. The thunder that followed every strike was getting louder and sounding just seconds after each brilliant flash. Larry and Scully had obviously been through this before, and quickly had the jib furled and the main tied to the second row of reefs. Larry said they could expect some short but vicious wind squalls, and might have to take down all sails depending on the squalls' severity.

"I'm more worried about getting struck by lightning," Artie said, looking up at the mast. "We're the tallest thing out here."

"Yeah, but we're properly grounded. The way that works, the lightning doesn't see any difference between the top of our mast and the surface around us. We could get hit, but if we did, it would mainly just be bad luck."

"I'd say it would be worse than bad. I haven't seen an electrical storm like this since we lived in Oklahoma, and out here, there's nowhere to hide."

"Well, at least we don't have to worry about the electronics, because they're already fried!"

Despite Larry's reassurance, when the first of the seemingly endless line of thunderstorms swept over them after dark, Artie experienced terror such as he had never known from weather before. The storms brought torrential rain and winds that drove it sideways so that the drops stung their faces as if they were being pelted with BBs or pellets. At one point, the wind proved too much for heaving to with even a scrap of sail up, so Artie had to help Scully wrestle the sail down and secure it. This done, the *Casey Nicole* was lying ahull to the wind, pushed off course but safe from damage to the rig. Worse than the wind to Artie, though, were the horrific lightning strikes that tore across the sky seemingly right over the deck, so close that the deafening thunder was nearly simultaneous with each flash. He fully expected them all to die at any moment, lit up by hundreds of thousands of volts of electricity as they crouched in the wet cockpit in their drenched foul-weather gear. But despite hours and hours of opportunities that lasted until the following dawn, the lightning missed them every time, and somehow they came out of the storms unscathed. The feeling of relief Artie had at the sight of clearing skies the next morning exceeded even the feeling he had had when he'd first set foot on dry land in St. Thomas after that first offshore passage.

"You freakin' sailors are absolutely insane!" he said to Larry as his brother handed him his first cup of coffee of the day.

"It's all in a day's work, Doc. You gotta weather a few storms if you want to drop anchor in paradise. Hell, if it weren't for a good gale now and then, the sea would be crowded with landlubbers sailing all over the place."

"I've never been so scared in my entire life."

"A hot electrical storm like that can get pretty intense, but we really were in no danger. What's bad is when you get caught in those kinds of squalls close to land. Then you're in real danger of getting blown ashore or run down by a barge or any number of coastal vessels. Out here, there's nothing to hit for a hell of a long way."

"So how far did we get blown off course, and how long will it take to make up for it?"

"It's not as much as you think. We might've got set about 10 miles east of our rhumb line, but I can't be sure without the GPS. If I can get a clear shot of the sun at noon with the sextant, I can tell you to within a mile, anyway. Of course we lost a few hours of distance made good on our heading, but we'll make it up as soon as the wind fills in. It looks like it's picking up now, so we'd better take advantage of it and get up all the sail we can carry."

Once they were back on course, after Larry confirmed their position with a noon sight shot with the sextant, they were able to take advantage of a steady southwest wind that leveled out around 15 knots in the afternoon and lasted through the next night. Steady sailing on a beam reach in this wind put them within 110 miles of the northern Gulf coast by the next morning. In this area, near the edge of the continental shelf, they began encountering offshore oil platforms, and by noon had sailed past dozens of these huge structures standing on stilt-like legs above the Gulf. All of them were shut down, of course, and there was none of the heavy boat traffic among them that Larry said would be a hazard to navigation in typical conditions. Nevertheless, he insisted on steering well clear of them, so that they didn't pass closer than a mile to any of them.

"Do you think any of the crews are still out here, stranded?" Artie asked.

"Probably not, after this much time. I mean, they certainly wouldn't be able to go home by helicopter, like they usually do, but these rigs all have some top-notch diesel mechanics keeping everything running. I would imagine that by now they've managed to get enough of the crewboats started to get everyone to the mainland. They certainly have enough fuel on hand, as well as tools and spare parts."

"They must have gotten as good of a view of the flash as I did, that first night."

"Yeah, I can imagine. Anyway, I'm just glad our timing worked out to cross this oilfield in daylight. You can see what a nightmare it would be to try to sail through here in the dark with all these rigs unlit. If this wind holds, we'll be past the danger zone before it gets dark again, but then we've got to worry about our speed, because we'll be making landfall before daylight."

Larry got out his chartbook for the northern Gulf coast and showed Artie a chart called "Mississippi Sound and Approaches." He pointed out the long chain of barrier islands that created the sound and paralleled the mainland from the Florida-Alabama state line to the entrance to Lake Pontchartrain.

"I never knew all those islands existed," Artie said.

"Most of them are reachable only by boat, and are part of a national seashore preserve. There's a lot of shoal water around them and inside the sound. This whole coast is hazardous to any deep-draft boat, in fact. We don't have to worry as much as most, with the catamaran, but we've still got to stay on top of where we are. You could run a skiff aground on some of the sandbars around those islands. Look, here's where we want to enter the sound." Larry pointed at a marked channel leading in from the Gulf to the west side of a barrier island labeled West Ship Island. The channel continued north for miles across the sound to the city of Gulfport, Mississippi. "I've run that channel before, and we can do it at night, as long as there's some moon- light, which we'll have plenty of. We'll drop anchor behind Ship Island and wait for dawn. From there, it's less than a day's sail to the west end of the sound and the entrance to Pontchartrain."

"I can't believe we're almost there. It seemed like we were a world away when we first talked about this voyage in St. Thomas."

"It's a pretty good trip, no doubt. A couple more like that, and I'll make a sailor out of you yet, Doc."

"One's enough, thanks. Except I know you're going to tell me we've got to sail away somewhere else once we pick up Casey."

"I don't have a better answer, do you? I don't know where we'd go or what we'd do on the mainland. You sure wouldn't likely be able to get to your house right now. But we'll figure all that out later. The main thing is to get to Casey first."

When the last of the oil platforms dropped astern, the sun was setting on the Gulf and they were once more in open water. Larry calculated it was less than 30 miles to

West Ship Island, but said it was so low lying, they wouldn't see it until they were within five miles of it. Once it was fully dark, Artie helped Scully put a reef in the main so they could maintain a slower approach while they waited for the moonrise. Two hours later, they were able to pick out the unlit markers indicating the Gulfport Ship Channel in the moonlight. On the horizon to the north, a faint line of white sand could be seen, and soon they heard the distant sound of crashing surf as they sailed closer to the island. Artie was eager and elated at the prospect of the end of the voyage. But he was also disappointed to see that there were no lights or even a distant glow in the direction of the mainland, where he knew, from driving it, that there was almost a solid line of urban sprawl from New Orleans to Mobile, Alabama. From what they could tell so far, the entire coast was as dark as the uninhabited barrier island they were approaching.

When they were closer to the island, Larry pointed out an odd, circular structure rising some 30 feet above the otherwise featureless dunes of the island. "In the daylight, we would have seen that before we could have seen the beaches. It's Fort Massachusetts, built after the War of 1812. It's a park now, and there is a dock near it on the north side of the island where excursion boats land to bring tourists out here. We can anchor around there on that side. It's the best harbor at any of these islands, which is why they built the fort there in the first place, to guard the approach to New Orleans."

Artie was surprised at how brightly the white sand beaches of the island glowed in the moonlight. It was almost like daylight against that white sand, and he could clearly see the outlines of the dunes and the sea oats that grew on them as they rounded the west end of the island and entered the sound to turn east to the anchorage area. The long excursion boat dock came into view, and as they sailed past the end of it, they saw something else—a small campfire on the beach, situated in a hollow between the high dunes that had made it invisible to them from the Gulf side of the island. A few yards out in the water from the fire, leaning over several degrees from upright, was a small monohull sailboat that was apparently aground on the bottom. Two anchor rodes could be seen leading from its bow and stern out to deeper water, and there was a third trailing off towards the beach. As soon as the *Casey Nicole* appeared past the pier, someone by the fire jumped up and began yelling and waving for help.

"Sailed dat boat too close to de beach, dat mon," Scully said.

"Or, he could have been out here and dragged anchor when those squalls blew through the other night," Larry said.

"Could it be a trap?" Artie asked. He'd seen enough at Isleta Palominito and the Cay Sal Bank to be suspicious of everyone they encountered on the water.

"I don't think so," Larry said. "But why don't you bring the shotgun on deck anyway, just in case. I think what we have here is simply a fellow mariner in need of help, and he may be able to give us some useful information about the conditions ashore, if he's local. Scully, let's come about and sail within hailing distance on the other tack. I don't see a dinghy of any kind on the beach, so he must have waded ashore when he couldn't get it off."

Artie laid the shotgun in the cockpit and helped Scully with the sheets. There was just enough wind to power the sails and allow them to maneuver, but with the ocean swell blocked by the island, the water was nearly smooth. They came around and sailed to within 50 feet of the beach. Then Scully put the bow through the wind again, allowing the jib to go aback momentarily and stall the boat long enough for a quick conversation.

"I've been stuck here for two days!" the man on the beach yelled back in response to Larry's inquiry. "We had some hellacious thunderstorms that came through in the night, and once my anchor started dragging, I couldn't get another one set before I was swept onto that sandbar. I went aground at high tide, and there's no way I can get her off by myself."

Artie started to relax. The man's story certainly seemed plausible, and the boat *was* hard aground. Though the depth at this distance was probably three feet and no issue for the *Casey Nicole*, this man's monohull obviously had a deeper keel. Larry yelled back that they would try to help, and then pointed to an area of deeper water out beyond the stranded boat where he wanted to anchor.

"What can we do?" Artie asked.

"We can try to pull him off if we can get a firm set on our own anchors. He doesn't have a windlass or a decent winch on board, besides being alone. I can't do much with this arm, but if you can work our winch, and Scully and the owner can get on board the boat and try to heel her over some more, then I think we can drag her to deep water. That's just a little J/27, not very heavy for a keelboat, but draws almost five feet."

When anchor was set, Artie helped Scully launch the two-seat kayak and, once he was in sitting in the boat, passed him the end of a long length of spare anchor line. Then Scully paddled away, first taking the line to the bow of the stranded boat, then continuing on to the beach to get the owner and explain what they were going to try to do. Artie and Larry waited until Scully and the owner returned to his boat and climbed on board from the kayak. Scully secured the end of the line to the main bow cleat of the J-boat, and at Larry's direction, Artie took up all the slack from the other end and wound several turns around the big drum winch mounted in the center of the catamaran's cockpit. This centrally mounted winch served mainly to handle the jib sheet and halyard loads, but Larry had sized it to do double duty as a windlass in just such emergencies. As Artie began putting tension on the line by cranking the winch handle, Scully and the boat's owner used their combined body weight to heel the boat much farther over on her side by hanging on to the boom, which Scully rigged to stick out perpendicular to the hull. By leaning her over and getting some of the weight off the keel, it was a fairly simple matter to pull her free of the sand, but it was still a lot of work for Artie, who was sweating profusely by the time the job was done. Scully helped the owner reset his anchor just downwind of the catamaran, then the two of them paddled over and came aboard.

"I can't thank you guys enough," the grateful sailor said as he shook hands with everyone. "I didn't think I would ever get out of this fix. I'm Craig, by the way." Craig went on to explain that he'd decided to take to the water as a last resort, but really wasn't prepared to do so and didn't have much experience cruising or much of what he needed on board.

"I bought the boat for day sailing, mainly, with the idea of getting into racing later. I never thought I would try to go somewhere on it, but as things got worse, it occurred to me that leaving by water might be the best option. Trouble is, I didn't have paper charts for this area, and of course the GPS is down. I knew some people from the marina that used to sail out here to these islands all the time on long weekends, though, and they talked about what a good anchorage this was. It was my first time to sail out of the lake, believe it or not, but I found my way here okay, I just wasn't counting on those storms."

"Lake? Do you mean Pontchartrain?" Artie asked with great interest.

"Yeah. I kept my boat at South Shore Harbor Marina."

"Is that on the New Orleans side of the lake, I'm guessing?"

"Yeah, it's just a few miles east of the Causeway, but west of where the I-10 bridge crosses the lake."

"Oh man, that's fantastic!" Artie said, then seeing the look of confusion on Craig's face, he explained: "We've sailed all the way from St. Thomas to get to New Orleans to find my daughter. I can't believe we were lucky enough to run into someone out here who's just come from there since the lights went out."

Craig shook his head. "I feel for you if your daughter is still in New Orleans. There's nothing good happening there, and I would hate to know I had to go back there looking for someone I loved. What a nightmare that would be!" Craig went on to describe his experiences in the city since the pulse had occurred. If what he said was true, and they had no reason to doubt him, the entire city had descended into anarchy and chaos. Craig described gun battles between the police and large gangs, and rampant, unchecked looting, burning, and rioting. He said some people began trying to leave the city by the second day, mostly on foot, and then a much larger number began leaving within a week, when everyone finally realized help wasn't on the way and the grocery stores were cleaned out. Craig said he would have been completely out of food, too, with no way to get any more, if not for the fact that he'd had a key to his dock neighbor's larger cruising boat. The absentee owner lived in northern Louisiana and kept the boat at South Shore for vacation cruising. Knowing they would never be able to get to the marina until all this was over anyway, Craig said he didn't feel bad about going on board the boat and taking the left-over provisions that were still there after her last Florida trip. He said he'd often driven to the marina in the middle of the night during storms to check the vessel's dock lines, and he knew the owners were grateful for that and would want him to utilize supplies that wouldn't do them any good.

"After that, I thought I might be able to just hang tight there at the marina for a while and see if things got better, living on my boat and keeping a low profile. But it didn't get better; it just got worse. I knew I had to leave when some guys came in at night and stole a Catalina 42 that was a few docks over. It was just a matter of time before every boat in the marina would be taken, as people got desperate to get out of the city. I was afraid they'd just kill me and take my boat, so I got out of there the next morning, as soon as there was enough wind. I didn't know where I'd go, but I knew I had to get out of Pontchartrain, because it's just a big bowl surrounded by land. I knew about this place and planned to hang out here awhile and then decide about going to Florida, or who knows where. But then that storm blew me aground, and I've been on the beach ever since, until you guys found me."

Artie was growing more anxious and restless the more of this he heard. "Did you hear anything about what was going on down in the Garden District, or around Tulane?" he asked.

"No, I haven't been in that area at all since the lights went out. All I know is there are fires everywhere and for days there was so much gunfire it sounded like a war zone. It's got to be bad down there. It's bad all over the city."

"Have you heard *any* news from other parts of the country?" Larry asked. "Does anyone know for sure what this event was, and exactly how widespread it was?"

"Everyone says it was a cataclysmic solar flare. They say it was something scientists have been claiming could happen for years, but few people really took seriously. There are rumors that some people have been in contact by ham radio with operators in Europe and Asia and that there was some damage there, but nothing like in North America, and from what you guys are saying, in the islands too. I don't know where I'll go from here now. I had thought about trying to make it down to the Caribbean myself, but if nothing's different there, I don't know now."

"We'll probably head south again ourselves," Larry said, "only not to the eastern Caribbean, but down to the Yucatán, or maybe somewhere among the islands off the Mosquito Coast."

"That sounds good. I hadn't thought of that," Craig said. "Hey, I know I'm not going back to New Orleans any time soon, if ever. I'm sure you have charts on board for these waters, but I just remembered, I've got a street map of the city and a Louisiana state road map. They might come in handy if you don't already have them."

"That's fantastic!" Artie said. "I've got a map of New Orleans, but it's in my car, of course, and that is parked at the airport."

"Those will be much appreciated," Larry said. "As you know, nautical charts show almost nothing of the details on land, and we've got to come up with a plan for quickly getting in and out of the Tulane area to look for Casey, without wandering around guessing which is the best route."

"It's the least I can do, guys. I *really* appreciate your taking the time to help me out of this bind. I don't know if I would have ever gotten the boat off without your help."

The next morning, Artie, Scully and Larry said goodbye to Craig, who was now securely anchored in deep water and had decided to stay at Ship Island for the time being, at least as long as it was safe there. They sailed off the anchor and headed west in the Mississippi Sound, passing to the north side of Cat Island, another large barrier island in the chain that protected the mainland coast. Their destination was a pass into Lake Pontchartrain called the Rigolets. After discussing all the options with Craig, and studying his city street map, they decided that the safest way to look for Casey was to make use of the many man-made canals that penetrated the city from Lake Pontchartrain. Larry could wait safely offshore in the lake with the boat while Artie and Scully paddled into the city in the kayak at night, keeping a low profile and hopefully remaining out of reach of the dangers that they imagined plagued every street. The canal that would take them closest to the university area emptied into the lake near West End Park, right around the corner from the marina where Craig had kept his boat. They decided that before going there, they would first paddle up a smaller canal to the west of the Causeway—one that would take them right to the New Orleans International Airport where Artie's car was parked, and, he hoped, still locked, with his .22 pistol in the glove compartment.

"I know it's going to take some extra time," Larry said when Artie protested, "but having an opportunity to grab another weapon, *any* weapon, is not something we can afford to pass up. You know what we've already been through, and you heard what Craig said. I think you and Scully need to take both my shotgun and your pistol for your trip to Tulane. You're going to need every advantage you can get."

* * *

Grant glanced over his shoulder one last time before they reached the canebrake where they'd left Casey with the hidden bikes. The solitary canoeist was disappearing from sight far down the river, carried swiftly by the current and his steady, practiced paddle stroke. Grant was envious that his destination lay downstream, while theirs entailed nothing but a struggle to go upstream. He steered the bow into the mud at the best landing spot and held the canoe against the bank by jamming his paddle into the bottom.

"Okay, you can step out now, then I'll get out and pull it up on the bank."

Jessica stepped ashore and immediately called out to announce their success: "Hey Casey! Guess what? We got a canoe!"

"Hey! Keep it down!" Grant whispered. "We don't want anyone who might be crossing the bridge to know we're down here."

"Oh, sorry!" Jessica whispered back. She called Casey's name again, this time in a quieter voice. When there was no answer, she turned back to Grant. "Where is she?"

Grant got out of the canoe and pulled the bow up far enough to tie it off to a small riverside bush. He pushed past Jessica into the dense cane to find the bikes just as they'd left them. "She probably walked over in the woods nearby to use the bathroom or something," Grant said, then he called out to her too, in a loud whisper: "Casey! We're back."

Jessica joined him and looked at the bikes. "Hey, look, Grant. Her backpack is gone."

"She must have taken it with her, then. I told her to keep the gun handy. She shouldn't be far, though, because I told her we'd be back in about an hour, and we were. Let's take a look around, but no more yelling, okay?"

"All right. She can't be far. I know I wouldn't wander off far into these woods alone, and I can't imagine that Casey would either."

Grant grabbed his machete and led the way out of the canebrake and back to the open area under the bridge. Casey was nowhere in sight. When they reached the sandy area at the end of the dirt access road that led up to the highway, he examined the ground and pointed out the footprints the three of them had made coming down the hill, as well as the tracks made by the bicycle tires as they had pushed them along. He walked closer to the river and then waved Jessica over to look at something else.

"She went this way," he said, pointing at a separate set of tracks leading under the bridge along the sandbar that made up the riverbank here. The tracks were so obvious in the rain-swept sand that Jessica probably would have seen them too, if it had occurred to her to look for footprints at all. Grant said he'd learned a bit about tracking from the hunters he'd spent time with in Guyana, so it was second nature to him to try to figure out where Casey had gone by the trail she would have had to leave, especially in all this open sand, which he said was the easiest kind of terrain for finding and following footprints.

As they walked the route she'd taken upriver, Grant called Casey's name several times in a slightly louder voice than he'd warned Jessica about before. After they passed under the bridge, it was obvious that no one else had come down to the river from the road, as there were no new tracks other than their own. But the farther Casey's trail led upstream, the more surprised Grant was that she would walk so far alone when she was supposed to be watching the bikes. Once the bend in the river took them beyond sight of the bridge, he suddenly saw the reason she had come here. Hanging on a branch at the edge of the woods was a pair of black panties and a white sports bra. Casey's New Balance walking shoes were sitting side by side on a log near the branch, her socks spread out next to them, along with her open backpack and a bottle of shampoo.

Grant suddenly stopped, not wanting to walk up on her if she were undressed. "Casey! Where are you?" When there was no answer, Jessica called loudly too, and still there was nothing but the sound of the river gurgling by. It was impossible that she would not have heard them by now if she was anywhere in the vicinity of her stuff. Grant rushed ahead to the log where her shoes were and looked around carefully at the sand. Casey's bare footprints clearly led into the water at the edge of the river, and another set showed she had walked back to where her clothes were, but there were no other clothes in sight but the underwear, shoes and socks. There were many other prints circling around and covering up the first ones she'd made, indicating to Grant that she had probably been moving around while she dripped dry from her bath before putting at least some of her clothes back on. He saw other footprints as well, some of them covered up by hers, and figured someone had been here before the rain. The other footprints looked older, because they did not have a clearly defined shape or tread definition.

Looking beyond the immediate area, he then spotted another line of Casey's barefoot tracks leading off up the sandbar, even farther upriver, but as soon as he started following them, a chill ran up his spine and he grabbed Jessica's hand while motioning her to silence with a finger over his lips. Superimposed over some of the prints made by Casey's bare feet were more of the larger, smooth tracks that he had mistakenly thought were old. The fact that some of them were on top of Casey's tracks made his previous conclusion impossible, and upon closer examination, he determined that the shapeless, smooth footprints could have been made by a person wearing moccasins or some similar footwear. One thing was for certain: the tracks were made by a man. Grant could judge by their size compared with Casey's tracks and his own that the person who made the prints had to be a man, as they were slightly bigger than the impressions left by his own size 11 hiking shoes.

His eyes swept back over the trail of larger tracks they had passed, and he could see where the person who made them had stepped out of the dense woods that began at the edge of the sandbar just a few feet uphill from the log where Casey had left her things. Someone had been walking around on this sandbar before she got here, and then must have been watching her from the cover of the trees while she bathed. When she walked farther upstream, he had re-emerged from the woods and followed her. It was the only explanation for the fact that some of his tracks were covered by hers, while these last were made on top of her trail. As this realization dawned on him, he wondered if the man who made them had been on the sandbar when they rode down the bank from the highway, and had hidden in the woods watching as he and Jessica left Casey alone and went to get the canoe.

Grant gave Jessica a serious look that conveyed the importance of keeping silent and then motioned downward with his hand, to tell her to stay put while he tried to figure this out. He crept over to the backpack and felt inside it for the Ruger pistol. *It was gone!* He could only hope that Casey had it with her. But now that he was looking for them, he saw moccasin tracks near the log as well, and realized the person who made them could have taken the gun if she had left it there when she walked away. Following along beside, but not touching the two sets of tracks, he moved as fast as he could while still remaining silent, which was easy enough in the damp sand. He gripped the machete so tightly his knuckles were white. Surely this person who had followed Casey had heard them calling her name. Surely she would have heard them too, but why didn't she answer? Fear and worry gripped him as he struggled to find the answer while he followed the tracks, ducking under the river birch trees that leaned out of the forest over the sandbar.

He didn't have to go far to reach the end of the narrow beach, where he found Casey's trail obliterated by a large area of disturbed sand where both sets of footprints had been erased by something. Only the man's tracks led beyond that point, and following them a few more steps, Grant's heart nearly stopped when he saw the answer to the puzzle. There was a deep grove in the mix of sand and mud that extended from the water's edge several feet up the bank, and on both sides of it, a flattened mark made by something smooth and heavy sliding into the water. On one side of these impressions were more of the larger tracks, but none of Casey's. Some of them were deep and distorted from slipping and digging into the mud. Grant had done enough canoeing to know exactly what he was looking at. It was the mark made when someone pushes a heavily laden canoe into the water from the bank.

Almost as soon as it became clear what he was looking at, he whirled back the way he had come, knowing that the canoe they'd seen heading downriver less then twenty minutes ago had to be the one that had made these marks. *Casey was in that canoe,* he thought, probably hidden from their view under the camo tarp that Grant had assumed was covering the lone paddler's gear! No wonder the man paddling it had not taken his eyes off them as he passed, much less shown any indication of wanting to stop and talk. With the strong current in his favor and his obvious experience as a paddler, there was no telling how far downriver he'd gotten by now. Grant was horrified by the thought of what his intentions might be. He turned and raced back down the sandbar, yelling: "Jessica! Quick, we've got to go!" The he grabbed Casey's backpack, shoes, and underwear, and shoved them into Jessica's hands as he hurried her back in the direction of the bridge.

"What happened? Where is she? Why are we going back this way?"

"That canoe we passed. She's in it! That man we waved at must have stopped here for some reason before we all got here. He must have been in the woods when Casey walked up here to take a bath. He was probably watching her the whole time, and then followed her when she walked upriver to where he'd left his canoe. He grabbed her and put her in it, and she must have been hidden in that pile of gear he had when we saw him."

"How do you know all that?" Jessica asked as she ran to keep up with Grant on the way back to where they'd left the bikes and the canoe.

"I'm no expert, but in this sand the tracks are easy to read. All the rain over the last two days would have swept away any tracks other than new ones made in the last couple of hours since it stopped. Her footprints leading upstream are covered by his, which makes it clear he was walking behind her. Then hers completely disappear and only his lead to the canoe. I could see where his feet dug in as he was pushing it back in the river. And, besides, there's no other explanation. She can't be anywhere near here or she would have heard us calling out to her."

"But wouldn't we have heard her scream if someone grabbed her?"

"Maybe not. He must have gagged her somehow. This probably happened when we were still trying to get the canoe and gear together at that camp. So we might not have heard anything even if she screamed as loud as she could, especially over the sound of the running water."

"What are we going to do? How will we ever find her? We've got to help her, Grant!"

"We *are* going to help her. We've got to try to catch that guy, and that's why we've got to go *now*, no time to waste! Let's just throw our stuff in the canoe and go! He's got a big head start, but he has to stop to rest somewhere."

"Why would he be going downstream anyway? Doesn't that go back the way we came, towards New Orleans?"

"No, not to New Orleans," Grant said as he steadied the canoe while Jessica got in and got situated in the bow seat. "It runs to the Gulf eventually, of course, but first it joins the Pearl River, which is the biggest river in this region this side of the Mississippi. The lower reaches of the Pearl split apart into three rivers and lots of branching bayous that spread out to be more than five miles wide. For about 20 miles it becomes a maze of waterways, and runs through a vast river-bottom forest that is the closest thing I've seen in the States to a jungle. The general area is called the Honey Island Swamp, but this forest covers some 250 square miles, most of it protected as a national wildlife refuge. If he is headed there and gets there with Casey before we catch him, it will probably be impossible to find them."

"How far is it from here?" Jessica asked. They were now afloat, with all their belongings, including Casey's, stowed in the middle of the canoe between them. The bicycles were left where they'd hidden them, in the dense canebrake.

"By canoe? I've only done the trip once, and I think it took us about four days to get to the Pearl River from my parent's cabin. But we weren't in a hurry and we were stopping a lot to explore and take pictures. Then we paddled another three days through the swamps and took out almost at the coast. From here, somebody paddling like this guy was doing could be in those swamps in two days, not to mention the help he'll get with the river up like it is after all this rain."

"The current will help us too, won't it?" Jessica asked as she frantically dug into the water with awkward, choppy strokes of her paddle, doing everything she could to help them go faster.

"It will, but we've also got to be careful. We don't want this guy to know we're following him, but since he saw us going upstream in the canoe, he knows we have a boat and that we *could* try to follow. But he probably doesn't think we would be able to figure out that he has Casey, unless we were just guessing."

"Isn't the gun still in Casey's backpack? Maybe when we catch up with the creep he'll give up when he sees that you have it, like those gang-banger punks in New Orleans did."

"Are you kidding? Any guy like that who has loaded up a canoe to live out here on the river probably has at least a hunting rifle or shotgun, and likely several firearms and plenty of ammo. But it doesn't matter anyway, because I don't have the pistol anymore and he's likely got it too. It wasn't in Casey's pack, and even if she was carrying it when she left her stuff on that log, he must have taken it from her."

"What are we going to do when we catch up with them then?"

"I don't know, Jessica. I guess we're going to have to play it by ear and figure something out. That's why we need to keep a sharp lookout ahead, down the river. I don't want to run up on this guy all of a sudden if he's stopped around a bend or something. And if he suspects we're following him, it would be easy enough for him to ambush us and we'd never know what hit us."

"You really think he would just shoot us like that?" Jessica had stopped paddling now while thinking all this over.

"Sure, why not? He obviously doesn't care about the law or what's right or wrong. He took Casey by force. Like a lot of other people we've run across since those guys tried to grab our bikes, this guy has decided that he can do as he pleases now that society has broken down and the rules cannot be enforced. I doubt he would stop at murder if he's already gone as far as kidnapping with the likely intention of rape."

"I'm scared, Grant. I'm scared for us and I'm scared for Casey too. She doesn't deserve this. We've got to try to help her, even if it is dangerous."

"Of course we will. And of course you're scared. You have every reason to be. I'm scared of what he will do to her if we don't find her soon, but more than anything, I just feel like a complete idiot for bringing you two out here and getting you in this situation to begin with."

"You didn't know, Grant. You did the best you could, and we saw how things were when we left New Orleans, just as you predicted they would be. I think you were right that we needed to leave. It could have been even worse if we were still there."

"It would be hard for it to be much worse than it is now, Jessica. We may not even be able to find Casey, especially if he leaves the river somewhere and takes off with her on foot. And besides the problem of trying to help her, we're almost out of food. Like I said before, I was counting on reaching the cabin by now, and we started out with about all the supplies we could carry on the bikes. Now we're going to be in survival mode and we're going to have to find more, but at least that will be easier on the river than it would be if we were still on the road."

"I don't really see how, unless we can find blueberries or something like that in the woods."

"No wild blueberries here, I'm afraid. There are plenty of blackberries, but they won't be ripe until May. It's too early for a lot of things like that, but there are always cattails, and this time of year there are other edible greens in these bottomlands. But mainly, there are fish—fish and crawfish. Oh, and frogs, turtles, snakes, alligators, armadillos, beavers, raccoons, squirrels, rabbits, turkeys, deer.... Everything that lives in these parts is either in the river or attracted to it because whatever it eats is in or near the river."

"I know you've got the fishing rod, but I hope you're not serious about eating some of that other stuff. I mean, really, *snakes? Alligators?*"

"All reptiles are good to eat, and easier to catch than real game like deer. Of course I'd only be interested in a small 'gator, and then only if its mama weren't around."

"I'll stick to those cattails you mentioned, whatever they are."

"You'll like them. But here, you need to eat something now, we need to keep our energy levels up for paddling." Grant handed her a Ziploc bag with almonds in it. "Eat a big handful of those. That's the last of them, but we still have some raisins, three more of the rice dinners, and a little bit of oatmeal. We can make it last at least through tomorrow."

TEN

LYING BOUND AND blindfolded in the bottom of the
canoe, jammed among the packs and bags crowding the
narrow hull, Casey felt she had lost all sense of equilib-
rium and time. Only her hearing was unimpaired, and the
sound of her abductor's relentless paddle strokes and the
bow of the canoe cutting through water told her that they
were moving downriver at a steady pace. She had no idea
how much time had passed or how far they might have
traveled. It seemed like a long time, and she was sure that
Grant and Jessica must have returned to the place where
she was supposed to be guarding the bikes by now. She
wondered if they had been successful in getting a canoe,
but most of all she wondered what they must have thought
when they did not find her where she was supposed to be.
Would they even be able to guess she had walked upstream?
Was there a chance they would find her shoes and other
things she had left there? What would they think if they did?
It would have to appear to them as if she had simply van-
ished. They might be able to figure out that she had gone to
the secluded sandbar to find privacy for her bath—after all,
she did leave her shampoo on the log beside her shoes and

backpack, and her underwear was hanging from a nearby branch. But what would they conclude from that? She wondered if they would think she got swept away in the river and perhaps drowned. She felt awful thinking about how upset they would be, and how she had ruined everything by getting herself in this situation. Would they even try to get to Grant's cabin now, or would they spend who knows how much time looking around for her in vain in the vicinity of the bridge? One thing she was sure of was that they would have no way of guessing what had really happened. And if *they* didn't know, there was absolutely no one who would.

She was all alone in her predicament, in the hands of this person she had not seen or even heard speak since she was grabbed from behind. Where was he taking her, and what did he plan to do to her? Casey shuddered to think about it. She had heard all too many news stories over the years of young women and girls being taken to entertain any thoughts that his intentions were anything but the worst. She knew she would have to fight for her very life, but so far she had failed miserably at that. The man was so strong, and his attack so sudden and unexpected, that her resistance to being bound and gagged had been futile. She could only hope she would have another chance whenever they got to wherever he was taking her to carry out his evil intentions.

She decided then and there that she would fight to the death and do everything in her power to defend herself. She would claw his eyes out, kick him in the groin, bite, scratch, and gouge—whatever it took to stop him. It angered her that she had been through so much in the past few days only to become a helpless victim, and she vowed to resist and not give up. Just as she resolved these thoughts and made up her mind to survive, she heard the paddling stop and felt the canoe slow down, drifting with the current. There was a bumping sound of the paddle being set down in the hull, and then she heard the rustling of the plastic tarp or whatever it was covering her being pulled away. For the first time since she was grabbed, her captor spoke:

"No need to keep you all covered up like that any more," he said. "We're a long way from the bridge or any other roads now, so you might as well enjoy some fresh air. It's a nice afternoon to be on the river."

Casey was startled by the voice. Far from sounding like some crass backwoods redneck, as she expected, the man spoke clearly and precisely, with correct pronunciation and a calm, steady voice. She twisted and tried to turn her head in his direction, tried to demand that he untie her and let her go, but managed only to make unintelligible noises through the cloth gag that was in her mouth.

"I'm sorry about that, but I couldn't have you scream-ing back there for your friends and whoever else might be nearby to hear. I know you've got to be thirsty, and I'm going to give you something to drink soon, so just hang tight a bit. I can't have you hollering out loud while it's still daylight. It'll be dark in another hour, and I'll take it off then. I don't think there's much danger of seeing anyone on the river at night once we get past Franklinton. We'll stop somewhere past there for a few minutes, then keep pushing on through the night. I want to put a lot of miles behind us before daylight." Casey heard the dipping of the paddle as he resumed his relentless stroke.

"I know you're not very happy with me right now, but the time will come when you will thank me for what I did today. I want you to know that you are safe now, and that nothing or nobody can hurt you as long as you are with me. I don't know where you and your friends came from on those bicycles, but I do know that if you were on the road, you've seen how crazy things have gotten out there, and how dangerous it is to travel. It makes a whole lot more sense to be on the river now than on the road, and traveling the river at night is even better. Where we're going, two people in a canoe can disappear without a trace. You don't have to worry about running into gangs of looters and hordes of desperate refugees from the cities out here, because the ones that make it to the country are going to be too busy trashing the houses and stores they come across in the small towns and along the road. They're not thinking about long-term survival, because in their ignorant and naïve minds, they still think everything's going to be fixed and they'll be able to watch their stolen flat screen TVs again just like they used to. While they kill each other over things that will never work again, you and I will be just fine, living in harmony with nature, and wanting for nothing that we really need."

Casey couldn't believe what she was hearing. This guy was even scarier than the abductor she had first imagined. He talked as if he actually thought of himself as her savior. What could possibly make him think he had a right to take her anywhere?

"Oh, and my name's Derek, by the way. I guess you can tell me yours later. You know, you couldn't have possibly run into anyone more prepared for what's going on than I am. No, you don't have anything to worry about now. I've been expecting something like this for years. I knew things couldn't go on the way they were, I just didn't know exactly what was going to happen to bring it all down. As it turns out, it seems that a massive solar flare was pretty effective. I think in the long run this will take out about 90 percent of the population of this country, and really clean things up for a new start in the aftermath. You can bet that we'll be in that 10 percent or whatever the exact number is that ultimately comes through this. You'll see when we get to my little piece of paradise. I've been getting ready for this for a long time, and you're going to appreciate all I've done in advance. There's still a lot to do, but time is one thing we'll have no shortage of now. I'd always hoped to find someone to share it with me, and it looks like you're that person. Of course I was hoping for a pretty girl, but you're way more than that—you're absolutely beautiful."

Casey squirmed and struggled, and kicked at the bags near her bound feet in protest. Her efforts got her nothing but a cold splash of water in the face, dipped from the river by the man's paddle blade.

"Now just calm down before you capsize us. I like your fighting spirit, but I'm not going to argue with you right now. If you keep that up I'm going to have to lash your legs to the thwarts. I imagine you're uncomfortable enough as it is, so just stay calm and I won't bother. Like I said, soon as it gets dark, I'm going to take that rag out of your mouth and I might even take that blindfold off and let you get a look at me. We might as well start getting to know each other, because we've got a lot of time to spend together, just the two of us."

Casey had little doubt now that she was in the hands of a psychopath, whether he spoke articulately or not. It was clear now that he had no intentions of letting her go, but it really scared and angered her that he seemed to think that she should somehow appreciate what he was doing—that in his mind he was saving her from a world gone mad. *He* was mad, of that she was certain, and the way he talked of how he had been preparing and practically hoping for something like this very thing made it seem that in his case, unlike those of many they had seen, it was not a condition brought about by the recent events. Now she was more afraid than ever about where he might be taking her. From what he said, she could only deduce that it was someplace remote and far from roads, likely some cabin or camp like Grant's that was deep in the woods somewhere along the course of this river. She did know that it wasn't in Mississippi, though, because they were still downstream of the state line, and Grant had said it would be a real struggle to paddle up the river to his cabin from the bridge where they planned to begin. She could tell from the sensation of speed and the feeling that they were moving even when her captor wasn't paddling that they were riding the current of the river downstream. But she had no idea where this river went. Casey hadn't given much thought to the geography of the local waterways since she'd moved to New Orleans, at least none of them beyond the shores of Lake Pontchartrain and the banks of the Mississippi River where it wound its way through the city not far from campus. She was at a loss as to whether the Bogue Chitto might empty into the lake or directly into the Gulf of Mexico, and she wished now she'd asked Grant more questions as they traveled together. All she really knew now was that no matter what, her top priority was to escape from this man. The chances of Grant and Jessica finding her and helping her could be little better than zero. Sadly, she realized that even if she escaped, she might be unable to find them. Every mile the canoe traveled downriver was just that much farther in the wrong direction from Grant's cabin, and even if she could find a way to travel back upriver, they might not be there by the time she made it. Her thoughts turned to her dad and her Uncle Larry as well. She wondered what they were doing and knew her dad would be thinking about her constantly and doing his best to find a way to get back to New Orleans, but she doubted it would be possible until the electricity was somehow restored. She didn't know how she was going to make it happen, but she was determined to see him again as much for his sake as for hers. She knew what he had gone through when they lost her mom, and she couldn't let him down by failing to survive this and putting him through the loss of his only daughter as well.

Derek, if that was really his name, had not spoken again after he started back paddling for what seemed to Casey like much longer than an hour. She hadn't really wanted him to either, as she was lost in her thoughts of escape and of Grant and Jessica, and of her dad and Uncle Larry. When he finally did, his voice startled her as much as it had the first time.

"We're going to pull over to the bank and stop for a little while just ahead here. It's getting dark now."

Casey's stomach knotted up as she wondered what he had in mind. Was he going to try and drag her out of the canoe and rape her here and now, as night had fallen and they were in a sufficiently remote place? She thought it was highly likely. In the silence after he said this, she noticed for the first time the sound of night insects, a distant hum from the riverside forests that surely must be surrounding them in this lonely place. She clenched her teeth as she felt the bow of the canoe slide onto something solid, then felt it rock and surge forward as the man stepped out and pulled it farther up on the bank.

"I want you to understand something, okay? I have no intention of hurting you or doing anything else to you. I don't want to keep you tied up and gagged like this, but I can't have you screaming and trying to fight me either. So if you and I can reach an understanding, I'll get that gag out of your mouth so you can drink some water, and eat something too, if you like. Then maybe we can have a conversation like the newfound friends that we are. The first thing I'm going to do is take that blindfold off of your eyes though, so you can see that I'm not the monster you probably think I am. I really am a nice guy and you'll see that and appreciate it more and more as we get to know each other."

Casey didn't believe for a minute that he wasn't going to try something, but she did want the blindfold off, and especially the gag. She was dying for a drink of water and really needed it, but the thought of eating anything that he might offer her made her sick. Food was the farthest thing from her mind right now. She tried to shrink away as she felt his hands near her head, but all he was doing was untying the knots. He removed the blindfold and she could see partly over the gunwale of the canoe into a starry night sky—the first stars she'd seen since the night they had camped on the Causeway before the rainy weather moved in. She couldn't see her captor because he was behind her, but presently she felt his hands lifting her from under her back until she was in a sitting position against the packs. She could see the outline of the treetops on the far bank, and the glint of the river as it rippled by in the faint starlight. Then he walked around the canoe to face her, squatting on his haunches to get down to her level where she sat propped up. It was hard to see his features clearly, but she could tell just from his silhouette against the night sky that he was tall and lean, and that he had a full beard and thick, shoulder-length hair. His movements were fluid and powerful, and squatting there he looked as comfortable as most people would look sitting in an easy chair. She got the impression that, even more than Grant, he was in his element in the outdoors.

"Okay, I know it's dark out here, but you can see I'm just a regular guy. I'm not some creepy serial killer or something like that you may have seen in a scary movie. I'm just a man who happens to have a lot of experience living off the grid, and to tell you the truth, I couldn't care less whether the power ever comes back on again—in fact, I sincerely hope it doesn't. The world will be a better place without it, but we can talk about all that later. First, I just want you to relax a bit and I want you to be more comfortable and to know that I'm not going to hurt you. I'm going to take that gag out of your mouth, but I warn you, if you scream, I'll put it back just as fast as I did the first time. What do you say? Can I trust you to keep quiet?"

Casey looked at him and nodded, indicating that she would. He reached behind her head with both hands to undo the knot, a movement that drew his face much closer to hers. She bent her head down as much as possible to avoid eye contact with him, and then felt the awful dry rag pulled away from her mouth. She tried to spit, but her mouth was so dry she couldn't. It was all she could do to resist the urge to scream at him, but she feared he would do exactly as he said and stuff the rag back into her mouth if she did.

He reached for something in the canoe and she saw it was a canteen of some sort. "I know you need some water." He unscrewed the cap and held it up to her lips. She tilted her head back enough to allow the water to flow into her dry mouth. She took several deep drinks and turned away when she'd had enough, causing some of it to spill on her shirt before he moved the canteen away.

"Why did you do this to me?" she yelled. "Let me go!"

His hand was over her mouth before she could utter another word. "I told you to keep it down. You can talk, but there's no need to shout. Do you understand?"

Casey nodded again and he removed his hand. "You can't do this to me," she said much more quietly. "I've got to get back to my friends. They're looking for me."

"It's not safe back there. It's much more dangerous up there around the state line than it is where we're going. I don't know where the three of you were trying to go, but you wouldn't have made it on those bicycles. It's a wonder someone hadn't already killed the boy you were with and raped you and your friend, then killed you both; that kind of thing is happening everywhere, whether you know it or not. I don't know what you three were thinking, traveling the roads like that."

"We were fine, until you came along," Casey said. "I don't know who you think you are, and why you think you're above the law, but you're going to pay for this when you get caught! You can't take someone prisoner against their will just because the power is off."

"You still don't get it, do you? Here's a news flash for you: *everything* has changed now, in case you and your friends didn't figure that out on your little bike ride. Where did you come from, anyway? Covington…Mandeville? None of you look like you are from around here."

"New Orleans!" Casey spat. "And we *were* getting where we were going. We knew there were scumbags like you everywhere trying to take advantage of the situation. We even passed the bodies of people who were murdered. But we weren't stupid. Grant knew what he was doing, and we had a gun too."

"You mean this one?" Derek reached for something in one of the bags in the canoe. She saw that it was her father's pistol. "Rule number one in using firearms for self-defense: Always Have it With You! You walked off and left this in your pack for anyone to come along and pick up. What good did you think it would do you there? You've got a lot to learn about survival. You're lucky you've found the right teacher."

Casey realized that if he had taken the gun from her backpack, he had obviously been watching her from the woods while she was bathing. She shuddered at the thought that she had been walking around naked on the sandbar, oblivious to having been watched the entire time.

"If I'm going to be that teacher, and we're going to be best friends someday, as I'm certain we are, I need to know your name."

"Screw you!" Casey said. Her voice was defiant, but not quite a shout. She didn't want his hands on her again so she restrained herself from provoking him by yelling it too loudly.

Derek laughed and rose to a standing position, putting the gun back wherever he'd stashed it in his bags. "That's okay, you can tell me later. As I said, we've got *plenty* of time to get to know each other, so it's not a problem." He took another small bag out of the canoe and squatted down in front of her again.

"Hungry?" he asked, taking something out of the bag and taking a bite of it. "I shot a deer and smoke-dried most of the meat before I put in upriver a few days ago. I've got enough to last for a couple of weeks. It's good; have some," he said, tearing off a chunk of something she could barely see in the dark and holding it up to her face. Casey turned away. It did smell a lot like the beef jerky she had been sharing with Grant, but she was far too upset to have an appetite at this point.

"I'm not hungry!" she said when he didn't take it away.

"Okay. You will be soon enough, but you can decide when. Do what you like, but I've got to paddle all night. We'll make another 15 miles before daylight. I'll feel a lot better then, the closer we get to the big swamp. That's where I feel most at home, and I've been going there so long that it's like it's my world down there. It's one of the best, most unspoiled places in the whole Southeast, and there's no way to get to the best parts except in a canoe. I can't wait to show it to you."

"You're insane! I'd rather die than go see some swamp— or anyplace else with you," Casey said.

"You may think that now, but you'll change your mind. And you're not going to die; I intend to make sure of that. If anyone tries to do you harm, it will be *them* doing the dying. I've been doing this kind of stuff alone for too long, and I'm through with that. I need you to stay alive, and you need me in order to do that, so let's just say we've got ourselves a mutually beneficial relationship here, and see if we can't just get along."

Casey still couldn't believe what she was hearing, and she was even more surprised when Derek pulled the canoe back into the river and resumed paddling without touching her again. She had been certain that he would do something to her immediately, but now, after listening to him talk, she concluded that he must be even crazier than she imagined. She was beginning to think that he actually *believed* she would somehow start to like him, look upon him as her protector, become his lover, and live happily ever after with him in some remote swamp! As dangerous as his delusions likely made him, however, she was overwhelmingly relieved that he had not tried to do anything to her yet, and because of what he thought would develop between them eventually, she could at least half-believe that he wasn't about to kill her at any moment, as she'd feared when she was first abducted.

* * *

Artie couldn't recall ever seeing so many vultures in one place. They were wheeling overhead by the hundreds, gliding in tight spiraling circles, while hundreds more congregated on the concrete railings of the two massive bridge spans they were about to sail under. Connecting New Orleans East to the north shore city of Slidell, the Interstate 10 Twin Span Bridge was one of the major traffic arteries out of the city, and had apparently been the scene of a massive exodus sometime in the previous days. Their first glimpse of this bridge pretty much confirmed all that Craig had told them about conditions in the city. Aside from the grotesque sight of so many of these big black birds of death, stalled vehicles were strung out along the overhead lanes for as far as they could see from their perspective on the water. Some of them appeared to have been burned in the days since the pulse left them stranded there, and lots of smoke could be seen off in the distance in the direction of the city to the southwest. A few haggard-looking people were walking on the bridge among the abandoned cars and vultures, all of them apparently headed away from New Orleans, using both the north and southbound lanes as escape corridors. Some of them yelled down at them like the teenagers on the Overseas Highway near Marathon had done, while others just leaned over the rail and stared, but at least here no one threw anything at them. Because of that incident in Florida, Larry had asked Artie to bring the shotgun on deck before they sailed under the bridges. He hoped they wouldn't need it, but said they needed a means of deterring anyone who might have a similar idea here, as rocks the size of the one that had barely missed them that night, thrown from a height, could do serious damage to the boat or even kill someone.

Beam-reaching on a light breeze out of the south, they soon cleared the bridge and the overpowering smell of death that surrounded it. "I sure hope Casey didn't try to leave," Artie said, his face pale and his stomach twisting as the horrific scene on the bridge receded astern.

"I doubt she would have," Larry said. "After all, the only way she could have gotten out would have been to try to walk. I'm sure she and Jessica and maybe some of her other friends are holed up somewhere on the campus and are just fine. I think she's too smart to do anything stupid."

"I hope you're right, but this is one unbelievable scene. I can't imagine how frightened she must be. I just hope she and Jessica stayed inside out of sight and have had enough to eat all this time."

"I think we'll find that she's just fine, but a lot of these people must have really suffered. It looks at least as bad here as Craig said it was, doesn't it? And I'm sure it's only going to get worse, but at least we're here. Now we just need to get in and get out while we still can."

Despite his worry and dread, Artie could scarcely contain his relief when he first saw the skyline of downtown New Orleans come into view from the deck of the *Casey Nicole.* They were sailing parallel to the south shore of Lake Pontchartrain from a couple of miles out, Scully steering for the elevated span where they could pass under the Causeway in the channel closest to the south shore. According to the chart, there was a vertical clearance of 60 feet at that point. Looking south to the distant, familiar buildings, Artie could dare to believe that Casey was really within his reach. After sailing some 1500 miles and surviving all the dangers they had encountered along the way, maybe they really were about to achieve what they'd set out to do.

"We won't waste any time," Larry said as they talked over their plan while sitting in the cockpit. "We'll be off the south shore near the airport by mid-afternoon if this wind holds. You and Scully can paddle up that canal and find your car as soon as it gets dark enough to cover your movements. That should still give us time to sail back over and maneuver the boat as close to the canal at West End Park as possible, and hopefully you two can be on your way to the campus before midnight. With any luck, you can get her and Jessica back to the boat and we can be out of here before daylight tomorrow."

There were a lot of unknowns and variables that could impact their plan, and as they sailed west through the lake, they discussed what they would do if things were not as they expected. One question that came up was the possibility that Casey would be taking refugee with several other friends, and would not want to leave them behind. Artie asked Larry what they would do if that were the case, and they decided that they could take as many as four more people on board, including Casey and Jessica, but any more would put too much of a strain on their supplies and the space available on board.

"We could shuttle a few more than that across the lake, or drop them off somewhere on our way back out to the Gulf, but we couldn't accommodate them long-term. I really hope it's just Casey and Jessica, because keeping enough food and fresh water on board is going to be enough of a challenge as it is."

"What *are* we going to do about water?" Artie asked. "We're getting low already."

"I know. We've got to take on more before we leave the mainland. The good thing about this area is that there are several freshwater rivers that empty into the Mississippi Sound. Since our draft is not a problem, we can sail up one of them, maybe the Pearl, just far enough to get beyond the tide range and top off our tanks. Thankfully, I've got plenty of filter cartridges for the galley pump filter, so we don't have to worry about getting sick from it. When we get to wherever we're going to hang out until this is over, I've got what we need to set up a rain catchment system for longer-term use."

Sailing under the Causeway illustrated the severity of the situation in New Orleans yet again. Like the Interstate 10 bridge, the lanes above them were full of abandoned vehicles and apparently the bodies of some of those who had waited too long to try to leave the city. There were the telltale flocks of circling vultures, though not in the concentrations they had seen on the Twin Span. They sailed under it without incident and continued some five miles farther west until they reached the point adjacent to the south shore that was nearest to the airport and the entrance to the canal that ran near it. Scully rounded up into the wind and Artie lowered the anchor from the bows. They were approximately a mile from land, far enough out to be safe from swimmers and to have a good escape route if someone ashore started heading their way in a rowing or sailing craft. While waiting for darkness to fall, they all stayed on deck to keep a sharp lookout for such dangers, and Artie changed his brother's bandages and inspected his wounds.

"You're doing good, little brother, considering the lack of proper medical treatment."

"What do you mean, 'proper'? I know you're a little rusty when it comes to ER trauma work but I think you did a passable job," Larry laughed. "It still hurts like hell, especially when I'm trying to sleep, and I still can't use it much, but at least it hasn't fallen off."

"Yet!" Artie said, "But, seriously, you're doing fine. Give it a little more time and you'll be good as new."

"Yeah, I know. I'm not complaining, I just wish I could go ashore with you and Scully. I'm worried about you, Doc."

"Well, as you said before, we have to worry about the boat too. We couldn't leave it alone in a place like this even if all three of us were able. I'm also worried about how you're going to defend it if someone does come out here while we're gone. We're going to have the shotgun."

"That's why we're anchored out this far. I know it's a pain in the ass for you and Scully to have to paddle an extra mile both ways, but if the breeze holds at all, as I think it will, at least I can sail off the anchor from out here if I have to. I don't think I can haul it in with one arm, but I can cut the rode. I know I can get the jib up, and that's enough to get going."

"I hope it doesn't come to that," Artie said. "I hope we can make this quick and get back out here so we can get over to the West End Park canal and then go get Casey."

"Me too, Doc. Me too."

They ate a meal of rice with rehydrated dried fish steamed on top of it as they watched the sun go down and twilight fall over the city spread across the land to the south of them. As in all the populated areas they had seen since arriving at Charlotte Amalie on St. Thomas, when darkness fell there were no streetlights, vehicle headlights, or any other significant man-made lights. They could, however, see the glow of countless fires in the increasing darkness, some of them apparently large and burning homes or buildings, and others scattered near the shoreline, pinpricks of light that were probably the campfires of frightened survivors. Artie and Scully lowered the kayak from the forward deck and climbed down into their seats, with Scully in the stern and Artie in the bow position. Larry handed down their gear before casting them off. Artie had the shotgun tucked under his legs, close at hand, and a small canvas shoulder bag of Larry's that contained his key ring, extra shotgun shells, a large fixed-blade dive knife, a hand-bearing compass, two LED flashlights with fresh batteries, and a pair of heavy-duty wire cutters from the ship's toolbox. Scully had his machete, the same one that had proven so effective in the fight against their unexpected visitors at Isleta Palominito.

Artie wasn't familiar with the use of the awkward, double-ended kayak paddle, but with some quick tips from Scully, he was soon able to contribute to their forward motion, though Scully's paddling was so strong and efficient it hardly mattered if Artie paddled at all. As they approached the shore, Artie began to feel nervous. There was no telling what they would find, and he feared a confrontation with desperate survivors who might want to take the kayak if they were seen.

"Got to stay quiet now, mon," Scully said as the opening to the man-made canal appeared in front of the bow. "Bettah if you don't paddle. I an' I don't make no splash. Got to creep up in dis place like a thief dem don't hear. Jus' keep dat shotgun ready," he whispered.

Just as he said, Scully's solo paddling was virtually silent, even from Artie's position just in front of him in the boat. He slowed down and carefully controlled each stroke, letting the blades enter and exit the water with as little disturbance as possible, exerting force only when each one was fully buried. In moments, they were off the open lake and within the confining banks of an arrow-straight, man-made ditch with undeveloped marsh on the west side to their right, and a high levee on to the east, forming the bank on their left. Beyond this grassy levee on the east side were the warehouses, office buildings, and city streets the levee was supposed to protect from rising waters in flood events such as the storm surge of hurricanes. From their perspective low on the water in the kayak, they could only see the rooflines of most of these structures, as well as the overhead power lines strung from poles running parallel to the avenues below them. Artie relaxed a bit, seeing that they were blocked from the view of anyone on the other side of the levee by its elevation, and that under the cover of darkness in the silent kayak they would likely be able to transit the canal unnoticed unless someone just happened to be on top of the levee looking out over the water. The marsh on the right side of the waterway was nothing but a flooded wetland of grass and low bushes, completely inhospitable to any kind of travel on foot, so they didn't have to worry about threats from that side. There were also numerous side channels leading off to the west on the marsh side of the canal, and these gave Artie even more comfort as they offered the possibility of an escape route other than just going back the way they had come. As they paddled, Scully also kept their course as close as possible to that marshy edge of the waterway, where they would be farther from anyone throwing or shooting something at them from the levee.

But, to Artie's relief, the entire area in the vicinity of the canal seemed lifeless and abandoned, as Larry had suggested it might when they were studying Craig's city map earlier as they planned their route. Few residents would have a reason to hang around a place like that, and the gangs would be more interested in controlling the busier streets where there were plenty of abandoned houses and stores that might still have useful goods in them.

Scully paddled steadily without speaking, while Artie scanned the water ahead for any signs of movement. Using the street map, they had calculated that the distance to the airport from where the canal began at the lakeshore was about three miles. It took them approximately forty-five minutes to reach the overpass of Interstate 10 where it crossed the canal, and from there it was another half mile or so to the edge of the airport property. The main waterway turned west just beyond these bridge spans, but there was a flooded ditch that continued on south in the direction they needed to go. What they soon discovered, though, was that it wasn't deep enough even for a kayak, much less any other kind of boat, and in places they had to both get out and wade in the muck, pulling the kayak along beside them as they slipped and stumbled along, sometimes sinking up to their knees in the soft mud of the bottom. It was tough going and took them twice as long as it would have taken to paddle the same distance in deep water.

When they came to the edge of the no man's land of empty, grassy space surrounding the airport, they found the expected perimeter fencing, a 12-foot-high, chain-link barrier with three strands of barbed wire at the top. Very conspicuous "No Trespassing" signs were wired to the fence at closely spaced intervals that no one could miss. Though they could have walked around the perimeter of the airport property and perhaps found a way into the long-term parking lot where Artie had left his car, they had decided in advance that would take too long and expose them to too many opportunities to be seen by people who might be on the nearby road. Going through the fence and proceeding in the most direct route was the best option. Airport security would have been out of commission since the first day after the event, and worrying about trespassers on that kind of property would be the last thing on anyone's mind now.

Artie took the wire cutters out of the backpack and went to work on the fence while Scully kept watch with the shotgun. As far as they could tell, there was no sign of life around the airport. Once they were inside the fence, they continued east, staying in the grassy perimeters of the property beyond the runways. Passing the terminals, they could see the outlines of the buildings and grounded jets that had been stranded when the pulse hit. They were too far away to see the details, and didn't want to pass any closer to the buildings than necessary, in case there were people still holing up in them. The walk to the parking area took nearly fifteen minutes, and in the darkness, Artie had to stop and try to get his bearings in order to remember the approximate location where he'd left his silver Chevy Tahoe.

As they made their way through the hundreds of vehicles parked there, he was surprised to see that only a few of them had smashed windows. But then it made sense that most looters would focus their attention elsewhere, as vehicles parked long-term at the airport would be unlikely to contain food or money. When he finally spotted his own, he was relieved to see that all the glass was intact. Knowing the electronic door opener on his key ring would be useless, he inserted the metal key into the door lock instead.

"Nice truck, dis," Scully whispered.

"It was at one time. I guess it's just a useless pile of junk now, like all the rest of these overpriced vehicles."

Artie slid behind the wheel into the driver's seat and unlocked the glove compartment. He was certain the pistol was still there, because not only was the compartment locked but so were his doors, with no glass broken. He felt around under the owner's manual packet and then pulled everything in the compartment out in disbelief. The pistol was *gone!* He was absolutely certain it had been there when he left the vehicle to check in for his flight, as he had consciously put his hands on it and covered it up with the manual before closing and locking the compartment door and getting out.

"Give me one of those flashlights, Scully!" he whispered. Turning it on, but keeping a hand cupped over most of the end of it to minimize the chances of it being seen from a distance, he directed the beam around the vehicle, onto the passenger seat and passenger side floorboard. Nothing else was out of place. Artie opened the lid to the center console compartment, despite knowing for certain that he had not put the pistol in there. As soon as he lifted it, a folded piece of notebook paper lying on top of his CDs and everything else he kept in there caught his eye. He took it out and turned it over to reveal what it could possibly be, knowing he had not left anything like that there.

His heart nearly stopped when saw that it was a letter and read the opening salutation: *"Dear Daddy."* Casey *had been here! It was a letter from Casey!* "Scully! She was here!" he whispered, barely able to contain himself from shouting out loud. "Hold on…let me see what she said." He continued reading.

I don't know if you will ever read this or not, but if you somehow find a way to make it back to New Orleans, I know you will be worried to death about me and will be looking for me everywhere. My friend Grant is leaving this in your car in case you couldn't get to my apartment for some reason and find the note I left for you there. If you read this before I see you again, I won't be here on the campus or even in the city. Things have gotten really bad here just one day after the lights went out. Jessica and I are leaving with Grant, who was here through Katrina and says that it would be far too dangerous to stay here with no power. He says that if we don't get out now, we may not be able to. My car won't start, of course, and hardly anybody has one that will. We are going to leave later this afternoon on our bicycles, because riding them is much faster than walking. Grant's family owns a cabin in the woods not far across the state line in Mississippi. He says we will be safe there, and I believe him. It is on a secluded river called the Bogue Chitto, and they have a well and lots of food and other gear stored there. He says we can stay there as long as it takes for the power to be restored. He drew a map that will tell you how to get there in case you find this before the power comes on. The map is on the back of this page. We won't be coming back here (until/unless?) that happens.

I have been thinking about you all the time since this happened and worrying about you out there on that boat, but I know you are with Uncle Larry and I'm sure he knows what to do and that you two are okay, wherever you are. I love you, Daddy, and I can't wait to see you again!

Love, Casey

Artie's hands were trembling as he read the last line. There was another note at the bottom of the page, written in a different handwriting that he knew was not Casey's.

Dear Dr. Drager:

I hope to get to meet you someday soon, I've heard a lot about you from your daughter. I want you to know that I will do everything in my power to keep her and Jessica safe. That's why we're going to my parents' cabin in

Mississippi. It is far off the beaten path and safe from the looters and desperate people who will soon be going crazy anywhere near the cities. I came here to leave this note for Casey before we get on our way. I hope you don't mind, but I found your .22 pistol and a box of ammo in the glove box. I know how to use it, so I borrowed it, because it is dangerous to travel now and I thought it would be a good idea to have it. I know it's unlikely you will be able to get here and read this, but I wanted you to know I will take care of it until I can meet you someday soon and return it to you in person.

Grant Dyer

Artie turned the letter over and for the first time saw the drawing on the back of the piece of paper. It was a map, just as Casey had said, roughly sketched, but with carefully printed labels in Grant's hand identifying roads along the route, which led north over the Causeway to the other side of Lake Pontchartrain, and continued on beyond the state line. Artie looked at the squiggly line denoting a river and the tiny square that showed the cabin. It was at the end of a long private lane that was labeled "dirt," which in turn was at the far end of a curvy country road labeled "gravel." In the margin, Grant had made a note that the approximate distance from Tulane to the cabin was 90 miles.

"Ninety miles!" Artie whispered to Scully. "She says she and Jessica left here on their bicycles with a guy friend of theirs, heading for his parents' cabin 90 miles to the north, on a remote river in Mississippi. They took my pistol for protection. They say they left the day after the lights went out."

"I t'ink she and Jessica smart girls, dem. Goin' to de river, dem havin' watah to drink, an' in de bush like dat, dem got some place to hide. Dis New Orleans dangerous place, mon."

"But you saw what I saw when we sailed under those bridges today." Artie couldn't imagine his daughter traveling in such conditions; the thought was too horrifying to contemplate. But aside from that, he could scarcely imagine her traveling that far on a bike even in normal times. "I don't know if Casey could ride a bike that far or not. She's never done anything that extreme that I know of, but she is reasonably fit."

"I t'ink she can, mon. When she and Jessica on de boat last summer, dem swimming strong every day. Paddle de kayak too. Not like most of dem tourist comin' to de island from Bobbylon on de cruise ship, layin' 'round on de beach like dem fat white whale, not to move 'cept goin' back to de buffet table to eat."

"Maybe so. At least I hope so. But I was counting on seeing her later tonight. I can't tell you how it feels to come this far, and think I'm so close, only to find out she's not here, though I've feared all along that might be the case."

"It's good dem got de young mon wid, and de pistol too. You said de note was written jus' de day after Jah strike down de lights. I t'ink we gonna find dem safe in dat cabin he put on de map."

"I hope you're right, Scully, but getting there will probably be a lot harder and more dangerous than trying to get to the Tulane campus. It looks like that cabin is way out in the middle of nowhere across the state line in Mississippi. One thing is for sure, we can't *sail* there, and it sure is a long way to walk. What are we going to do?"

"First t'ing, Doc, is we get outta dis place an' bok to de boat. De Copt'n probably gonna have a plan when we discuss dis problem wid he. But we knowin' now de girls dem not here. Too dangerous to stay in here for no reason now."

"Yeah, let's go." Artie closed the glove compartment and center console, and reached into the back seat to get a small bag with an extra change of clothes he usually kept there when he traveled. Other than that, there was little of use in the Tahoe, so he got out and locked the door, and they hurried back across the airport property to the kayak. Thoughts of Casey's journey with her friends ran through his mind with every step as he tried to picture the scene on that day when they left New Orleans on their bicycles. He had heard Casey talk about Grant, but had never met him. He could only hope that he was a young man who had a good head on his shoulders. The fact that he found and took the pistol showed that at least he was somewhat resourceful and recognized the possible need for it. It was also comforting that he'd written in the note that he knew how to use it. Artie could only hope that was true, and also that Grant wouldn't have the need to prove it.

ELEVEN

"WHAT ARE WE GOING to do when it gets dark?" Jessica asked Grant. "Are we going to keep going, or stop?" The sun had dropped behind the tops of the trees in the forest surrounding the Bogue Chitto and the day was quickly fading into twilight.

"I would keep going if I *knew* he was still paddling, but at night there's too much chance of running up on them in the darkness or even passing them if they stopped to camp somewhere out of sight of the river, which is what I would do in his place. Considering that, I don't want to risk missing them entirely and somehow getting ahead of them on the river, or worse, getting shot."

"But if he does keep going, we'll never catch them, will we?"

"That's always possible, but there's no way to know what he might be thinking. I know the farther downstream we get, the more we'll begin passing side creeks and sloughs that connect to the river. Most of them don't go very far, but someone in a canoe could easily hide in any of them. I don't want to pass them in the dark, because I want to stop at every creek and look for signs that they may have turned off the river. We really have no way of knowing where this guy may be going, Jessica. The big swamps down on the lower Pearl River are a good guess, but a guess is really all we have."

"I'm so scared for Casey," Jessica said. "Trying to find one person out here is like looking for a needle in a haystack, even if she is in a canoe. And what if he has already raped and killed her! He could have dumped her out in the river or hidden her body in the woods by now and we would never know."

"I don't think he would have done that, Jessica. He knew we were still in the vicinity and that we had a canoe. He may not think we could have figured out he had her when we saw him, but he wouldn't take a chance by stopping right away to do anything to her. And besides, I don't think he would kill her any time soon anyway. If that had been his intention, he wouldn't have bothered to take her with him. I think he's trying to take her somewhere and take his time doing what he wants to do to her. At least that's what it seems like guys like that do from the news stories I've read and crime documentaries I've seen."

"I'll never understand those sickos. What could be so wrong with someone that they think they can do horrible things to another human being? How can anyone not have a conscience?"

"They're psychopaths, I guess."

"I know one thing, it doesn't matter if we stop for the night or not, or how tired I am, I won't be getting any sleep tonight thinking about what she must be going through. I just can't believe this is happening, Grant."

"Me either, and I will worry about her all night too, but we've got to try to get some rest since we can't travel anyway. Tomorrow will be a long and hard day, and we may need every ounce of our combined strength both to catch this guy and to help Casey when we do catch him."

Grant slowed his paddling as the darkness increased, carefully guiding the canoe among the many snags of fallen trees that protruded from the current, waiting to tip an unwary or unskilled canoeist. He was looking for a good place for them to stop for the night, not out on one of the exposed sandbars, which would be his first choice if this were a mere recreational camping trip, but someplace that would allow them to pass the night out of sight of anyone else who might chance along by river or afoot. He found the perfect spot at the end of a long horseshoe bend, where a sandbar tapered to a narrow sliver and a clay bank three feet high bordered the river. The hardwood forest here was made up of mature timber, and the undergrowth was sparse. Grant guided the canoe alongside the bluff and held it while Jessica climbed out. Then he stepped out and pulled the boat up over the bank and away from the river until it was hidden among the trees. It was much darker within the edge of the forest—so dark they could barely see each other. Grant crept back to the riverbank and reached out to take Jessica's hand, guiding her to where he'd pulled the canoe.

"I can't see *anything*," Jessica whispered. This is just like that place we camped last night."

"Yeah, but at least it's not raining, and I think we're going to have good weather for a few days. I'm not going to bother with the tarp, if that's okay with you. We can just spread it out on the ground and sleep on top of it."

"I'm scared of snakes after what you said last night."

"I don't think we have to worry too much. You see how quickly it's gotten cool since the sun went down. That's one good thing about these weather fronts that come through this time of year. After the rain passes it always turns cool for a few days afterwards. I'll bet the temps will drop into the low 50s or high 40s tonight. Reptiles generally aren't moving at night when it's that cool—same with bugs. It'll be nice not to have to worry about mosquitoes, because in hot weather in the woods along these rivers, they would eat you alive at night."

"It *is* getting cold. Can we build a fire tonight since it's not raining?"

"I don't think we should. I wanted to camp out of sight in the woods to be on the safe side, even though I think it's highly unlikely anyone would be coming down the river at night. And although I'm pretty sure we're still a good distance behind this guy who's got Casey, building a fire would defeat the purpose of camping up here instead of out in the open. There is a little bit of propane left in the one canister we have, though. We can use the stove to make some hot chocolate and cook the last of the rice packets. Maybe if we do that quickly, there will be enough left to heat water for oatmeal in the morning. You can have what's left of that too. I'm going to try and catch a fish tonight for my breakfast."

"How are you going to see to fish in this dark?"

"Not the kind of fishing you're thinking about, Jessica. There were some hooks and trotline in that tackle box where we got the canoe. I'm going to take some small pieces of the beef jerky I have left and use it to bait some drop hooks. What you do is tie them to a branch hanging out over a deep, still hole in the river, like the one just upstream, and leave it out all night. With any luck at all, a catfish will come along and smell the bait and hook itself when it swallows it. Jerky isn't ideal, but that's all I've got. I hope soaking it in the water for a few hours on the hook will soften it up and it will still have enough smell to work."

"Well, good luck with it, but I hope we can find a riverside salad bar for me tomorrow. I'm looking forward to trying those cattails you were talking about."

Grant left her for a few minutes and carefully picked his way along the riverbank in the dark. He had been trying to maintain a positive attitude as much as possible in front of Jessica, but he was overwhelmed with fear of what would become of Casey, and full of doubt that they could ever even find her, much less rescue her, out in the vastness of these river woodlands with no help. More then the fear though, he felt guilt for his own failure to protect her. He realized now he should have never left her alone to guard the stupid bicycles. They should have all stuck together and none of this would have happened. He had brought them both out here to the middle of nowhere with the promise of a safe refuge, and now look where that had gotten them. Not only was Casey in immediate and grave peril (if she were still alive), but he had now gotten Jessica, who was completely inexperienced in any life outside of a city, into a hardcore wilderness survival situation. It was up to him to somehow provide for her safety, shelter, and food, as well as take care of his own needs.

He found branches from which to hang four drop hooks. It was hard to tell in the darkness if the locations were ideal, but all he could do was hope for the best. This wasn't a method he'd learned from the Wapishana in Guayana, but rather a technique used by the locals on the Bogue Chitto and most other rivers in the South to catch catfish. The beauty of it was that it was passive—setting out hooks was like setting a trap. You could forget about it and do other things and it would either work or it wouldn't, depending on whether the quarry took the bait.

He returned to Jessica's side by the canoe as quickly as possible, knowing she was terrified to be out in these dark woods and devastated by what had happened to Casey. She said she wasn't hungry, but when the last of the cheddar-broccoli rice packets was cooked on the stove and he offered her most of it, she wolfed it down. Then he heated water for hot chocolate and they sat close together sipping it, leaning back side by side against the hull of the canoe, talking about Casey and trying to reassure each other that she would be okay. Grant knew the next day would likely be long and hard and they would need their sleep, but neither of them could relax because of their worries. He spread their sleeping bags on the tarp, putting Jessica's next to the canoe and his close by on the other side, shielding her from the dangers she was certain lurked in the inky blackness surrounding them. Before lying down, he stuck the point of his machete in the soft ground so that the handle was within easy reach, though he knew there was nothing in the wild to fear here and the chances of a human intruder stumbling across their camp in the night were slim to none. But they had barely settled into their bags to try to rest when a barred owl unleashed its demonic, half-laughing, half-screaming, and utterly ear-piercing cry into the forest close by. Jessica grabbed him in a panic and nearly suffocated him in her arms, terrified by a sound that he had assumed everyone was familiar with.

"What in the *hell* was that?" she whispered, barely able to breathe in her choking fear.

Grant laughed a little and hugged her back to reassure her. "It's just an owl. They're common here in these big hardwood forests. We'll probably hear them all night. They're perfectly harmless."

"That was worse than something from a horror movie! I'm so scared, Grant. I believe you that it was an owl, but I'm so scared after what happened to Casey." Her tears flowed freely as she clung to him, and soon she was sobbing uncontrollably. Grant felt his own eyes moisten as he stroked her hair as if she were a little girl and tried to reassure her.

Jessica stayed snuggled up against his shoulder the remainder of the night, and when he opened his eyes, he realized they both must have fallen fast asleep. The impenetrable darkness of night was replaced by a thick morning mist that hung over the river like heavy smoke. Birdcalls and the barking chatter of gray squirrels echoed through the forest.

It was cool enough that Grant thought about a hot cup of coffee with great anticipation, but he then he remembered his hooks and gently pulled himself away from Jessica to go check them.

When he got to the river's edge, the first two hooks were just as he'd left them, and when he pulled them up the jerky had swollen to the consistency of raw bacon, but was untouched. He pushed his way through the river cane to the next hook and saw that the branch he'd tied it to was bobbing up and down. When he grabbed the line, there was strong resistance as he pulled it in and he found on the other end a nice, sleek catfish that he guessed weighed at least two pounds. He grinned as he hooked a finger through one of its gills so it couldn't get away, and checked the last hook with heightened enthusiasm, but found it empty. He was thrilled with his success nevertheless, as this fish represented a good meal that would make a fine breakfast for both of them—if only Jessica could get over her aversion to eating things from outside the plant kingdom.

Back at the canoe, he used the machete to cut a small sapling down and quickly cut three equal-length stakes from it, about a foot long. The propane left in the single bottle he'd brought was barely enough to heat some oatmeal for Jessica. He decided to save it since it wasn't enough to cook the fish with anyway. In this heavy morning mist, he felt it was safe to build a quick twig fire that would put out very little smoke, so he made a tripod of the green sapling pieces by pushing one end of each one into the ground so that the tops were spaced just a few inches apart—just the right distance to support the cooking pot.

Jessica was awakened by the whacking of his blade and sat up to watch him build the fire. "I can't believe you caught a fish that easily. That's amazing."

"Not really. Any good fisherman in these parts who knows what he's doing would have probably caught at least two or three, if not four, with four sets. I hate to waste time cooking anything, but this will only take minutes. If we don't eat, we won't be able to paddle all day. I sure wish you would try some of this."

"I'm okay, really. You said there was oatmeal."

"Yeah, but only enough for today. After that, it's gone, and we're down to a few almonds and raisins."

Grant put the pot on top of the tripod and collected a handful of pencil-sized dry twigs from dead branches still on the trees in the vicinity. He got the fire started and instructed Jessica to feed it with just a few twigs at a time while he went to the riverbank to clean the catfish. There wasn't time to do it right, so rather than worry about trying to remove the tough skin typical of the species, he simply gutted it and cut off the head, then split it into two halves and washed these in the river. He was so hungry for meat he could have eaten them raw, but a kiss of the flames for a few minutes would make the fish much tastier and would be simple and quick enough. When the pot of water was boiling, he poured enough for Jessica's oatmeal in her bowl, then added some ground coffee to the rest. Then he laid the fish halves over the flames.

"So, what made you decide to become a vegetarian? Casey told me you made that choice before she met you at Tulane."

"Yeah, I had thought about it a lot since I was in about the seventh grade, I guess, when we learned in school how animals were treated in modern factory farming. The more I learned about it from reading on the Internet and all, the more I realized how cruel it really is to raise animals for meat. I decided to give up eating all chicken and beef and things like that first, then the more I got into the vegetarian lifestyle, the more I realized I didn't even want fish or seafood, or any kind of animal foods that require killing the animal. I still eat cheese, and occasionally drink milk. I just don't eat meat. It's been four years now, and I feel fine."

"Well, I can understand how the details of factory farming could be disturbing, but you do realize that humans have been eating meat as well as plant foods since the dawn of time, don't you? The thing that bothers me about vegetarianism is that it implies we are somehow 'above' or 'better than' the other species, when in fact, we are animals too, and are subject to the laws of nature just like all species, despite our technology, which, as you can see, has failed us miserably now. Anyway, as an anthropology student, I find it a fascinating topic. I'm not trying to put you down or change your mind, I'm just trying to understand, that's all."

"I know most primitive people ate meat. But it's just not necessary today. We don't have to live that way because we have infinite choices available to us now."

"*Had* infinite choices," Grant reminded her as he used his pocketknife to turn the two slabs of fish over in the flames. "Everything's changed now. Getting all that variety of fruits, veggies, and grains delivered to your neighborhood grocery store is a thing of the past until the whole system gets rebuilt, as you are well aware by now. Regardless of that, we are presently in an environment not unlike that of our distant primal ancestors. I can assure you that I have learned through my extensive studies of the subject, and my time spent living among the Wapishana, who are among the few truly aboriginal people left in the world today, sustaining human life from plant food alone is extremely difficult, if not impossible, in the wilderness. I hope you can see the difference between eating this fish, caught from the wild in the river, compared to fattening up chickens or hogs on growth hormones in inhumane cages for slaughter. If I didn't eat this fish, chances are a hungry alligator or a bigger fish would."

"I can see your point. I'm not saying I'll *never* eat it. I'd much sooner eat that than a rabbit or something. I just hope it doesn't come to that."

"I'm afraid that it will, Jessica. That's my point. Our situation isn't going to change, and I don't want to see you get weak or sick as a result of clinging to an unsustainable lifestyle." Grant lifted the fish off the flames and quickly put out the fire by kicking sand over the burning twigs. He poured them each a cup of coffee and squatted next to the canoe, where he began pulling chunks of half-cooked fish off the bones and skin with his fingers. It was the best meal he'd had since leaving New Orleans.

"It *does* smell good cooked," Jessica said, as she ate the last bite of oatmeal. "I'm not saying I won't eat fish, I'm just not ready today, okay?"

"I'll tell you one thing I'm going to miss the most about civilization," Grant said, "and that is coffee. What we have left will last three, maybe four days, and then we'll be caffeine-free for good, unfortunately."

With no tarp or tent to take down, breaking camp and getting back on the river took only minutes. The mist hanging over the water limited their visibility, so Grant took it easy and paddled as silently as possible, instructing Jessica how to do the same. He felt sure that they were still a good distance behind Casey and her abductor, but he didn't want to take a chance. The sun would soon burn away the fog, and then they could focus on making up lost time.

As they paddled around the wide, looping bends of the river, they passed huge sand and gravel bars on almost all of the inside bends. Grant knew that this part of the Bogue Chitto was the site of extensive gravel mining, but that most of the operations were just out of sight of the river. Paddling this way before in normal times, he'd heard the sound of bulldozers and other machinery off in the distance almost constantly in the daylight hours. He knew all this must have shut down the first day after the lights went out, and didn't expect to see anyone associated with that work out on the river. Other people that would use the sandbars before the solar flare occurred were recreational weekend canoeists and some of the local country folk who loved to ride four-wheeler ATVs across these wide beaches and through the shallows.

As they paddled by these wide beaches, Grant kept their course as close as possible to the edge of the sand, scanning for signs that the man who had Casey had stopped on any of them. Grant knew he had to stop sometime, if for no other reason than to get out of the canoe and relieve himself. Since it had been less than a full day after the heavy rains let up, Grant figured that it was unlikely anyone else had visited any of these sandbars, except for those that were near the occasional camps that were scattered along the river course here and there. Stopping at each one and getting out for a close examination would take far too long, but he surmised that if Casey's abductor had indeed stopped, the evidence would be right at the water's edge anyway, and his theory proved correct after they had been paddling about an hour or so.

"There!" he said, as he quickly dug his paddle in and did a correction stroke to turn the bow into shore.

"What is it, do you see them?" Jessica asked, as she scanned the river ahead, thinking Grant was looking that way.

"He stopped right here!" Grant said as he leapt out of the canoe and pulled it up for Jessica. As soon as she was out he warned her not to walk over the tracks and then he crouched down to see if he could make sense of them.

"Yep, it was him! Look, it's the same footprints, those moccasins or whatever they are that he's wearing. The tracks are identical to the ones on the sandbar where he took Casey. Now we know for sure he's still ahead of us, somewhere on the river. See, there's the mark he made when he pulled his canoe up, like I just did with ours." Grant followed a straight line of the tracks off across the sandbar to where a lone, stunted cypress tree stood weathered and broken out in the open. "He walked over here to pee," he called back to Jessica, then he went back to the canoe.

"I don't see any other tracks," Jessica said.

"He probably didn't let Casey get out. That could be a good sign. At least he didn't make her get out so he could try to rape her or something." Grant was still bent over, looking carefully at the tracks. The man had walked back and forth around the place where he stopped the canoe quite a bit, and the details were vague as there were prints on top of prints.

"I'm amazed at how you can tell all this just from looking at the ground. I would have never thought of any of that."

"I only know the very basics. If it wasn't for all the sand along this river, I wouldn't know any of it—even that Casey had been taken. Real experts, like the Wapishana hunters I spent time with, could find and read signs even in dense jungle where you can't see the ground. But that's what they do for a living. At any rate, I know he stopped here, and I'm sure Casey must still be with him, but then again, I can't even prove that without a single track of hers to be found. And I'm afraid I'm not good enough to tell if these prints were made last night or sometime earlier this morning."

"So, you think they're still somewhere ahead of us?"

"They pretty much have to be downstream, the question is how far. Come on, let's go."

Over the course of the next four or five miles they paddled before noon, the character of the river and its surrounding forest began changing somewhat. Occasional
areas of high bluffs with pine trees on them gave way to
almost unbroken hardwood forest and large stands of cypress. In many stretches the sandbars disappeared, with the
river's edge running right up to the bases of the cypress
and tupelo trees. They passed several sloughs connecting
the river to dead oxbow lakes left behind long ago when the
river had changed its course over time, and at the entrance
to each of these, Grant stopped to investigate and look for
any clue that the man who had Casey might have turned off
the river. He looked for tracks in the mud and on both sides
of each tributary, but only near their entrances, as it would
have killed the entire day to paddle each one to where it
came to a dead end. Each time he stopped he came to the
conclusion that the mysterious paddler must be still ahead
of them, and each time they got underway, he dug in and
paddled hard with renewed determination not to give up
until they caught up with him.

★ ★ ★

The hours of darkness seemed to Casey to go on forever, lying bound in the bottom of the canoe, watching the trees go
by overhead against a backdrop of starry sky while worrying
about what was to become of her. This man who had taken
her against her will, who called himself Derek, relentlessly
and tirelessly paddled hour after hour, expertly guiding the
canoe among the countless snags and fallen logs that were

everywhere in the river. Sometimes he spoke to her, but for the most part he was quiet while he paddled, and she was glad he was. She had no idea how far they'd come since he had found her the afternoon before, but at this pace she knew it had to be many miles, and with every hour they were on the river, she was being taken deeper and deeper into a land of swamps and forest that separated her from everyone and everything she knew.

When the first pale grays of dawn replaced the darkness, he turned off of the river into an opening in the forest, and paddled into a stagnant, smelly slough of still water. At the far end he ran the bow of the canoe into the stinking mud and hopped out to pull it aground. "We'll stop here awhile," he said, "and rest and eat."

Casey didn't want to acknowledge him, but she *was* hungry and thirsty, and more than anything, her bladder was about to burst and she couldn't hold it any longer. "I have to go to the bathroom," she said.

"Of course. I'll untie you so you can go over there in the bushes. But don't get any ideas. This is an island with the river on one side and a dead lake on the other. There's no way out of here on foot, and I'm going to be right over here. Believe me when I tell you, you cannot outrun me out here, so don't bother trying."

Derek squatted behind her and worked at the lashings binding her wrists, and then he untied her ankles. "I'm sorry I've had to keep you all trussed up like this, but you understand I couldn't have you jumping out of the canoe or something."

Casey avoided eye contact with him as she rubbed her wrists and ankles and tried to get the circulation going in them again. Now that the morning light was getting brighter, she could see a bit more of what he looked like. He was tall and lanky but it was hard to tell much about how he was built because of his loose-fitting clothes—olive drab military fatigues and an untucked, long-sleeved shirt that was a couple of shades darker green than the pants. The most unusual thing about the way he was dressed was his foot-wear—tall, over-the-calf moccasins that looked to be home-made from some kind of animal hide. From what she could see of his hands and bearded face, he was deeply tanned, as if he spent a lot of time outdoors, and his shoulder-length hair was shaggy and somewhere between blond and light brown. His movements suggested that he was fit and at ease in this environment, as he showed no signs of fatigue despite paddling all night without rest.

After he untied her, he ignored her while he pulled one of his backpacks out of the canoe and rummaged through it for something. "Go ahead and do your business," he said, "just don't go far."

Casey was both surprised and greatly relieved that he would offer to let her have her privacy. She had been hold-ing it all night because she was so afraid that he wouldn't and had decided she would sooner pee in her pants than have him see her naked, though she knew he had seen her bathing. She pulled herself up out of the canoe with dif-ficulty, and nearly fell back down as she waited for the numbness to go away in her feet. She stepped over the gunwale into the muck and wet leaves of the forest floor, still barefoot because she had left her shoes on the log where she had undressed for her bath. She picked her way carefully over fallen branches and around thorny vines, feeling the disgusting, foul-smelling mud of the swamp squishing up between her toes with every step until she had gone far enough to screen herself from his view with foliage.

When she stood again, she thought about running as fast as she could in the opposite direction, but peering through the trees and bushes that limited her view to just a few dozen yards, she could see that there was indeed more water that way, just as Derek had said. With no shoes, she knew it would be hard for her to walk fast, much less run with all the protruding cypress knees, fallen branches, and twisted briar vines covered with thorns that were everywhere on the forest floor. From the ease with which Derek moved and paddled the canoe, she knew he was in good shape, and she doubted she could outsprint him even in open terrain. She resigned herself to the hard truth that there was no use trying to escape right now. It would be better to wait for another opportunity when she had a better chance of succeeding, and she was determined to find one, and not miss it when it presented itself.

When she made her way back over to the canoe, Derek had just finished tying a dark green cloth hammock between two nearby trees. "I've got to get some sleep," he said. "I hate to have to do it, but I've got to tie your hands and feet again. You can sleep in the bottom of the canoe if you like. I'll move my stuff out to give you more room. I don't plan to stay here more than four or five hours though, and then we're going to be on the move again."

Casey had no choice but to submit to being tied up again. At least this time he tied her hands in front of her body instead of behind her back, so she could lie down comfortably. He had also tied a piece of light rope between her bound ankles and one of his own wrists, so that when he fell asleep in the hammock he would know if she was trying to get away. She resigned herself to wait. The only way to escape now would be to somehow untie her wrists with her teeth without waking him, and then launch the canoe and paddle away in it. She knew that was hopeless, as his hammock was strung squarely in the path the canoe would have to be dragged to get it afloat again.

They were back on the river around noon, and to Casey's surprise she too had dozed off to sleep in the bottom of the canoe while Derek slept in the hammock. Fear had kept her awake the entire previous night, but today exhaustion had caught up with her, and in a more comfortable position, she probably slept at least two hours. As they traveled through the afternoon, she was once again low in the canoe among his gear bags, and more than once he pulled the tarp over her head to hide her when they passed riverside cabins. He did refrain from using the gag or blindfold again, but he told her any outcry in the vicinity of anyone they happened to pass would be met with a swift blow from the paddle that would knock her out. She had no reason to doubt that he would do it, and kept quiet, even when he exchanged a few words with a man who was fishing on the bank near one of the weekend getaway camps they passed.

Just as she could no longer resist sleep, hunger overcame her that second day as well, and the next time they stopped she accepted some of the smoked venison jerky he had offered her before. It was surprisingly delicious, even better than the processed beef variety Grant had bought that first day when they had stocked up at the grocery store near campus. She knew it could have been simply that she was really hungry, but this stuff was delicious. After trying it she ate another piece.

"Venison," Derek said. "I eat it year round; it's much better than eating fat, grain-fed cattle. I hunt year round too, even before, when it was illegal and there were people trying to enforce their idiotic laws. Now most of the people that thought up laws like that are probably dead already— too stupid to survive in a world without a government to take care of them."

"This isn't going to last forever," Casey said, "and it's no excuse to break the law and do as you please. But I don't care if you kill deer out of season and want to live in a swamp. Just please let me go. I'll walk back to where you found me, and you can just go on and do whatever you want to do."

"You know I can't do that. I can't let a beautiful young woman like you take off walking on the roads the way things are now. You still don't get it, but I'm *saving* you. I'm doing you a favor and saving you from the fate that would have awaited you if I hadn't come along, and will still catch up to your two friends. I don't think you understand, but most people are going to die as a result of the power grid going down. Most of them don't have the will to do what it takes to survive, but I'm different, and always have been. I've been literally *living* for a time like this. I've been *preparing* for it and *knowing* it would happen eventually. The artificial lifestyle you and everyone you know has been living is just that—*artificial.* It's not *real,* and it could not go on indefinitely. Now, at last, we get a chance to live a life that is real, and I've chosen you to be my partner in that life. I know it's all new and unfamiliar to you and maybe a little frightening, but I'm going to teach you. You're going to love it when you get used to it, and we're going to live in a beautiful place—a nearly perfect place that is wild and natural—where we will have everything we need, and be free, like our ancestors were before modern civilization screwed everything up."

"You're insane," Casey said. "I would rather die than be anywhere, even in a paradise, with someone who would do what you did to me. I don't know where you came up with your fantasy, but it doesn't involve me! Why didn't you bring your wife or girlfriend, or whatever? Oh, never mind, you probably never had one. You're too weird to get one! And you're completely wrong if you think I needed 'saving' from anything. My friend Grant knew what he was doing, and we had a place to go where we would be safe and have everything we would need until this was all over."

Derek's only response was to laugh. He was genuinely insane, of that she was certain—insane in a dangerous way, but she felt more confident than ever that he wouldn't hurt her, at least not deliberately, unless she tried to escape or cry out to someone. It seemed that he really believed his delusion that she would eventually be grateful to him for 'rescuing' her, and that they would somehow live off the land deep in some swamp hideaway, like some kind of happy pioneer couple or something.

Back on the river, Derek continued to rant about the evils of civilization as he paddled the canoe. He told her that he had never fit into modern society, and had known he was not meant to live that way ever since childhood. Instead of playing sports in school, he spent every spare minute hunting and fishing, and often played hooky to get in more time doing so. He said that as an adult, he hated working for money, and didn't want most of the things it could buy anyway. He mostly did odd jobs on a friend's farm and then took off for weeks at a time to live in the woods and do what he really wanted to do. In between these excursions he read everything he could get his hands on about the way the Indians and later the white trappers and explorers had lived before the whole country was settled and tamed and completely ruined, as he saw it. He practiced their skills and learned to use every part of the animals he killed, pointing out the deerskin moccasins he wore as an example to her. Then he said that he had a brain-tanned deer hide rolled up in his bags and promised that once they got to his secret camp he would make her a pair of nice moccasins like his, since she didn't have her shoes.

He talked about the solar flare and how everybody in modern America was so dependent upon electric power that they didn't know how to do anything else but go apeshit crazy when the lights went out. He said they were all so stupid they would just sit and wait for the government to bail them out and only a few would take any initiative to do anything, and then, if they did, it would be the wrong thing.

"I may have hated school," he said, "but I'm not some ignorant dumbass backwoods hick like most people around here. I didn't like somebody else telling me what to read and having to take a test on it, but that doesn't mean I didn't like to read. I studied what I wanted to learn about on my own and one thing that always interested me was the history of various cultures and especially the decline of ancient civilizations. I was into a lot of philosophy too, especially Thoreau and the ancient Chinese Taoist teachings. Do you know who Lao Tzu was? Have you ever read the Tao Te Ching? Would you like to hear what my favorite quote of his was? "Water flows in the places men reject." You can see now how true this is. Look at this river, for instance. It winds and twists for more than a hundred miles through some of the finest woods and wild lands left anywhere in these parts, and what do all those 'civilized' idiots do? They sit in those square boxes they call houses or take off down the road, stuck in their way of thinking that nature has to be shaped and conformed to their needs, and not the other way around. All the while, this river flows nearby, twisting quietly and unnoticed through these for-gotten 'places that men reject,' offering a route of travel, a refuge, food to eat and water to drink. Yet they're just too blind to see it. That's why they will die, and that's why they deserve to. We're entering a new era now, and those who can't figure out fast that they've got to give up on their technology are not going to be a part of it. It might be hard for a while until the die-off is complete, but give it a good year or so and we won't have to lie low in one area anymore. There'll be so few people around that there will be room enough for everyone who is smart enough to still be here. Then we can live the way we were meant to—free—as nomadic hunter-gatherers roaming whenever and wherever we please. There will be others like us too, and it will take time to reconnect, but someday we will eventually join together and form new tribes. By then, we will be fully adapted to the old ways, and this transition period will be a distant memory."

Casey had to listen to this for hour upon hour as Der-ek paddled. The longer they were together, the more he talked, but he wasn't really trying to engage her in conver-sation. For the most part she didn't bother trying to argue with him, and had given up on asking him to let her go. They traveled through the rest of the afternoon and another night, and the farther downriver they went, the lower and swampier the terrain surrounding the river became. By now, the wide sandbars that were in nearly every bend upstream were non-existent, replaced by low, muddy banks where the forest reached right to the river's edge and the understory was a green wall of head-high palmettos. The current in this lower part of the Bogue Chitto was much slower, but Derek's tireless stroke kept the canoe slicing through the nearly still water at the same relentless pace. Before dawn they passed a man-made canal extending north and south, and the Bogue Chitto reached the end of its course, becoming less defined as a separate river as it joined a maze of channels and bayous of a much larger river system flowing south to the Gulf.

"This is the Pearl," he said. "We're home free now. There are miles and miles of winding little bayous in this swamp that are so small a canoe can barely pass through them. I've been coming here for years, and I've found one of the most remote spots in the entire basin that I always figured would be my go-to place when the shit finally hit the fan. You couldn't find a better hideout anywhere in the state, you'll see. There's no way in and no way out except by canoe or pirogue, but everything we need is already there."

Casey saw nothing but woods and water. She found it hard to believe, but the entire time they had been in the canoe she had seen little else but woods and water, save for the occasional cabin built on the riverbank, and a couple of highway bridges they had passed under. If she had not seen all this for herself, she would have never believed there could possibly be so many endless miles of woods and water along a river course so close to the huge urban sprawl of New Orleans.

Now that they were in this swamp where even the boundaries of the river disappeared in walls of flooded forest on either side, Casey felt more lost than ever. When Derek turned the canoe off of the broad waterway they had been following and into a narrow bayou barely two canoe-widths wide, she knew that she was utterly and thoroughly hidden away from the outside world and completely out of reach of anyone who might save her from this man who was determined to keep her that way.

The canopy was completely interlocked overhead on this route, so it was so dark Casey could barely see a few feet beyond the bow of the canoe. Derek slowed down to a drifting pace, using his paddle only to keep them from banging against trees as the current flowing beneath the boat carried it deeper into the forest. When dawn finally came, Casey saw that they were gliding among hardwood and cypress trees of tremendous, primeval proportions. It was a place like no other she had ever seen, with long, wispy curtains of Spanish moss hanging from almost every branch and limb, creating a mysterious, haunting atmosphere that was both beautiful and foreboding.

The waterway they were following lost all definition in a labyrinth of narrow swift sections interspersed with lagoons where it spread out and surrounded the boles of the giant trees, making it impossible for her to understand how anyone could find their way through it. Derek paddled as if he knew exactly where he was going, though, and here in the hush of early morning in this cathedral-like forest, he remained silent once again, much to her relief, after having heard hours of his indictment of modern civilization the afternoon and evening before. In places the canoe was swept by low-hanging branches, forcing her to duck even from where she was seated in the bottom of the boat, propped up against a duffel bag. When this had happened several times, Derek stopped and cut her hands loose so she could fend off branches before they hit her in the face. She knew he wasn't worried about her escaping now, as there was absolutely nowhere to go in a place like this without a boat.

They had been traveling in this manner for a good two hours since they left the main river, when Derek turned off to their left onto yet another branch of the bayou they had been following. This one was even narrower, but to Casey's surprise, the water was clear and the bottom was white sand instead of mud. Small sandbars, miniature versions of the huge beaches in the bends of the Bogue Chitto, lined the banks intermittently, and at last Derek stopped and pulled the canoe onto one that had a flat shelf at the top just wide enough to accommodate it.

"We're here," he said. "Welcome to my little piece of paradise."

Casey said nothing as Derek untied the ropes holding her ankles together and began taking his duffel bags and packs out of the canoe. She climbed out, grateful for the opportunity to stretch her stiff joints, but when she looked around, she saw no sign of a camp. There was a narrow path leading off through the palmettos, though, and she could see that somebody had made it by cutting their way through there. Derek stepped into the path and motioned for her to follow.

Not wanting him to grab her arm and lead her or touch her in any way, she complied. The terrain rose slightly and the vegetation in the understory changed from the tropical-looking fronds of the dwarf palmettos to a dense thicket of sweet bay bushes, their waxy emerald-green leaves screening from view what might lie ahead at the other end of the path until they pushed their way through.

"There it is," Derek said. "My perfect bug-out hideaway."

Casey had not expected anything quite like this. When she looked where Derek was pointing, she saw a shelter that blended in so well with its surroundings that it would be easy to miss even from a short distance unless you were specifically looking for it. It was the primitive construction of mostly natural materials that made it blend in so well, though the camouflage tarps that made up the roof and one side certainly did their part to help.

The most unexpected thing about it was that it was built about 10 feet off the ground, on a platform of poles cut from small trees, lashed horizontally between four much larger hardwood trees, like a much bigger version of a child's tree house. As they walked closer, she saw a crude ladder going up to it, also made from lashed poles, and then saw that the floor was made up of very old and weathered-looking planks of wood. Rolled up mosquito netting was hung from the edges of the roof all the way around and a tarp formed a single wall at the back, but otherwise the structure was open-sided. She could see that that the only things in there were some camo-colored five-gallon plastic pails with lids on them and a stack of large, square metal boxes, the olive-drab green kind that Casey knew were Army surplus ammo cans.

Beneath the platform, a heavy wire was stretched on a diagonal between two of the supporting trees. Suspended from it hung several skillets, cooking pots and utensils, and an axe and shovel. A fire pit was dug in the sand nearby, framed on both sides by chunks of heavy logs that obviously had been chopped to length by the axe.

"It's built above the forest floor like this to stay above high water in times of flooding," Derek said. "This is an island we're on here, though you can't tell because of all the trees. It's one of the highest elevations in the area, and it's rare that the bayou gets over the bank, though I have seen it happen in the years I've been coming here. But regardless of floods, there are always plenty of big cottonmouth snakes in these palmetto thickets, and everywhere else in the swamp. It's a lot better sleeping off the ground, and a lot cooler in the summer too. This is the way the Indians that lived in these parts built their houses, and it makes sense to do the same."

"How can you plan to *live* in a place like this?" Casey asked, tears starting to roll down her face as she slapped at the mosquitoes that were buzzing around her head and neck. "There is nothing here but *trees*. You can't even see the canoe from where we're standing, and it's just a few yards away. I feel like I'm going to suffocate." She slumped to the ground and sat with her head in her hands, gripping her hair with both hands and trying to resist the urge to yank it out as hard as she could. She was so frustrated, terrified, and exhausted. Every day since her alarm had failed to go off that morning that now seemed so very long ago, her life had gotten harder and scarier with each new passing day. Now that she saw this place that Derek had been planning to take her, the prospect of coming up with an idea for escaping his clutches and finding her way out of this nightmare seemed truly hopeless. And here at his camp, their journey on the river done, she feared time was running out before he would try and force his way on her.

TWELVE

ARTIE'S MIND WAS RACING with worry as he and Scully quietly paddled the kayak out of the dark canal to the open waters of Lake Pontchartrain. Had Casey and her friends left New Orleans early enough to avoid the horrors they'd had a vivid glimpse of today? If they had left in time to get ahead of the worst of the panicked exodus from the city, what would they have faced on the other side of the lake, and along the highways leading north? Was the cabin really in a safe enough location, or would they be in danger there too? Most of all, he wondered how he was going to get there and how long that would take. If they had to walk, traveling 90 miles would take days. And if things had deteriorated a lot more in the days since Casey and her friends made the trip, what dangers would they face trying to follow their route now? Artie had lots of questions; what he didn't have was answers to any of them.

The map Grant had drawn was just a simple sketch, with highway numbers and turning directions. It was hard for Artie to grasp what the journey would really entail without seeing a real map, and he was anxious to get back aboard the catamaran so he and Larry could study the Louisiana state road map that Craig had given them. He was unfamiliar with the towns along the north shore of the lake, and especially with the countryside north of that. His route in and out of New Orleans had always been Interstate 10, which crossed over to the north shore at Slidell, but then continued east through the Gulf coast cities of Gulfport and Biloxi and on to Mobile. He hoped Larry might have some ideas, but doubted he knew the area to the north either because his only visits to New Orleans in decades had been a couple of yacht delivery trips in and out by the route they'd just sailed on the *Casey Nicole*.

Larry was waiting anxiously on deck for them when they paddled back alongside the boat. "Did you get your pistol?" he asked.

"She left," Artie said, as he climbed aboard. "She and Jessica and their friend Grant. Grant left a note from her in my car. He borrowed my gun as well, and I'm glad he did, I just hope he hasn't needed it and hope he never does." Artie helped Scully pull the kayak back on deck, and when they'd secured it, he sat down with Larry to tell him about Casey and her friends' plan to ride their bicycles to a cabin in Mississippi.

"Wow!" Larry said. "That's quite a trip, but you know, it also sounds pretty smart to me. If this kid Grant had enough sense to lead them out of here that soon after the grid went down, I'll bet they made it just fine. You know most people would just be confused and disoriented, not knowing what to do or where to turn in the first few days after an event like this. Chances are all the real problems and violence didn't crop up until about four or five days into it. They probably got across the Causeway ahead of all that and made it to that camp with no problem. I've never heard of that river, the Bogue Chitto, but let's check it out on the map...."

Crowding over the chart table in the starboard hull, the three of them looked at the official state road map of Louisiana and compared it to Grant's hand-drawn sketch. His route made sense and seemed to be the most direct way to reach the state line while avoiding as many major highways and urban areas as possible. The level of detail on the road map showed only highways, because of its small scale, though there was enough overlap in the coverage area across the state line to include the corner of Mississippi where Grant's sketch indicated the cabin was located, but none of the county roads or unpaved roads leading to it were shown. They would have to rely solely on his drawings to find their way the last few miles, once the route left the highway.

"There's the Bogue Chitto," Larry said, tracing it with his finger. "Look at that, it's a tributary of the Pearl. See here, it empties into the river there, just downstream from this Highway 21 here."

"So?"

"So that means we might be able to get a lot closer with the boat. I've heard that some of the shrimpers and other boat owners in the area sometimes use the lower reaches of the Pearl for a hurricane hole, so at least part of it is navigable. I don't know how far up it we could get, but it looks like a big river to me. Let me get my chartbook and see what it shows for the entrance."

"Yeah, but we could only go up it so far, right? Wouldn't that take too long and wouldn't it be better to try to follow the same route Casey and her friends took on the road?"

"How you goin' down de road, Doc? You gonna walk 90 mile wid all dem hungry people? How you gonna take enough to eat an' den keep it safe from a thief? What you gonna do den, mon, if you find dat place? You gonna want de girls to walk back all de way dem come, when t'ings more dangerous now?"

"Scully's right. I think it would be crazy to try and hike it from here, and besides, that would take days, one way." Larry pointed on the map, "Look, even if we sailed to the north shore and started here, you'd have to get through all this urban sprawl for miles and miles—Mandeville, Covington, and then more small towns to the north. And besides that, what would we do with the boat? We couldn't all go and leave it behind, and I think it's a real bad idea to split up for a long time like that, especially since we have no way of knowing how bad things are inland. If you go wandering off on the road, either alone or with Scully, I won't have any idea when to expect you back and no way of knowing if something happened to you or if you just got delayed. And likewise, you'd have no way of knowing if I would even still be here with the boat when you get back. Someone could kill me and take it if I just sat here anchored in the lake that long. You heard what Craig said was happening in his marina, and I don't have to remind you about Puerto Rico.

Would you want to bring the kids through all that danger to get back to the north shore, only to find out that you didn't have a ride when you got here? I don't think it's feasible at all to do it that way."

"Well, what are you proposing then? It's not like we can sail all the way to cabin, can we?"

"No, but with our extremely shallow draft, our working outboard motor, and our untouched fuel supply, not to mention the ability to easily lower the mast to go under bridges, power lines, and other obstacles, we may be able to get a hell of a lot closer to it than we are here." Larry pulled out his chartbook for the northern Gulf coast and flipped through it to the appropriate page. "Here it is. Look, the main mouth of the river is here, this easternmost entrance. This chart doesn't show it, but you can see on the road map how the river splits into two major branches, the West Pearl and the East Pearl, way upstream but below the place where the Bogue Chitto empties into it. The nautical chart doesn't cover that part of the river, but you can see that there is a marked channel on the East Pearl, and it shows enough water even for much bigger boats than ours all the way north of Interstate 10. So we know we can get that far. It's impossible to tell from the road map, of course, but I'm betting we could motor on upstream for quite some distance beyond the marked channel, maybe to here even, where Interstate 59 crosses the river. That's almost halfway to the mouth of the Bogue Chitto. The closer we can get to that cabin with the boat, the easier it will be to get to them and get them all out of there. Once we're that far upstream, you can see that there's nothing but a few small towns and hardly any development along the river. The map shows that most of it is a national wildlife refuge."

"What good would it do to go all the way up there and only get halfway to the Bogue Chitto? That still leaves a long way to go, and then it looks like even farther on the Bogue Chitto itself to get to the state line."

"Well, in the worst case, from that point, it would probably be feasible for you and Scully to strike out on one of these smaller roads that roughly parallel the course of the river and go overland the rest of the way. That's far from ideal, but much better than leaving from here. We could tuck the boat into one of these smaller bayous or oxbow lakes and I could stay with it and hope no comes along that far out in the swamp who would realize the potential of a boat like this. I think it would be much safer there anyway, as anyone we encounter up there on the river is likely going to be more self-reliant and probably not desperate like all these folks here in the cities. But as I said, that's the worst case. Here's what I'm hoping: on all these Southern rivers, aluminum johnboats are everywhere. All the locals in the area use them for fishing, and you see them tied up or pulled up on the bank everywhere there's a camp or cabin. I'm sure that given this situation, most people who have one are not going to want to let go of it, but we might find someone who will. Whether we're able to borrow one, barter for it, or buy it outright, if we could get hold of a 14- or 16-foot johnboat, it would be a simple matter to mount our 25-horse outboard on it, and then you and Scully could probably reach Grant's cabin in a day. We've got enough fuel on board to do that, and you'll use less coming back downriver. Anyway, that's the best plan I've got, and I think it's our best shot. What do you say?"

"How long do you think it will take to get to the river mouth, and then motor up it to that point?" Artie wanted to know.

"You can see on the chart that it's roughly 50 miles east of here to the mouth of the Pearl. We passed it yesterday on the way here to Lake Pontchartrain. We could be there tomorrow morning easily if we sail back to the eastern end of the lake tonight, and at least get to the other side of the Twin Span Bridge. We can get a few hours of sleep, then get up and go. We should be within the mouth of the Pearl before noon. We can then assess the situation better and make sure the outboard is ready for the trip upriver."

"We could run into delays and obstacles on the upstream part, of course, but I figure, if the Pearl is typical of the rivers that empty into the Gulf, the current won't be very strong. The outboard ought to push us at least three knots—maybe five if the current's real sluggish. And if it proves to be slower, maybe we'll get lucky and find a johnboat before we have to go that far. I mainly just want to take the big boat upriver far enough up to get it out of sight of anyone who might see it as a grand opportunity to sail the hell out of Dodge, and that mostly means getting inland of the coast."

"So it looks like all day tomorrow to get the *Casey Nicole* situated, and then if we're lucky and find a boat, the day after that Scully and I might make it to the cabin. I guess that's not bad at all."

"No, and even if we lose an extra day, you'll still get there faster than you could walk from here. Even if you could walk 20 miles a day, which you probably couldn't given the conditions, it would take you four and a half days to get there from here, and at least as long to get back."

Once Larry had made his case Artie needed no further persuasion. Scully was certainly happy about the plan, as he had no desire to be walking any distance from the boat in 'Babylon' and just wanted to get the girls and their friend and get back to sea as soon as possible. With this settled, they hauled in the anchor and sailed back under the Causeway the way they'd come, and later in the night cleared the Twin Span Bridge and its awful smell of death. Once they'd gone a few miles farther east, they anchored to get some sleep and wait for daylight to navigate the Rigolets out of Lake Pontchartrain into the sound. But in the morning, when they were ready to leave, the wind had died down to a flat calm, and Larry said they might as well go ahead and use the motor; because of the land masses surrounding them it might be afternoon before the wind filled in again.

The 35-year-old Evinrude hadn't inspired much confidence in Artie when he first saw it in Culebra. But since that day, it had been out of sight and out of mind, hanging below decks under the cockpit with the cover fixed over the well. With the favorable winds that had carried them everywhere they had wanted to go for more than a thousand miles, the motor simply had not been needed.

"It's as good as new," Larry assured him when he expressed his doubts. "Scully rebuilt the carburetor last time we used it to move somebody's boat when a tropical storm was coming into Culebra. It ran like a top. One thing about these old two-stroke Evinrudes: they're dead-nuts simple to work on and there's little to go wrong."

Scully proved him right when the engine cranked and ran on just the third pull of the starter rope. Once they put it in gear and got up to speed, the small outboard was able to push the *Casey Nicole* along nicely at seven knots, owing to the slim, knifelike profiles of the twin hulls that presented little resistance to the water.

"It's not as fast as sailing, but it'll get us there," Larry said.

They motored on through the morning, droning along over the opaque, brown waters between Lake Pontchartrain and the clearer waters of the Mississippi Sound, and by late morning reached the marked channel that designated the entrance to the navigable part of the Pearl. Turning north into the river, before they even got to the first bend they encountered their first potential obstacle: a low bridge that spanned the channel. It was far too low to clear in any sailing vessel with a mast, but it was a railroad swing bridge, so it was kept in the open position most of the time when a train was not expected. Luckily it had been open when it was abandoned sometime after the pulse hit, because they found it out of their way now. For a few bends beyond the railroad, the river wound through an expansive marshland of tall grasses, snaking along through the transition zone between salt and fresh water. The Evinrude outboard was proving its reliability and had consumed only a few gallons of gas from their supply. Larry did some calculations based on how much it had taken to get this far from Lake Pontchartrain and was certain they had enough fuel to make the trip upriver and back, considering both the distances they planned to go on the catamaran, and by small boat the rest of the way.

"We probably won't have much left after the trip, and I doubt we'll ever be able to get any more, but if it enables us to get those kids and get back to the Gulf, it will have served its purpose," he said. "After that, we'll be real sailors like in the old days when no boats had an 'iron staysail' to fall back on when the wind died."

"Hey Copt'n, what we gonna do 'bout dis otha drawbridge up ahead?" Scully asked. "Dat one's de highway and she closed, mon."

"Yeah, that's what I figured. It wouldn't have been open that day unless there happened to be a barge or something coming through, so it got locked down in the closed position. We're going to have to lower the mast. Let's drop the hook right here in the middle of the channel and get it done. We might as well stow the sails below. We won't be stepping it again until we come back out under this bridge."

The way Larry had the rig set up, with synthetic Dyneema shrouds and stays tensioned by simple dead-eyes, rather than turnbuckles, and the mast stepped in a tabernacle with a pivot, lowering the entire affair was a relatively quick and simple task. To bring it down in control, he connected a four-part tackle to the forestay, with the tail led back to the central cockpit winch. The total time lost in the operation was less than a half hour, and soon they were motoring north again, passing under the steel suspension bridge that the chart identified as Highway 90. As on all the other bridges they'd seen, abandoned cars were scattered along its length, but they saw no sign of life, nor the evidence of death that had been so clear from the presence of vultures on the long bridges leading out of New Orleans.

Immediately to the north of this bridge, they passed the small town of Pearlington on the right bank. It appeared that many of the residents here had chosen to remain in their homes, and they saw a few people as they motored by, all of them stopping to stare at the unusual catamaran going upriver. At a dock in front of a waterfront house, a middle-aged man was loading crawfish traps into a slightly larger version of the kind of johnboat Larry was on the lookout for. At his signal, Scully cut the throttle back to idle so that he could make him an offer to either buy or rent it. The man in the skiff just laughed out loud.

"Are you kidding? How you think I'm going to feed my family without a boat? A boat's the only way anybody can make it around here now. I wouldn't trade it for nothin', not even that fancy yacht of yours there."

Larry said he understood, and for the brief moments they were drifting within speaking distance, he plied the man for local knowledge of the river conditions upstream.

"You might make it as far as I-59, I don't know. I've never run the river that far myself. If your draft is only two feet, like you say it is, you can probably find a channel. The only problem is that thing is so damned wide you may not find a place to get through with both of them hulls. Good luck trying to find a small boat, though. I can't imagine anybody letting one go right about now, but there's a fool born every minute, so you never know."

Artie was beginning to second-guess his brother's plan as they motored on upriver after hearing this bit of advice. What the man had said made perfect sense. In a world where the grocery stores were cleaned out and the delivery trucks were not running, anyone living on a riverbank with a functional boat would have a distinct advantage over those less fortunate souls who had no way to access the abundant food sources the river offered. And if they couldn't find someone willing to part with the right kind of boat that could negotiate the smaller waters of the Bogue Chitto, they would end up walking once they reached the limits of where the *Casey Nicole* could go.

After leaving what was left of civilization behind at Pearlington, they motored upriver the rest of the afternoon, winding through the endless bottomland forests lining the banks on both sides, while carefully watching the muddy brown current for signs of sandbars, hidden logs, and other dangers. These hazards made it necessary to go slowly, and when the sun dropped below the trees, they had not covered as many miles as Larry had hoped. They were well to the north of the Interstate 10 bridge over the swamp, but still several miles downstream of the next bridge at Interstate 59, at least by Larry's calculation. The I-59 crossing was the last bridge spanning the river basin between them and the mouth of the Bogue Chitto, and Artie could feel a growing sense of anticipation at being that much closer to Casey, but he was also overwhelmed with frustration about not having an appropriate boat and having to stop for the night. Larry insisted it was too risky to navigate the river in the dark, though, and steered them off the river into a wide slough that led into a large dead lake bounded by tall cypress trees. As they were maneuvering about to find the best place to drop the anchor, Scully spotted something washed up in the debris of logs, plastic bottles, and other trash that had been deposited by the last flood among the cypress knees at the lake's edge. Upon closer inspection through Larry's binoculars, they could see that it was a boat—or at least part of one—turned on its side and halfway submerged in the shallows. As soon as the anchor was down, Artie and Scully off-loaded the kayak and paddled over to check it out. It was indeed a battered and abandoned aluminum boat, jammed in between two cypress knees, its stern end sunk and its port gunwale bent and twisted. Upon closer inspection, Artie saw that there was large hole punctured through the thin aluminum hull, which was why it sank and probably why no one bothered to salvage it. It looked to be at least a couple of decades old, and Artie knew that such boats were cheap to buy even when new. It likely had washed downriver from some camp upstream, and probably was already neglected and abandoned before then.

Scully said Larry could fix the hole, though, and if they could get it out, he thought it was big enough to carry the outboard. But try as they might, because of the way it was jammed between the cypress knees and weighted down with water inside, the two of them couldn't budge it. They paddled back to the catamaran; Larry passed them one end of a long mooring line and handed Scully his machete. After cutting one of the cypress knees that had it hung up and fastening the line to the bow, they were able to winch it free just as they had pulled Craig's sailboat off the bottom at Ship Island. Once it was alongside, Artie and Scully muscled it aboard the forward deck.

After a close examination, Larry was ecstatic. "Sure, it's all beat to hell and ugly as shit, but I can fix this. We'll straighten the bent gunwale as much as we can and hammer the aluminum flat around the hole, and then sandwich the damaged area between two pieces of quarter-inch marine plywood, which I've got plenty of."

"How will we attach the plywood so it won't leak?" Artie asked.

"It'll be a quick and dirty job—not pretty—but simple enough. We'll just slather the plywood pieces in 5200, one of the toughest marine adhesives on the planet, and bolt 'em together right through the hull. It'll keep the water out long enough to get you where you're going. This hull is twisted some too—not much we can do about that—but at least it's big enough to mount the outboard on. I say let's get it done tonight and then you and Scully can take off in the morning. This is as good a place as any for me to wait with the *Casey Nicole*. If you go from here in the skiff, you'll get there before tomorrow night, easily. I think that makes more sense than trying to navigate this big-ass catamaran any farther upriver, don't you?"

Artie did think it made more sense, and he was thrilled that he could possibly be reunited with his daughter by tomorrow night! They set to work and got the repair done after dark, leaving the boat upside down on the deck so the adhesive could at least partially cure. Larry said it wouldn't fully cure for days, but it was thick enough to keep the water out anyway, and the screws they bolted the plywood together with would keep the patch in place. The only thing left to do was pack some food, water, and emergency gear, along with the shotgun and ammunition. Artie and Scully were going on an expedition!

★ ★ ★

More than a week had passed since Grant and Jessica had seen any sign of Casey and her abductor. He didn't even know exactly how long it had been, maybe even longer than ten days. The days all ran together, now that every one was just the same struggle to survive and keep looking. Though they scanned every likely place someone might land a canoe during their entire descent of the Bogue Chitto, the tracks they had examined on that one sandbar their second morning on the river were both the first and the last that they found. That seemed like the distant past now to Grant, almost like another place in another time, miles and miles upstream on the banks of a river they had long since left astern. Today they turned once more down yet another twisting bayou in the lower Pearl River basin, looking for anything that might be a clue to Casey's whereabouts. But each waterway they traveled in this labyrinth of flooded forest confirmed what he'd already known. Searching for two people, in one small canoe, in 250 square miles of swampy forest—was a daunting prospect. There was simply no way he and Jessica could try all the possible routes that the man who had Casey could have taken, and he knew there was also a chance that he had left the river and taken her somewhere overland. They could have missed any sign where he did this and continued on downriver without knowing it.

Of course Grant didn't have a map of the river basin with him, and he'd only paddled through it once, several years ago, and along just one the dozens of possible routes that a canoe could take to the river's end at the coast. Now he was faced with trying to explore all these possibilities, without the benefit of a map, and each time they reached the end of one bayou, they had to backtrack upstream against the current to check out others that branched off on different routes. It was incredibly frustrating, not to mention physically exhausting. Grant knew that even if he had a boat with an outboard motor and could zip up and down all these waterways at speed, it would still take days to cover them all and there was no way to account for the endless changes in route that the man he was pursuing might take in the meantime.

On top of the difficulties of trying to find Casey, Grant had the even bigger problem of trying to forage and catch enough food for them both to eat while they traveled. This was proving to be a greater challenge than he had imagined, despite the fact that they were in a rich ecosystem with great diversity of plant and animal life both in the water and in the forests it flowed through. The biggest problem with trying to find food while also looking for Casey was the amount of time it took away from their search for her. While he'd had been lucky that first night he set drop hooks and caught a catfish, night after successive night he was unsuccessful in catching another by this method. He did manage to land a decent-sized bass on one occasion with the rod and reel and one of the lures he'd found in the canoe shed, but other than that, fishing was not as productive as he'd hoped.

Jessica finally succumbed to hunger and ate a sizeable portion of fish when he cooked the bass in the coals of their campfire that night, and that was a big relief to Grant, as he was worried about her getting weaker. Just as he expected, it was proving really difficult to find enough food to support her vegetarian diet in the swamp, especially this early in the year when a lot of seasonal wild plant foods simply were not available. It was the right time of year for tender cattail shoots, though, and they both ate their fill of these whenever they came to a patch of them at the water's edge. They were tasty and easy to gather, but not very sustaining for the kind of effort they were expending each day paddling the canoe. When they reached the swamps of the Pearl, he was also able to gather hearts of palm from the dense thickets of palmettos that grew there, but getting to these required a lot of effort with the machete for the small reward in each plant.

The easiest source of available protein in the swamp, he soon discovered, were the abundant freshwater crawfish that were everywhere in the still backwaters and slow-running creeks. At first, catching them by hand proved nearly impossible, but then he tried wading in the edges of the shallows at night after they'd made camp, using his flashlight in one hand to spot them and cause them to back away from the beam. This made it possible to grab them with the other hand and eventually collect enough to make a meal. Jessica was reluctant to try the bug-like creatures at first, but again, her hunger was becoming so constant that she gave in and discovered she liked them almost as much as the fish. Grant said they were exactly the same as lobsters, only smaller, and having crawfish boils was a long-standing tradition among the locals throughout the region. The only problem with this food source was that he only had one more set of batteries for the flashlight, and using it for a couple of hours at a time would soon deplete those. He also saw bullfrogs along the bank at night, but could never get close enough to even attempt to grab one. If only he still had the .22 pistol, he knew he could shoot them before they hopped away, but then again, if he had that, he would be able to put a wide variety of meat in the pot fairly easily.

They frequently passed chattering squirrels from just a few feet away and saw many small birds, rabbits, and even wild turkeys that would have been in range of a well-placed shot, but they were all out of reach without a projectile weapon. Grant had seen the Wapishana hunt with primitive bows and arrows and the blowguns they made from materials collected in the jungle, and while he knew a lot about the theory of primitive weapons from his anthropology studies, he lacked any practical experience in making them. He did know enough to know that producing useable weapons, especially bows, required not only skill in choosing materials and crafting them, but also time for the wood to season properly. It was not something he could invest that much time in yet, but after seeing all those frogs at night he did fashion a rudimentary spear out of a large section of river cane in hopes of getting lucky and impaling one. They also saw plenty of big garfish in the shallows practically every day, and he knew that with patience he might be able to spear one. At this point, he was ready to eat anything that moved, and also kept a lookout for snakes and turtles, both of which were abundant, but difficult to approach close enough to catch.

The coffee had run out a few days ago, and following more than a year of caffeine addiction in graduate school, he suffered headaches for a couple of days, but now seemed to be over it. He doubted he'd get another cup of coffee any time soon, even if they had not been combing the swamp looking for Casey. Coffee was one of those luxury commodities imported from afar that simply would no longer be available after the collapse of the power grid and easy transportation. He knew that a lot of things wouldn't be available, but he still felt that if they had made it to the cabin according to their initial plan, they would have been better off than most. With enough canned foods to last a few weeks and the pistol for hunting, as well as a better selection of fishing gear that his father had left there, he felt they could have hung on long enough. And though it might have been difficult, the difficulty would have been nothing compared to trying to survive with hardly any equipment while paddling and searching for someone day after day, always on the move.

With what would soon be two weeks of fruitless searching behind them, Grant had to admit to himself that they might never see Casey again. He still felt guilt for letting the abduction happen to begin with, but he also told himself that he had done everything that anyone could reasonably expect in his efforts to track down the man who had taken her. He knew that they couldn't go on like this, and that he couldn't provide for Jessica indefinitely with so little equipment. He knew it was time to start thinking about their future, both in the long term and in terms of what they should do next. One thing he was sure of—it would be out of the question to turn around and travel upriver all that distance they'd come and then some to try to reach his cabin in the canoe. If they were well fed and had their full strength, that would be one thing, but before they could even contemplate such a journey, Grant knew they had to try to find some supplies and equipment. He didn't know if that was within reason or not, but it seemed that if they traveled on downriver, closer to the coast, they might find people in some of the rural areas who were in a better situation than most and could help them. The other option was to try to find more uninhabited weekend camps like some they had seen on the Bogue Chitto, where they might be able to pillage some canned goods or other groceries. He knew that if the owners of any such retreats had been unable to get to them by now, they likely never would, and would not need them anyway. Thinking about this, he realized it was just as likely that some desperate refugees might have taken up residence in his own cabin and made use of the goods stored there. If so, going all that way would prove a waste of time and effort. Considering all this, he didn't really know what to do.

Another consequence of the long days of being completely alone in such close proximity to Jessica was a growing attachment to her that he could tell was mutual on her part. He supposed it was inevitable, considering the situation into which they had been cast, but the more time he spent with her and got to know her, the more he liked what he discovered. Though he had felt they were as different as two people could be just a couple of weeks ago, the challenges of life in the woods brought out a part of her he hadn't seen before, and he liked it. He thought her chances of adapting to life in this altered new reality were slim when they had first been preparing to leave New Orleans, but here on the river, she surprised him as she quickly conquered her fears of the dark and the local wildlife and even overcame her reluctance to try new foods.

The realization that he was feeling something more than mere friendship towards her gave him a twinge of guilt and brought nagging doubts that he was really as committed to finding Casey as he had been when they started out. On the one hand, he felt he had done the best he could and had put Jessica in even more danger by bringing her deep into this swamp on a fruitless chase. Continuing on to the cabin without trying to find Casey wasn't an option he had considered for even a minute, and he knew Jessica wouldn't have either. But after all this time, it was becoming clear how hopeless the search really was, and each day that went by with no sign of her at all made that realization all the more evident. He couldn't help but think about what the future would bring, and right now Casey simply wasn't in that future and he had to accept the fact that she might never be.

Whatever it was he was feeling towards Jessica, he had managed to keep it well in control, and did his best not to let her know. He certainly didn't want to discuss it, as he wasn't even sure if it was real or just a natural reaction to the stress of the situation. Not only did he feel bad about it because of Casey, but he knew that Jessica must be going through her own wide range of emotions considering how close she was with Casey as friends and roommates. And in the beginning, he *had* been much more attracted to Casey than to Jessica, as they seemed to have mutual interests that were apparent when he first met her at the freshman anthropology field trip he attended as an assistant.

But night after night, as he shared a camp with Jessica, and she slept close to him in their sleeping bags against the canoe or under the tarp, depending on the nature of the campsite, he felt a growing desire for her. It had started that first night when she wrapped her arms around him in terror at the shriek of an owl. He couldn't deny that it felt good to comfort her then, and that he took comfort in the closeness of their embrace as well. The whole world had changed practically overnight, and they were only human, after all—a young man and a young woman—trying to survive without any of the systems or structure that had always been a part of their lives until now. As he steered the canoe from the stern, guiding around the twists and bends of this new bayou, he pondered the implications of these things as he watched her wield her paddle with the new skill she'd mastered so quickly.

This particular route was proving to be one of the most interesting yet. They had followed a series of dead sloughs that led them off of one of the main branches of the Pearl River. The route led through several still lakes, connected by sections of running water flowing generally southward. Paddling through this deep swamp, he'd almost overlooked a tiny channel that split off in a clear-running branch. They'd had to backtrack a few yards upstream to check it out, and at first it didn't even look big enough to accommodate a canoe. But there was a strong current flowing into the entrance, evidence enough that it was indeed a bayou and not merely a slough. It had to come out again somewhere downstream, so Grant suggested they push on through a little ways and see if it was passable. Once they'd followed it for a few bends, it opened up a bit, and surprisingly, the water was clear enough to see the white sand bottom anywhere from a few inches to three feet below the surface. It was one of the many unexpected surprises of the swamp and one they would have completely missed if they had relied on first impressions. The little bayou led them into a magical stand of old-growth cypress and Tupelo gum, with huge flaring buttresses and almost solid sheets of Spanish moss hanging like curtains from their lower branches, nearly touching the water.

"This is magnificent," Grant said. "This is a glimpse of what this entire river basin forest would have looked like back before they logged most of it over a hundred years ago."

"It's kind of creepy too," Jessica said, looking around at the moss-draped giants in awe. "It has an otherworldly quality or something."

"I know what you mean. It's *primeval*, that's what it is. Most people today have never seen anything like it, because in most places there are only tiny remnants like this scattered here and there. But a lot of the jungle I saw in Guyana was very similar."

After that exchange, they drifted on in awed silence down the narrow bayou, staring up at the huge trees and only occasionally dipping their paddles to avoid hitting something. Being in this place made Grant think about the Wapishana people again. Their lifestyle would be totally unaffected by this solar event that had disrupted the world for everyone else. For them, life would be the same today as it was before, and they would likely be unaware that anything had happened. He was snapped out of his contemplation of this by a whispered, excited cry from Jessica:

"Grant! Look!"

He saw that she was focused on the bank to their left, where there was a small sandbar in the inside bend of the bayou, maybe four feet wide and several yards long. The edge of the sandbar, sculpted into a smooth-faced bluff by high water the last time the river level had been up, was collapsed and broken, and piles of it had fallen off and slid down to the water's edge. At first, Grant thought maybe an alligator had pushed itself off the bank into the river, but the tracks that were everywhere on the sandbar were no reptile tracks—they were human footprints! And not only that, as he looked closer, he could see that what had collapsed the edge of the sand was the weight of a canoe being pulled over it, into the water. There was the unmistakable area of smooth, flattened sand that could only be made by the hull of a canoe or the belly of a big gator, but the sharp, central groove down the center of the slide mark told him for sure that it was the keel of an aluminum canoe. And he was certain the mark was just like the one at the place where Casey was taken and the last one they'd found so many days ago.

He was shocked, almost unable to believe what he was seeing. He immediately motioned Jessica to silence as he quietly jammed his paddle into the bottom to stop their forward motion. Stepping over the side of the canoe, he hung onto the gunwale while he pulled it closer to the bank and bent over the disturbed area for a closer look. There were many tracks in the sand, some old and shapeless and impossible to decipher, but the more recent ones made it clear to Grant that they had been made by two different people—a large man wearing moccasins and a person with significantly smaller bare feet! The latter could be Casey's, and they could mean she was still alive! Furthermore, the barefoot tracks seemed to the be the most recent, as several of them were superimposed over the top of the moccasin prints, including a few that were alongside the slide mark made by the canoe. He wondered what that could mean as he crouched down beside the canoe and told Jessica that he was sure Casey had been here, and recently.

Looking beyond the sandbar into the dense undergrowth of palmettos and bay trees, he saw that someone had cut a path leading away from the bayou. Moving as quietly as he could, he stepped ashore to get a closer look. Some of the cut stems and saplings had turned brown and died long ago. Other cuts were fresh, with dripping sap and green pith showing inside. Someone had used the path both recently and sometime well before the pulse event. Could it be that this was the place Casey's abductor had planned to take her all along? If so, where were they now, and why were Casey's tracks the only ones visible where the canoe had been pulled into the water? Grant trembled a bit to think that the man might be nearby, and likely armed to the teeth as well as intimately familiar with the area. He knew it was extremely dangerous, but he had to follow that path and see if he could find any clue to this mystery. Though he was reluctant to expose Jessica to the possibility of running right smack into this man who had taken Casey, he had learned his lesson before and was determined not to leave her alone or out of his sight, even for a few minutes. He tied the bow of their canoe to a cypress knee near the little sandbar and took her hand in his, his machete in the other. Warning her to silence, he crept forward along the path with Jessica in tow, stopping to look and listen every few steps, just as he'd seen the Wapishana do when they were stalking game in the jungle.

There were more tracks in the deep carpet of leaves covering the ground along the narrow path, but none were clear enough to decipher or even to tell if they were made by Casey or by the man in moccasins. The presence of so many tracks made it all the more likely that the two of them had been here for much longer than just an overnight camp. Grant knew for certain his hunch was right when he emerged on the other side of the thicket into an open area of forest with little undergrowth. There, on the far side, was a platform hut built between four trees, not unlike those he'd frequently seen along the rivers of Guyana. A mix of man-made and natural materials, the hut's log support beams and plastic tarp roof were an unusual combination he hadn't seen before. A few feet away, hung upside down from a rope stretched between two trees, was the skinned carcass of a small deer. He froze at the sight of the camp, watching and listening to be sure no one was in the vicinity. Thanks to the fact that the tree house itself was open on all but one side, he could easily see that there was no one hiding inside it.

After waiting for what seemed like at least five minutes, he crept out into the clearing with Jessica's hand still in his, his machete upright and ready for action in the other. There was something lying on the ground not far to one side of the tree house, opposite the side on which hung the deer carcass. He let go of Jessica's hand to walk a little closer, giving her a look that told her not to follow. Even before he was close enough to really be sure, he heard the buzzing of flies and then could see them swarming by the countless hundreds. The object on the ground was the body of a man, sprawled face down onto an animal skin that had been staked out next to a fire pit. When he walked closer, Grant saw that next to the dead man's head, bloody and thrown aside on the ground, was a full-sized axe with a weathered wooden handle. The man's skull was split from a blow to the back of the head that surely must have been delivered by the nearby axe, and the thickest congregation of the flies covered the oozing mess that spilled out of the wound. Looking over the rest of the body, Grant's eyes were immediately drawn to the man's feet, which were clad in crude, handmade deerskin moccasins.

Grant took a couple of steps back, feeling a touch of nausea and shock at the violence of the man's death. Though he couldn't see the face to be sure it was the man they'd passed on the Bogue Chitto that day, the moccasins left no doubt in his mind that it was him. But who could have done this? Was it even possible that Casey could have done such a thing herself? To spare Jessica from the gruesome sight, he turned around and warned her to stay back, speaking in a normal voice now that he knew the man with the canoe was dead. Then he began calling Casey's name, yelling at the top of his lungs, joined by Jessica, until their voices were hoarse. When they finally stopped, there was no answer, only the indifferent stillness of the swamp gradually replacing the fading echoes of their shouts.

Grant quickly scaled the primitive ladder to the platform floor, looking for clues among the duffel bags, backpacks, buckets, and ammo cans scattered around the floor. He searched through all the bags looking for the pistol that belonged to Casey's father. It was gone, and there were no other firearms to be found, though upon opening the military surplus ammo cans he found that two of them were still packed with individual boxes of ammunition in three different calibers: .22 Long Rifle, .357 Magnum, and 7.62 x 39 steel-jacketed Czechoslovakian military surplus.

The plastic five-gallon buckets stacked along the one tarp wall of the shelter were empty except for one. Opening that one up, Grant was delighted to find that it was packed with cans of tuna fish, vegetable soup, chili beans, and one-pound bags of rice. If Casey *had* been the one who took out her abductor with the axe, it appeared she had the presence of mind to take all of the weapons and most of the food supplies in the shelter before leaving in the canoe. Grant resealed the bucket and the ammo boxes and carried them all down the ladder and over to the edge of the clearing where Jessica was waiting. Then he returned to the fire pit, trying not to look at the corpse beside it. He put his hands on top of the dead coals in its center and felt for heat. They were cold on the surface, but when he dug into the pile with his fingers, he found warmth just a few inches deep. He didn't know how to estimate for sure how much time might have passed since there was a fire here, but he figured it couldn't have been much more than about 24 hours at the most, and maybe a good bit less. It was clear that Casey had left the scene of whatever had happened here in the canoe, and the tracks they'd seen when they first got here made sense now. There was only one way she could have gone, and that was downstream. Since there was no one here who could have kept that fire going after she left, Grant was hopeful that she wouldn't have had time to go very far.

He rushed Jessica back to the canoe and quickly loaded the supplies and ammunition he had taken from the tree house into the bottom of the hull with their own gear. He had been so hungry before they got here that, if not for the sight of the dead man, he would have surely wolfed down some of the soup, beans, and tuna right out of the cans to replenish lost calories that had been so hard to come by in the swamp. He would have also eagerly thrown most of the deer carcass in the canoe for later too, but right now, he was still feeling queasy from what he had seen and had completely lost his appetite, especially for meat.

They followed the current downstream as it twisted its way out of the old-growth forest and back into hardwood bottomland forests more typical of the rest of the river basin. Visibility was limited to a few yards, as the banks of the stream here were overgrown with head-high palmettos. They had paddled less than an hour when Grant spotted a sign that the canoe had been pulled up in the mud. He stopped and got out, and immediately noticed a small pile of charred wood on a patch of ground where the leaves had been cleared away. There were faint footprints, but the harder surface on the top bank did not leave clear impressions.

"I'll bet this fire was from last night!" Grant said to Jessica. "She must have stopped here after she left the camp because it got dark. If that was the case, she wouldn't have left here until daylight this morning, and can't be too far ahead of us. Come on, let's go!"

They worked their way around the twists and turns as fast as possible, but by the time the bayou emerged from the forest and rejoined one of the main branches of the Pearl River, it was late afternoon, with little time left before sunset. Grant was at a loss as to what to do next, but he had to assume that if Casey was indeed alone in the canoe, she would head downstream, as there was simply no way she could retrace her route back upriver against the current. He and Jessica paddled into the middle of the river and had only gone the distance of one big, sweeping bend, when she stopped mid-stroke and pointed at something in the distance ahead.

"Look! Is that a canoe?"

It *was* indeed a canoe, its bow pulled up halfway onto a small sandbar! And it was the common aluminum model, like the one the man who had taken Casey had been paddling when they saw him that first day of this ordeal. It had to be the same canoe, and if so, she surely must have paddled it there. But why was there was another boat pulled up alongside it? Grant could see that the other vessel was not another canoe, but rather a small johnboat, the type of watercraft most favored by the local fishermen in these parts. He could also see that it had an outboard motor hanging off the stern. Such a rig was too heavy to paddle far, so he assumed the motor must still be operable for the boat to be here in such a remote place. But who could it belong to? Could the owner have been the one who did that to Casey's abductor? And if Casey had been in the canoe next to it, where was she now, and was she in danger yet again from these new strangers? Grant whispered to Jessica that the situation merited a cautious approach, though he could barely contain his anticipation to find out whether or not Casey was indeed finally within reach. With slow, deliberate strokes of the paddle, he maneuvered the canoe over to one side of the river, careful not to make a splash or any excessive movement that would attract attention from a distance.

"Don't use your paddle, and keep quiet," he whispered. "I just want to let the current carry us slowly, close in to the bank where they can't see us. I want to get a good look at whoever it is in that other boat before we show ourselves."

Using the paddle blade as a rudder, Grant steered the canoe as it slowly drifted downstream in the sluggish current. A thick stand of cattail marsh grew on the bank just ahead, between them and the two boats they were approaching. Grant aimed for the edge of it, and when the bow knifed into the tall grasses, he grabbed a handful to hold them in position, where they could observe the scene while staying hidden. For several minutes there was no movement or sound at all, and he wondered if whoever it was in that boat had taken Casey into the woods away from the river. He was about to paddle on ahead to find out when two men stepped out of the trees and walked over to the johnboat, one of them stooping down to get something out of it. Grant was glad they were well hidden by the tall grass when the other one turned and looked upriver, straight in their direction.

"Oh my God!" Jessica cried out loud. "I can't believe it! How could this even be possible?"

THIRTEEN

EVERY DAY SINCE THEY had arrived at Derek's hidden camp, time had slowed to an excruciating pace for Casey, the hours dragging endlessly by as she felt the confinement of the deep forest closing in around her. The nights were even worse, as she was only able to sleep for those brief periods when she was too exhausted to lay awake in fear or worry any longer. She had no way of marking time other than by the cycles of dark and light, and sometimes the position of the sun on the days it wasn't cloudy or raining. Derek had no watch, nor did he care what time it was or even what day, week, or month, for that matter. He said that time was a stupid invention of civilization designed to imprison people who had to work for others. From now on, they would live free of time and free of all the other conventions and restrictions of society. But regardless of whether or not she could track the hours, Casey had some idea of the number of days she'd been there, and she thought it was at least nine or ten.

After spending this much time in such an inaccessible pocket of the swamp, among a forgotten remnant of old growth trees that were somehow spared the logger's saw a century or more ago, she knew that it was highly improbable anyone would ever find her. The camp was essentially on an island, a slightly higher area of mostly dry ground surrounded by miles of sloughs, bayous, dead lakes, and, farther away, the two forks of the Pearl River that bounded each side of the basin. Practically all of the basin seemed to be unbroken forest, with trees growing on both the dry ground and in any water that wasn't moving. There was no way in or out of it except by boat, and there was no boat that could negotiate the tiny bayou that led to the camp other than a narrow canoe or pirogue. Casey doubted anyone other than Derek had stumbled across it in decades, even before the supposed solar storm, when fishermen from nearby towns frequented the more accessible parts of the swamp in their bass boats year round. Derek had chosen his hideout well, and he had hidden the rough-built tree house platform far enough back in the forest that even if someone did by chance find the tiny creek, they would pass right by, unaware a camp was there.

One thing she discovered he was not exaggerating about was the amount of preparation he had done in his expectation that civilization would eventually collapse and he would someday be living in a place like this, surviving off the land. His skill as a hunter became readily apparent once they stopped traveling, and every morning he was gone before dawn, usually returning within a couple of hours with several squirrels, or sometimes a rabbit, and once, a wild turkey. When they'd arrived there and he had unpacked the big duffel bags and backpacks he had been carrying in the canoe, she discovered that among his gear were several firearms for different hunting and defensive purposes, each of which he showed to her and bragged about with great enthusiasm. First of all, there was a scoped, bolt-action Marlin .22 caliber rifle, which he said he would use for most of his hunting because it was relatively quiet and the ammunition was small and lightweight, allowing him to store enough to last for years. For larger game such as deer and wild hogs, which he said were plentiful in the swamp, he had a short lever-action Winchester carbine that looked to Casey like the typical cowboy rifle seen in old Western movies. Derek said it was chambered for the .357 Magnum, a cartridge that would kill anything that lived in these parts with one well-placed shot. Finally, he had an all-black gun that looked like a machine gun to Casey. He said it was a Saiga semiautomatic AK-47, and that its only purpose in his arsenal was to kill intruders—or anyone else that might present a threat in any way. He told Casey that one day, when he knew he could trust her, after she finally acknowledged that his bringing her here was the best thing that had ever happened to her, he would teach her how to use the guns and how to be a hunter too.

Despite his near-daily wanderings away from the camp to find game, Casey had no opportunities to escape. Although he gave her a bit of freedom around camp during the day, when he was there to watch her, he still bound her hands and feet each night before he went to sleep and left her that way until he returned from the hunt each morning. Casey knew that it wouldn't have made much difference even if he hadn't taken this precaution. Each time he left to hunt, he took the canoe and paddled it to other nearby islands of dry ground in the swamp, leaving her effectively cut off from the outside world, as it would have been impossible to walk out in any direction. She wondered if, left free, she would even be able to wade and swim, given a long enough opportunity to get a head start, but the number of large alligators they had seen on both the lower Bogue Chitto and in the waters of the Pearl on the way here made her push that idea to the background as an ultimate last resort. Besides, even if the alligators didn't bother her and she didn't get bitten by a snake, she had no idea how far she would have to go to get to solid land, and if what Derek had said was true, the swamp basin they were in was bounded on both sides by the two major branches of the Pearl River. Casey knew that in order to escape and find her way to help, she was going to need the canoe. And to get the canoe, she was somehow going to have to take Derek out of the picture. She didn't know how she was going to do it, as he was much bigger and obviously quite agile and fit as well, judging by the way he moved. From what she had learned of his life, he had spent most of his adulthood hunting and practically living in the woods between odd jobs, and she had no doubt that he was plenty tough.

But, despite these doubts, Casey knew it would soon come down to fighting for her life anyway, as Derek was beginning to lose patience with his fantasy that she would somehow voluntarily come to like him and want to be his wild woman, enjoying the life he had dreamed of even before the lights went out. She could tell by the way that he looked at her that her time of being left alone was coming to a close. When he had first taken her captive, she would have never believed that he would have restrained himself this long, especially considering that he had already watched her naked, bathing in the river that first day. She could only surmise from listening to him talk that he had little, if any, experience with women, having lived most of his life as a loner, and never fitting into any social groups as an adult or teenager. Apparently his ideas of relationships were skewed by the many fantasy adventure novels he'd read along with his philosophy books, and he thought that winning her heart would be as simple as demonstrating his prowess as a hunter and woodsman—skills no one could deny were more valuable at the moment than the ability to earn a high salary.

But along with his ill-informed notions of romance between men and women, it was also clear that he regarded her as his property. It was one thing that he had taken her against her will, but now he expected her to follow his orders and do whatever work needed doing around camp. This included chopping firewood from the dead branches he dragged to the fire pit from the surrounding woods, cooking their meals, and washing pots and utensils in the bayou. On occasion, when she was awkwardly trying to swing the heavy axe to cut up the wood, the thought crossed her mind that she could use it as a weapon. The only problem was that every time he made her do this work, he was standing there watching her, out of range of the axe but easily close enough to rush in and disarm her if she tried anything. She also considered the guns. If she had to kill him to escape, she could imagine herself shooting him from a distance a lot more easily than she could contemplate something as violent as hitting him with an axe. But he was careful to keep the guns out of her reach in the tree house when she was untied, and never let her near them unsupervised. In addition, while in camp he often carried the short lever-action carbine hanging from one shoulder on a rifle sling. Though she looked for opportunities, there was never a time when she would have had a reasonable chance of making for one of the firearms and turning it on him before he could stop her. But Casey was determined to escape, and determined to keep looking for that opportunity and to take it when it presented itself. She was not going to give up and become this man's slave and worse.

Today he was gone longer than usual, giving her lots of time to think about all these things as she pondered her dismal future. When he did return to the camp sometime around mid-day, she saw the reason. Apparently, he had traveled farther to hunt that day and had taken the time to hide and ambush a young female deer. He walked into the clearing with the bloody carcass slung over one shoulder, grinning with pride at his accomplishment. Casey had gotten used to eating the wild game that Derek brought in, and had even gotten good at cooking it over the fire, but she still didn't like the sight of the dead animals before he dressed them. The deer was much worse than the small game. It was a pathetic-looking remnant of a once-beautiful and graceful animal, hanging limp, one glazed eye seemingly staring back into hers.

"We'll be eating well for a long time now. I'll rig up a shelter for smoking all this meat and then I won't have to go hunting for a while. I know you'll like that. I won't have to leave every morning and we're going to have a *lot* more time together. Now get over here and help me hang her up off the ground so the ants won't get on the meat."

Later that afternoon, Derek went back to work on the deer and finished the job of removing the skin, carrying the bloody hide to the edge of the bayou to wash it. Then he returned to the fire pit where Casey was sitting, watching the venison steaks roasting on green branches directly over the coals.

"Now I'm going to be able to make you a nice buckskin dress, to go with that pair of moccasins I've been working on. First this hide's got to be scraped; then we'll tan it with the deer's brains. I bet you didn't know it, but every animal has enough brains to tan its own hide. That's how the Indians did it, and it makes the finest buckskin that can be had. I want you to watch closely, because this is women's work and you'll be doing the next one."

Derek had cut some stakes from a small sapling with the axe. He used the blunt side of it to hammer them down, then laid the axe back down behind him, on top of the pile of firewood Casey had prepared earlier. Punching holes in the corners of the hide with his knife, he stretched it out between the stakes until it was tight, the hair side down, against the ground. Then he showed Casey how to scrape away the fat and bits of meat that still clung to it, using the edge of his hunting knife, turned at a 90-degree angle to keep from cutting into it.

"Here, you try it," he said, holding the knife out to her.

"Okay, but can you give me a minute? I need to go over in the woods and use the bathroom."

"Make it quick!"

When she was done, Casey returned to the fire, knowing she would be forced to do the disgusting work of scraping the deer hide. As she walked nearer, it suddenly struck her that Derek was totally preoccupied with the hide, not bothering to look up when she approached. His back was to her and he was bent over it on his knees, pulling the knife across it in long, two-handed strokes. She glanced at the woodpile and saw the axe. It was lying there forgotten, completely out of his field of view.

Casey realized that at last she had a chance to do something decisive about her situation. It was the best opportunity she'd had during the entire time she'd been this man's prisoner, and there might not be another like it for a long time, if ever. There was no time to be squeamish or even let herself think about the fact that her captor was a fellow human being, just like her. There was only time to act, and that's what she did. Without making a sound, she bent over and picked up the heavy tool, then shifted her grip to grasp the handle with both hands. She brought it back over her shoulder to gather all the strength she could muster, and swung it as hard as she could, knowing she had only one chance and that she'd better not miss or hold anything back.

She felt the shock of the impact all the way through her arms and into her shoulders. The axe blade struck with a dull thud and she could feel something give as Derek's head absorbed the blow. His body slumped forward onto the stretched deerskin, and she wrenched the handle back to free the axe in case she needed to hit him again. But it was clear that there was no need. One of his legs was twitching, but he would never get back up. She could see that she had split the back of his skull with one blow, and she threw the axe aside in horror, turning away from a sight that she knew she would never be able to forget. She looked nervously around the clearing, as if she expected to see witnesses that would testify to this brutal murder she'd just committed, but she was all alone. She told herself again that she had done what she had to do. She'd had no choice if she wanted to ever be free to leave.

Casey stepped away from the fire pit and quickly climbed up the wooden ladder to the tree house. She began collecting the things she knew she would need, starting with Derek's lever-action carbine, the .22 rifle, and the AK-47 with the folding stock. Then she rummaged through his backpack and found her father's pistol. Once she had all the guns gathered up, she opened one of the ammo cans and sorted out a few boxes of shells, reading the labels to make sure she had some for each weapon. Then she opened the five-gallon buckets to go through the food supplies, and filled one to the top with bags of rice and canned goods before resealing the lid. She then put the guns and ammo in one of the big duffel bags and loaded a smaller pack with butane lighters, insect repellent, a cooking pot, a can opener, and other necessities Derek had among his gear. It took her three trips to carry all this stuff from the tree house to the edge of the bayou and load it in the canoe. Each time she walked back into the camp to get another load, she couldn't help but glance at the body beside the fire pit, just to make sure Derek was really dead and no longer a threat to her.

The afternoon light was rapidly fading when she finally got underway in the canoe, and she knew she wouldn't be able to go far before the swamp was enveloped in darkness. But she was determined to go as far as possible from that awful place while she could still see. She pushed off the bottom with the paddle and struggled to steer the long canoe through the twists and turns of the winding bayou. Frequently banging the bow into trees and getting the keel stuck in the mud along the edges, she made slow progress, but at least she was moving.

When the deepening twilight finally overtook her, Casey pulled the canoe onto a muddy bank and hurriedly scrounged some dry leaves and broke dead twigs off of nearby branches to start a fire. She managed to get it going before full nightfall, but there was not enough dry wood in the immediate vicinity to build it up to any size or to keep it stoked until morning. She huddled in its glow as long as she was able to keep it burning, using the can opener to open a can of mixed vegetable soup, which she placed near the flames to warm before eating it and drinking the broth from the can. In her haste to leave, she had not thought to include even one of Derek's cooking pots as she gathered the things she thought she would need.

She had no idea what she would do when morning came; her only plan was to follow the bayou downstream. It had to come out *somewhere*, either on a bigger river or directly on the coast. Either way, it didn't really matter. There was no way she could find her way back to the Bogue Chitto, and even if she could, she knew it would be impossible to travel back all the way they'd come, paddling alone and upstream against the current. Though she wanted to get to Grant's cabin and be with Grant and Jessica more than anything, she knew she couldn't get there by that route, and she sure couldn't stay out here in the swamp indefinitely. She would have to take her chances with strangers somewhere downstream in what was left of civilization, and she could only hope that she could find other people with decency and morals remaining despite the collapse. If so, maybe she could get help in eventually making her way to the other side of the state line and finding her friends.

She sat by the fire thinking about the prospects for her future and worrying about Grant and Jessica, as well as her father and her Uncle Larry. After what she had gone through with Derek since that day he'd taken her by surprise, she couldn't imagine that she would face anything worse. Even sitting there alone, surrounded by the blackness of the night forest with her firewood nearly depleted, she was not afraid anymore. She had turned the tables on her captor and rescued herself completely on her own, and she knew after that experience that she could overcome any other obstacles that might loom in her path tomorrow or beyond. When the fire finally burned down, she sat propped against the canoe, and finally dozed off.

She awoke with a scream, her rest shattered by a nightmare of Derek looming out of the blackness to grab her, half of his brains spilling out of the bloody wound in the back of his head like some specter from a horror movie. After that vision, she knew there was no hope of getting more sleep, so she spent the rest of the night awake, huddled against the canoe and waiting for dawn.

When the light finally came, she lost no time getting on the move again. She wanted to get to the end of the little bayou as quickly as possible, and away from the closed-in feeling of the dense forest that surrounded it. In less than an hour of paddling, she reached that goal. The bayou suddenly opened up ahead of her and its clear waters merged with the muddy brown current of a big river, which she was certain had to be a branch of the Pearl. She drifted out onto its broad, sunlit expanse, feeling as if she had suddenly stepped out of a darkened room into daylight after days of confinement. But despite her relief at the relatively wide-open space before her, she could see that she was literally not out of the woods yet. There was nothing on either bank but walls of greenery bounding the waterway on both sides, much the same as the river upstream had appeared before they turned off to go to Derek's camp.

She resumed paddling, easing into a steady rhythm that would eat up the miles, but hoping to find a place to land soon so she could eat something and take a short nap to make up for losing so much sleep during the night. She had only rounded one big bend of the river when she came to a good-sized sandbar. Knowing now that such nice places to stop would be few and far between in the swamp, she landed and tied the canoe off to a big piece of driftwood. The warmth of the morning sun was so pleasant she stretched out immediately on the soft sand next to the canoe and fell fast asleep.

How long she slept there, she had no idea, but when she awoke it was to the sharp clang of metal on metal as something banged against the side of the canoe. At first she thought she was still in the boat and that it had drifted down the river and bumped against a log or something, but she was really too tired to care and just wanted to go back to sleep—that is, until she heard voices—*men's voices.* Still thinking she was in the canoe, she reached for her paddle, and her hand grasped only sand. At the same time, she opened her eyes and saw a grinning apparition looming over her, squatting just an arm's length away. She cried out as she sat up, and then she heard her name uttered from the lips of a completely unexpected black face, a face framed by wild cords of matted hair hanging down and draping across the man's shoulders and arms. A shock of recognition swept over her—despite the utter impossibility, she knew that she was looking at none other than her Uncle Larry's friend *Scully!* Before she could open her lips to form a question, she heard her name called again in another nearby voice that trembled with excitement and joy. There could certainly be no mistaking that one, and when she turned her head to look, beyond her canoe to the boat behind it, Casey knew for sure that she was not dreaming.

★ ★ ★

When Artie and Scully set out in the battered johnboat at daybreak from the lake where Larry would wait with the *Casey Nicole,* Artie fully expected to spend the entire day winding their way upstream, first to the mouth of the Bogue Chitto, and then up most of its length to beyond the state line to the north. He could only hope that the old Evinrude would continue to run as smoothly as it had while pushing the catamaran, and that the quick and dirty patch job they'd done to the battered johnboat would keep the water out long enough to get them there. He also worried that there would not be enough depth in the Bogue Chitto, or that they would hit something such as a submerged log and damage the engine. It was going to be a long journey, well over a hundred miles, and a lot could go wrong. Still, he felt hopeful that he would be reunited with Casey before dark, because finding the boat was more of a lucky break than he'd dared to hope for after what the fisherman in Pearlington had said of their chances of buying one.

Early morning mist hanging over the river forced them to run at idle speed for almost two hours, Scully sitting in the stern and steering the boat with the outboard's combination tiller and throttle, while Artie crouched in the bow, straining to see through the fog to direct him around stumps and floating debris. They passed under the double overpass bridges of Interstate 59 at around the same time the sun began to burn off the fog. The river here was still wide, but in many places there were logjams spanning almost bank to bank, forcing them to pick a channel to steer through. At one of the worst of these, Artie realized that if they had brought the catamaran this far upriver, they would have been blocked from further progress at this point. With the narrow johnboat, it was tedious, but not too difficult to thread their way through all these obstructions. They would typically come to one every third bend or so, and then enjoy a mile or more of open river where Scully could open up the engine enough to get the johnboat up on a plane. They had just sped up again in this manner when Artie spotted a sandbar far ahead and what looked like a canoe pulled halfway out of the water onto it. He pointed it out to Scully, and the Rastaman slowed the engine back to idle as they approached the sandbar from downriver. Not wanting to take any chances on being ambushed by someone who might be hiding in the woods near the canoe, Scully steered them to the far side of the river to keep as much distance as possible between them and the sandbar when they passed. Both of them watched the woods for movement, Artie cradling the loaded shotgun at ready in his lap, just in case. They were adjacent to the upper end of the sandbar, where they could see on both sides of the canoe, when Scully shifted the engine into neutral and pointed.

"Take a look wid de glasses, Doc. I t'ink mehbe dat's some dead mon in de sand by dat canoe."

Artie reached behind him and took his brother's binoculars out of his bag, bringing them to bear on the canoe and the body lying beside it as the johnboat started slowly drifting back downstream.

"It is someone, but I think it's a woman. I can't tell if she's dead, but I don't see any movement. I think we ought to check it out."

"Could be a trap, mon," Scully warned. "Keep dat Mossberg ready." Scully put the outboard back in gear and idled across the river, killing it when they were within 10 feet of the canoe and allowing it to drift until it bumped into the stern of the other aluminum hull before Artie could fend it off.

"Sit tight wid dat gun," Scully whispered as he hopped out. "I an' I checking if she dead."

From where he sat in the bow of the boat, the canoe blocked his view of the body on the sandy beach. That was just as well for Artie, who didn't really want a close-up look at some unfortunate dead woman if he could help it. He was happy to let Scully check it out, and he was totally unprepared for what happened next as he tried to see into the dense woods beyond the sandbar, half-expecting to find they had fallen for a setup. There was a sudden movement and a female voice cried out. He heard Scully suddenly say the name *Casey* and then, from behind the canoe, he saw *his daughter* rise to a sitting position on the sandbar, the look on her face as amazed as he knew the one on his own had to be. Artie dropped the shotgun and leapt out of the canoe.

The three of them spent the heat of the day sitting in the shade of the woods beyond the sandbar. When Artie learned of all that Casey had been through, and saw the condition she was in from her many days of captivity in the swamp, the last thing he wanted to do was hurry her back downriver. She had been sleeping soundly on the sandbar, totally wiped out with exhaustion, and undoubtedly in shock from what had happened to her and what she'd had to do to escape her captor. On top of all that, she was worried sick over what might have become of her friends, Grant and Jessica, who certainly must have spent a lot of time frantically looking for her. Scully suggested that since they had everything in the boat they needed, they should let her rest longer, camping here overnight and then getting a fresh start back to where Larry waited with the *Casey Nicole* early in the morning.

It was later that afternoon, when he and Scully were getting their gear out of the boat to set up camp, that the second miracle occurred. Artie had stopped to stare absent-mindedly upriver for a moment, and was about to turn back to the boat to grab his bag, when he heard a female voice cry out: *Dr. Drager!* Straining to see who it could be and where it could possibly come from, he was startled when the bow of a canoe suddenly emerged from a dense stand of cattails along the riverbank some 50 yards upstream. The smiling girl paddling in the bow was none other than

Casey's roommate, Jessica, and the young man in the stern had to be Grant!

"What were the odds we'd all meet here?" Artie asked again as they sat around the campfire that evening, everyone full from a big meal of rice and beans they'd cooked just before dark and shared as they told their separate tales of what had transpired since the event.

"I just can't believe you guys found your way here," Casey said. "I knew you would come looking for me, and that Larry would find a way to get you to New Orleans, but wow, I wouldn't have hoped in my wildest dreams you'd find me on this river."

"Now the rivers are the natural highways," Grant said. "Just like in Guyana, where there are no roads to begin with. I'm glad you guys didn't try to follow us on foot. You wouldn't have made it through on the roads, and even if you had found the cabin, you would be so far behind us now that we would have never found each other."

"My question is, what do we do now? Is it still a good idea to all go to the cabin and wait until the power is restored? And if so, how do we get there?" Jessica wanted to know.

"No, Jessica. That's not the best plan. Larry has a much better idea, I think. With the boat, we're not limited to staying anywhere in this country. He thinks it will be too dangerous to be near any populated areas, or even anywhere around the mainland. He says that because the U.S. is such a technologically dependent country, and most people here are ill-equipped to live otherwise, it would be safer to sail to some place much more remote, somewhere that we can live on the boat but have access to the resources of the sea and the land nearby, preferably where there are few people, or at least people who live a simpler life."

"Some place in de sun," Scully said. "A mon not supposed to be dis far north."

"This is hardly what I'd call North, Scully. But yeah, Larry is talking about sailing south again, maybe to the Yucatán, or somewhere farther south along the Central American coast," Artie said as he looked around to see everyone's reaction.

"Hey, we could sail to Guyana!" Grant said. "If the catamaran can get up this river, it can get up the Essequibo, and I know a lot of the villages there. One thing about it, that's one place that's definitely off the beaten path to anywhere."

"You can run that idea by Larry," Artie said. "He's the captain and I think he's far more qualified than any of us to make that decision. But regardless of where we go, just be glad we've got a boat and a knowledgeable skipper that can take us practically anywhere in the world. I don't know about you all, but I'm going to feel a lot better as soon as we are back aboard tomorrow."

"I an' I feelin' mo' bettah when de wind fill de sails, Doc, an' put dis Bobbylon astern in de wake."

"That too, Scully. That too." Artie put his arm around his daughter and squeezed her close to him. "I've got what I came here to find, so that sounds good to me."

ALSO BY SCOTT B. WILLIAMS

Bug Out: The Complete Plan for Escaping a Catastrophic Disaster Before It's Too Late
$14.95

Warning sirens are blaring. You have 15 minutes to evacuate. What will you do? Being prepared makes the difference between survival and disaster. Guiding you step by step, *Bug Out* shows you how to be ready at a second's notice.

Bug Out Vehicles and Shelters: Build and Outfit Your Life-Saving Escape
$15.95

A cataclysmic disaster strikes. Do you have a vehicle you can count on to evacuate your family safely? *Bug Out Vehicles and Shelters* zeroes in on the key considerations and essential equipment for planning all your bug-out needs.

Getting Out Alive: 13 Deadly Scenarios and How Others Survived
$14.95

Every year, ordinary people find themselves in extraordinary life-or-death situations. Delving into 13 harrowing scenarios, *Getting Out Alive* combines riveting narratives with expert advice and real-life accounts of savvy survivors.

To order these books call 800-377-2542 or 510-601-8301, fax 510-601-8307, e-mail ulysses@ulyssespress.com, or write to Ulysses Press, P.O. Box 3440, Berkeley, CA 94703. All retail orders are shipped free of charge. California residents must include sales tax. Allow two to three weeks for delivery.

ABOUT THE AUTHOR

SCOTT B. WILLIAMS has been exploring wild places and seeking adventure on both land and sea for most of his life. At the age of twenty-five, he embarked on an open-ended solo sea kayaking journey from his home in Mississippi to the islands of the Caribbean. His nonfiction book *On Island Time: Kayaking the Caribbean* is a narrative of that life-changing journey. His pursuit of adventure travel led him to further develop his wilderness survival skills that began with hunting and fishing while growing up in rural Mississippi. After his Caribbean kayak trip, he spent years testing his skills in a variety of environments throughout North America, using both modern and primitive methods, and traveling both on foot and by canoe and kayak. His enthusiasm for travel by water fueled an interest in a variety of boats and led him to learn the craft of wooden boatbuilding. In addition to building boats, paddling small craft, and offshore sailing, he enjoys backpacking, bicycling, martial arts training, dual-sport motorcycling, and photography. He maintains several blogs related to these pursuits and occasionally writes for magazines including *Sea Kayaker* and *SAIL*. His most popular blog is *Bug Out Survival* (www.bugoutsurvival.com), which expands on his books *Bug Out: The Complete Plan for Escaping a Catastrophic Disaster Before It's Too Late* and *Bug Out Vehicles and Shelters*. More information about Scott can be found on his main website, www.scottbwilliams.com. He lives in Prentiss, Mississippi.